LETHAL SPOILS

a novel by

Keith Short

Trafford
PUBLISHING

ISBN: 978-1-4120-7211-3

 www.trafford.com

North America & international
toll-free: 1 888 232 4444 (USA & Canada)
phone: 250 383 6864 ♦ fax: 250 383 6804 ♦ email: info@trafford.com

The United Kingdom & Europe
phone: +44 (0)1865 722 113 ♦ local rate: 0845 230 9601
facsimile: +44 (0)1865 722 868 ♦ email: info.uk@trafford.com

10 9 8 7 6

READERS COMMENTS

Blitzkreig of a read. You don't have to be a student of second world war history to read Keith Short's new book, but if you are it will add just a little bit more to the enjoyment. The book's atmosphere and pace reminded me of an amalgam of The Third Man and Indiana Jones with a touch of Georges Slmenon's Inspector Maigret thrown in by way of Short's Chief Inspector Steiner. It might make a good movie.

By **Rumblebunny** (Toronto) ★★★★

A great "read"! An intricate plot about repatriating a World War 11 treasure combined with fascinating characters and a bit of irony makes this one of the most interesting and entertaining books of the year.
If you're a heavy reader and are bored with redundant plots, you'll find Lethal Spoils a refreshing change. My comment to Mr. Short is: "More books, please."

By R.C.Bush (Fairfield, Ct.) ★★★★★

Bravo! to this new author! LETHAL SPOILS is everything I like in a mystery/thriller. I loved the detail and vivid imagery, especially the descriptions of the war. The irony of the Lancours owning stock in a company that manufactured the rounds that killed them was delicious! The way all the characters' lives were intertwined added depth to the story, and it indeed is a page-turner deluxe. I savored every word of it!

By P.Polansky (Asheville, N.C.)★★★★★

I have read LETHAL SPOILS by Keith Short. This work was written in a style that was like a motion picture forming in your mind showing every detail. It is a gripping tale dealing with temptation and corruption.....
I couldn't put it down.

By J.Perrin, (Adelanto, California.)

This book is dedicated to Yvonne...
a fantastic wife whose
perseverance and encouragement
made it all possible.

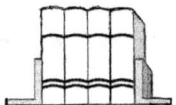

The best way to enjoy a book requires
keeping the bath water
at the right temperature.

AUTHOR'S NOTE

IN MAY 1940 PANZER COLUMNS OVERRAN France. Many of its citizens wept at the débâcle brought about by their government and its inept military leaders. Following the defection of the cabinet from Paris, the writing was clearly on the wall. It had taken only five weeks for the 'Blitzkrieg' to overwhelm the vaunted French forces. The world was stunned by the event.

Many people spend years searching for bonanzas while a few simply stumble across them. 'LETHAL SPOILS' focuses on a sensational treasure secreted by a French aristocrat ahead of the advancing invaders. The dying words of an old man would guide two German soldiers, Sgt. Freiburg and his younger companion to its recovery.

Neither soldier is imbued with military fervor but they soon develop an entrepreneurial spirit and strong bonds of friendship. Prior to being drafted to different theaters of war, the men know they must await an end to hostilities before cashing in on their find… unfortunately a third party has other ideas for its distribution.

The lives of three men undergo radical change before the war grinds to a halt. Life in Europe is bleak after five years of slaughter and deprivation. But for those grabbing opportunities the pay-off is rewarding.

In the 60's era, politics, sex and greed result in the death or ruin for those associated with the St. Lucien treasure. A bizarre murder becomes a problem for Chief Inspector Steiner and creates an embarrassing political scandal for the German government before the saga draws to a close.

LETHAL SPOILS

Part I

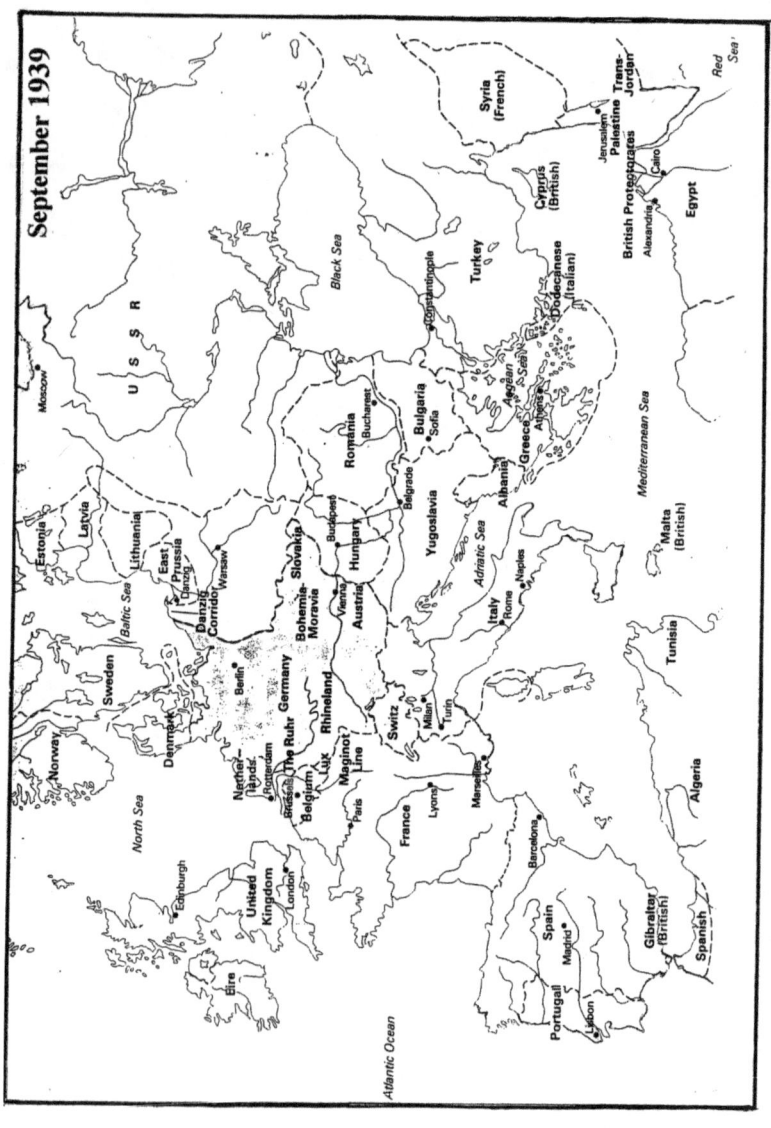

PROLOGUE

FEELING FULL, PASSENGER LEO STEINER PUSHED his chair away from the dining table.

A walk on deck was needed to let his stomach settle, and then later he'd drop by the Neptune bar before returning to his cabin to finish a book. So far the weather had been good and as a land lubber he'd quickly acclimatized to life on board, but an unexpectedly choppy sea could change all this. A deep-sounding voice broke into his ruminations... "Going to get up for the sunrise?" The question was raised by a stocky man Leo had noticed earlier, when they were both watching the setting sun. Leo gave a noncommittal grunt... certainly the scene had been spectacular, an artist would have had difficulty matching such colors.

The two men were near the bridge, gazing at the darkened sea roiled by the breeze. Spume-flecked water slid quickly past the hull and more boisterous waves were highlighted by the lights of portholes. The whole scene mesmerized Leo. Straightening up from the rail, he turned to the other man, "I've often let my senses become dulled, but this time seeing the sunset was incredible." His companion nodded: "Distractions in life create barriers, and we become the losers."

Hannah, Leo's girlfriend, had planned their cruise in celebration of his retirement as a chief inspector in the West German Police. At the last moment she had to cancel, due to her sister in Stockholm becoming seriously ill. Leo had boarded the 'Malaysian Star' alone, sailing out of Southampton. In spite of the circumstances he thought some reflective time would be helpful in adjusting to a new life style.

Going down another deck, he headed aft which brought him to the Palm Lounge just as its door burst open. A bevy of middle-aged women engulfed him as he tried to enter. An attractive brunette gave him a dazzling smile while adjusting a shawl over her sequined evening dress. He patted down his silver hair ruffled by the sea breezes, and while still maintaining eye contact, nearly tripped over the raised threshold.

Once inside he ordered a large brandy. Tasting it, he noticed the approach of the talkative woman he'd sat next to at dinner. Clutching his glass Leo strode towards a row of slot machines and escaped via double doors on the starboard side. Leaning against a ventilator cradling his drink, Leo became aware of company. An aromatic smell of an expensive cigar wafted past his nose.

After a few minutes the stranger spoke. "On such nights one could imagine a world minus problems, eh?" Leo nodded. "True but before long we'd probably invent them, knowing the perversity of human nature." The stranger remained quiet a few moments, enjoying his Cuban 'Hoyo de Monterey.' This small conversational exchange had been conducted in German... did the man know him? When asked, he laughed. "No, I happened to see a label on your luggage when we embarked, so I know your name and domicile." Leo extended his hand and hoped the man wasn't an ex-cop.

"Peter Ricardo, I'm from Argentina." They talked for a while on various topics and eventually Peter mentioned he was divorced, and the cruise was to give him time to sort out his priorities, and take a break from an accountants job. "Since coming aboard I've noticed the uneven ratio between the sexes. It tells me to hurry if I have unfinished projects. Mathematically our gender appears on the endangered species list." Leo laughed. It was a viewpoint he hadn't thought about. After chatting a while longer they decided to watch a new film about to be shown in the ship's theater.

The days passed pleasantly for most passengers on the Malaysian Star. Entertainment and various shipboard activities were first rate, during the course of which new friendships formed. People found they now had time to relax in a different environment. Leo danced several times with the woman he'd first met exiting the Palm lounge, and surprised himself to find his expertise had not entirely left him.

Occasionally, Paula joined Ricardo and Steiner as they explored various ports of call, returning to the ship hours later clutching junky souvenirs, laughing over shared experiences. Several weeks into the voyage, the threesome lay sprawled on chaise lounges positioned to catch the shade afforded by a lifeboat. Leo was on the point of nodding off when Peter tossed over a newspaper purchased during the last shore visit. "Interesting article on the back page... do you believe any of these stories about hidden treasures? It seems one reads of some expedition or other, then after they've grabbed your attention, that's the last you hear of it."

Leo was about to shrug before trying to nap, but instead levered himself up on an elbow. "I don't know what I believe quite frankly, but I know for certain a cache is occasionally discovered having a content that is priceless. The odd thing is, it doesn't always provide the happiness most people expect. At least that's what happened during my final case." Peter had stood up while listening to Leo but sat down so quickly he spilt his drink. "My goodness Inspector, I need to be told about your experience... my curiosity wouldn't be satisfied otherwise. It must be due to my training as an accountant, balancing everything to come out not a penny under or over! The idea of anyone coming across hidden wealth is fascinating."

Leo inwardly groaned, "I think not Peter, it would take too long." Ricardo snorted, saying "I reckon we're about a quarter of the way around this globe and I could start and finish War and Peace before disembarking." Leo wondered if that mightn't be such a bad idea, having noted Ricardo's expectant look. He'd seen the same rapt expression on Hannah's face when something intrigued her. Leo paused a moment: "O.K. Ricardo... I'll tell you about the San Lucien case, with the following conditions." Ricardo inquired what these might be. "I will need you to be responsible for ordering me a steady supply of drinks, and in addition, to remain patient whenever the raconteur dozes off." Peter Ricardo made a mock pretense of mulling over these duties before nodding his assent.

Leo pushed his sunglasses onto the top of his head and glanced across at Paula who was fast asleep and motioned to Ricardo not to wake her. The couple seemed to be hitting it off... maybe a shipboard romance was underway? Leo smiled reaching for his suntan lotion feeling like an actor awaiting his cue. He searched his mind for a beginning as nowadays it seemed as if the whole thing had never happened. "My role in what became known as the 'St Lucien affair' culminated in solving a bizarre murder. I retired shortly afterwards and tried out hobbies I'd never had the time for previously. I managed to adapt to my new life style quite quickly but one day I started thinking of the magnificent artifact which had featured so prominently in the case. Suddenly I wanted to know the story behind the treasure and perhaps write about it. I had the time and money to indulge any whims within reason... are you ready Peter?"

1

PARIS 1929

PERHAPS LE TRÉSOR LUCIEN MIGHT BE considered fairly insignificant compared to a few of the world's treasures, but for its owners it represented a wealth most men would envy. In fact, Claude Bauten didn't even know its true worth. His daughter Lucy had heard of its existence since early childhood. It was occasionally discussed at her parents' dinner table, when out of the servants earshot. Only once had she actually seen it. She was thirteen years old at the time. Her father had taken her into the office maintained at their house on the Rue Felix Conte, in the Paris suburbs. Walking across to a wall facing the garden, he removed the picture obscuring a wall safe, dialed the combination and removed a large box with reinforced leather corners similar to the kind used for filing records and manuscripts. She guessed it had cost more than her monthly allowance.

"Lucy, I don't think I will provide another sister or a brother to keep you company, and I want to show you what will be yours one day." Slowly he removed the ribbon securing the lid, exposing a cloth-wrapped bundle. Moving to his desk, Monsieur Bauten carefully unwrapped the package containing 36 items. Lucy looked at the objects revealed. Most were fairly small, but one drew her prime attention. It was a large cross encrusted with jewels, or so she presumed. At the age of thirteen, articles of antiquity don't usually inspire much more than fleeting interest, and this was now the case. But remembering the discussions between her parents regarding the objects, she stared hard for a few minutes, more out of curiosity than anything else. Her father also looked down at the desk, but with an intensity not present in Lucy. He lit his pipe and sat down in a chair and motioned his daughter to also be seated.

Late afternoon sunshine streamed through the windows and a faint smell of burning leaves occasionally came through the partially opened windows.

"Lucy, let me tell you something about what is in front of you. The treasure is named for the Maison St. Lucien, which no longer exists, except for a few grass-covered humps on the slope where it once stood overlooking the Mediteranean. In the 12th century it was occupied for a time by an order of monks noted for their piety and succor to the poor of the region. According to records kept in the Vatican archives, several English and French knights had stayed there en route to their homes after campaigning in the Crusades. One of the knights, Henri de Beaumaris, suffering from wounds inflicted outside Jerusalem and from the rigors of traveling for many months, stopped at St. Lucien to recuperate, but after a few weeks suddenly died and was buried in the grounds by the monks. On his deathbed he entrusted a leather portmanteau to the Abbot with instructions it was to be delivered to his wife in Bordeaux. He also gave a sum of gold coins to the Abbot in gratitude for the care bestowed upon him. Very little is known about the life of Henri except his age at the time of death, and the fact that despite having very poor health, he'd acquitted himself with distinction during his campaigns. How he obtained this collection can only be guessed, but often knights returned with enormous loot from the Middle East which laid the foundation for many ancestral properties in Christian Europe.

Research of some church records in Bordeaux close to the original Beaumaris Estate, noted the deaths of Henri's children. What is known for certain is that the portmanteau was returned by the Abbot to the Beaumaris family, as 160 years later a letter records that five rings and two jewel boxes, part of the original St. Lucien hoard, were donated to the papal envoy at Grenoble by a certain Paul Beaumaris. The donation was used toward the cost of building a new church in that city. I myself heard nothing of the treasure from my own parents. After your grandfather died and his will was read, I was given a lead box which needed two people to carry. There were instructions that I be alone when breaking open the seals to inspect its contents. Inside the box was a smaller wooden one containing the treasure and a small leather bound book written in Latin describing each of the artifacts in detail. A letter in my father's handwriting had been tucked behind its fly leaf, and provided the information I've just imparted."

M'sieu Bauten bent down and unlocked the middle drawer of his desk, then withdrew a brown paper package secured with string and sealing wax. Opening it, he handed Lucy the two books inside. One was evidently the book to which her father had just referred to. The leather was cracked and the color faded to the point that only traces of the original pigment remained. A peculiar clasp retained its covers, but her father made no attempt to open it. The other book was larger and was obviously newer. He pointed towards it saying "Lucy, inside are photographs of each item, and I have translated the other book in order to try estimating a value of everything in present day francs." Having said this, M'sieu Bauten carefully returned the books to the drawer, and placed the tresor back in the wall safe. Turning to Lucy, he spoke in a soft manner. "Truly this is the first time you haven't fidgeted during one of our talks." A smile had creased his countenance. "You will probably pay more attention now in history classes, and maybe the crusades will take on greater significance." Lucy straightened in her chair. "I noticed your last school report on the subject was somewhat disappointing." He reached over and patted her forearm.

"Well mon cheri, that is the story of the St. Lucien. When I die it will be yours, although I hope you won't be moved to make many donations later in life, as you can see it has become somewhat of a tradition to hand it down through the ages, and I'm certain you will feel well enough provided for with what I've managed to acquire during my career." Lucy suddenly felt a little frightened. The idea that her father wouldn't always be there seemed remote at her age, and the responsibility of having valuables to safeguard was somewhat disturbing, but now she wanted to get back to her latest film magazine which had just arrived in the afternoon post. Her father got up noticing that long shadows were now spreading across the garden. With his arm around Lucy's shoulder, they both walked out of his office.

* * * * * * * *

Paris during the late twenties was a marvelous place for a teenage girl, especially one like Lucy enjoying a generous allowance from her parents. She was glad to have finished at the Catholic Lycée. She'd only been an average student, but it had provided a circle of friends for company, especially at the weekends. The burden of school work absorbed too much time during the week, in Lucy's opinion, and the discipline imposed by the Nuns had begun to make her sullen, despite a normally sunny nature. Having met two boys she really liked, this added minor complications to a rather structured life. One day walking home, she pondered whether to ask permission to invite one of them, Paul Rocard, to her home, but decided it wasn't worth having to field the sort of questions that would inevitably be asked by her Mother, so dropped the idea. Anyway, she'd soon be going to the finishing school in Lausanne that her father had picked out, and once settled would make a new collection of friends. Having never been to Switzerland, the prospect excited her and as it seemed so far away, Lucy went to a library and thumbed through a big atlas and one or two travel books to learn more of the country.

The information her father had shown her regarding the school really didn't tell her too much, but a listing of the rules of behavior seemed less strict in nature than those endured at the Lycée. She would start after an August vacation spent at the Nieuport Hotel in Cannes that her parents loved so much. This would make the fourth time they'd booked there, always choosing the same room overlooking the Mediterranean.

The capital was all but deserted during the month of August, when vast numbers of the population headed to vacation spots, needing to enjoy a respite from daily routine and stress. Lucy enjoyed the bustle and seemingly organized chaos of the Gare de Lyon. Piles of baggage, with an occasional fishing rod or tennis racquet strapped to the exterior of bulging suitcases were sorted and stowed in capacious baggage cars. Her mother didn't like Lucy wandering off once they settled in the compartment, but agreed to a request for taking a look at the locomotive… adding an admonition to be back at least ten minutes before departure time. For Lucy, the huge black monsters represented untold power and a sense of freedom, standing ready to make the long run south. Eddies of smoke and steam enveloped their bulks, and crews dressed in blue bibs sometimes gave a wave as she stood gazing up from the platform. Hurried conferences between S.N.C.F. officials standing alongside the train terminated with glances at their pocket watches and the long train pulled out right on time. M'sieur Bauten stretched, then settled back in his seat with a grunt. His mind was still on affairs of the shipping line he headed, but he quickly began to relax and nod off, contemplating the meal they'd soon enjoy. Few found cause for complaint with fare served on these crack trains of the French rail system. Madame Bauten sat upright, knitting a cardigan for her husband... he'd have preferred buying his own, but years of married life had taught prudence in such matters!

As the train sped through the countryside, industrial backgrounds had given way to vastly different terrain. The land became rugged with rivers snaking along valleys or rushing between rock faces. To Lucy, the further south they traveled seemed to intensify the quality of light, putting her in a happy frame of mind.

Lucy loved Provence, and on the final leg of the journey, first glimpses of the Côte d'Azur gave her a sense of elation. The blue of the Mediterranean was almost indivisible from that of the sky and most passengers felt a sense of well-being looking out of their windows. The first sighting of a palm tree was always cause for comment. Looking at the Mediterranean briefly turned Lucy's thoughts to the maison St. Lucien, and she wondered if she might one day see where it had stood. These musings were interrupted by her fathers' announcement that they would be arriving at Cannes within the next ten minutes.

The train pulled alongside a crowd of people waiting to greet arriving passengers. M'sieu Bauten supervised two porters loading his luggage onto one of the station carts, and within a few minutes they were climbing into a large Renault taxi for the short journey to the hotel Nieuport. After arrival formalities were taken care of and luggage distributed to their rooms, Lucy decided to walk around the hotel gardens and try out a new box camera given to her by her mother as a graduation present. Both parents had decided to take a nap before tackling the bouillabaisse at dinner, which was a noted specialty of the hotel. As they headed up the stairs, she heard her father exclaiming "A premier bouillabaisse is due to the racasse, a hog fish which is an extremely ugly creature."

Lucy bumped into Sophie on the landing. They had met last year and become good friends. Both were overjoyed at their reunion and spent the next hour catching up on each others' news. Suddenly they realized it was time to change into evening dresses for the formal dinner. Both girls liked Cannes, but found the hotel tended to be full of older people with tastes different from their own. A few of the other guests had children of the same age, but during previous visits Lucy found most of them were pretty dull. It occurred to her that she too might be considered dull because of the similarity of well-heeled backgrounds.

She wondered if something was missing in her life but couldn't exactly put a finger on it. The evenings were the worst when her parents played endless card games with acquaintances who always came to the hotel at the same time of year. Back in Paris they never associated, but when August came around they picked up the threads from the previous year as if there'd been no passage of time. World events played little part in their conversations, and quite a few things were absolutely never mentioned. The men always wore similar dark suits and ties, occasionally sporting the ribbon of the Legion d'honneur in a lapel. The women dressed in the latest Parisian fashions, although in Lucy's eyes none of the dresses surpassed outfits of the stars shown in her film magazines. She really didn't like her own clothes as her mother decided what looked most becoming for a girl of her age. Still, life was very pleasant and she enjoyed tennis parties and occasional yacht cruises her parents took her on. Sometimes Lucy spotted a celebrity she'd read about in the papers or in one of her magazines.When this occurred the fact was duly noted in the diary she kept which even Sophie wasn't allowed to see.

Lucy sat down in the lounge. She'd chosen a wicker chaise next to a potted palm and was listening to a mediocre ensemble churning out popular melodies when her parents entered after a stroll along the beach. "Hello Lucy, I forgot to tell you that your mother has decided to accompany me to the Casino in Monte Carlo tomorrow." This surprised her as she'd never heard of her father playing at cards for money. "I've rented a car to take us there and bring us back... we'll be gone quite some time." Taking an envelope out of his jacket, he passed it to his daughter. "Your birthday is next week, and we thought you might like to spend the day shopping with Sophie, who seems to be a great friend of yours." Lucy's mood changed instantly. "Thank you Papa, that will be fun." Lucy's mother astounded her by telling her she might like to buy a couple of dresses 'of the right sort.' The idea of freedom to choose for the first time added to her excitement. She stood up and kissed her mother. "We are going upstairs for a moment and will meet you in the dining room later." Lucy immediately went in search of Sophie to relate the news, but not finding her sat down to mull over any implications of her parents trip to the Casino, and the pleasures of spending the contents of the envelope which felt satisfyingly fat. Perhaps she wasn't living in a vacuum after all. Finishing dinner, she left a note on the door of Sophie's bedroom asking her to meet for breakfast. She then went to bed and listened to a program from radio-Paris, before drifting off to sleep.

Early next morning, Sophie tapped on the door and the two girls decided after much giggling to have breakfast sent up. They sat on the balcony overlooking the sea, enjoying their cafe au lait and croissants. After planning what they would do during the day that lay ahead, Lucy went downstairs to the dining room, knowing her parents would already be seated. She wanted to wish her father luck at the Casino.

After exploring every clothes shop they could find, the girls finally ended up in the older part of town. Sitting at one of the sidewalk cafes sipping an aperitif and listening to a Corsican with an accordion entertain the patrons,

Lucy decided that Cannes had more to offer than she'd supposed. They discussed boys and parents, and when Sophie announced that she hoped to attend the Sorbonne later on, Lucy for the first time let her thoughts project further than the finishing school which was next on her agenda. The Sorbonne might also suit her. They arrived back at the hotel exhausted. Each had bought a dress in the old quarter at a third of the price they would have paid at the places visited earlier.

For the rest of the vacation the girls were inseparable and found many things to do which filled each day. Lucy began to realize that a whole world existed which she knew very little about, and suspected Sophie was somehow more sophisticated, even though only two months separated them in age. Suddenly the vacation was at an end. After the mandatory exchange of addresses and phone numbers, Lucy and Sophie promised to meet again after their return to Paris.

2

WEIN 1934

KARL BAYER GREW UP IN THE Heilgenstadt district of Vienna which provided many things of interest for a small boy in the years before the upcoming war. Frau Bayer promised to make a favorite cake for her son's eleventh birthday, and his father had already bought the model aeroplane he'd been hankering after for several weeks. One more day to wait, then his best friend Hans would go with him to the park in order to give it a test flight.

Dawdling his way back from school, Karl made the usual brief stops in front of the windows of his favorite shops, before reaching home. Climbing the steps to his parent's apartment, he reached the top flight and pushed open the outer door to be greeted by his mother "Hello Karl, did you have a good day at school?" Mumbling something indicating an affirmative, the boy headed to his bedroom while his mother returned to the kitchen table where the rich ingredients for making the birthday cake awaited attention.

Karl picked up a pile of Märklin train catalogs and started to browse through the latest issues, but mostly his thoughts were on the model aeroplane soon to be his.

His parents had always made previous birthdays match his anticipation of the event. He wasn't greedy, but like all boys his age, having decided on what presents he wanted, thoughts of the minor sacrifices his parents must make never entered his head. Karl's father Heinrich was an ardent socialist who was born and grew up in the same district they now lived in. Times were hard in Vienna for the majority of workers, and the city had many unemployed. War profiteers and people who'd prospered under the Hapsburg regime still gave the city a veneer of gaiety, but it was apparent to visitors that the lustre of former years had all but dissipated, making its appearance more like that of an elderly dowager.

Heinrich worked as a clerk in the office of one of the larger construction companies located in a western suburb, which entailed a long trek each way from his apartment. He walked with a slight limp, the result of shrapnel wounds incurred serving with a mountain artillery unit at Caporetto. Luckily, with an early discharge from the army he was able to obtain a job straight away as most soldiers were still at the front, and Vienna was woefully short of manpower. After the armistice, veterans flooded employment agencies, prior to gathering at soup lines set up by charitable organizations. Sometimes these men would meet old comrades they'd lost touch with which brought a fleeting moment of joy. However, like the thousands of ex-soldiers throughout Europe, they were part of a brotherhood without hope or luck, struggling to survive one day to the next.

Heinrich considered himself fortunate, and with the passage of time had become a senior clerk. The pay wasn't much to speak of, but he was reasonably happy with his lot. He still maintained a vision for a better life within a future prosperous Austria, which hopefully the Socialist party would provide. The ideology of the communists and Nazis didn't suit his bourgeois taste. Heinrich deemed it better not to discuss political leanings with fellow workers, especially his membership in the Shutzbund which had been banned the previous March. His hobby consisted of buying and swapping old prints, usually discovered in the vicinity of the Turmstrasse. Sometimes he kept one he liked and gave it to his wife who also shared his enthusiasm, and these were displayed on their living room walls. Occasionally he dropped in at a bier stube with an old friend. His life was uncomplicated even if slightly dull. Heinrich was quite content the way it was.

Headed by Dr. Seitz, the burgomaster, Vienna's municipal government was solidly Socialist. Although support for the party was weaker in Austria as a whole, in the capital they held sway at the Rathaus. It was becoming increasingly obvious that a clash would soon erupt between the party and the Heimwehr, a paramilitary fascist organization which had many supporters throughout the country. The Heimwehr had fully supported the diminutive Dr. Englebert Dollfuss, as chancellor of Austria, when he'd assumed dictatorial powers. The Heimwehr was as equally opposed to the socialists as to the embryonic Austrian Nazi party officially dissolved in 1933, but had hopes that antagonism between the socialist party and the Nazis would further its own aims in a bid for power.

Taking advantage of a temporary absence from the country by Dr. Dollfuss, a planned strike against the Socialists was initiated by the Austrian vice-Chancellor and Prince Starhemberg, leader of the Heimwehr. On Karl's birthday, the Socialist party was declared illegal, and street fighting broke out between the government forces backed by the Heimwehr, and armed members of Shutzbund squads.

Hostilities were mostly confined to working class areas, but the majority of the population thought it wise to remain indoors throughout the city. The fighting between opposing forces increased in intensity as the day wore on, with small arms and machine guns employed on both sides. Later on, field guns were brought up by government squads to subdue the more stubborn pockets of Socialist resistance and the number of dead and wounded was beginning to mount rapidly. Heinrich heard reports of the disturbances at the office, but decided rumors had overblown the seriousness of the situation, and he really needed to finish the pile of invoices in front of him before leaving work. He looked forward to seeing his friends and attending his son's birthday party. Heinrich was just leaving the Karl Marx Hof when the first salvo of shells hit the upper floors behind him, sending chunks of masonry and glass in all directions. His instincts from war time days made him duck back quickly into the nearest opening on the ground floor of the apartments. Almost immediately a second salvo raked the lower floors. His life ended at that precise moment.

Afterwards part of his head and a severed leg were found by ambulance workers amid debris created by the shell. The books for exchange he'd been carrying lay scattered next to some overturned dustbins, ignored by two dogs searching for food scraps. A sad and obscene end for a son of the city. A city which itself had become obscene on February 12, 1934 with Austrian killing Austrian. The Flag of the Heimwehr was hoisted on the Rathhaus tower and people became fearful as to what would happen next.

Frau Bayer was worried sick when her husband had not come home at the usual time. She had tried telephoning him but the switchboard didn't answer. She knew her husband didn't like her calling him at work, but this was different. Suddenly she remembered his intention of dropping by the Karl Marx Hof, a huge block of workers apartments where one of his Schutzbund friends lived. He'd assured her this would only be a quick stop in order to pick up some books. Momentarily her anxiety lifted, it had been a hard day. She'd listened to the radio blaring news of the Socialist Party being banned and various reports describing the outbreak of fighting in the streets, not only in Vienna but also in provincial cities such as Linz and Graz. Although she didn't play an active role of any kind in her husband's political activities, Frau Bayer was aware of mounting pressures building up over the past few weeks, and noted a certain tenseness in her husband listening to broadcasts.

Looking at the clock, a prized wedding gift from her mother, Frau Bayer began fretting once more, picking up and putting down objects absentmindedly, refusing to turn the radio back on for fear of hearing more news that would frighten her. Earlier she'd heard neighbors on the landing discussing the days events, but felt too tired to join the babble of conversation, and had retreated to her bedroom to lie down. She hoped to rid herself of a pounding headache which always started after becoming unduly nervous. Despite his mother's warning to stay indoors, Karl had slipped out to fetch his friend Hans in good time for the celebration. He would get a preview of the parcel Hans would have ready, knowing that it wouldn't be opened until after they'd eaten. Just seeing the wrapped present would allow speculation and heighten the feeling of anticipation. Frau Bayer was distraught her son had disobeyed her, and wondered if she should tell her husband or not. Even though he was an only child, she still believed in a code of discipline imposed on herself as a child. Not wanting to cast a black mood on the upcoming party, she decided to defer the decision until later on. Returning to the kitchen, she put her finishing touches on the cake. At that moment, the two boys burst into the room. "Mutti, that looks the best cake ever." Both boys stared admiringly at the confection making Frau Bayer pleased with their reactions. She had a soft spot for Hans, and he was always welcome in the Bayer household. "Go and play with your train set while I go and get changed." After an hour had elapsed, Frau Bayer's headache receded, but her anxiety was worse, if anything, so she decided to let the boys start with the meal.

Karl and Hans were engrossed in conversation about their upcoming flying exploits. Karl would take the part of the 'Red Baron' and Hans decided his role would be that of

'Max Immelman', both admired aces of the war, but after a time their enthusiasm began to wane. Karl was restless due to his father's absence. It was so unlike him to be late. His mother had gone back to her bedroom. At 8:40 p.m. the doorbell rang, and Karl rushed to greet his father, but saw a policeman and another man in plain clothes standing at the threshold. Frau Bayer, hearing the bell, also ran to the door pushing Karl to one side exclaiming "Liebe Gott, what can this signify?"

"Frau Bayer, would you please accompany us to the police station… I am afraid it is very bad news."

* * * * * * * * *

Following the death of his father, Karl became 'the man of the house'. After school he worked long hours at a nearby grocery store in order to help the family budget. Finally, a small state pension was awarded to his mother and coupled with a pittance received from the construction company, things became a little easier. During this period, Karl's schoolwork suffered considerably. He was always tired and often during class he'd nod off only to be awakened with a sharp rap on the knuckles administered by a teacher. Initial sympathy shown at the time of his fathers' death had long worn off and Karl was longing for the time when he could leave the place he'd begun to detest.

3

ALGERIA
MAY-JUNE 1940

THE MARQUIS JEAN DE LANCOUR LEANED on a rail of the 'L'Aigle' as the ship made its approach to the harbor at Oran. He always enjoyed watching the sun glint on the sea water and the rainbow effect in the plumes of spray. The sun would be setting shortly, and it would be dark by the time Tony Gambetti met him at dockside, before transporting him to the hotel for a drink. At times Jean de Lancour worried about how much profit from the Lancour holdings ended up in the Gambetti bank account. However, Tony was a delightful companion, besides being his Chef de Bureau. His encyclopedic knowledge of all the best clubs, and the women he introduced to his boss were usually highly desirable.

Jean was not enthused with having to make the present trip. Other pressing business affairs caused by the war demanded his attention, but Marcel Cordon his financial director had pointed out some rather disquieting reports with regard to their Algerian operations. Jean deemed it necessary to personally investigate matters rather than delegate the task.

Lancour et Cie was in the business of importing base metals, animal hides, and food stuffs in bulk, which were then processed and packaged at a central complex outside Paris. The company had been founded in 1830 by a Lancour and had gradually expanded over the years to be ranked 27th in the whole of France in terms of net worth. Any money scandals would upset the shareholders, not to mention the military procurement heads who could jeopardize present and future contracts. Maybe Marcel was too much of an alarmist. However, he'd often been the one who had saved Jean from making poor decisions.

He left the rail and returned to his cabin in order to prepare for disembarkation. Jean had a feeling of foreboding over happenings in Europe which made him wonder if this might be his last business trip for a very long time. He also had a touch of indigestion which was put down to the oysters he'd eaten at lunch in the ship's dining room. It was either that or the insufferably pompous Egyptian business man who had sat opposite regaling him with the charms of Alexandria and its' fleshpots.

Jean had been there in his younger days and ended up with a dose of clap... some charm, and a painful episode was the way he remembered the place. The damned war was unsettling him. At least he had been exempted this time from having to serve for the 'Glory of France.' His spell at Verdun in the last world war had taught him about the stupidity of generals and politicians. Over 700, 000 dead... and for what?

He'd witnessed the political rising in Paris that took place on February 6, 1934 creating a night of terror for the city... Thousands of ex-service men with war flags flying, marched down the Champs Elysees yelling 'Mort a Daladier' the then prime minister. The rioters consisted of extremist factions from the right and of the left, who were battled by the Gardes Mobile, and regular police. Finally the Gardes Republicain on horseback using drawn swords charged the demonstrators. Many prominent buildings along with overturned buses and cars were torched. The next day the Place de la Concorde was littered with makeshift weapons used by the rioters. Daladier faced pandemonium in the Chamber of Deputies, and although he won a vote of confidence, it was doubtful he would survive much longer in power. It had been the worst civil strife since the days of the commune. Millions of francs' worth of damage resulted, besides the deaths of several of those who took part.

Jean tried to absorb the events that were beginning to affect the social order of France. The rise of the Nazis led by Adolf Hitler in Germany coupled with the Fascists in Italy made him wonder if the seeds of disaster had again been sown, just a few years after the horrors of world War I. To him everything pointed that way. In September 1939 listening to the declaration of war, he was saddened but not surprised.

The 'phony war' over the next few months tended to lull the populations of France and England into a 'business as usual' mentality. Even the troops sitting behind the Maginot and Siegfried lines were relaxed. It was really only the dress rehearsal, not the 'real thing.' True, the Finns were beating the Russians in a 'hot war' and the spectacle of the communist bear getting its arse kicked only reinforced the people's view that somehow things would all be settled soon in a civilized way, and any minor disruptions to their lives would be obviated. Paris carried on as before. Smartly uniformed officers and their women folk strolled down the Champs Elysees, attended theaters and the racetracks at Auteuil and Vincennes. Restaurants and hotels were doing a booming business. Tickets for exhibitions and concerts were at a premium. The diplomats at the Quai D'Orsay went back to sleep, while the wives spent their money at the houses of haute couture. Suddenly things took a very nasty turn.

* * * * * * * *

The Anglo-French campaign in Norway had been a disaster. On May 11, the day after the Germans had launched their offensive against Belgium, Holland and Luxembourg, Jean sailed to Algeria from Marseilles. While there was not much he could do about it, he thought it best not to remain away from Metropolitan France for too long. His wife, the ex Lucy Bauten was a capable manager and ran the affairs of the chateau at Dreux without much help from himself. Mostly his time was spent in the capital where the headquarters of Lancour et Cie was situated. He maintained a pied a terre in Auteil, and although his personal fortune was quite meager, combined with that of his wife he was able to enjoy the life of an aristocrat which he truly believed was his due.

Quickly spotting Tony from the forward deck, after the 'Aigle' had been made fast, he waved. The man was dressed in an immaculate suit and jaunty hat, with a newspaper tucked under one arm. The sun tan and dark glasses had the effect of making him stand out from the small crowd awaiting the disembarking passengers. Jean was pleased to have remembered the box of cigars which were a favorite of Tony's.

"Bonjour mon ami" Tony grinned as he greeted him at the foot of the gangway. He thought his boss looked a little grayer at the temples since the last visit. "I want to invite you to the Moulin St. Pedro tonight, the seafood is superb" Tony confided as they waited for the taxi to take them to his place for predinner drinks. Jean enjoyed the vintage brandy that always sat on the heavy sideboard facing the window overlooking the street. No doubt Lancour et Cie subsidized the outrageous price that must have been paid for laying in such a fine cellar. C'est la vie. He looked out at the lights of the city. The heavy walls of the building effectively shut out the street noises which were always raucous in a North African city. The constant ebb and flow of people of all kinds with the occasional deals concluded after much haggling, could all be watched day or night from this vantage point.

They finished the usual toast to each other and replaced the snifters on the sideboard, retiring onto the rear balcony with their cigars to discuss business matters. Jean took care not to mention his suspicions, or the real purpose of his trip. If Tony guessed the intent he certainly didn't betray any outward sign. Maybe things would be clarified at a board meeting Jean was going to convene. He would think up some reason to have Tony absent when that took place. He hoped his instincts were wrong, but he would resolve things either way, the quicker the better. Soon the conversation turned to lighter topics.

"By the way Jean, another surprise for you tonight. I have invited Madame Delacroix to dine with us, and of course Peppi will be my companion." Tony stood in the doorway holding a tray with a second round of brandies. "Who the hell is Madame Delacroix" Jean queried. "You don't remember the party at the end of your trip in '38... the one at the Italian consulate?" Mon Dieu, he remembered that one all right. He'd had an almighty hangover the following day. "Well Yvette Delacroix was the one you were getting very cozy with, until that little fat slob of a husband put in his appearance, and yanked her away." Now he recalled exactly to whom Tony referred. A fascinating petite creature in a strapless black dress who had stood no higher than his chin which had given him a distinct advantage in admiring her décolleté. She had described some outrageous happenings at the same time jabbing a jeweled cigarette holder in such animation that a shower of ash dropped into his champagne glass... so this was going to be his dinner companion. Delightful. He looked at his watch, then raised his glass toward Tony, "Bon Appetit. Let's be on our way."

After stopping at the hotel for Jean to take a quick bath and a change of clothes, the two men arrived at their destination. Set back from the Rue Dennis in a lush garden complimented by ornate fountains the Moulin St. Pedro proved to be exceptional, as did its prices. Once inside, the ambiance was not lost on the party of four awaiting their meal. Tony and Peppi were laughing about the latest sex scandals in the Oran newspapers. Jean was delighted by Yvette's chitchat, and as she placed another Turkish cigarette in her holder, he reminded her of the incident when she'd ruined his glass of champagne. Her infectious laugh startled diners at the next table. "But that's a small price to pay for my company M'sieu, n'est ce pas?"… He replied that indeed it was. She proceeded to tell him a small part of her life over the meal. Both parents were French and she had been born in Syria. Jean suspected that more than pure French blood ran in her veins, but kept the notion to himself. Often the combination of several ethnic lines produced the most alluring females around the southern Mediterranean coastline. Both women were wearing garlands of hibiscus, bought from street hawkers earlier in the evening. At the end of the night they would be thrown away, having had one brief moment of glory around the neck of a beautiful woman.

The effect of the drinks coupled with the smell of hibiscus and Turkish cigarettes were making Jean feel slightly heady, and glancing at his watch he realized they'd been in the establishment over three hours. A piano in the corner was being played by a sad eyed man, as both couples got up to dance on the small floor across from the bar. Jean's wife Lucy infrequently danced with him and he felt out of practice, however tonight with Yvette he could have gone on forever as they glided in unison.

She told him of being bored living in Oran without much sense of purpose, intimating that she'd married her husband for his money. Perhaps children would change things, but so far this had been denied her. Jacques, her husband, was away on a business trip to Dakar, and wouldn't be back until the middle of June. Jean bent over her as they danced, looking down the front of her dress, before whispering in her ear. Glancing at him she hesitated a moment, smiled and nodded. Both parties hailed separate taxis after the pleasurable evening the Moulin St. Pedro had provided. Tony exchanged a brief quizzical look with Yvette, just as the first taxi pulled up, but this went unnoticed by either Jean or Peppi as they departed.

4

SOLDIERS OF THE SPADE

KARL READ NEWSPAPER ARTICLES ABOUT THE rising economy of the third Reich and wondered if that would be a better place to seek employment. With a full time job he would be able to send money to his mother on a regular basis, and still be able to come home occasionally... it was not like going to China! His mother was upset when he told her about his plans and she immediately felt an oncoming headache. Trying to dissuade Karl only made it worse, as she knew he'd made up his mind. Finally she sat down at the table cupping her chin with both hands. She was going to miss him, let alone his friend Hans, but Karl could be stubborn so she did her best in adjusting to the situation.

Later that month Karl took the train to Augsburg, stopping en route in Linz for a couple of days in order to visit an aunt at his mother's behest. He had saved a little money working at the grocery store and a couple of other jobs. He had packed what he thought was needed inside two old battered suitcases. The farewell at the station proved somewhat traumatic as he kissed his mother goodbye and gave a hug to Hans. As the train gathered speed he felt grown up and in charge of his destiny.

In less than six months German troops would stream across the Austrian border initiating the 'Anschluss' the annexation of Austria. As Adolf Hitler explained to the citizens of Vienna, 'as leader and chancellor of Germany I report before history that my homeland has now entered the German Reich.' Perhaps if Karl had only known what was about to happen he could have saved the cost of his train ticket. Germany didn't exactly turn out to be the promised land. Lacking an apprenticeship or more formal academic qualification Karl found himself drifting from one menial job to another. He cleaned offices and painted houses generally working at whatever presented itself. He'd enjoyed one job working on a farm. He was strong and a hard worker, but the farmer had caught him eyeing his daughter so once again he was looking for work.

After a few weeks things were becoming desperate. The landlady at his lodgings was demanding the unpaid rent and he always felt hungry. Walking by a department store he entered to escape the rain. After looking at a counter displaying clothing he surreptitiously pocketed a pair of gloves while the clerk was engaged in conversation with a customer. Later he couldn't decide if he really needed them or whether it was the opportunity which presented itself that got him into trouble. Just as he was about to leave the store a hand tapped him on the shoulder. "Would you mind stepping this way, Sir?" The floor walker was an elderly and gaunt looking individual with a pince-nez perched on a long nose. Karl thought of making a run for it but by then it was too late as two other shop assistants were between him and the exit. He came before the local magistrate who went through the usual formalities. Karl was confused and ashamed as he thought of his Mutti. He imagined the look of grief on her face as she heard the news, and cursed himself for being so stupid.

The sentence was a month in jail. As it was a first offense, an option was offered. A suspension of sentence if he signed a document enrolling him in the Reich Labor Service... 'Soldiers of the Spade.' Karl decided this might be the lesser of two evils. Later he wished he'd spent the four weeks in jail. He was issued a uniform and blankets after reporting to the barracks housing a large contingent of other men doing compulsory service. The place was located several kilometers outside the city.

Groups marched to waiting trucks each morning, with their standard issue government spades held over their shoulders, as a soldier would carry his rifle. After a while, Karl couldn't remember how many different building projects he'd worked on. Every day his feet hurt wearing the military style boots, and each of his hands were permanently blistered hefting the heavy spade. The military discipline was alien to Karl, but at least he had a roof over his head and three square meals a day. The worst thing was getting up at 5 o'clock each morning. He enjoyed the comradeship even though the others tended to make fun of his Viennese accent.

One day they were mustered in front of the main building and told they'd been honored by being chosen to attend the National Socialist Congress at Nuremberg. It was to be held that year under the title 'Rally of Work' and Der Führer himself would be present. The opening ceremonies were to be conducted by Rudolf Hess, Hitler's deputy, later a march past of 40, 000 'Soldiers of the Spade' was to take place. Everybody was told that this was to be the most spectacular show amongst the various events at the Congress, and exemplary behavior was required by all participants.

An excited buzz of conversation took place after their dismissal. The rally as such meant little to most of them, but the prospect of a break in their daily toil plus a trip to the city sparked their interest. Maybe there would be a chance of free beer... and even girls if they got lucky! To Karl, the rally was an eye-opener. The great mass of spectators, fiery speeches, insignia and banners, coupled with military precision impressed him. The wild enthusiasm on the part of the crowd made it something he wouldn't forget in a hurry.

The months rolled by and Karl began to weary of becoming a drone for the Third Reich. During one of the allowed visits to see his mother he told her that he was now thinking of joining the Wehrmacht. Life should be easier and the pay better… after all, now they were all members of the greater Reich. Hopefully he would be taught a trade in the army as he didn't want a lifetime doing odd jobs when he returned to civilian life. Hans agreed with his decision and wished him luck.

His request to meet the Squad Commander was duly granted and he was ushered into the Camp Headquarters Office. Standing smartly at attention he put forth his request. The commander ruffled through his meager file, looked up and made the comment "It's a good job you spent your time in the Labor Service, the Wehrmacht is not in the business of accepting common criminals." Karl stared hard at the man's Iron Cross pinned to his tunic, and thought of his father. "Case granted. You've done quite well since coming here Bayer, just remember to keep your nose clean and serve the Fatherland with pride." With that Karl stepped back, saluted and then returned to his bunk. Later that evening, accompanied by three comrades, Karl's forthcoming career change was celebrated in a nearby beer cellar and everyone got uproariously drunk. Two weeks after the binge Karl received his discharge papers and after saying his good-byes, slung his meager belongings into the back of a truck which would drop him off at the local station. As the Albert Ritter barracks faded from view his mind turned to the prospect of the ten days of leave he'd accrued which would be spent in Vienna before reporting for army service. The grin on his face lasted until he clambered down from the truck.

* * * * * * * *

Recruit depot No. 11 was sheer hell. The Albert Ritter discipline was a bed of roses in comparison. Fortunately he'd been prepared for most of it by his conversations with old sweats. Still the vindictive close cropped Prussian drill masters made him long for the time when he would be sent on the next assignment, which he hoped would be better. The Medical Officer diagnosed Karl as having flat feet and this was entered into his file… the powers that be decided this would make him an ideal clerk.

After several weeks on detachment at another camp, he was indoctrinated into the labyrinth of army paperwork and Pvt. Karl Bayer was posted to the 12th infantry support group. He wore a newly issued feldgrau uniform and stahlhelm. At least the helmet didn't have the ridiculous spike on top. He'd seen his father wearing one in a photograph taken in 1914, it always made him laugh.

* * * * * * * *

Spearheads rumbled across the Polish frontier not long after Karl joined the 12th infantry. The Blitzkrieg caused speculation and rumor amongst the newly minted soldiers, and suddenly all the combat troops of Karl's battalion were entrained for the front, clerks were not required as the bleeding of the Wehrmacht was still in the future. Later in the war, ancillary units would be thrown into the meat grinders of Russia and the battles for Berlin, until finally fifteen year old boys and pensioners formed the front line troops defending the Fatherland.

Karl applied for training as a teletype operator, not really knowing what this entailed, except it would mean a change from working through mountains of paperwork every day. His present boss was Sgt. Fritz Freiburg, an old-timer from the first world war. He liked Fritz, but also wanted to take advantage of any opportunity that might prove useful in civilian life. The Lieutenant vetoed his application pointing out that 'Sgt. Freiburg needs all the help he can get at present as who knows how long he'd have to wait for a replacement'. Karl wasn't unduly put out knowing other things would come his way. Walter Tisch, one of the other clerks in the section, came into the room and perched on the edge of his desk. "Don't forget we are playing tennis this evening after it's time to get out of this paper mill". Walter was a good player and had been teaching his comrade how to play. "O.K., but don't hit the ball so hard this time... I'm losing too much weight having to bend over to pick them up" Walter laughed. "If you want to enjoy the facilities of this country club you have to expend a little effort and cut down on your beer guzzling!"

* * * * * * * *

Lucy almost didn't gain her baccalaureate needed for university entrance. The school in Lausanne nearly stifled her from the beginning with constant reminders regarding the poise and deportment expected of it's students. Social events arranged by the faculty and the shallowness of some fellow students depressed her. Lucy shuddered thinking about what it must be costing her father in fees... at least she was learning to ride well as the establishment maintained first rate stables. The riding sessions gave an opportunity to be by herself... a welcome option from classes in table decoration or elocution etc. Very little was taught about things Lucy considered important. Maybe the Sorbonne would meet her needs. Finally the time came to say au revoir to Switzerland and thinking of what lay ahead, her spirits began to revive.

Life at the university proved to be stimulating, but required a lot more work than she'd bargained for in order to keep up with her peers. It was annoying to find that some students never appeared to study at all, then got much higher marks in exams than she did! She hoped her father was satisfied with her progress although he hardly mentioned it.

Lucy adored the Parisian cafe scene and often sat listening to students arguing about politics and philosophy for hours on end. She would gravitate between popular establishments, and her favorite was 'Remnics' patronized for the most part by aspiring artists.

Excited by these new avenues of experience which had opened up, suddenly everything fell apart. A phone call one night told her that her father had died of a heart attack. Somehow it seemed impossible, only last weekend she'd accompanied her parents to an art exhibition at the Louvre. Her father had laughed when told of her latest escapades and appeared to be in the best of health and now Lucy was mortified by his death. Depression and withdrawal set in during her third year at the Sorbonne. Fortunately she was close enough to look after her mother... but Madame Bauten was becoming increasingly senile, and since her husband's demise, appeared to be rapidly going downhill. Several people told Lucy she must be prepared to move her into a nursing home if things worsened. It wasn't as if the house was too large to manage as the two servants and a gardener were adequate, but the steep stairs became a problem for Madame Bauten who was now hobbling around with the help of a cane.

Lucy felt crushed with the responsibility of having to manage all the family affairs and wished she had an older brother or sister to help. Somehow she struggled through her final year but had nearly reached the point of exhaustion. Her mother seemed slightly better, but secretly Lucy thought it wouldn't be too long before having to attend a second funeral. Louise Bauten passed away peacefully in her own home eighteen months after the death of her husband. The family lawyer took care of everything.

Afterwards Lucy was immensely relieved by having someone to lean on especially as Charles had been a lifetime friend of her father and felt obligated to his daughter. He assured her that the house would fetch a good price and asked how she wanted to dispose of all the contents. In sudden alarm Lucy recalled the tresor and the following week had it transferred into a vault at the Banque Salomon, along with a collection of keepsakes having sentimental value. Charles had arranged to have most of the household contents auctioned off and was trying to find alternative employment for the staff who had served the Bautens loyally over the years.

Lucy decided to lease an apartment and chose all new furnishings to counter memories of the recent past. The house would be missed, but then it would be ridiculous to remain living there by herself.

After several months everything was finalized and Lucy felt a weight had been lifted off her shoulders. Her depressions seemed a thing of the past, and Charles informed her she was now a wealthy woman dictated by her father's will and sale of the house. He advised investing the major part of the money in gilt-edged holdings, and offered Lucy an introduction to a director of one of the more conservative financial institutions in the city.

The new maisonette Lucy found was perfect for her needs. It was in a quiet tree lined cul-de sac, and was within easy reach of the Bois de Boulogne where she could ride every day if the weather permitted. Maybe later on she would buy a horse but for the moment decided renting was easiest and less troublesome in the city.

At present there were several boyfriends she could choose from when needing an escort to attend various social functions. Vaguely, Lucy felt an inner sense of drift from everything that recently comprised her orbit. Maybe a job would provide new interests and friends, but this could wait awhile. The present freedom was a heady drug so why not enjoy all that Paris had to offer in the meantime?

It was a glorious spring day and everybody who could

mount a horse appeared to be in the Bois that morning. People strolled along footpaths enjoying the sunshine and small children clutched paper bags containing bread crumbs for ducks on the lake. Couples seemed animated and even Lucy's mount appeared more sprightly than usual. Stopping at a drinking trough, the horse began its usual ritual then brought it's head around for the proffered lump of sugar. Lucy momentarily closed her eyes and turned her face towards the sun while the horse drank. The horse gave a small whinny indicating it was time to move on as Lucy leaned forward to pat his neck. Straightening up, the noise made by another horse slurping water attracted her attention, and half turning in the saddle she noticed its uniformed rider. Bon jour, Mademoiselle... the rider raised his cap. As he spoke Lucy stared, then smiled. "Good God I don't believe it... Paul Rocard." "Cadet Rocard, at your service... is it the one and only Lucy Bauten?" Both laughed uproariously, dismounted and embraced. After the initial questions and answers were disposed of, Paul remounted his horse saying. "Come on Lucy, let's turn these old nags in, and then we'll go to Rupert's for lunch and rehash our lives."

Over the next few weeks they saw one another whenever Paul was able to get away from the military school of St. Cyr. Final exams were coming up prior to his gaining a commission making it doubly hard to meet in the final stretch. Once graduation was over he'd have a month of freedom before joining his regiment, the 159th Alpine infantry stationed at Briançon. Two days after becoming Lieut. Rocard, the couple dined in an intimate restaurant close to the left bank.

Neither Paul or Lucy stopped to realize they were not so much in love with each other, but in love with a form of romance... a kind of carryover from earlier times together when Lucy had hesitated in inviting Paul home. She was happy footing the bills and did so as discreetly as possible.

Paul apparently did not mind.... with his pay he didn't have much choice, but with an occasional loan from his uncle he splurged and Lucy was quick to notice his generosity. Suddenly Paul leaned across the table and proposed. She nearly giggled as he was grinning crazily at her... the effect of the wine was taking it's toll. Trying to compose a suitable response and ignoring a twinge of hesitation, she accepted.

5

THE HONEYMOON

LUCY STILL FEELING SADDENED ABOUT THE death of her parents decided the wedding should be a low key affair which suited Paul who had no living relatives apart from his brother. Invitations were sent out at the end of the month to a small circle of their special friends and Lucy was kept busy with a host of minor details for the approaching occasion.

It was a bright sunny day for the happy event. Following the church ceremony, the bride and groom walked under an archway of crossed sabers held aloft by eight St. Cyr cadets, an embellishment Paul had kept as a surprise. As part of the military establishment Lucy knew she'd probably endure long periods away from her new husband but right now this all lay in the future.

The honeymoon was spent in Italy and during this time they often made love, even when Lucy reminded him not to act as if he was "in the saddle going full out in the Bois." He would become slightly sheepish, promising to remember for next time. They spent a few days in Venice where Paul having drunk too much one afternoon all but fell out of their gondola, much to the amusement of onlookers. Lucy began to notice some rough edges regarding her new husband, but in general she was happy and decided it was early days for now. Later, as daily routine supplanted the present glamour, she would find ways to smooth out any bumps in the road.

After hours spent at the Lido, art galleries, and many drinks in the cafes around St. Mark's Square, they were feeling fatigued so decided to move north and stay a few days at Lake Como for a change of pace. While at the hotel overlooking the lake their first quarrel erupted. The row itself didn't particularly upset Lucy as it was over some trivial matter, but the darker side Paul displayed gave her misgivings about similar happenings in the future. At the end of the month it was time to return to Paris where they would spend a few days at the maisonette prior to Paul reporting for duty with his regiment. They talked about whether Lucy should move down to Briançon, but as he had no idea how long he would be stationed there, it was decided she'd continue living in Paris and visit occasionally for long weekends. Lucy resumed her life without unduly missing her husband. At first she looked forward to visiting Paul, but found Briançon tedious after awhile, and always felt relieved climbing into a taxi to catch a train back to Paris.

Paul introduced her to several of his fellow officers, and once or twice she had accompanied other wives visiting their husbands. Generally she found little in common with them, and it reminded her of the days spent at the Hotel Nieuport in Cannes when she'd often been bored with the people staying there.

Lucy sighed and wished Sophie was around to enliven the various functions she was forced to attend. Paul never ceased telling her these were events that would 'advance his career but she couldn't take seriously a society hermetically sealed off from the outside community. Perhaps this was unfair, probably the Army was not so different from other professions, but it seemed military regimentation and mindless rituals pervaded her life nearly 24 hours a day whenever she was with Paul. He was fitting into the mold with no trouble at all, or so it seemed.

She'd just got back from a party in Paris when the phone rang. "Lucy, I hate to tell you, but part of my regiment is being sent to Indochina at the end of the month. I spoke with my colonel to see if the married ones might be exempted from going, but was told duty comes before personal matters in the Army. In fact, he was quite frosty at the idea of my suggesting it." Lucy realized she wasn't exactly sincere in telling him how upset she was with this piece of news, but reassured Paul they would survive the upheaval. She even thought a trip to the Far East might prove a pleasant diversion someday in the future. At least she could forget about having to see Briançon again, which was one consolation.

Paul wasn't exactly a prolific correspondent. Occasionally when he wrote to her a black and white photo with an exotic background would fall out of the envelope, but the contents of his letters hardly revealed anything about the kind of life he was living, and all references to her coming out had been dropped months ago. At first Lucy corresponded on a regular basis, but lately had lost the urge to write, other than the occasional note.

She had made an arrangement at an exclusive store to have small luxuries sent to Paul every three months. At first a hand written card was always enclosed, but now the parcels were sent without this personal touch. Lucy realized it had been almost eight months since they'd corresponded. This was ridiculous, she was married but in name only, though the situation wasn't too displeasing.

How long was he going to stay in that far off place? Finally, after another three months had passed without contact, she decided to phone Paul's colonel, only to be told by the adjutant that Colonel Besson was on a visit to Paris. Having obtained a phone number where he could be reached, she arranged to meet him for dinner the next night. Lucy thought Col. Besson sounded constrained when answering her call, but seemed pleased to have the opportunity of dining with her, as he was alone in Paris.

Lucy had met Besson once at a cocktail party. The wife was a mousy little woman who left no impression on her. He was tall and thin. His rugged suntanned face had seen many hard African summers spent at lonely outposts of the French empire. A small bald spot showed through his closely cropped white hair. Two rows of medal ribbons adorned his khaki tunic. He reminded her a bit of her father in his mannerisms, but behind the austere countenance was revealed a kindly and understanding man.

After the main course, Lucy came to the point of why she'd requested the meeting. Colonel Besson looked at her for a brief moment, finished his wine and laid his napkin to one side. "Madame Rocard, having listened to what you've told me, I feel I should have spoken to you long before now. I take it your husband didn't tell you about the reason for my sending him to Indochina?" Lucy replied that all she knew was what Paul had told her on the phone. "In that case, " Besson continued, "I must be frank. Paul got himself involved with the wife of a brother officer, and later I had to straighten out an embarrassing deficit in the regimental mess funds for which Lt. Rocard was partly responsible. To avoid scandal, I thought an immediate posting overseas was called for."

Lucy was stunned. So this in part was the explanation for the infrequent correspondence… the fool, why hadn't he asked her for money? On second thoughts she became angry at the idea that if she'd given it, no doubt it would have been spent subsidizing an affair. This was a novel situation for Lucy, and her ego began feeling slightly bruised. Col. Besson reached across the table and laid a hand on hers. "Lucy, I'm sorry to have had to tell you all this. A man in my position quite often has to be the bearer of distasteful news."

After ordering more wine, Besson told her the rumor

that Paul was suspected of having picked up an opium habit since being in Hanoi, and it was very probable that he was about to be cashiered. Lucy swallowed her brandy quicker than she meant to and coughed. Forcing a smile, she thanked Besson, and added, "Under the circumstances, I think the court will find due cause for a divorce. I'm sorry that my husband has caused a black mark upon the affairs of the regiment." Colonel Besson returned her smile and said "C'est la vie. Think nothing of it for my part. The Army is good at sweeping its own dirt under the carpet."

Outside the restaurant, Besson kissed her hand and saluted. "Don't hesitate to contact me if I may be of any assistance in the future. Remember, so long as one retains one's health and money, most problems can be solved given a little time. "Lucy watched him as his taxi departed, sitting ram-rod stiff in the back seat, with his kepi worn at a slight tilt. He turned and gave Lucy one last glance. She shrugged, turned and crossed the road, deciding to walk awhile allowing her thoughts to settle before returning home. Thank God no children had resulted from the union with Paul. It was now a time to re-evaluate her life, and head in a new direction. She had a feeling of being both relieved and disappointed by what Col. Besson had told her.

Emerging from the Metro on the Rue de Vaugirard, Lucy bumped into Sophie Deschamps, her friend from days spent together on vacation in Cannes. Both girls were delighted by this chance meeting... it had been a long time since they had seen each other, and they hugged in greeting. "Lucy, let's go for coffee and a long talk. When I first spotted you, did I detect a thoughtful look on your face?"Lucy laughed, "well, it was probably more of a mixed up expression." She began to relate her news as they walked along. After the second cup of coffee, Sophie sighed. "It seems we all have our troubles. I've just broken up with Jean Boulet." Lucy knew him from her time at the Sorbonne. He was now a well-known radio announcer. After a few more minutes discussing the perfidy of the male species, the two girls agreed to meet the following day for lunch at Lucy's place in order to continue catching up on each others lives.

* * * * * * * *

The Paris paper was two days old, dated May 28th, 1940. The headline bore two words in large print, 'BELGIUM CAPITULATES.' With a sinking heart, Jean continued to read on about the events leading up to this débâcle. Two days previously the British Expeditionary Force had started 'Operation Dynamo.' British and French troops were being evacuated to England from Dunkirk. On the 19th, General Weygand had taken over as commander of the French armies. Jean deLancour hadn't much respect for the man, having met him at different functions before the war. On the 26th, Weygand had told Baudoum, Secretary of the War Cabinet "If we succumb, I shall have the ghastly job of meeting the Germans, just as at Rethonde 22 years ago, but with positions reversed."

Reading the paper's editorial, he noted the absence of any reference to the 'Entente cordiale, ' but a use of the word 'betrayal' in talking about the evacuation underway at Dunkirk. Too dismayed to read further, Jean ordered another brandy to bolster his morale. Other patrons of the bistro were busy discussing the latest turn of events, and he realized how stupid he'd been not to pay more attention to the news over the past few days. A slight sense of panic began to take hold. Truly it was a catastrophe so he'd finish up things immediately and get back to France before it was too late. What an idiot, completely taken up in his whirlwind affair with Yvette since returning to Algiers. The question of Tony was still unresolved, its implications and ensuing scandal being pushed to the inner recesses of his mind, while he'd indulged himself like an adolescent with this seductive woman. It must be a softening of the brain.

The board meeting convened two days after his return to Oran. The Marquis was dressed in a linen tropical suit bought during a visit to London, and wore a boutonniere in the left lapel. Sporting a colorful bow tie, he looked immaculate and could have been mistaken for a colonial governor of any one of a number of African colonies. On entering through the familiar heavy oak door bearing a plaque proclaiming 'Conseil d' administration' he greeted members seated around the table. It seemed like a case of déjà vu. No hints of wrongdoing were brought up by any of those in attendance, despite some probing questions on his part. He didn't want to show his hand and was hoping for someone to broach their suspicions. But no, the whole thing seemed almost a repeat of the meeting held during his previous trip to Algeria.

* * * * * * * *

Yvette got out of the taxi and hurried over to his table where she leaned over and kissed his cheek. Jerked out of his musings, Jean appreciated the view of her superb breasts displayed before him. After ordering their lunch and chatting awhile, he pushed his newspaper across the table without comment. Yvette scanned the headlines and then frowned. Looking up at him she said "It is too bad... what fools these men are who presume to control us, but it will pass. Life is meant to be lived, not squandered." Having said this, Yvette raised her glass and smiled. "Don't be so sad cheri, as the saying goes, the more things change the more they stay the same." Jean stared back at her for a moment not sure if the woman was a dumb version of Aphrodite, or indeed a lot smarter than he gave her credit for.

* * * * * * * *

Reaching into his jacket pocket, he extracted a small box containing the bracelet bought in Algiers from an expensive jewelers on the Blvd. Anatole France. It was owned by a nephew of Pierre Manville, so he was confident that the price he'd paid wasn't unduly inflated, even though it would take care of Jamail's salary for a couple of years or so. Her delight at the gift was worth all the time spent looking at the innumerable trays of gems before selecting his choice.

Two women at an adjacent table glanced with envy as Yvette outstretched her wrist displaying her gift. The light flashes given off by the diamonds reminded him of standing on the steps leading to the Sacre Coeur and watching Paris illuminated after dark. Yvette spoke softly, "Let's go back to the hotel, I would like to thank you properly mon cheri."

6

THE BETRAYAL

"Unzip me cheri," Jean didn't need telling twice aware that a rigid member has no conscience. After Yvette emerged naked from the bathroom, he watched her walk slinkily towards him… she knew the effect it was having. Jean surmised he'd already died and gone to heaven. For a time they kissed and fondled on the bed before Yvette rolled on top and began making passionate love.

Exhilarated and spent, the couple sprawled out and Jean reached over for his cigarettes. Lighting one for himself and Yvette he propped himself against the headboard watching smoke eddies wafted by the ceiling fan. He thought of other women in his past who'd shared his bed, but none compared with the one beside him. She was incredibly different one moment tender, and the next a wild animal. He realized it excited him more than he cared to admit.

Having cooled off Yvette stuck the tip of her tongue in her lover's ear before whispering "Mon ami…I think we are both exhausted and need to save a little for next time. Thank you for a most marvelous evening." Jean, stripped of everything except his watch agreed, noting it was now 3:50 a.m. and that the evening referred to was now history. Laying back, he glanced at his companion before sleep engulfed him.

Awakening just before noon Jean was conscious of street noises penetrating the hotel room through the shutters. Trying to marshal his thoughts, he stretched and sat up in bed. Suddenly, aware of being alone his eyes focused on a note propped against a glass on the dresser. Opening the envelope he read a few digits scrawled in lipstick. It took a second to realize it was a telephone number, Yvette's.

Relaxing in his bath, a couple of thoughts penetrated his hangover. The first dealt with his being infatuated so quickly, the other that he'd arranged to dine with his cousin aboard the 'Surcouf', a huge submarine docked at the Mers el Kebir naval base.

His cousin Jules, employed by a civilian contractor, was on temporary attachment to the navy in order to monitor and calibrate navigational equipment. The vessel was impressive, even having a watertight hangar on its deck, housing a tiny reconnaissance airplane. It was a special honor to serve on this vessel which was the pride of Admiral Darlan, and the entire French fleet.

Jean now dressed for dinner, walked downstairs and ordered a coffee and campari. His thoughts turned back to Yvette. Maybe it was his vanity causing his present euphoria, after all he must be quite a few years older than the woman, or so he surmised but whatever the cause he was delighted how she'd responded to his lovemaking, and it took someone special to make him feel the way he did. He would phone her before his visit to the 'Surcouf'. When he called, there was no reply.

Arriving at the huge base he was greeted by Jules whom he hadn't seen in years. Alongside the 'Surcouf' was moored the 'Richlieu', a gigantic battleship that made the submarine appear small in comparison despite its bulk. Jean felt a tinge of pride seeing this naval might. Only the British fleet could match the French, and fortunately they were allies at this point in history. Thank God for the 'Entente cordiale', as it would take care of those new madmen of Europe. He was taken on the allowed tour of the vessel, and could only guess what was contained in the areas they bypassed. Jules offered few comments as maybe he didn't know either, perhaps only concerned with his own field of expertise. At each forbidden zone a bored marine with a side arm stood guard to comply with standing orders while the 'Surcouf' was in port.

The dinner in the mess was excellent. Only one or two officers were present, as the main body of the crew were ashore. He was glad he hadn't eaten anything since the 'Moulin St. Pedro' enabling him to do justice to each of the courses, served by stewards wearing white monkey jackets. Jean had envisioned cramped quarters on a submarine, and was surprised by the spaciousness of the surroundings. Over cigars and brandies, a pleasant glow of bonhomie settled in on both men, but pleading tiredness Jean took his leave wishing Jules "Bon Voyage, and make sure you come to stay with Lucy and myself at Dreux, in the near future." Jules replied "I hope it won't be long, its been good seeing you after all this time." Jules was no sailor and these damned sea trials his company sent him on were something he could do without. His views of the war situation depressed Jean and he was glad to be alone again with his thoughts of Yvette. It was rather like the tornadoes he'd read about wherein one was sucked up into the vortex. One moment feet firmly on the ground, and then 'Voila,' complete loss of control over the situation. The taxi deposited him at the hotel. Flinging off his clothes he collapsed on the bed and was instantly asleep. Things were going a little too fast, and his body was reminding him it was trailing a few lengths behind.

He slept soundly until 10:30 a.m. After dressing it seemed some exercise might help clear his mind and refocus his thoughts on the prime purpose of his trip. Stopping off at his favorite Arab cafe for a lunch of couscous, fruit and wine, his conversation with Marcel Cordon before leaving

Paris resurfaced. He knew he couldn't procrastinate much longer, but where to start? Then it came to him, a visit to the sub office in Algiers and a talk with Pierre Manville, the deputy Chef de Bureau might be in order. He knew that Tony and Pierre disliked one another, which was one of the reasons he'd separated their business operations in the first place. Pierre was a loyal old stick who'd been a friend of his father when he'd run Lancour et Cie. It was over 400km to Algiers, but it might just be worth it. Having come to a decision, Jean got up from the table and paid his bill. Perhaps Yvette would come too? Dismissing the idea, he deemed infatuation was one thing, but business and pleasure didn't usually mix.

Back in his room at the hotel, Jean picked up the phone and gave the number Yvette had scrawled in lipstick to the hotel switchboard. "Bon jour, ici la Villa Miramar." Ascertaining it was the maid who had answered, he asked to speak with her mistress, but was disappointed finding that Yvette had gone out and was not expected back until late. Having established the address of the Villa Miramar, he decided to send a bouquet of roses with a billet doux, and would now try phoning from Algiers.

After a second call to Pierre Manville arranging his visit, Jean spread business papers out on the bed and began studying their content. After a time he dozed off, and when he awoke he realized it was quite late. Pierre had arranged for a chauffeured car to pick him up early, as it would require several hours of travel. Jean decided that after arriving, he would meet Pierre over dinner, before going into the office the following morning. Finishing a rather indifferent meal in the hotel, he returned to his room and finished reading the hand written reports given him in Paris by Marcel, the financial director. Getting up, he gathered together all the scattered paperwork and returned the pages to a folder on the dresser. The oppressive heat of the room was unrelieved by the solitary ceiling fan. Jean unlatched the shutters and stood by the open window to make the most of a faint breeze. Standing there reminded him of nights spent on sentry duty at Verdun in 1917, occasional periods of relative calm, then all hell would let loose. The sour feeling in his stomach was the same as then, however now the face of the enemy was familiar.

* * * * * * * *

Jamail, the chauffeur, tapped on Jean's door just as he snapped shut the suitcase containing what was needed for the trip. Jamail saluted, and picked up the case. Jean privately thought his gray uniform and leather boots were slightly ridiculous for the climate of Algeria, but perhaps convention demanded it along with the many other trappings of Lancour et Cie. Jean smiled remembering a newspaper cartoon which had shown him standing on the apex of a pyramid, he felt it apt or a bore depending on his mood.

Jamail had five children, was discreet and an excellent driver. Having formerly served Jean's father, he was considered a valuable and loyal employee of the Company. Life for an Algerian was hard under the French Colonial government and Jamail considered himself truly fortunate to have his steady job and an income far greater than many of his compatriots.

As the car passed the 89km marker, Jean closed his eyes and slumped back in the seat after sliding the glass partition that separated him from Jamail in both a physical and symbolic manner, realizing he didn't even know the man's surname. The approach to the city always lightened Jean's mood. He preferred it to Oran, and wondered why the main office was located there. No doubt his father originally had some good reasons for the choice. As the car passed the Lancour office on the Rue el Azoun, he noted it had been repainted and generally spruced up since the last trip.

* * * * * * * *

Algiers had been founded by the Phoenicians, and the sun glinted on its white buildings giving a hard reflected glare to its streets. The winters were cool and wet, with hot and dry summers. Jean was born in 1898 at a house his parents maintained on the outskirts of Algiers. At the age of three his parents had taken him back to metropolitan France. Later on as a young man he'd returned many times on business, and always felt affection for the vibrant city. He married Julie Cassour in 1920. They'd had a wonderful two years together, before her tragic death in a train accident and he always regretted that they'd never had children. After his second marriage, Lucy Bauten had given him two boys in quick succession, so at least there would be an heir to the Lancour empire. As the car pulled to a halt outside the hotel, he instructed Jamail that he'd be required to take him to the Lancour office in the morning, and that Pierre Manville would notify him of the time to pick him up.

Striding into the hotel bar, he saw the distinctive back of Pierre's head as he sat sipping a glass of wine. Manville seemed pleased to see him, but with his creased features, it was difficult to ascertain what emotions were portrayed. After about an hour pleasantly spent discussing family matters, with an exchange of photos showing domestic scenes, both men went into the dining room. Jean realized that after the fourth drink he'd better broach the reason for their meeting, before Pierre lost his powers to concentrate, and Jean his clear head for the task at hand. Pierre bent over and extracted a notebook from his briefcase resting against the table leg. "M'sieu, I have kept this record of transactions covering the past eighteen months, but until now have been hesitant to show them to anyone before having positive proof of the anomalies contained. It is a great relief to be able to bring them to your attention." Jean took the book and placed it next to the menu. "Please don't concern yourself further mon ami, but never breathe the slightest suspicion to anyone regarding what you've compiled." Jean leaned back in his chair and stared at Pierre for a moment. His instincts made him trust the man. Manville seemed to suddenly relax as if an inner spring had been released. They both drank another brandy before wishing one another adieu.

The following day Jean ensconced himself in Manville's office at the Lancour building. The night before he'd told Pierre to take the day off, and borrowed his office key. "Please inform your secretary to have the relevant files available." Shortly after noon, he knew his journey hadn't been wasted. His morning perusal of the company files, in addition to Pierre's notes left no doubt. He ordered coffee to be sent in then slumped in the chair making sure in his mind the evidence was conclusive. It didn't need a detective to pin point that thousands of francs had been embezzled.

Curiously the money had been siphoned off with hardly any attempts at a cover up which amazed Jean as he yawned and stood up. He felt saddened thinking about ending a friendship on such a sour note... however the question was how to handle the next move, as perhaps others might be involved. He needed to wrap the whole thing up as quickly as possible before the press got a whiff of scandal which in turn would depress the Lancour share prices.

7

JUNE 10, 1940

JEAN ARRIVED BACK IN ORAN IN the early evening. He had been to Mascara in order to see an old friend, Henri Roux, who had run the credit Lyonnais in Oran until ill health forced him into an early retirement. He was married to a charming Algerian woman and both of their children were at school in France. The couple had bought the house they now lived in back in the late twenties, and over a period of time had turned the place into an oasis of cool tranquility bordering a harsh arid hinterland. After finishing a superb lunch, Henri and Jean returned to one of the inner courtyards where the only sound was the splashing of two fountains.

Jean related the events of the past few days, before pushing a small pile of documents across the table towards his friend. Getting up, he went in search of Henri's wife, whom he found on the back verandah. They talked of family matters and current topics for almost an hour before Jean went back to Henri who'd neatly piled the documents and was leaning back in his chair smoking a cigar. Nodding towards the papers, he said "Your suspicions are well founded... a sad case of greed... what will you do?" At this point, Jean still wasn't entirely sure.

Jean kissed Henri and his wife on the cheeks. "Thank you for your time and hospitality." Each of them wondered if they would see one another again. Jamail brought the car around to the front entrance.

* * * * * * * *

It was humid and oppressive back in the city and he felt tired. Dismissing Jamail outside the hotel door, he bought a paper at the kiosk and went up to his room. Scanning the front page was enough to deepen his present depression. He felt irritable and slightly nervous, and regretted having made the trip to Algeria, although an inner self told him it was a damned good job he had. He could catch the night boat, and told the front desk to have the bill made ready.

Everything was coming apart at the seams. The hyena Mussolini had stabbed France in the back by declaring war, and German troops were closing in on Paris. He sat on the toilet trying to collect his thoughts. After a quick bath he wrote a letter to Tony informing him he was fired. He regretted not being able to do this in person but events didn't allow time for this. If he made restitution to Lancour et Cie for what he'd stolen, Jean would be prepared out of old friendship to drop the matter, otherwise all the evidence implicating his Chef de Bureau would be turned over to the police for criminal investigation, and the courts would decide the outcome. It was his choice.

He then wrote a quick note to Yvette, ending with the fact that it might be a very long time before they next met, but he would do everything possible to make sure they did. She knew how he felt, and no doubt understood why he must depart now before it was too late. He stamped and addressed Yvette's envelope, while leaving Tony's blank. Having dressed, he left the hotel and on the way he dropped Madame Delacroix's letter in a mail box.

* * * * * * * *

Tony had provided him with a key. He would put the letter on the mat just inside the door, and leave the key on top. He felt a slight revulsion on opening the door, and at the same time was startled to hear subdued music coming from the bedroom down the passage. Tony wasn't supposed to be back until the 12th! That had been the arrangement when he'd sent him on the bogus trip to El Affroun, ostensibly to look at a potential supplier for Lancour et Cie, at the same time, keeping him out of the way when the board meeting took place. So why was he here now?

A small amount of light was visible at the bottom of the door. The rest of the apartment was in darkness. He paused, his hand half way extended to the light switch. The headlights of a vehicle illuminated the foyer long enough for him to see a woman's shoe and a long dress strewn across the floor. Next to the shoe lay a diamond bracelet, which he knew with sickening certainty was bought a few days ago in Algiers. He stooped down and retrieved the letter and key he'd already placed on the mat, eased open the door and left. Reaching the first street corner, he leant up against the brickwork to catch his breath. He knew his blood pressure was skyrocketing, and a blind rage was beginning to develop. The bastard, the whore... they were in it together. Suddenly, he calmed down. He knew now exactly how things had to be settled.

In his room the pig skin suitcase was propped up with the other pieces ready for his departure. Putting it on the bed, he paused for a moment then with a quick movement released two concealed catches behind the inner lining. He'd had the bag especially made in the souk at Tangier a few years ago. The old Arab had crafted it with loving care and it had been worth the price they'd struck after a great deal of haggling.

The hidden compartment secured by the latches revealed a 9m/m P35 automatic. This gun had been issued as the Belgian service side arm in 1935, and Jean had obtained one from a business associate during a visit to Brussels. The gun lay nestled in its recessed leather tray. The case had never been any cause for concern to Jean when passing through many customs inspections. The gun always remained loaded.

Jean retraced his steps to the apartment, making sure nobody was around as he inserted the key in the door lock. Stepping inside gripping his gun, he flipped the safety catch. The gleam of light was gone from under the bedroom door, and the radio had now been turned off.

Very slowly, Jean crept along the passage. His eyes had grown accustomed to the darkness and a faint light came through the apartment window. Pile carpeting, plus the fact he'd left his shoes by the door allowed him to move silently forward, his left hand gently touching the wall for guidance. Opening the bedroom door just a crack, he heard heavy breathing. Momentarily the thought occurred that he wasn't sure where to find the light switch, but reaching carefully along the inside wall the tip of his finger contacted a toggle. He froze for an instant, before illuminating the bedroom.

Tony was face down with the sheet pulled almost completely over him, while Yvette lay naked on her side, with one arm dangling over the edge of the bed. The aroma of a Turkish cigarette still lingered in the air. Jean was an excellent shot. The Army had given him plenty of practice. He fired twice into the back of Tony's head and after the second shot, Yvette opened her eyes and looked at Jean in horror... he paused momentarily before shooting her once through the forehead. Her body lay like a rag doll. By now a deep pool of red had already seeped through Tony's shroud.

Strangely calm, Jean took out the handkerchief from his breast pocket and carefully wiped the handles of the bedroom and front door, then left the apartment feeling nothing but bitterness. He didn't imagine he would get away with it, but there was always the chance.

Perhaps the plea of 'crimes de passion' would be appropriate. Yvette's husband might get back in time from Dakar so maybe the police could pin it on him. He hardly thought so, but really didn't care. A feeling of numbness set in. He would have to hurry if he were to catch the ship for Marseilles.

8

CHAOS

After the decree nisi had been granted, Lucy celebrated by splurging at one of the great fashion houses in the city. A week later, after returning from a more mundane shopping trip to 'Printemps' she kicked her shoes off and plopped down on the sofa. An invitation from Jean de Lancour had arrived in the morning mail, and he'd enclosed two tickets for the Opera.

The couple had been introduced recently at a buffet lunch before the start of horse racing at Vincennes. Susie, a mutual friend who had made the introduction told Lucy he was a handsome widower and also amusing. Susie had known his wife Julie as they had been at school together. Once the two were alone, Lucy found they had many things in common and began to feel quite smitten with her new beau.

After an evening of dinner and the Opera, they strolled along the Seine for over an hour. She found Jean almost the exact opposite of Paul and realized how attracted she was becoming. Although enjoying her life of freedom, the idea of marrying a man that loved her, and the prospect of having children began to take hold. They had been seeing each other for three months and were out in the park when

Jean Lancour proposed. She was almost certain he would, and had decided beforehand what the answer would be.

* * * * * * * *

A year after their marriage, the first child, a boy, had been born. The second another boy, soon followed. Adjusting to a life at the chateau was difficult for Lucy in the beginning partly due to its size. The maisonette had sold for an excellent price and with the money Lucy bought a large block of shares in her husband's company. They had agreed to keep Jean's apartment in Auteil as a pied-à-terre when they wanted to spend time in Paris.

She'd persuaded François who'd worked for her father to move to the chateau along with his family and they now occupied the old gate keepers cottage. She was delighted when he'd agreed, as François had always been a favorite of hers. Having him around made the rambling building seem much more hospitable. The chateau had been fairly well maintained, but it was due a major renovation. Lucy now had the money to pay for it and this would provide a birthday gift for her new husband.

The Lancours entertained frequently, and mostly the guests were business associates of Jean, but she was also careful to include friends from the time she'd been single. Fortunately Jean wasn't the jealous type even when he knew some of the men were former escorts. Her husband's business trips often left her on her own, but the children and affairs of the chateau left little time to be lonely. When the war started, their life had hardly been affected, but now things were getting serious and Jean's present trip to Algeria had come at a bad time.

Until recently she'd hardly bothered with the news, but now made it a priority reading the Paris newspapers as soon as they were delivered. The radio was left on continuously, as one disaster after another unfolded. She knew she must do something about the San Lucien tresor and other things stored at the Banque Solomon. Jean was unaware of this matter as his wife's mind had been focused on other things since her marriage. It would be too late if the Boche marched into Paris, and that increasingly looked to be a possibility. If it was confiscated by the Germans, she'd never forgive herself and her father would turn over in his grave.

That afternoon Lucy phoned the bank manager about withdrawing everything deposited in the vault. The man sounded harried and advised her to come as soon as possible due to the deteriorating situation. An appointment was fixed for 2 p.m. the following day, when all the necessary paperwork would be ready. Driving into the city, Lucy noted that many army vehicles were headed west which seemed odd to her. Why weren't they going in the other direction, unless the unthinkable was about to happen?

François had been delegated to pull up several floor boards in the gazebo fronting the lake and rose gardens. Lucy had not given any reason to the old man for this task, and after returning from the bank asked him to help carry the contents of the St. Lucien from the car, and stow them under the gazebo floor. François laid some old blankets on top of the concrete foundation slab then placed the wrapped items on top. A few potato sacks were finally thrown over the entire pile before the floor boards were replaced.

François stood up clutching his back and Lucy told him to sit in an old rattan chair pushed into a corner. "François...I owe you an explanation." Lucy told the old man why he'd been exerting himself, knowing she could trust him implicitly. For François, the knowledge that the treasure was part of the heritage of 'La belle France' was all that mattered to him. When Lucy made him swear never to tell a soul, he was even a trifle miffed asking, "Has Madame ever had cause to doubt my loyalty?" She took both his hands and kissed him on the cheek. "Never, my old friend, and we have known one another for a good many years."

As they walked back through the grounds, François felt pleased thinking he'd been instrumental in preventing the Germans from ravishing something of his beloved France.

* * * * * * * *

Jean's boat docked at Marseilles in the early hours of the 13th of June. The ship had been packed, but the customs check was only perfunctory because of the unusually heavy influx of people. Everybody appeared tired and anxious due to the débâcle moving to its climax on the mainland. Nobody realized how much their lives would be changed by these dramatic events rapidly overtaking them. Paris had been declared an 'open city' and on the 11th of June, Pétain, de Gaulle, Churchill and Eden met at Briare to discuss the situation. An English expression crossed Jean's mind hearing about this......something about the futility of shutting the stable door after the horse had bolted, and wondered how much longer France could hold on.

He took a taxi to the Matour garage to pick up his Citröen which had been left there for storage and minor maintenance. Thank God he'd decided to drive down from Paris in the first place. The trains would be impossible with all these people on the move. His old friend Jules, a dentist, lived outside Lyons, so driving would enable him to have a brief rest stop on the journey. Paying his bill at the cashier's office, the latest government communiqué was being broadcast on the owner's radio. It announced that French troops were about to abandon Paris making Jean extremely apprehensive.

The fat garage owner took out a dirty red handkerchief, and wiped his sweaty brow. "You'll have to drive like the devil M'sieu if you are headed for the Paris area. You may find the Germans there before you." Jean had the man place two metal containers of gasoline in the back of the car in case of unforeseen eventualities, then pushed another large denomination bank note across the counter. "I need your phone and a map, vite." As he waited for the woman on the switchboard to connect with Dreux, he perused the map. Finally Lucy answered... she sounded close to being hysterical. After she'd calmed down somewhat, he continued... "Pack the barest necessities and make sure the car's tank is fueled up. Turn all the keys over to François and give him six months wages in advance." He'd worry later about what was to happen after that. "As soon as possible, take the children and drive to Tours. Stay at the Hotel Gerard. I'll be there whenever I can make it." With that he rang off... every moment counted now. Thank heavens Lucy had been at home when he called. With the map on the seat beside him, he headed in a northwesterly direction, pushing the Citröen as hard as he dared.

* * * * * * * *

After many hours on the road, he drove into the hotel courtyard. The last 200 km had been the worst. Remnants of the French 10th Army along with streams of civilian refugees clogged the highways. Occasionally he had resorted to little more than dirt tracks through farms, in an effort to circumvent the worst of the gridlocks, the whole thing was a nightmare with constant delays.

Some of the troops had amazed him with their look of abject defeat...was it possible this was the same proud army of France in which he had once served? Now a beaten and disorganized rabble it saddened and disgusted him, but it was of little consequence, his sole concern was in reaching his destination before it was too late.

* * * * * * * *

He spotted Lucy's Bugatti parked behind some other cars, as he unloaded baggage from the Citröen... it was the only positive thing that had happened since leaving Marseilles. The courtyard was jammed with vehicles of every description, most of them with piles of household effects strapped onto their roofs, and a few had mattresses overhanging fore and aft. The smart hotel had become another refugee depot. Striding into the entrance, he found many people milling around, or perched on whatever they could find to sit on. It was close to pandemonium.

A distracted member of the hotel staff gave him Lucy's room number which she'd been lucky to find considering the present chaotic situation. They fell into each others arms while the two boys held onto his legs. Lucy's journey had been even worse from her account and she'd only arrived two hours prior to Jean. They ordered drinks from the bar and took them outside where he told her his plan of action. They would leave the Citröen in a garage at Tours, and use the larger car to head for Nantes where Jean's sister lived. She had a large house and he was confident they could stay there for a while until they'd worked out a direction for their future. Any thoughts of living under the German heel was anathema to him, but then, what was the alternative?

He tried phoning his sister but the switchboards were jammed solid and he gave up... she would just have to be surprised when they rolled up in front of the house. Formalities could be foregone during these times of crisis.

After buying a few supplies from the local shops, they headed west out of the city. The children started to be fractious being too young to fathom these sudden disruptions in their normally placid routine. Little conversation took place between husband and wife and Lucy's thoughts were on the chateau being left to an unknown fate, along with the St Lucien which she could only hope would remain undiscovered. Jean's thoughts fixated on the last visit to the Gambetti apartment. He had blanked out the episode during the journey to Tours, but now the full significance of his actions struck home like a thunderbolt.

Within a few kilometers short of Saumur, the congestion on the road forced their pace to a crawl. A majority of the refugees probably had no idea of where they were headed. Their only thought was to put as much space between themselves and the relentless advance of the Panzer columns moving unimpeded towards them. German troops had entered Paris on the 14th and the cabinet had already transferred to Bordeaux. Two days previously, General Weygand had visited the President of the War Council and proposed asking for an armistice. Marshal Pétain had spoken of 'the necessity for requesting this to save what remains of France, and to permit rebuilding of the country.' France by now had become a corpse, and all that remained was for the funeral arrangements to be finalized.

The Lancour's Bugatti ground to a halt and Jean switched off the engine to conserve fuel. They'd just have to sit there until the latest choke point unsnarled itself. Staring out of the window Jean felt a sense of nausea overtake him. Both of the children were asleep and Lucy dozed fitfully. It was unusually hot for June making it unpleasant inside the car. Through a break in the hedge, Jean saw two Renault whippet tanks in the adjoining field. They were headed for the road. Irritably he knew they'd only worsen the bottle neck. Jean swore then closed his eyes in disgust.

Suddenly he heard the noise of an aircraft engine and glimpsed a shadow pass across the field. The leading tank erupted in a fireball, and the second careened wildly to one side. The explosion had thrown up a huge column of dirt which obscured his vision. Jean flung an arm around his wife just as four 20 m/m cannon shells ripped through the car's roof. Both adults were killed instantly, but the two boys lying on the back seat escaped without a scratch. The truck a few meters in front of the Bugatti burned with an intense heat. It had been carrying gasoline for the military depot outside Saumur where the tanks had been heading... For a brief second, an eerie silence ensued before a roar of flames drowned out the departing sound of the Me109's which had strafed the column. Ironically, the Marquis de Lancour still held 1, 700 shares in the German company who'd manufactured the 20 m/m rounds which blew away the top of his head splattering blood and brains on the dash.

9

THE FLYER

Unteroffizier Otto Steiner was feeling good. It looked as if the war in France was just about over. He didn't really think much about death at his age, but then there was always the possibility, life as a fighter pilot could be very hazardous. So far he'd attended the funerals of four comrades, an abrupt reminder of what could happen. Today any such thoughts were the last thing on his mind. A letter had arrived from his mother telling him the family news he so liked hearing about, and a post script told him a parcel was on the way for his birthday.

On Thursday, he would be twenty-four and two weeks later he would be going home to Halle for a ten days leave. He planned to give Anna, his girlfriend, the engagement ring he'd already bought, and couldn't wait to show it to her. Life couldn't be better as he loved flying, and getting paid for it wasn't hard to take. At sixteen he'd joined the Hitler Youth enabling him to obtain proficiency certificates from the glider school near his hometown. After completing his training, he'd joined the newly formed Luftwaffe. He had flown several different types of trainers before joining his first staffel which was equipped with Heinkel He51's. These biplanes seemed so outdated in comparison with their new equipment, it was hard to believe so little time had elapsed since piloting one. It must have been in 1937, when serving for a short time in the Condor legion during the civil war in Spain. He had even shot down a tubby little Russian-made 'Rata' belonging to the Republican side, before his bad crash landing in a rainstorm outside Salamanca.

The crash resulted in his being sent back to Germany for recuperation, sailing on the 'Robert Ley', one of the 'Strength through Joy' passenger ships owned by the Reich. Although being on crutches, it was like a tourist cruise, and he was almost sorry when the ship finally docked. After a spell at home and a long series of medical checks, he had finally been pronounced fit by the Luftwaffe doctors. He was assigned to a newly formed unit where he was kept busy on conversion courses in order to fly the new Messerschmitt Bf 109. Some of these had been used in Spain when it became apparent the He51's were inferior to the opposition. Most of his comrades were fresh out of flight school and Otto felt like a veteran with the experience gained in the Condor Legion.

He loved the 109, it was a beautiful machine to fly, and was fast. It had a few quirks, but he hadn't taken long to master them. The crash at Salamanca had made him a little more cautious than formerly, but his reflexes had quickened, and inwardly he felt he was becoming the kind of pilot he wanted to be. His flight dossier was starting to have the right remarks, but naturally Otto didn't get to see these.

The Gruppe had been assigned to Norway after their training on the new aircraft was completed. A few had 'washed out' and were sent back to other units, but the majority had made it, and were now front line fighter pilots eager for action, having just missed the initial assaults on Denmark and Norway. The Kommandeur of the Gruppe, Major Bernburg, had commended them on their flying qualities, shortly after arriving at Stavanger. Germany's northern flank would remain secure for the continued import of iron ore from Sweden, which the Reich so desperately needed for its ever expanding war machine.

The 'Sitzkrieg' or phony war came to an end after May 10, 1940. On the 25th Otto's staffel, along with one other was seconded to operate from a base in occupied Belgium. The Belgian army had surrendered a week previously, and it had been decided that more fighters were required for the knockout punch against France. Otto was sorry to say goodbye to his ground crew who would remain in Norway. The flight to Belgium was made in several easy legs during daylight, and was uneventful except when landing at Bremen one pilot made a hard landing and wiped out his undercarriage. Otto was glad it wasn't him. There would be hell to pay for that one!

Otto's staffel settled in at a former Belgian Air Force base. Planes bearing the unfamiliar black, yellow and red roundels still stood clustered near a hangar. Civilian workers were patching up the concrete aprons which showed evidence of recent bomb damage. Having barely unpacked, new orders came through to relocate at a forward base in France. This one turned out to be an abandoned civilian flying school outside Argentau which had recently been overrun. The whole place consisted of just a couple of dilapidated wooden buildings and a long grass strip. They would be living in tents from now on.

The 109's had been dispersed close to a nearby wood, and camouflage netting helped conceal them from any unwelcome visitors. On their second day a flight of British Hurricanes swept the field, but must have concluded the place was disused. In the morning Otto shaved and showered in the temporary bathrooms which the ground crews had rigged up, then ran a couple of laps around the field. His friend Bruno kept a small dog as a mascot, who eagerly joined them on the run. The dog kept spotting rabbits who had little trouble eluding him. Arriving back at the tent,

Bruno reminded Otto of their briefing at 08.15 hours.

Oberleutnant Kessler outlined the planned activities for the day. Due to ground fog in the sector, the patrol assignment was rescheduled for the afternoon. They were detailed to attack road transportation in the triangle formed by Alençon, Tours and Angers, and time of take-off was now dependent on ground visibility which was expected to improve later in the morning. Meanwhile, he informed them they were expected to attend a lecture on engine maintenance given by Oberwerkmeister Hensen, starting in twenty minutes.

A collective groan went up from the group of pilots. Nobody really disliked the Chief Engineering Officer, but his meetings were renowned for sending everybody into a rapid state of drowsiness. Otto and Bruno chatted awhile, enjoying the morning sunshine, before making their way to the big tent where the lecture was to be held.

Having just finished lunch, Kessler called Otto's group over to one of the vacant tables and announced take-off was now set at 14.30 hours. Staffel Kapitän Peter Rossmann would lead the patrol. The Met. people had informed him that the general target area was now clear of fog, and visibility was excellent. By 14.15 Otto had completed his checks and 'walk around' of the Bf 109 he was to fly. After a few words with the crew chief, Otto climbed into the cockpit and strapped himself in. The staffel consisted of ten aircraft, and today Rossman decided they would fly in a V formation made up of three aircraft at each point, separated approximately 60 to 80 meters apart. Rossman would fly in the center of the formation.

After forming up over the field, the staffel started on its climb and sector heading. Approaching the target, they ran into small cloud banks. After emerging from one, Otto spotted a lone French Morane-Saulinier fighter cutting across on their beam. He was considerably lower, and apparently going all out. Otto noted its blue, white and red tail markings. It disappeared into cloud as the radio crackled and Rossman, who'd also seen the fighter, notified the others. "Let him go, I have better hunting." A minute later, Otto caught sight of the city of Le Mans over the starboard wing.

Once again Rossman came on the radio. "Otto, Steffi, Bruno, fly the leg Tours to Angers, then head back along the Sarthe river. The rest of us will see what the roads around the Le Mans and Alençon area have to offer. See you back at base... good luck." Otto transmitted his acknowledgment, reset his trim and checked his instrument gauges... everything was normal. Noting that Steffi and Bruno were in position, they began descending shortly after passing Le Mans, leveling off at 1100 meters. Approaching Tours Otto decided to skirt the city just in case any flak units were active, but with the French in complete rout he very much doubted it. Heading on a south westerly course, the three aircraft picked up the road to Saumur. Coming down to 300 meters they were amazed looking at the scene below. It was like watching a huge snake composed of people and vehicles of every description. The 'final curtain' of the campaign was being pulled down, ending in mass confusion.

Sweeping across the road Otto saw a couple of small tanks making for the stalled stream of traffic. He called his wingmen telling them "I am going in for a strafe keep me covered." The camouflage of the tanks was ineffective... Otto thought they looked like slow moving ducks on a pond.

Banking to the right and gaining a little height, he made a 280 degree turn, and came in low. The tanks had almost reached the road when he fired. Two long bursts and a short one, the latter aimed at the vehicles on the road. Opening the throttle, he climbed and once more repeated his turn. The lead tank was upside down on fire, and a huge column of fire and smoke engulfed a rapidly disintegrating tanker truck towing a trailer. People were running in panic toward the fields, headed by three galloping horses which had somehow broken loose.

Otto had a feeling of compassion at the added devastation he'd caused, then remembering his mission, called up his companions on the R/T. "Finish off the second tank, then strafe further up the column." After the second attack, they formed up and flew on past Saumur toward Angers. Spotting five large trucks below, the three aircraft attacked in line astern. Otto had decided to dispense with the precaution of his comrades giving cover… it was like a clay pigeon shoot. Having expended the majority of their ammunition, Otto thought it prudent to head home. He had trouble locating the field for the final approach, until picking up rail tracks close to a church. These forward bases were tricky at times.

Hauptman Hans Bartsch conducted the debrief. After Steffi and Bruno had made their reports, it was Otto's turn. He disliked Bartsch. Fat, and with rimless glasses, he reminded him of a frog, sitting across the wooden table. "Well, Steiner, did we shoot down any Tommi's today?" He smirked at Otto, who was standing at attention as he gave his report. The Hauptman paused momentarily "Hardly deserves the Ritter Kreuz, eh?"

Otto never knew that two of his victims that afternoon were French aristocrats… such is the impersonal manner of war. All he wanted now was a shower and quick snooze prior to heading off to the mess. Within the space of five minutes he was snoring while his cigarette smoldered in the ashtray.

10

DREUX

KARL NEVER SAW ACTION IN POLAND. Things had settled into a routine for the soldiers at Langerfeld, the 12th infantry regimental H.Q. The camp was close to Freudenstadt, a small country town in Baden-Wurttemberg. Recently he had been sent on a course learning to drive and maintain army vehicles, which had proven an enjoyable diversion.

In civilian life he might be able to save the 250 marks for a down payment for a 'Strength through Joy Car' which were being built at Fallersleben. The government had announced a plan whereby the purchaser could put so much down, and pay off the remainder in weekly installments. At the start of the war this was all put on hold, and as it turned out, not many became proud owners of a V.W... or had their deposits returned. For Karl the idea of owning a car represented unbounded freedom. He hoped he wouldn't have to wait too many years before his wish became reality.

All in all, life wasn't so bad for Pvt. Bayer. The boil on his neck chafed on his tunic collar, but other than that, his life was devoid of any real anxiety. Returning to his billet, he thumbed through a copy of 'Signal' featuring a hero of Das Reich on its front cover. Switching on the radio the first news regarding the assault against the Low countries was being broadcast. Karl listened for a bit then changed to another station. It all seemed so unreal and far off at that moment for him to feel any involvement.

Soon the soldiers at Langerfeld camp were being dazzled by the stupendous victory in France... it seemed as if the Wehrmacht was invincible. He looked at the school atlas which he'd kept since leaving Vienna, and the way things were going it would soon be outdated.

Walking back from the pharmacy to pick up ointment for his boil, he was accosted by Tino Jackel, another clerk. "Well, you'd better get your swimsuit packed, we might spend our next leave on the French Riviera! Personally, I would like to get a sun tan on one of those beaches" Karl grinned. "You would peel like an onion with your lily white skin, besides, I bet places like that will be reserved for the 'battle heroes.' Pen pushers like us will end up in some dump similar to this one." Tino replied, "You could be right, but maybe we'll get lucky." Tino had a more optimistic nature than Karl. The two men strolled for a bit, then decided to have a beer at the soldiers club. Karl let Tino pay for the drinks as he owed him ten marks from the previous week, and with the way things were going, he might not be around to collect!

That same evening, Lieutenant Sondel informed Sgt. Freiburg to get his detachment made ready for an unknown destination at 23.00 hours the following Thursday. Christ, that only left them two days to sort and pack up the rat pile of documents that filled the office, let alone complete the end of the month reports. Early on the day of departure a small convoy of trucks and one or two cars assembled adjacent to the building in which Karl worked. A few more crates were loaded, then finally the vehicles began to move off. Karl glanced at his pocket calendar noticing it was the end of June.

On the 21st of the month, the French delegation signed an armistice. Adolf Hitler had ordered the same railway coach to be used as in 1918. The irony and humiliation of the act was not lost on the French population. Many wept, watching the news reel showing Der Führer dancing a jig of joy in front of his cohorts outside the coach. The German propaganda media made sure full coverage was given in the news films distributed around the world. Most people in Europe were now filled with dread as the unthinkable had happened, but for some it was a time of celebration.

* * * * * * * *

Freiburg pushed back the canvas flaps at the rear of the truck and looked out as the driver lurched to a halt. They had arrived at the Strasbourg crossing point. The Lieutenant got out of the cab and was conversing with a gendarme who spoke German. Fritz facetiously announced to the other occupants of the truck that their destination would be somewhere in 'La belle France' according to his reckoning, but this didn't illicit much response as most of the men were asleep. The sergeant glanced at his watch and saw it had just gone 10.00 p.m. yawning, he went back to a pile of greatcoats wedged between some boxes and made himself comfortable.

At 7:40 a.m. the convoy stopped near Troyes, southeast of Paris. Tired and stiff, men relieved themselves at the side of the road, while waiting for a captain to roust out the cooks of a nearby field kitchen who'd been told to prepare hot meals. The men took advantage of the brief respite to stretch their legs and take stock of their immediate surroundings but disappointingly there wasn't much to look at. Talking and smoking some speculated on how long it would take before the next stop. No one seemed to know, not even Fritz who was usually pretty good at ferreting out this sort of information. Karl supposed destiny was moving him along a line roughly due west from Vienna where he'd started out not so long ago.

Later that day they pulled into a small town and halted in the main square. Some of the buildings fronting one side were badly damaged either by bombing or shell fire. One structure still smoldered creating occasional sparks. A small group of civilians had gathered gawking at an overturned bus, and two burnt out cars were jammed up against the side of a disabled French tank which had taken a direct hit on the turret. Karl and his sergeant jumped down from the back of the truck and walked over to take a closer look. After a few minutes a motorcycle and sidecar pulled up with an officer and corporal wearing Feldgendarmerie uniforms and were taken to confer with the convoy commander. Pulling out documents from his brief case the officer pointed out various directions on a map. Shortly thereafter, a shrill whistle blast had the troops scrambling back into their vehicles and the convoy lumbered off.

Karl mulled over his first look at battle damage, wondering what had happened to the tank crew. To Fritz it was all old hat as he sat filling in requisitions with a pencil stub. He remarked to nobody in particular "Liebe Gott, this army is the same as the Kaiser's. Paperwork for everything. Soon they'll make you sign a chit to take a crap". As the convoy rumbled along, Sgt. Paul started to whistle the 'Horst Wessel.' Fritz glared at him muttering Nazi bastard under his breath. Only Karl heard this but was slightly taken aback as one needed to be extremely careful expressing any negative thoughts about the third Reich, especially in public. He respected Fritz who'd seen a great deal more life than himself and seemed to march to his own drummer. Soon they slowed at a major road intersection with signs erected by the Feldgenarmerie directing military traffic. The convoy split up with the main body heading for Orleans. The three remaining trucks including the one in which Fritz and Karl sat playing cards, continued on towards a place called Dreux.

On the outskirts a long column of poilus were being escorted by German troops on motorcycles riding up and down it's flanks. Fritz remarked that they were all headed towards P.O.W. camps and he reflected on the time he'd been captured after a French counter attack in 1917. Looking at the column reminded him of shepherds herding sheep and indeed the bucolic countryside provided the right setting. After a few more minutes the lead truck turned off the narrow road they'd been traveling on and entered a long curving driveway. Karl wondered how the convoy had been able to find it's way, forgetting the military police escort which had joined them at the last stop. The arrival at the chateau de Lancour was without fanfare.

* * * * * * * *

It took Karl by surprise realizing a single family could have occupied such a vast place but he supposed that if you had the money you could do as you pleased. Now the estate had been requisitioned by the Wehrmacht, its former occupants gone. Real estate changed hands quickly during a Blitzkrieg. A small detachment of Kriegsmarine had taken over the lower floors of the building and were busy erecting a temporary antenna on the tennis court. Soon they would move on to Cherbourg to set up permanent communication bunkers for the navy. On the adjacent lawn a lanky Kapitänleutnant was sprawled in a deck chair smoking his pipe watching two soldiers unload a black and white striped sentry box from one of the trucks in the driveway. The chateau had witnessed many changes since it was built and it now looked as if it was to embark on another role.

The other floors were delegated to members of the 14th Panzer Corps who had been part of the iron fist which had recently punched into France from the north. These were the first battle hardened troops Karl had come across and their high spirits and confidence were new to him. Most of these troops looked at the new arrivals with a faint air of amusement and in some cases disdain. He put it down to the natural pecking order of things witnessed when working on the farm during the labor corps stint. The only other unit stationed at the chateau formed a section of the Propagandastaffel headed by an elderly colonel. These people occupied a portion of the top floor and kept mostly to themselves. No doubt they would soon relocate to Paris in order to teach the decadent French the benefits of being occupied by the master race!

* * * * * * * *

Karl went to Vienna on leave at the end of July. It felt good to get away from army life for a while. The ever increasing paperwork could be forgotten over the next ten days, and he looked forward to seeing his old friends. His mother was excited at having him home again, and prepared a big meal to celebrate the occasion. She insisted he wear his uniform when they went out shopping, although Karl would have been happier in his old civilian clothes. Having put on weight, he found most of these didn't fit anymore.

The day after he got back, Hans came to the apartment and they headed off to a bier stube in order to catch up on each others news. Hans had signed up for the navy and expected to be inducted within three weeks. The only drawback was having met a girl he'd fallen in love with. "Karl, why don't we go dancing at Mellers tomorrow night? Gretchen has an older sister, a good-looker. I'm sure she'd like to meet you." Karl thought a moment then nodded. He hadn't had much female companionship the last few weeks… the local girls around Dreux hadn't proved much of an attraction, in fact the German uniform often engendered hostility.

* * * * * * * *

The following evening turned out to be more fun than Karl had expected. Lilli, Gretchen's sister, certainly was the good looker Hans had promised. They danced until the three man band took a break, then drifted back to the table. Hans and Gretchen were holding hands and hardly noticed their return. Karl ordered two bottles of champagne. What the hell, he was on leave and for the first time in his life didn't have to worry over spending a little money. He told Lilli about Dreux, and she laughed at his jokes and told a few of her own. After dancing some more, they went back to finish off the champagne. The dark beamed cellar with its white washed walls was jammed, and pretty soon the noise level became deafening. After ordering more drinks and listening to his companion describe her life, Karl was beginning to feel a little unsteady. Effects of the champagne were making him act like a real war hero.

God, it was good to be with ones own kind, listening to Viennese music instead of that French stuff on the radio back at Dreux. Observing Gretchen and Hans had seemed to have disappeared, he looked around at the couples on the dance floor. Lilli laughed, and said they were probably out in the garden. "Let's go and find them." Mellers' garden was a great favorite with courting couples. Several chairs made out of old wine casks and ornate wooden tables dotted a half acre behind the building and were interspersed among linden trees and several overgrown flower beds. One or two lanterns with colored glass hung from poles giving a romantic touch.

Making only a half hearted search for the other pair, they sat down at one of the tables. A couple of waiters stood discreetly in the entrance to the garden ready to take any orders. Most of the regular patrons had nicknamed it the 'Garden of Love'. Lilli slid onto Karl's lap, and soon he said a silent thanks to the person who'd conceived the idea of making the garden.

Lilli worked in her father's business, as did her sister, and she'd talked him into letting her have a few days off to be with her new soldier boy during his leave. Twice they'd borrowed bicycles and picnicked in the Viennese Woods, afterwards riding through the outlying pretty villages before making their way back to the city. Apart from the uniformed personnel in the streets, it was hard to tell it was wartime. Occasionally, wall posters and propaganda films at the cinemas reminded residents of the fact, but generally it was business as usual and the crowded shops and traffic gave the capital a prosperous new look. Towards the end of his leave, Karl invited his mother to accompany them for a boat trip on the Danube. Both she and Lilli appeared to like one another, and Karl pondered what it would be like being married, when thoughts on the subject were interrupted by Lilli. "Karl, stand over by the rail next to your mother so I can take a picture." She had borrowed Gretchen's old Agfa box camera, and had already taken too many of him. This time he insisted she should be in the photo with Mutti and asked one of the passengers to oblige. Karl's ten days were nearly up and for the last night the foursome went back to Mellers. This time he felt despondent putting it down to leaving Lilli, and because he wasn't sure of his emotions. Hans had confided he'd ask Gretchen to marry him after he'd completed six months in the Navy. Karl felt happy for his friend, and back in the garden Lilli made Karl forget his earlier mood. Hell, she was terrific… it was more than the champagne working this time. Later when Hans and Gretchen came by, Lilli's skirt was around her hips and Gretchen giggled while looking at Hans. "Du liebe Gott, what an example my sister sets!" Karl glanced at the open fly of his friends' trousers then at Gretchen, before replying. "Look who's talking with such a moral tone!"

* * * * * * * *

Heinz Wittich's parents ran a successful art and antiques gallery on Berlin's Gustav strasse. For many years the Wittich family had barely scraped by until promulgation of anti Jewish laws helped make them financially secure. They had bought inventories at rock bottom prices from people desperate to flee Nazi Germany. Nowadays, being of Ayran stock had its distinct advantages, and the familiar faces of Wittich's competition who'd dominated the trade, were disappearing fast.

Secretly, Wittich senior didn't have much time for Der Führer, but realized the man had his points so far as business was concerned. Despite being disinterested in politics Wittich senior deemed it advantageous to join the party, and new clients more than made up for the inconvenience of having to attend various meetings. Frau Wittich was the perfect wife for her husband. Once pretty, she'd grown coarse and fat and had an inordinate attachment for money. It wasn't surprising her son inherited some of the same traits. The only one of the family that might turn out differently was the youngest child, but for now it was too early to tell.

Heinz enjoyed visiting the library, and having looked up all the information his father required, he wandered over to the section of books he never passed up. Several of the volumes contained information regarding treasures recovered throughout history. Karl delighted in studying the color plates depicting objects from collections around the world… he tried to imagine what it would be like having a few displayed in the gallery. His thoughts turned to documented loot hidden by pirates. Perhaps one day he could go to Spain and delve into the government archives that dealt with manifests of sunken and plundered cargo. Stretching, Heinz looked at his watch and saw it was getting late. Putting fantasies aside he gathered up his notebooks, and left the building.

His father was slightly annoyed over the time he'd taken, but the notes Heinz had made were just what he needed. Putting an arm around the shoulder of his son, he said "Excellent… we can now make that arrogant Gauleiter pay through his long nose. You are indeed a great help to your Papa." Heinz was pleased hearing this. He suspected that he was the apple of his father's eye, and proving useful would one day be to his benefit when inheriting the gallery. Heinz had joined the Hitler Youth at his fathers urging, but hated the regimentation. The thought of joining the Nazi party inwardly revolted his senses, and the thing that scared him now was his imminent call up. His father had tried to pull strings but nothing developed which would exempt Heinz from service. Having an impediment would help, but in his case this didn't apply. The idea of combat was highly distasteful to Heinz, liebe Gott, he might even get killed! The only thing his father had come up with was a promise by a fellow party member to facilitate having Heinz sent to an army clerical unit after boot camp which at least should keep him out of harms way. Heinz wasn't overjoyed, but it was better than most of the alternatives. He wondered what antiques had been proffered as a bribe to obtain this dubious favor? Recruit basic training seemed like utter madness to Heinz. It was appalling to realize that for some it was quite enjoyable despite the endless grumbles regarding the sadistic N.C.O.'s who ruled their present lives. At least he was reasonably fit, but doubted his feet would last out to the end of the course. All the endless marching and drills seemed so bloody pointless. Finally it came to a finish and after a short time at home, he reported back to camp and was told that he and four others were being sent to France.

* * * * * * * *

Karl Bayer had been detailed to meet new arrivals outside the guard gate at Dreux. He watched as they tossed out their kit and jumped from the back of the truck. Forming them up, they marched across the grounds to four billets erected by the lake. After allocating them beds, he told them where they would eat, and the location of the bath house. The five were then free until the morning, when they were to report to Sergeant Freiburg in the clerical section at 07.30 sharp. Karl noted that the only one who seemed to take any apparent interest in his new surroundings was Pvt. Wittich. In general, the new intake looked to be an unappetizing lot. In fact, the thick lensed glasses two of them wore hid any expression whatsoever. Help was what was needed in Bldg. 2B as the chateau was filling up with ever more personnel. Karl supposed beggars couldn't be choosers as he hurried off to check the mail hoping for a letter.

11

LAST WORDS

THE TRAIN RIDE FROM VIENNA FELT boring, how could his leave have gone so quickly? Karl had forgotten to bring a book to help pass the time en route, and was reduced to flipping through a copy of 'Der Adler'. He found it uninteresting, then dozed off thinking about Lilli. Suddenly, the train jerked to a halt with a screech of brakes, and after a few seconds slowly began moving backwards. This was the second time they'd been shunted onto a spur line. Fully awake now he left his seat and lowered the window. A huge locomotive hauling a long line of flatbeds loaded with tanks was passing. Finally, after nearly an hour elapsed, Karl's train began moving again. He was aware the Reichbahn gave priority to the Wehrmacht, but why had the tanks been headed in a westerly direction when the war in France was over? Farther down the line he saw the same train again. Somewhere it had looped around and was now headed east. This direction made more sense to Karl, who wondered if a new blitzkrieg was in the works, if so he hadn't the slightest idea where or when it would take place.

Back at Dreux, one of the first people he encountered was Sgt. Freiburg who gave him a warm welcome, and told him "I have good news and bad." Reading the teletype message Fritz pulled from his pocket, he read of his promotion to Gefreiter. Fritz grinned, and said "It's hardly a commendation from O.K.W. but it will give you a few marks to spend on booze and women! The bad news is that a special section of the Abwehr moved into the chateau a few days ago along with General Klaus Strecker, no less. Being the senior officer at the chateau, the clerical section would come under his jurisdiction."

Fritz didn't like this upset having heard the man was a Prussian martinet, and no doubt it would be an end to the relaxed atmosphere around the chateau, supplanted by more 'spit and polish.' Karl laughed, telling his friend they would have to find ways to avoid any unwanted aggravation.

Fritz enjoyed hearing details of Karl's leave and suggested they should visit Paris on a four day pass while an opportunity existed. "Spend some of your pay increase in the brothels reserved for the Wehrmacht." Karl smiled, Fritz might be getting on in years but he was still a randy old dog. They strolled towards the billets passing the new parking area laid out close to the lake. Two big Henschel tractors hitched to 88m/m guns had recently arrived making Karl wonder if 'Tommi' was expected to bomb the place.

Parked on the grass were three new 'Ziegewagens' a military scout car produced in occupied Czechoslovakia. Reference to a goat in the name of the vehicle reflected its exceptional agility over rough terrain and ability to conquer steep slopes. Two of them were camouflaged and bore red cross insignia. The third, was unmarked and had been assigned to the clerical section. According to Fritz a Zündapp motorcycle and side car was also due to arrive. Fritz suggested that the new general might want to sponsor a race around the lake throwing in a French tart as a prize for the winner. Karl pursed his lips doubting such a morale booster would ever be sanctioned.

* * * * * * * *

Lt. Hugo Langfried was in charge of medical personnel temporarily posted to the chateau until reassignment to various base hospitals being set up in the Paris region. Most of these medics lived in tents pitched on the grounds, but Langfried had a tiny office in the chateau itself, in what had been the former housekeeper's sanctum. There had been just enough room to squeeze in a small iron bed and table, which seemed preferable to being under canvas, especially as it had drizzled with rain for the last two days.

Hugo had befriended François and his granddaughter Mimi when strolling around the chateau grounds. The old man now retired, had been employed by the Lancours, the former occupants of the place. François lived with his son and family in the gate keeper's house and spoke a passable German picked up in a POW camp during the last war and a spell working in the Saar. Hugo Langfried learned French in school, but had trouble with the local accent, and preferred his own tongue. The old man was full of interesting tales about his youth, and some of the locales he described were familiar to Hugo and evoked pleasant memories.

Shortly after Karl's return to Dreux, Lt. Langfried had the chore of duty officer. Hugo reckoned since moving into the chateau his name appeared more frequently on the roster, but didn't feel like complaining to the new commander, who initialed the lists. Grunting, he propped his boots on the table. It was close to midnight and things had been slow. Probably it would remain that way for the rest of the night. Part of his checks included monitoring the communications console installed in the foyer. Apart from routine teletype messages, nothing of importance had developed since his coming on duty. Schmidt, the clerk had gone downstairs to make coffee. Getting up from his chair Hugo stretched out on an old chaise in the corridor. He felt a small lump beneath the cushion and retrieved a child's metal toy and wondered to whom it had belonged, and where the parents had ended up.

Christ, what a boring war! Just as he had finished adjusting the chaise cushions, the sound of running feet on the hardwood floor in the passage surprised him, it was Mimi the twelve year old granddaughter of François. The child looked red in the face, and Hugo realized this was due to her running nearly a kilometer from the gate-keepers house. Civilians were strictly 'verboten' inside the building, but to the girl this was of little consequence. "M'sieu, my grandfather has fallen and hurt his head. My mother sent me to get help, it is urgent." Lt. Langfried sat the girl down in his chair, while deciding what was to be done.

Picking up the phone, he called through to the enlisted men's billet. Karl Bayer answered. "Bayer, get down to the motor pool and pick up the Ziegewagen right away. I need you to take François down to the Holy Cross hospital on the east side of Dreux, macht schnell." "Jawohl, Herr Lieutenant, I'll be there straight away." Karl had often exchanged pleasantries with the old boy but knew it was strictly forbidden for civilians to ride in military transport. However, the urgency in the lieutenant's voice over-rode any misgivings. He grabbed for his pants and boots then glanced at his watch realizing he'd only been asleep just under an hour, for the second time.

Earlier he had been awoken by Oberfeltwebel Willi Ahrens telling him of a forthcoming work detail. "The 88 m/m gun has to be set up at the end of the stables... I'll be looking for 'volunteers' at 0.900 tomorrow to dig a foundation. I'll need some muscular types for filling sandbags." The sick joke about 'volunteers' riled Karl. The stupid pig, as if this clap trap couldn't wait until later. The man's bad teeth and breath revolted Karl, and to be awoken out of sleep added insult to injury. He could 'stuff' his course on operating the 88 m/m... hopefully the bloody thing might blow up and wipe out his tormentor. In contrast to this brute was Lt. Hugo Langfried. Militarily he was always correct but his orders were given in a civilized manner. Buttoning his tunic Karl jogged to the Ziegewagen thinking what he would like to do to Willi Ahrens.

* * * * * * * *

Karl jerked to a halt leaving the engine running and bounded up the steps of the chateau. Lt. Hugo Langfried returned his salute "I can't raise the civilian switchboard in Dreux… it appears the phones are all dead. Here is a note explaining the situation for the head nurse at the hospital. I would come with you but it is impossible to leave." As Karl turned to go Hugo said "stay with François for as long as it takes, at least you are someone he knows." Karl reached the gate keepers place as François emerged from the front door supported by his wife and son. Easing François into the vehicle they propped him up with cushions. Mimi also wanted to go but was dissuaded by her parents.

The rain abated slightly as Karl approached the hospital. Holy Cross stood at the end of a cobblestone driveway. It was a large stone edifice with ivy covered walls. A plaque attached to the main door indicated the place opened in AD 1745. Karl entered having made sure the patient was safe to leave unattended. A sullen faced orderly sat behind the receiving desk. Bayer spoke German to him, but quickly found out he was wasting his time. The man said "Je ne parle l'Allemand." Karl glanced at the note from his lieutenant, and was relieved to see it was written in schoolboy French, and despite the frequent crossings out, the orderly seemed to understand the situation. Pressing a buzzer, the man stared at Karl Bayer. This was the first time he had seen one of the new conquerors close up. He noted the cut of the uniform and quality of his boots. The few 'poilus' that had been in Holy Cross had looked shabby in comparison. In response to the buzzer, an elderly head nurse appeared with a male orderly pushing an ancient wheelchair.

After an explanation was given her, Karl with help from the orderly maneuvered François into the chair and the group proceeded along a dimly lit passageway leading to a row of offices at the rear of the building. A light shone through the corrugated glass window panel of the end office. The head nurse tapped on the door, and a voice called for them to enter. Inside stood a tall elderly man sporting a goatee and wearing a long white coat. After listening momentarily to the nurse, he took Lt. Langfried's note and pulling out a pince-nez from his top pocket the doctor quickly scanned the content. After consultation with the nurse he paused for a moment then started to speak in a fractured German. "I will make my examination of the patient, and I presume you are able to wait?" Karl nodded in the affirmative as he could always report back to Hugo when the telephones were back in action. For the first time he noticed a gash at the back of François' head. Dried blood had clotted and some of his white hair was already matted in the area of the wound. He looked pathetic and very frail at this point. The doctor measured his pulse. "How serious is it doctor?" The man grunted, then replied. "I think it best you remain in the foyer until I'm finished then I can give you an answer. The orderly will come and collect you after the patient is settled in the ward."

* * * * * * * *

After a while the smell of disinfectant had become overpowering, and Karl went outside to smoke and stretch his legs. The hospital was dirty and unkempt, and religious symbols hanging everywhere on the walls depressed him. He compared the place unfavorably to the two hospitals he'd visited in Vienna. After forty minutes, the orderly beckoned for him to follow. By now, François was asleep on one of the iron cots. He could just make out the craggy features under the faint blue ceiling light.

Pulling up a chair alongside the bed, Karl stared at the old man for a while thinking that one day he himself might end up in the same situation. His eyes grew accustomed to the subdued light in the ward and he realized only seven of the twenty-four beds were occupied, judging by the shapes he could discern. After ten minutes, the nurse reappeared and looked at François to make sure he was sleeping. The sedation had done its job and tapping Karl on the shoulder, she indicated the direction of the door leading to the doctor's office. Doctor Pagnol spoke as he entered the door. "Your friend has a very severe concussion. How bad, we can't know until I do tests and x-rays in the morning. It is so late now, I think it best if you could stay." Karl nodded, and said, "Please ring my superior Lt. Langfried at the chateau, as soon as the phones are in order." The doctor yawned and replied, "I'm told they will be fixed in the next hour or so. The police called round and told me an army truck hit a roadside junction box. A crew is working to repair it as of this moment."

François was gently snoring when he returned to his bedside and Karl felt exhausted. Lying down on top of the adjoining bed, he fell instantly asleep. At five a.m. he awakened. Afterwards he wasn't sure if it had been a bad dream, or François starting to babble. For a few seconds he hadn't the faintest grasp of his present surroundings, then it came to him. François had flung the bed sheets to one side, his hospital smock rucked up to expose spindly legs. He rambled in French interspersed by an occasional groan before stopping and staring at the ceiling... Karl straightened the old man's bedding somewhat, then lay down again.

To get more comfortable he kicked off his jack boots, and decided to light a cigarette. Just as he reached for his matches, the old boy started up again, but this time in German. It was all disjointed, but curiosity made Karl listen while he pulled on the cigarette. Reaching for the ashtray by the bedside, he caught the word 'tresor' and something about Madame Lancour, followed by several unconnected words, the only familiar ones being 'Mimi' and 'Dreux'. Karl's hand froze holding the ashtray, there was no mistaking what Francois had said. "The treasure is safe under the floorboards, the 'Boche' won't violate a gazebo as they surely will our womenfolk." He ended up with a raspy cackle followed by a coughing spasm. Karl hurried off to find the orderly and get the old man a glass of water. When they returned, François was lying on his side, sleeping like a baby.

Karl didn't hear any more rambling… he was in oblivion. He awoke to find a new nurse shaking his shoulder, and a cup of coffee had been laid on the table. As his eyes refocused, he saw the doctor standing at the end of the bed with a clipboard under his arm. He coughed and said "M'sieu, I regret to inform you the patient died at 6:15 a.m. There was nothing more I could do. I have already informed your officer of the situation." On returning to Dreux Karl asked Lt. Langfried if he could be excused from Oberfeldwebel Ahren's digging project pleading lack of sleep. Hugo nodded his head, saying he'd take care of the matter and thanked him for his assistance. "It will be a sad day for Mimi and the others, I appreciate what you did…."

12

MID-AUGUST 1940

WITH THE 'HOT WAR' NOW OVER, the routine of occupation duties became established at Dreux. Several weeks after Karl's arrival all the 14th panzer troops moved out to rejoin their corps H.Q. at Rennes. An old auto assembly plant outside the city had been taken over by the Wehrmacht to be used as a repair depot, and all armored vehicles which had taken part in the sweep through the Low countries and France were scheduled for regular maintenance and overhaul.

A portion of the newly vacated space in the chateau was assigned to the clerical section. Karl helped Sgt. Freiburg make a layout for placing the office furniture, and on the following day everybody helped move and set up under Freiburg's watchful eye. "Well Karl, what do you think?" Sgt. Freiburg lit a cigarette and gazed out of a window overlooking the spacious grounds below. Karl was struck by how much the view improved at this higher level.

"I think we'll be fairly comfortable here provided they don't send us any more of those idiots from Langerfeld." Freiburg laughed, and continued smoking with a look of concentration on his face. Flicking his cigarette butt out of the window, he said quietly almost to himself, "I bet the previous owners stashed away lots of wine somewhere in this place over the years, we ought to nose around a bit, it would be a shame to miss out on any opportunities that might be available." Karl reckoned Fritz was pretty savvy and this sounded an interesting idea needing to be looked into.

* * * * * * * *

On Sunday the 18th of August, early morning sunshine dappled the chateau's facade as Gefreiter Bayer and Sgt. Fritz Freiburg ate a hearty breakfast, picked up their passes and headed off to catch a train for Paris.

Later on that same day, Otto Steiner flew his final mission. Two weeks earlier he'd been transferred to fighter Geschwader 51, flying out of St. Omer in the pas de Calais. By early afternoon formations of bombers began attacking R.A.F airfields at Biggin Hill and Kenley. Stuka dive bombers hit the naval airfield at Ford and the radar station at Poling. Göering had decided his mighty armadas must wrest air superiority from the British, and elimination of fighter bases and radar chains were given top priority. Heavy damage was inflicted on the targets although it wasn't a complete knockout blow hoped for by the Luftwaffe commanders. Losses on both sides were heavy in crews and aircraft, but the greatest shock for the Germans was finding they'd finally met their match, in contrast to the earlier victories in Spain, Poland and France.

Otto's Geschwader wasn't involved in the initial assaults, and mechanical difficulties with the fuel injection system on his Me 109 made it doubtful he'd be in the next strike. No spare aircraft were available, so all he could do was wait while the ground crew struggled to fix the problem, however by mid afternoon his aircraft was combat ready. Currently, Otto had four 'kills' to his credit which qualified him for an Iron Cross, first class… he just hoped he would be around long enough to receive it... At 5 p.m. he was airborne forming up over the Pas-de-Calais with other segments of Air Fleet 2. This time selected targets were the R.A.F. fighter bases at North Weald and Hornchurch. Otto's staffel was to provide cover for the bombers, and look for targets of opportunity over southeastern England before turning back towards France. If he lingered too long his fuel would run dangerously low risking a bale out over the channel.

* * * * * * * *

There would be no rest for the Hurricanes and Spitfires. Otto's briefing outlined a plan for a force of fifty Heinkel 111's to batter the North Weald airfield, while another formation of Dornier 17's would attack Hornchurch. A total of 140 Me 109's and Me 110's were assigned for protection of the bombers in this two pronged effort. Altogether, over 250 aircraft would be thrown into the assault. The most the R.A.F. could offer equated to a ratio of three British fighters for every five German aircraft sent to hammer these bases. Having to ride herd on the Heinkels was difficult because of the relative speed differential, leaving escort fighters at a disadvantage should the R.A.F. take them by surprise. The bombers lumbered along at less than 200 m.p.h. and low cloud totally obscured the airfield when they arrived.

Formation leaders were under strict orders to bomb only if they were able to see their target area, and heavy cloud forced the bombers to turn back. On the outward run to their objectives the Heinkels escaped casualties, however on the return leg of the flight it was a different story. Off the Essex coast Hurricanes swarmed for the attack. In the general melee that followed the Luftwaffe formations began splitting up, making it easier for the R.A.F. fighters to select individual prey.

Otto watched a group of three Hurricanes diving

towards the Heinkels, one of which had smoke trailing from it's starboard engine. Opening his throttle wide he turned with the intent of catching the tail end Hurricane making its run on the crippled bomber. Otto's adrenaline was working overtime, now the enemy was located exactly where he wanted… and he had him in his sights. The fighter wasn't taking evasive action, intent on making it's kill. The other two Hurricanes were no longer visible obscured by cloud. Firing an initial burst, Otto briefly glimpsed rounds stitching along the lone Hurricane's upper fuselage. White identification letters on each side of the roundels looked huge as Otto pulled into a sharp climbing turn to avoid a collision. Coming around for another attack, he quickly scanned the surrounding sky. All seemed to be clear… the Hurricane had started a slow spiral, spewing oily smoke from its engine.

Otto's instrument panel exploded in a cascade of metal and glass, and streams of glycol filled the cockpit. The three rounds that penetrated his body killed him outright as he slumped forwards. Two Spitfires had 'jumped' him from out of the sun. Both pilots witnessed the Me109 and Hurricane vanish into cloud base, each one on a trajectory to final destruction. The wounded Hurricane pilot managed to slide his canopy back and bailed out. Seconds later his parachute deployed and he found himself floating gently down towards a school playing field. Otto's plane plunged almost vertically into some rolling farmland creating a pit seventeen feet deep.

At the 'Crossed Keys' a pub two miles from the Spitfire base, Sgt. 'Paddy' Lane and pilot officer Jim Lockerby argued the toss as to which one of the pair shot down the German plane less than three hours previously. Each man raised his glass marking respect for the dead before calling for the next round of drinks, and an exchange of ribald jokes.

Over the years rain storms kept the crater dug by Otto's Messerschmitt filled up with water. This provided an ideal gathering place for the Guernsey cows that were raised on the farm purchased by a young Bill Jennings several years after the war. He was unaware fragments of wreckage still lay embedded in the muddy bottom of the drinking pond.

* * * * * * * * *

Paris had always been a huge Mecca for tourists, and the armed services of the Reich continued the tradition. Hitler, Göering and Goebbels had already graced the city with their presence. It seemed as if an army of ants had overrun the place, busy buying up items in the well stocked shops, paying with occupation marks worth roughly half the value of any given item. Procurement officers from every department of the Fatherland set up establishments for purchasing goods in bulk. At this rate it wouldn't take long to denude the metropolis. Cabarets and night clubs were filled to capacity every night. Brothel owners vied with one another to have their establishments classified for 'officers use only' in order to maximize profits and had been helped by a relaxation of the curfew. Everybody walked, bicycled or took the metro. Bus services were infrequent, and generally jam packed. Private cars had been banned except for certain essential occupations, and the absence of street noise was quite unnerving for some Parisians. Bayer and Freiburg sat down at a sidewalk café and ordered beers then indulged in people watching for a while… Earlier they'd been to one of the newly set up 'Soldatenkinos' and saw a rather boring pre-war German film. During the following newsreel extolling the exploits of the army, Sgt. Freiburg dozed off. Later on, feeling hungry, they'd eaten at a large canteen reserved for the Wehrmacht at the 'Place clichy' where the food was plentiful and cheap.

The two men had already done a guided tour of the city, visiting all of the well known landmarks. Karl had brought a camera along in order to send pictures to Lilli and his mother. "Well what now Karl?" Karl put his beer down and looked at the leaflet distributed by 'Jeder einmal in Paris' (Paris for everyone, once) an organization formed to cater for the military tourists swamping the city. "How about the Casino de Paris?… someone told me they have the best looking girls performing there." This seemed to please Fritz. "OK let's go and buy the tickets before the high command requisitions the place!" The comrades sat back in the plush chairs and enjoyed watching the bare-breasted dancers perform. Very few civilians were evident in the audience, it seemed as if an enthusiastic sea of feldgrau was making the owners of the establishment rich. Napoleon might have referred to 'an army marching on its stomach' but forgot to add that the sight of near naked females did wonders for morale! On the way back to a dingy little hotel commandeered by the Wehrmacht, both men decided to visit the 'Maison Chanticler'. Earlier they'd heard a group of soldiers discussing the merits of this brothel.

In his next letter, Karl ignored certain aspects of his trip, certain his Mutti would rather hear about the cultural things. Doing some shopping, each of them had picked up good bargains at the flea market, and Karl had also bought lingerie for Lilli. Both enjoyed a good laugh in the shop when the buxom girl behind the counter had modeled various items by holding them up against herself. Karl mused that the Viennese shops selling such intimate apparel had a way to go before matching the allure of Parisian creations. Probably Lilli's mother would throw a fit when the parcel arrived… that's if the military censors didn't steal the stuff beforehand.

* * * * * * * *

The house of joy had proven a winner although the price they'd paid the Madame seemed atrocious. While waiting for the girls to make their appearance, the pair gazed around the reception parlor with its pink and white decor and overstuffed chairs. Karl tried to take a photograph, but Madame, making her entrance rushed across with an upraised hand as two high ranking officers descended the stairs. Karl wasn't sure if a salute was required in these intimate surroundings. He also wondered if the ornate chandeliers might come adrift some day due to the heavy traffic on the floors above. The girl Fritz selected seemed a little old, but the look of exhaustion Freiburg exhibited next morning suggested his money had been well spent. Karl's choice was a young girl from Brittany who spoke a few words of German. She had involved him in several acts of physical activity that had never entered his mind prior to the Maison Chanticler.

On leaving the establishment laughing and exaggerating their prowess, they were stopped by 'Feldgendarmerie' and written up for parading the streets of 'La belle Paris' with unbuttoned tunics and unpolished boots. Karl got an additional entry for not wearing his cap. "Too bad, " Fritz observed. "It's the shits having to leave this place and be harassed at the last minute." Heading toward the transportation center, they walked past the Hotel Meurice, where General Schaumberg was ensconced. The hotel was now the H.Q. for the German military government of greater Paris. Three large swastika flags flew from its facade. Fritz paused and jerked his thumb at the place. "Those fat cats can visit the Maison Chanticler every night if they wish and have a Mercedes drop them off, and we have to return to the charms of Dreux. There isn't any justice in this world."

13

LIQUID DISCOVERY

Sgt. Horst Wederman the chief storekeeper fancied himself a skillful poker player. This self-delusion usually depleted the contents of his wallet on a weekly basis. His moon-faced features were read like a book, by an old pro such as Fritz. Two other sergeants from the medical unit made up the foursome that met each Friday night to drink and play cards. This ritual was held in Wederman's store room located in the chateau basement. Fritz was amazed at Horst's lack of initiative. Here was the man sitting on a gold mine and not taking the opportunity to make some real money. He sighed, the dumb Prussian hadn't the sense to punch his way out of a paper bag it would seem. Along one wall of the room hung a double row of keys each tagged and identified in Horst's spidery handwriting. Placing his tunic on a hook Freiburg was able to read them quite easily.

Opening a large bottle of Courvoisier, Horst Wederman laughed nervously. "Sit down Fritz, I'm anxious to recoup the money you won from me last time." Fritz grunted and nodded towards several crates of Löwenbrau piled in a corner. "Where did that lot come from?" Horst grinned, "from the officer's mess but I doubt they'll miss it." Pulling up a chair Fritz wondered how someone took the risk of petty pilfering while keys to grand larceny hung just above his head. One of the sergeants offered cigars around the table while another cut a deck of cards.

After they had been playing a couple of hours, Sgt. Freiburg was no longer concentrating on the game... his thoughts posed a distraction, and if he wasn't careful he'd end up paying Horst. Shortly after midnight he reversed his losing trend and when the men decided to call it quits Fritz was ahead by D.M. 200. The two medics bid them goodnight after an exchange of jokes and exited the door. "See you next Friday." Fritz put his feet up on the table, belched, and lit up the last cigar. The smile had vanished from Horst's face... his brain still hadn't registered the point when things first started to go wrong. A mixture of beer and brandy hadn't helped matters. Pulling out his wallet he could only count D.M. 176. Hell, he was wiped clean yet again... but this time he couldn't even cover the debt.

Fritz looked at his agitated face a moment. "Don't worry Horst, I don't think you'll desert just because you had a run of bad luck. In fact, keep the 176 and forget the rest you owe me." A look of surprise was supplanted by one of disbelief. "Why would you do that?" "Just a small favor comrade, I want to borrow your keys sometime, and take a sniff around by myself to see what's hidden away in this rabbit warren of yours, OK?" Horst thought for a moment. "Is that all?" "Ja, just for my higher education" Fritz replied. Both men laughed. "Just let me know what you intend to 'liberate' that's all. That way I can square my paperwork accordingly."

Fritz had ideas beyond the contents of Horst's domain, still a good French ham and a bottle or two of the officers' brandy would provide an acceptable bonus. They finished up the last of the beer, then headed for bed each feeling a satisfactory outcome resulted from the get together. On the following Thursday Fritz noticed a large Opel van parked near the chateau. It bore the inscription 'WEHRMACHT FILM UNIT' painted on the sides. After making inquiries Sgt. Freiburg learned that instructional films and current news reels would be shown that evening in the former main reception salon. Mulling this piece of information over Fritz headed to the storeroom in search of Horst.

* * * * * * * *

Finishing a snack of bratwurst washed down with vin blanc, Horst picked up an old copy of the Beobachter newspaper which had been used as wrapping inside a crate containing refurbished typewriters. The reading matter was hardly calculated to excite anyone other than an ardent Nazi. Horst dozed off before having finished the second column of a speech by Dr. Goebbels. Fritz looked at the sergeant's reclining figure and smiled, then suddenly bellowed "General Strecker here, on your feet soldier, I've a good mind to have you shot." Horst caught in mid snore almost fell out of his seat. A shower of crumbs left over from his snack rolled down his shirt onto the floor. On recognizing Fritz relief lit up his face knowing the unthinkable hadn't actually happened. "Dummkopf, at the very least it might have been Lt. Mansbach and I'm sure you wouldn't want to forfeit this cozy little setup of yours, so next time lock the bloody door and we'll all be a lot safer."

Fritz sat down and reached for a beer. "You are going to the movies tonight my friend." Horst downed the contents of his glass and stared at Fritz. "Movies, what movies may I ask? I haven't been inside a cinema for two years or more." "Well, tonight your turn has come round again my friend." Fritz eyeballed the keys hanging on the far wall as he spoke, "If you haven't been for that long you'd be surprised at what's been happening in the world during your many naps. Make sure you don't miss the start of tonight's performance in the main reception salon, I understand Der Führer himself stars in the newsreels and he wouldn't want to be kept waiting by someone like you. Don't forget it starts at 20.15 hours… I'll be out of your storeroom by 22.00 hours."

The storekeeper wasn't too pleased as he'd planned on listening to a radio program in his den, but Fritz's tone, coupled with the possibility he might still have to repay a mounting debt, convinced him an evenings viewing was the better proposition

* * * * * * * *

After finishing supper Fritz met Karl outside the library. They then took a short walk in the grounds where Fritz told his comrade "if we split up our tasks of exploration we'll have more time to do a thorough job." Karl agreed, and they headed for the storeroom entering just as Wederman sat down to watch the film in the salon. Each man took a handful of keys from the rack and began their individual search… They were surprised by the amount of foodstuff and equipment accumulated since the Wehrmacht takeover, judging by manifests pinned on the inside of doors, but none of this particularly whetted their appetites. After thirty minutes Fritz began to feel irritated, especially as the last two rooms he wanted to check out had inoperable lights. He walked back to retrieve a flashlight left on Wederman's desk. Karl was already back in the room enjoying a smoke. "Any luck, Fritz?… I didn't find anything to get excited about." Fritz sat down looking rather cross. "When you've finished your cigarette, I want to take a peek in the last couple of rooms before we leave. Come to think of it I should have taken the 176 marks from that idiot Wederman."

Karl trailed his companion along the corridor. Shining their flashlights in the last room revealed nothing except two open crates coated with dust and mouse droppings. Fritz uttered an oath of disgust and was about to extinguish the flashlight when its beam illuminated a short length of rope hanging from the ceiling. It was attached to an eye ring fastened to a trap door. Judging from the filth encrusted edges it looked as if it hadn't opened in many years. Karl tugged the rotted rope but only succeeded in pulling it completely away from its mooring and bringing down a shower of crud onto his head.

Fritz returned to check out Wederman's junk box for a length of wire. He was unlucky, but saw a padlock and chain on one of the hooks. The chain was somewhat on the short side, but he reckoned it might work. Grabbing a chair he returned to where Karl waited. Standing on the chair Fritz was able to reach high enough to engage the chain's padlock with the eye bolt. Snapping it shut he left the chain dangling just above the floor... pulling on it nothing happened. Karl then gave it a try, but the result was still the same, the bloody door was stuck fast. Suddenly inspiration struck Fritz... he'd seen a piece of steel pipe roughly a meter long in one of the rooms, and went to get it. Inserting the pipe through a link of the chain formed a handle and both men were able to get a purchase on each side. With the third pull the trap door suddenly opened pitching both comrades onto the floor.

After picking themselves up, Karl chuckled saying. "This had better be worth it, otherwise we'll end up on medical leave... or worse." Fritz wasn't even listening, busy grabbing boxes which he piled up to form a rickety platform, and then precariously placed the chair on top. After pausing a moment he climbed to the top. Using one hand Karl pulled down on the chain and with the other assisted Fritz who clambered gingerly towards the ceiling. With Karl holding down the trapdoor, Fritz managed to poke his head and shoulders through the opening and shine his flashlight in an arc.

At least seven long wine racks were caught in the light, there must have been several hundred bottles covered in layers of dust. More racks were probably hidden by the immense forest of cobwebs. After Fritz regained his breath he called down. "It's worth it my friend, but we'll have to wait. I can't pull myself up inside, we need to find a ladder."

Fritz told Karl to ease the door slowly shut, then he removed the padlock and chain letting them fall to the floor. Having laboriously worked his way down, Fritz looked at his watch and reckoned the film show would be finished in about ten minutes. Turning to Karl, he remarked "I think the 176 marks will have gained a better interest than the Bayerishe Landesbank pays it customers, if my instincts prove me right the wine stashed up there is worth a bundle." The earlier frustrations seemed to evaporate like magic. Fritz replaced the steel bar and hung the padlock and chain back on the key rack in Wederman's room. Both men left feeling elated by the way things had panned out.

14

A COMMANDANTS VISIT

SHORTLY AFTER DISCOVERY OF THE WINE, Bayer and Freiburg were sitting on a bench overlooking the lake. Fritz's award of the War Service Cross had been recently announced, but he only wanted to talk about business. As Karl congratulated him, Fritz muttered something about one couldn't eat medals, and that the prospect of selling the wine at a fat profit appealed to him far more.

Fritz gave a sly look. "Comrade Wederman will be absent tomorrow, he has been given a 12 hour pass and is visiting a cousin at a Luftwaffe base... how about that?" Fritz yawned "I have a few days due to me so naturally I volunteered to cover for him as Wederman ordinarily can't leave the place unattended. I called in a favor to finagle the pass and Sgt. Wederman was overwhelmed by my generous offer to look after his fiefdom."... "Why you conniving old goat, it sounds like the fox has been put in charge of the hen house." Karl slapped Fritz on the back in admiration, the man certainly had balls. Lighting a cigarette Karl said "I'll get a pal of mine in the maintenance section to loan us a folding ladder. I won't even have to give a reason, he's not nosy so don't think you are the only one with any clout in this partnership." Fritz made a rude gesture in reply. The pair couldn't wait to get going on their project.

* * * * * * * *

Sitting in class for two hours listening to Oberfeldwebel Ahrens yapping about the 88m /m gun was sheer boredom to Karl. From the start the man delighted in singling him out to answer questions about this technical marvel, but somehow he was never able to satisfy him. Finally the class came to an end and Karl hurried off to his billet for a lie down prior to the evening meal. Waking from a nap he noted the light was already fading and his watch told him it was too late for supper… oh well he could fix himself something in the storekeeper's place. Fritz was to pick him up shortly after darkness fell.

When Freiburg tapped on the window Karl was pulling on his boots, and once outside retrieved the hidden ladder from space under the billet floor. His friend had brought a small knapsack containing flashlights, a coil of rope, candles and a steel spike. Once inside Wederman's place, reached without incident, they walked down the corridor and entered the room below the wine cache. Karl positioned the ladder under the trap door. Forming a double knot at one end of the rope, he climbed up to poke its length through the existing eye bolt until the knot snugged tight. Standing on the floor, the men grabbed the rope pulling on it until the trapdoor fully opened. Fritz held it in position while Karl hammered the spike into the wall and anchored the rope to prevent the door closing. Fritz climbed the ladder and placed two candles close to the opening and lit them before heaving himself onto the wooden floor boards. Karl quickly followed his partner, and with the benefit of illumination they were able to see what the room had to offer. Karl gave a low whistle of appreciation.

Fritz exclaimed "Liebe Gott… look at this, a feast for sore eyes, those aristocrats certainly knew how to live." Karl gazed at rows of bottles, there must have been several hundred lined up on racks. He turned to his companion and said "if we can somehow get these back to the Fatherland it will provide a nice little sum for a rainy day." Karl reached for one of the bottles and wiped off the grime on his pants to see the label. It read 'Lafite Rothschild Paulliac'. A thin wire attaching a lead oval was twisted around its neck with the date 1898 inscribed. Picking up another bottle he read 'Chateau Margaux' 1892. The room had a low arched roof and standing upright was difficult in places. The temperature was on the cool side, the place must have been built expressly for storage of wine. Two mice skittered close to a wall as the men surveyed their surroundings. Clumps of rotted straw lay scattered on the floor, and in one corner were four casks each with seals affixed to the spigots. Incised in the wood staves was an imprint hard to make out, but it looked like 'Cognac Freres Pretelat'. Karl sat down on a crate labeled 'CHAMPAGNE SEC DE LAUNAY & Cie' and reached for a bottle from the one next to it, wondering how long it had rested there.

He stood up and blew his nose finding the dust was bothersome. Noticing something on top of the casks he again walked over and realized it was an old smock on the point of disintegration. Carefully spreading it out on the floor a small pocket was apparent, and Karl pulled out a rusty key and two coins. Holding his flashlight closer, he made out the dates on them… the smaller silver one was issued in 1859 and the copper coin was dated 1865. Karl discarded the key and placed the coins in his tunic as a memento.

Pulling out a notebook he made a stab at calculating the quantity of bottles and wrote down the names of vintners and year of bottling. Fritz helped in the task until they decided it was time to go. Having removed the rope they left the spike in situ after rubbing dirt and grease over it. Karl yanked away some ancient wiring running to the broken light socket and stuffed it in the knapsack. It wasn't foolproof but it was unlikely the lazy storekeeper would enter the room. After returning to Wederman's den they made themselves ham sandwiches and opened some premier German beer. While munching their snacks the men speculated about the market value for their find. In their present mood one or two additional zeros increased a feeling of 'gemütlichkeit'... Karl tried to imagine the reactions of his Mutti and Lilli if he told them about the discovery.

* * * * * * * *

After returning the ladder they strolled over to the canteen, and Fritz asked "do you suppose some old duke kicked the bucket and forgot to tell his heirs what he'd stored away?" Karl started grinning, "No all along he meant for it to be there waiting for us... to the conquerors go the spoils." What was intended to be just a couple of drinks turned into something longer. The canteen wasn't crowded, just a few soldiers standing around talking. One or two were grouped at the bar and a couple were playing billiards. The late night crowd hadn't drifted in yet. The civilian bartender was busily polishing glasses in readiness for the eventual stampede. Collecting their order at the bar, Fritz and Karl went outside holding their drinks and sat at a table in the sheltered forecourt. Even though the canteen was nearly empty there was a risk of being overheard and Karl had something pressing on his mind. By now he fully trusted Fritz, especially after they'd become partners in crime so to speak, and the beer was making him feel expansive enough to take another plunge.

"Remember François the gatekeeper who died?" Fritz looked nonplussed for a moment, "Ah yes, the old boy who used to work cutting grass and other odd jobs... I talked to him a couple of times that's all, he spoke in an accented German, so what about him?" "Tonight's expedition could be chicken feed." On hearing this Freiburg's jaw dropped slightly, "what the hell do you mean?" Karl stretched his legs out and began relating the episode at the Holy Cross hospital. When he'd finished he felt a lot better having shared his experience. Freiburg briefly picked his nose and slid his chair back. "I've got to go and pee." Returning from his trip around the corner he sat without moving for a while before speaking. "O.K. Karl, what's the next step on the agenda? Gazebo, treasure, it all sounds a bit weird to me"… Karl interjected "No more so than today's happenings." Fritz grunted, slowly nodding his head. "I never thought the army might become so lucrative for its heroes, but I reckon our work is cut out before we celebrate, eh?"

* * * * * * * *

A frenzy of spit and polish was taking place throughout the chateau. General Schaumburg, the commandant of Greater Paris was to be the weekend guest. Rooms were being dusted and cleaned, while a horde of soldiers were cutting and raking the lawns in preparation for this event. Freiburg's earlier observation about their General was proving correct. The man was cast in the true Prussian mold. Worse yet, Karl's name was on the list of attendees for compulsory church service following a review of troops outside the chateau. Karl spent the previous evening pressing his uniform and polishing his boots, along with the rest of the billet, and the military barbers were working overtime. Next morning long lines of men waited to be pre-inspected by officers and senior N.C.O's. Everyone was cleanly scrubbed, even their finger nails had been examined for the slightest vestiges of dirt.

Stiffly erect the two generals walked between the assembled lines, while off to one side a small band, slightly off key, played martial music. Karl stood like a ramrod, eyes held steady in the approved textbook manner. General Strecker's monocle caught the morning sun making it flash like a small signaling light. The church service was held in the reception salon where the films had been shown as the family chapel was far too small to accommodate such a large assembly. A navy Kapitän conducted the service with a war flag prominently displayed in front of a temporary altar.

Both generals sat on high-backed padded seats in the front row. Karl wondered if previous owners of the chateau had used them for sitting down to dine... if chairs could speak what might they be saying about their present role? The collapsible steel chair Karl was perched on was hardly conducive to comfort, but occasional scathing glances from senior N.C.O.'s in attendance made sure nobody's posture offended the Almighty. Karl hadn't been to church for a long time. In earlier days he'd accompanied his Mutti who was an ardent Lutheran, now he felt ambivalent on the subject of religion. It reminded him of the monthly payments his father had made to an insurance company before his death... so long as the contributions were prompt everything would be taken care of when the time came.

The Kapitän reached a part of the sermon in which God was invoked to bring victory for the glorious endeavors of the Wehrmacht. Karl thought this sounded ridiculous... probably at this very moment across the English Channel people were requesting the same thing for their particular cause. Maybe God understood this anomaly, but Karl found it hard to accept.

The food provided at lunch was exceptionally good, helping relax the earlier tensions. It was just as well because he and Fritz aimed to examine a gazebo as soon as possible. In fact it couldn't be at a better time as most of the officers would attend a gala dinner for General Schaumberg at the chateau, and many N.C.O.'s and men had been assigned duties patrolling the perimeter of the grounds. The distinguished visitor rated this increased security and with both the outer and inner core taken care of scant attention would be focused in between according to Fritz. After Karl related the ramblings of the old boy in the hospital, Fritz reminded him there were two gazebos in the grounds, one by the lake near the rose gardens, and the other which was close to the Lancour chapel thereby complicating matters. Maybe their search effort would have to be doubled.

15

EUREKA

THE TREASURE SEEKERS FLIPPED A COIN to decide which of the gazebos should be investigated first. It happened to be the wrong call... the one nearest the chapel was selected. Using steel crate openers Karl had borrowed, five of the heavy floor boards were carefully pried loose and laid aside. They were taking their time, not wanting to cause any damage to the oak planks and leave traces of activity. Freiburg snagged his thumb on a rusted nail making him wince and say "O.K., that's enough for now." Lying along one side of the opening he reached over for the flashlight, with a sock over the lens, and peered down. "Shit, there's nothing but bits of rubble and wood, you take a look." Unfortunately nothing of value waited to be examined by the two eager searchers. Karl came to the same conclusion, "I guess you're right, it's got to be the other place". Fritz was still sucking his thumb after extinguishing the flashlight when both men heard a faint sound of voices. "Hell, just what we need" Karl whispered nervously. As the voices became louder they were just able to discern two figures in the semi darkness approaching the gazebo.

By now it was too late to make a run for it, so they hunkered down behind the balustrade. The trellis and foliage, coupled with partially obscured moonlight helped concealment, but if the two figures entered the gazebo the men would be in bad trouble. Karl gulped peering through a small gap, observing one of the figures appeared to be wearing a monocle. He whispered to Fritz "It's the bloody general." The pungent smell of cigar smoke was unmistakable and now he was headed straight for the gazebo, while the other figure remained motionless. At this particular point both soldiers wished to be magically transported to a place far away. To be caught with their implements and the uprooted floor boards would need a very imaginative explanation to avoid incarceration at the disciplinary barracks at Rennes.

Sweating profusely, hardly daring to breathe, Karl froze as the general stood at the bottom of the gazebo steps. Seconds later, he was startled by the sound of a loud fart followed by the noise of urine splashing against the trellis. Karl could even discern the broad stripe down the side of the trousers... only generals were permitted such sartorial elegance. After finishing, the unwelcome visitor gave a cough and ground his cigar out on the path before rejoining his guest. Both generals stood talking in muted tones a few minutes before moving off. Karl wiped the sweat from his brow... he had almost wetted himself moments ago.

"Screw old François and his supposed treasure" Fritz exclaimed following departure of the generals. "I've got cramp in my leg now, and that bastard Strecker almost pissed on us... can you imagine being hauled up in front of that candidate for potty training?" Karl tried suppressing a faint smile "frankly... no I can't." Regaining his normal breathing, Fritz surmised that General Strecker and his guest had something private to discuss having finished their dinner, and chance played a dirty trick picking this spot for their conversation! "Did you see Strecker's wife in church this morning?" Fritz queried. "If I was married to that tub of lard in braids, I'd have stood outside talking all night. Let's get these boards put back before anyone else shows up, the place gives me the spooks." By now he was looking towards the rows of tombs fronting the chapel. A momentary break in the clouds allowed the moonlight to illuminate their white marble. Karl was hardly paying attention as his heart still raced over the near disaster, just minutes ago.

* * * * * * * *

The soldiers spent several minutes discussing the merits of tackling the other gazebo, and decided now was better than later. In any case, the second should prove safer, as it was located further away from the chateau. This time the floor boards were easier to remove. Having lifted up the third one Fritz directed his flashlight into the opening, and immediately his hand trembled. "Du lieber, there's something down there." Following removal of two more planks there was room for Karl to step down onto the gazebo foundation. After their recent scare Fritz said he'd mount guard while his companion examined whatever was there. Hurriedly, Karl pulled aside a few sacks covering an irregular shape. Using a pocket knife he cut the straps around a canvas cover, and with rising excitement saw packages of various sizes. By now it was getting late, and he thought if General Schaumburg returned to Paris that night, the perimeter guards would stand down and some of the men might pass the gazebo too close for comfort.

Karl threw caution to the wind, opened the largest package and was totally unprepared for what was inside. His dimmed flashlight showed a large cross embedded with jewels, which glinted on catching the beam. Its beauty was breathtaking, and Karl could hardly wait for Fritz to take a look. Both stood silently awestruck before Fritz observed "Our benefactor not only left us a fine wine cache, but was also thinking of our retirement!" Laughingly Karl retorted "I don't think my nerves can stand any more for one night, whatever the old boy intended." The boards were quickly replaced, and Fritz packed a little dirt into each of the seams with his boot. Tomorrow the two men would celebrate, but for the moment all they needed was a shower and bed. Walking away, Karl told his companion he'd counted over thirty wrapped items besides the magnificent cross.

* * * * * * * *

The celebration had to be postponed, as Karl was forced to attend further tedious lectures on the 88m/m gun. With a feeling of dismay he learned the course would last another two days bringing it to the weekend. His mind drifted on and off about the gazebo, and how a man's dying words had proven to be true. Suddenly he felt Oberfeldwebel Ahren's hand on his shoulder jerking him around "Gefreiter Bayer, you'll be private Bayer at the end of this lesson if you don't pay more attention to what I'm saying". The man glared balefully and his hard fingers dug into the flesh beneath Karl's shirt. "Now stand up and explain to the class how to input the co-ordinates marked on the blackboard, then demonstrate to us on the gun predictor." As usual, Karl screwed up, but another student was even dumber, and Ahren's wrath became directed at this hapless soul.

Karl had seen Fritz Freiburg only once since General Schaumburg's visit to the chateau. They'd arranged to meet on the following Tuesday at 'Chez Martine' a small tavern roughly a kilometer from the chateau's main entrance. Karl walked there arriving just before Fritz, who was riding an old bicycle he'd borrowed from somewhere. The last time Karl had been there the place was crowded with uniformed men singing and talking as they stood around an ancient piano. Rings from the bottom of wet glasses over the course of years had given a decorative touch to the chipped and varnished top. Probably it hadn't been tuned since the first world war and tonight it remained silent. After Karl gave their order to the bald headed proprietor, the companions chose a corner bench and stretched out their legs.

A pretty girl with her hair in a pony tail sat drinks down on the table and Karl thought she looked to be about fourteen or fifteen. Fritz admired her trim little backside as she cleaned off surrounding tables with a damp cloth and Karl couldn't resist joshing his companion. "She's too young for an old sweat like you." Fritz snorted and remarked "When they are big enough they are old enough." He then raised his glass, "To our success." Karl clinked glasses and repeated the same words. Fritz inquired "So what's been happening the past few days?" Karl proceeded giving him an earful as to his views about flak guns, and what he thought of engineers who'd invented them, ending with observations regarding the ancestry of Oberfeldwebel Ahrens. Freiburg nodded his head in agreement "A dangerous crawler that man, but do your best not to aggravate him too much... it might cause difficulties regarding our enterprise, just try to keep out of his way if possible."

Karl thought this was easier said than done. "Cheer up, my friend the world is full of assholes like him but if we play our cards right we'll be eating his kind for breakfast!" A self satisfied grin spread over Fritz's face. "Now listen to my news." After taking another look at the girl's legs Freiburg swiveled round in his chair speaking softly. "Currently we have the services of a non paid expert who will appraise our gazebo inheritance... his name is Wittich." Karl was startled, what had the man been up to since they'd last met? "You mean private Heinz Wittich ?" Fritz belched "That's the boy, and what's more he'll never open his little trap with what I have on him "

Recently Karl had noticed a sour look on Heinz's face and mentioned this... "I'm not surprised, he knows you and I pal around together. Last Tuesday Paul Zeiss phoned me wanting to know if I could help him with some of those forms we churn out. Paul is an old buddy of mine and secretary of the officers mess. I told him I couldn't make it before 22.00 hours but he said that was OK and would leave the self locking rear door ajar using a wedge. I was on time, removed the wedge and went to Paul's office. After his queries were straightened out I looked at stuff he'd brought back from Paris and by then could hardly stop yawning, so wished him goodnight and arranged to meet him later that week".

"Ironically, during my visit Pvt. Wittich was also inside the building working a project of his own, namely 'liberating' items of regimental silverware! He is in cahoots with one of the mess waiters and the pair had struck up a deal. On the other side of the building from Paul's place is the Paymasters office where the silverware is kept". At this point Karl interrupted "How did Wittich get into the place?" "He told me the waiter brought him in through the kitchen entrance after all the staff had gone. The waiter left when Wittich showed up. Evidently the silver is stored in a fitted cupboard kept in a divided off section used for pay records. Wittich jimmied the lock of the Paymasters office door and once inside filled two pillow cases with the choicest small items from the cupboard.... our friend is sharp and knows what he is doing".

"After leaving Paul I walked down the corridor to the door I'd entered by. Before reaching it I noticed a toilet and decided to heed a call of nature... I must have sat on the pot for a good five minutes reading a discarded magazine. As I came out into the dimly lit corridor a figure was holding the exit door open with one hand while grabbing bags with the other. For a second I didn't recognize who it was, simply thinking it was a waiter dumping trash. Something made Wittich glance around, then I knew the man. I grabbed his collar and holding one arm behind his back marched him over to Sgt. Wederman's place with the loot. Luckily it was pretty dark and nobody was around. I had the spare key to the storeroom in my pocket and knew Horst was away. I shoved Wittich into one of those windowless rooms near Horst's office, barred the door reusing Wederman's padlock and chain, and left the little bastard to mull over his situation."

Karl was beginning to feel jumpy by these revelations, "So what did you do?" Freiburg lit a cigar before continuing. "I returned to my quarters to fetch a camera and my old Lüger." Karl downed his drink and went to the bar for another... it was beginning to seem like an old movie he'd watched in the past. Karl turned his attention back to Fritz. "What happened after you went back?" "As I opened the door Heinz Wittich looked like a rabbit mesmerized by a snake... I don't blame him as I probably resembled a King cobra at that point." Fritz glanced at his watch "Well, after he'd finished filling me in on his larceny, he kept staring at my Lüger which helped lubricate his tongue. I had him pile all the stuff on an old bench inside the room, and made him stand behind the display. I took several photographs and believe me he wasn't smiling in any of them knowing his finger prints were over everything. When asked if he had any idea of the silverware's worth, comrade Wittich had it down to the nearest pfennig."

Fritz paused a moment "Wittich's parents run an antiques gallery so he grew up in the business and I reckon the little turkey is more enterprising than most of the dolts we see around here. I told him he was needed for another appraisal, but of course I didn't divulge any details He seemed relieved when I said he might get to keep the silverware if his degree of co-operation proved satisfactory, adding should he get any big ideas he'd end up in a ditch with a bullet through his head. To emphasize the point I told him I'd swear on a stack of bibles he'd resisted arrest when caught with the evidence. I do believe he's convinced I'm serious... which of course I am."

Karl felt his head spinning with all this information to digest and glanced around checking to see if anyone was within earshot. Fritz continued "You know the funny thing about all this? Wittich chose the night for his robbery when I was in the building. If I hadn't wanted to take a crap the man would have been home free." Karl wasn't sure whether to laugh or cry, fervently hoping Fritz had stowed the silverware in an absolutely safe place. Fritz revealed nothing further, probably his way of protecting him should things fall apart.

Fritz undid his tunic and withdrew a manila envelope. "A good job my father taught me the photographers art. We owned a shop in Bremen at one time. Sgt. Keller lets me use his dark room at the back of the signals section. Photography is a hobby of his… it pays knowing the right people." Opening the envelope he pushed three photos across the table. "These are the best, I enlarged them and they are yours to keep." Pvt. Wittich's face stared bleakly from behind silverware piled on the bench… it was fairly easy to read inscriptions on most of the pieces.

A big hue and cry developed once it was discovered a good part of the mess silver had gone missing. Spot searches were common and the military police interrogated possible suspects but after a time things went back to normal. Occasionally Karl felt nervous thinking everything could blow up in their face, although Fritz looked as if he hadn't a care in the world, knowing the silverware was a good form of insurance. At one point he said, "The difference between Wittich and us lies in the fact that he's just a common thief, whereas we could be classified as archaeologists." Karl laughed, noting his partner's sanguine expression. He felt like applauding the man's modus operandi…

16

UNTOLD WEALTH

Towards the end of September Sgt. Wederman was again in debt. This time his losses at cards had skyrocketed and Horst couldn't understand it. At the start of each game things seemed to go well only to be followed by an inevitable slide. He didn't necessarily think he was being cheated, however he wasn't entirely sure so decided to cut down on his drinks during a session as the beer and schnapps must be dulling his wits. When the group broke up he was actually ahead by a slight margin. Fritz, sitting on the opposite side of the table, observed the storekeeper with a faintly amused smile. "Feels pretty good eh, Horst?" The storekeeper nodded despite the vague feeling of being manipulated, although laying off on the drinks enabled him to play better hands. The foursome pushed back their chairs and stood up. As if in unison everyone except Horst needed the toilet. Fritz started following the medics but after a few steps turned back towards Horst who was gathering scattered cards on the table. "Listen Horst, meet me in the canteen tomorrow at 20.00 hours as I have a small proposition and it will in be in your interest to show up. Counting your winnings should make you sleep better tonight." Horst wondered whether to question Fritz right then, but the man was already rapping the toilet door yelling at one of the medics to hurry otherwise there would be a flood on the floor.

* * * * * * * *

The meeting between Fritz and Horst had gone well. The overall debt he'd incurred recently could be forgiven with a little co-operation on the storekeepers part. This entailed ignoring some 'overtime' work which would take place in his domain, and he'd also need to supply one or two items Fritz required. This seemed like a 'no brainer' to Horst who in any case had a limited interest in the affairs of others. Horst Wederman usually quit for the day around 17.30 hours allowing the comrades time to get on with the task of packaging bottles. Horst procured several crates from a Wehrmacht repair center along with a load of sawdust which had been dumped in a room at the rear of the building. The crates originally contained engine parts and still had a distinct odor, and this combined with stale air in the musty room caused the comrades to cough frequently. Karl identified and listed each bottle in a thick notebook, before wrapping them in layers of newspaper. Everything was then cushioned inside the crates with sawdust. It was a tedious chore, but finally came to an end. The awkward business would be maneuvering the heavy casks down to the lower room. Thinking about the problem Karl suggested they construct a device using a tripod and pulley. This would entail buying the necessary material from a nearby town. At this point both the men were tired and decided it was time to call it quits.

The following day Karl had Fritz authorize a work order which was counter signed by the medic Sgt. allowing use of the Ziegewagen. Karl drove into the nearby town of Cherisy ostensibly to pick up office equipment. He parked outside a hardware store across from the Hotel de Ville. Having picked out various items from the shelves he dumped these on the cashier's counter. Hardly speaking French he let the proprietor deduct the cost from a bundle of notes he held out. Although the French might dislike the Boche, they seemed to have few qualms doing business with them. Karl's purchases included three coils of rope, several pulleys, fasteners and a quantity of wood. After a quick cup of coffee at a cafe he headed back to the chateau.

The following evening the two men labored at building a work aid. The first attempt at lowering a cask went according to plan, but with the second one it was near disaster as the tripod slipped. The cask almost slid out of it's sling onto the concrete floor, causing them to swear at thoughts of lost profits. When handling the remaining casks they used more caution. Wooden bracing was added between each cask and the sides of the crates minimizing any movement during shipment. After fastening all the lids down Fritz used locking wire as an extra precaution, then stenciled destination information in two places on every crate. It was hot and dusty work and Fritz straightened up wiping his brow "well I reckon that's it, we've earned our beer." Making use of Horst Wederman's utility trolley they trundled everything into the dispatch room, before leaving the building.

The following morning Horst looked over the new consignment uncertain about the content. Entering the sergeants mess just before lunch, he noticed Fritz Freiburg sitting alone and sat down beside him. Being assured again none of the stuff was Wehrmacht property, Fritz showed signs of impatience so Horst deemed it better to shut up. "Listen Horst, just you worry about doing a great job on those dummy shipping papers, and make sure to keep your tongue from wagging... apart from that you'd better quit cards from now on" Fritz got up and left, as Horst reflected on their meeting when Fritz intimated his debts could be wiped out. It wasn't any skin off his nose if indeed the boxes contained civilian articles that had been filched from somewhere. The additional bonus promised by Fritz allayed his misgivings. If the pair plundered bits of the chateau, good luck to them, c'est la guerre!

Horst had mentioned that several trucks from Rennes would collect cargo on the ninth, destined for the Reich, which made Fritz prick up his ears. Apparently the final destination would be the 11th army depot, on the outskirts of Karlsruhe. This was very sweet music to Fritz... his younger brother happened to be the depot quartermaster.

Leon Freiburg had been a farmer prior to the war, and his home was only 36 Km from the depot. After Horst mentioned his news about the trucks, Fritz shot off to make a couple of guarded phone calls to be followed by a letter. He couldn't believe his luck having Leon available to handle everything at the other end. The operation should work like a charm. Fritz told his companion that his brother Leon would take care of the cargo and have it transferred to his farmhouse. Karl wondered how this would be accomplished, but realized the fewer questions asked the better. It seemed both of the Freiburgs had an entrepreneurial spirit... words such as court martial simply weren't in their lexicon. The important thing was keeping the wine secure until Leon was able to sell it through a network of shady contacts, probably Nazi officials. Yes, Leon was definitely the man of the moment.

* * * * * * * *

Early on the morning of the ninth, three unfamiliar looking trucks arrived and parked alongside Wederman's building. They turned out to be ex-British army vehicles which had been repainted then pressed into Wehrmacht service. They'd probably been captured around the time of Dunkirk. Sgt. Wederman was busily supervising the loading operations and after everything was stowed to his satisfaction an exchange of paperwork took place. The trucks departed for a marshaling point north of Dreux where they would join up with a large convoy headed for the Fatherland. 'Operation Bacchus' was under way and its instigators could now start concentrating on the trickier problems associated with the gazebo.

Fritz observed that he now regarded himself primarily as a business man… and the army was just a part time job. Karl couldn't help laughing, and it was just as well general Strecker wasn't present to hear that little gem. Fritz turned to Karl "by the way I looked at the duty roster pinned up in Langfried's office and noted Pvt. Wittich is due for leave and is off to Berlin next week, so we've got plenty of work to finish in the meantime. He'll need photos of our gazebo artifacts to research while at home, and by the time he returns, the maggot better have all the answers."

Karl had been waiting for his partner to arrive at the gazebo closest to the chapel. He winced thinking how near they'd come to discovery the last time they were there. Lighting a cigarette he saw Fritz approach holding a black briefcase, what on earth did this signify? He already felt jumpy and didn't want more surprises, however so far Fritz had handled everything with aplomb. Greeting the younger man, the Sergeant sat down in a deck chair and stretched out his legs. After scratching a spot on his hand he began, "You know, I've a feeling our latest find is worth a king's ransom, and will make the wine consignment seem like a drop in the bucket. But it needs foolproof planning and execution when the time comes for it to leave the chateau." Karl nodded an affirmative response, relieved it wasn't something more dire. Earlier they'd run into one another at the orderly room where Fritz suggested a meeting at the gazebo, but before Karl elicited its purpose Lt. Langfried emerged from his office clutching a sheaf of papers needing Freiburg's help.

Fritz carefully placed his briefcase on the balustrade, slipped the catches and withdrew a bottle and two glasses…

so that was the reason for meeting at the gazebo, Karl realized. Taking a corkscrew from his pocket, Fritz carefully opened the bottle and said "I thought we should sample our wares to make sure it's O.K." Both men drank after having raised their glass towards each another. The wine was perfect and before Karl finished his glass Freiburg was pouring his second. "Here's to a profitable partnership" adding the old fashioned "Gott mitt uns." Karl grinned smacking his lips in full agreement. The men slumped in their chairs savoring the taste of a premier vintage.

Karl realized he knew very little about Fritz, despite telling him about his own life during the Paris trip… not that there was much to relate. He asked his companion where he was born. Fritz ran a hand through his already graying hair. He replied "Bremen 1899" Karl gave him a quzzical look and asked "then what?" Fritz lit a cigarette, "Well, I told you my parents ran a photography shop in which my younger brother and I helped out after school. Our mother died giving birth to a third child. In 1916 I joined the colors, the 87th Saxony infantry brigade to be precise. Almost immediately we were thrown into the slaughterhouse of the Western front. I was totally unprepared for the nightmarish events we were exposed to… this time around it was a blitzkrieg thank God, back then you waited in trenches of unimaginable filth for the next attack. If you survived, they had you go over the top on the orders of some moron safe behind the lines. It must have been the same routine for the Tommies… complete insanity. No doubt you'll have noticed I have a slight limp, a piece of shrapnel – a souvenir of an offensive ordered by Ludendorf in which we gained ninety blood soaked meters of France, only to give it back about a week later after incurring eleven thousand casualties. Freiburg gave a sour laugh, "Probably some of our general staff were sipping wine the color of our blood while planning such fiascoes."

After the armistice it was still hell, but of a different sort. Little food, unemployment, and inflation that was out of sight. Very gradually things began to improve under the Weimar republic, and I decided to move to the capital and try my luck. I got a job with a cabaret doing odd jobs, the pay wasn't too bad and I even took part in some of the acts. Many of my comrades weren't so lucky, those that survived the war that is. I'd see sleek ex-war profiteers come in every night to drink and ogle the girls, and they'd spend money as though there was no tomorrow, but never put a pfennig in the tin cup of the blinded veteran standing outside the entrance in all weather. I remember the iron cross ribbon pinned on his frayed jacket... the poor bastard had been terribly wounded on the Somme. How quickly people forget after the shooting stops.

Fritz paused to light a cigar and said, "I used to go out with some of the girls from time to time even though most of them were on the game. I also saw many tourists come by, mostly elderly Americans and British. The majority of these old boys couldn't wait to park their wives back at the hotel and have them go on a shopping spree while they got their jollies in the back room of the club... I guess they were somewhat repressed at home. There was a sign above the doorway reading 'abandon your inhibitions as you enter'. Berlin had supplanted Paris in terms of depravity. It was 'die goldenen zwanziger Jahre' (the golden twenties) when whatever turned you on was acceptable, provided one had the money to indulge. Anyway, eventually I quit and got a job selling insurance and didn't do badly for a while. I'd married one of the girls at the club and it was just great while it lasted. Then she took off with a banker she'd been meeting behind my back. I never saw hair nor hide of her again after that but technically I'm still married.

Later I was just starting to get established and enjoy things when the fricking Nazis came on the scene. Then I was ill for a long time and nearly died, after which I lost my job and started a quick slide down the economic totem pole. Finally, almost desperate, I rejoined the army in '36 in order to put food in my belly and have a bed to sleep in. Stupidly, I never thought another war would start as I didn't believe the events of eighteen years ago could be forgotten... I was dead wrong. Believe me I'd have gone into crime or the poorhouse before wearing this uniform again if I'd thought otherwise." Fritz paused and puffed on his cigar for a moment. "I curse the fact of not bothering to read the news and find out what was really happening in the early thirties. Too wrapped up in personal misfortunes to pay attention I suppose, and it was my own fault." Fritz again fell silent before continuing. "If I'd been smarter earlier on I would be a gauleiter by now, seeing I outranked the corporal who is now our lord and master." He began a coughing spasm after this last remark. "The only thing I've learned so far is to look after numero uno and then anybody who merits real friendship. Money, sex and power is what it's all about my friend, and generally if you have the first the other two become automatic."

Karl felt vaguely disturbed hearing all this as it was alien to his own life experiences, but realized Fritz had acquired his philosophy in the school of hard knocks. What did the future hold for himself, Karl wondered? There was no way of telling, in fact there might not even be one if the war hotted up. Fritz replaced the empty bottle and glasses in the briefcase. "Enough of my ramblings, we need to talk business. The first thing to be done are those photos for Wittich which means getting everything over to Keller's place as soon as possible. He's away for three days but I've got the key... lets make it for tomorrow, meet me outside the mess at nineteen hundred hours, O.K.?"

* * * * * * * *

They had already transferred the heaviest pieces to Keller's place using an old kitbag and returned for the remaining items hidden beneath the gazebo. It was risky but they hoped to avoid anyone in the dark and Keller's place could be approached from it's rear obviating the use of the main path. It was tedious removing the planks and replacing them each time, but they weren't about to take chances with so much at stake. Nearly all the artifacts were breathtaking in beauty and workmanship even to untrained eyes. Karl picked up a small chipped wooden box from the rest of the pile. Opening the lid revealed a worn leather pouch containing four heavy rings. Glancing at each in turn Bayer was astounded by their size and intricacy. One especially was so appealing that he was tempted to slip it on before realizing he'd hardly walk around displaying such an eye–catching object. Holding the ring between thumb and forefinger made him recall his mother's beautiful diamond bracelet. Later Karl was to learn the ring was comprised of a central massive ruby, cut in a marquise pattern surrounded by eight emeralds. A curious feature incorporated a tiny golden snake that intertwined the settings around the periphery providing a slightly sinister aspect.

Fritz spoke "Hurry up, we need to get moving." Reluctantly, Karl returned the ring wondering who in history had warranted such a valuable adornment. It wasn't until they'd nearly finished the task that Fritz let out a string of oaths, apparently one of the packages contained two books and the larger one was an album of sepia photographs showing everything in the cache. Well it was too late now, Fritz finished photographing the final three items anyway. At least his pictures could be enlarged and would be of a better quality. It wasn't so bad just a lot of work could have been saved if they'd looked at the book in the beginning.

The fatal mistake made by both men was in underrating Heinz Wittich. He knew Bayer and Freiburg would never show him the items for appraisal, but asking for pictures was necessary if he were to do an evaluation. Heinz had often seen the men together and knew they were good friends. Karl lived in the same billet as Wittich so he'd be able to watch one of the pair like a hawk. Soon they would lead him to their hiding place if photos were going to be made. He remembered an old adage his father had used... softly, softly catchee monkey. He didn't need to see the items for the moment, only the location was of prime importance. Heinz had the feeling it wouldn't take long. He'd avoided catching Karl's eye, but assiduously watched his movements so far as he was able.

* * * * * * * *

On the second trip to the gazebo the men had the misfortune of being seen. Wittich had almost missed his chance when the phone in the billet rang and as he was closest got off his bed to answer it. It turned out the caller was wanting Pvt. Padinsky who'd gone to the canteen. Wittich replaced the receiver and went for a pee as calls of nature couldn't be ignored even for a cat watching a mouse. When he returned and glanced across at Bayer's spot... hell, the man had vanished. Just moments ago he was lying back reading a magazine with his boots kicked off and didn't look as if he was about to move. This was a cardinal error Heinz might end up regretting. As he tore outside it was just in the nick of time to see Bayer disappear around a corner. At this point the light was failing so Wittich followed as close as he dared. Bayer reached the sgts. mess and waited until a figure emerged from the shadows which had to be Freiburg. The two headed off towards the lakeside gazebo without so much as a backward glance.

Keeping his distance in the poor light Heinz was able to make out the two figures kneeling on the gazebo floor. Approximately ten minutes later they departed carrying something between them. Wittich remained motionless hidden next to a tree until it was safe to move. He was pretty sure they were carrying their loot. He was going on leave in a couple of days and guessed some photographic work would soon be underway. A nasty thought struck, supposing they were simply going to hide the stuff in another place? It might prove impossible to follow them another time, but he dismissed this negative idea. When he saw the pictures he'd know if the items merited risking his neck. If they did it would need a foolproof scheme to spirit the stuff away from Dreux to avoid getting himself shot legally or illegally!

As Heinz stumbled his way back to the billet the last vestiges of light had disappeared. His mind was racing but he felt good and couldn't believe his luck. The two comrades had screwed up. When Karl Bayer climbed into bed Heinz Wittich had been fast asleep for nearly an hour snoring contentedly.

17

VIENNESE WEDDING

SGT. FRITZ FREIBURG APPROPRIATED THE STOREROOM for the last evening of the month. He found the lack of windows and dingy paint work gave the place a cell-like appearance. He switched on the lights and sat down. To make sure Horst Wederman absented himself, he'd arranged a date for him with a Luftwaffe girl from a nearby flak unit. Fritz suggested he take along one of the special hams as a present. The girl wasn't much to look at judging from her photo, but neither was Sgt. Wederman. Earlier he'd told Horst 'the girl might even hold the barrel of your gun, if you play your cards right.' Having said this Horsts lack of expertise at cards came to mind making this doubtful. Well, so long as he didn't bring her back too early was all that mattered.

Heinz Wittich entered the room soon after Fritz and Karl had arrived. Neither of the men greeted him, but after a moment of silence Karl handed over a beer. "Well Pvt. Wittich, what do you have to report?"Fritz spoke in a no nonsense manner noted by the other two. Heinz grumbled that nearly all of his leave had been spent working in museums and the library, but this elicited little sympathy from Fritz. "Just cut the cackle and get down to facts, remember what I told you when having your picture taken." Wittich's jaw dropped slightly eyeing the Lüger tucked in Freiburg's belt.

Pulling himself together Wittich reached inside a folder containing the photo's he'd been provided to work with. Clipped with them were several typewritten pages which he spread out on the table. "I haven't been able to check some of the items, they'll need further study, I couldn't obtain all the background material in the time available, but this is what I've managed so far." Wittich jerked his thumb at the manila folder. Freiburg glared at Heinz. "Enough of your bullshit, just get down to basics. Maybe you spent too much of your time in bars, and chasing after women. Don't try any stalling tactics with me!"Wittich recoiled slightly and paused before continuing, . "The cross... my God, it's unbelievable... the thing is priceless!"Freiburg snorted hearing this, his hand moving onto the pistol butt. "Let me inform you my friend... everyone and everything has its price." Heinz looked apprehensive and took a deep breath before replying "I know that, but you are not dealing with the sort of stuff found in a store. Take a look at this." Heinz produced a thin book with glossy covers, and pushed it towards the sergeant. Karl stood up in order to take a better look over his comrade's shoulder.

The book contained nine color plates depicting various jeweled crosses, each roughly the size of the 'St. Lucien'. Opposite each picture was a page of descriptive matter recording the size and weight of each object. The type and number of jewels were itemized, followed by the present whereabouts of each cross at the time the book was published. Four of the crosses were displayed in famous museums throughout the world and the others were presumed to be in the hands of private collectors. Five artifacts, including the St. Lucien, were stated to be priceless. Fritz looked somewhat annoyed as this bore out Heinz Wittich's earlier remarks.

Turning to the last couple of pages, both men were gripped by mounting excitement. Detailed were sums realized at one of the world's leading auction houses after two of the crosses came under the hammer. The last auction had been held in 1911. The winning bidder had paid 975, 000 D.M. for the 'Lorenzo' cross. Apparently there had been hectic international competition for this item. Hurriedly, Fritz flipped back to the color plate on page 11 featuring the Lorenzo, and read the description out loud. Both men were flabbergasted by the information, as Wittich had been when he'd come across the book in one of Berlin's smaller art galleries. After ascertaining it was no longer in print, Heinz had later returned and stolen it. Both Karl and Fritz remained silent until the shock began to wear off.

The typewritten pages dealing with the rest of the treasure items lay on the table, ignored for several minutes, before Fritz started reading each sheet and passing them to Karl. It was apparent Heinz had done a thorough job. Individual prices were listed and rationales given as to how they were arrived at. Sometimes this had been relatively easy, but many items required hours of perusing rarely opened books on library shelves. Each item had been indexed, linking the titles of the books researched, and suitable cross-references noted when applicable. Heinz had included newspaper clippings of noteworthy auctions saved by his father, most of which were yellowed with age. A few of them accompanied photos of the items put up for sale. These had occasionally been useful for comparison purposes with the pieces being appraised. Sometimes names of people attending the auctions were vaguely familiar to Karl. They all had one thing in common... celebrity and unlimited funds.

Heinz Wittich reminded them that "one doesn't just display this kind of stuff out on the sidewalk with a price tag, the police can be very curious if they suspect someone of handling stolen goods. It would require careful planning and discrete contact with the right people before making any trips to the bank." Fritz banged his hand down hard on the table. "Shut up you moron, don't you think we've already thought about all that?" Heinz mumbled "Sorry sergeant, I was only trying to be helpful." The meeting concluded and the three men left half an hour before Wederman and the girl walked into the room. Freiburg's assessment proved to be wrong, the table was used for an entirely different purpose. The storekeeper was beginning to feel his oats with enthusiasm…

* * * * * * * *

The swastika flag hung listlessly from its pole in front of the chateau. After weeks of glorious summer, patches of creeper on the walls withered and were turning brown. In former times, throngs of holiday makers on both sides of the English channel would have covered the beaches. Now mostly deserted they were left to groups of uniformed men, occasionally peering through binoculars out to sea. Barbed wire, interspersed with pill boxes and tank traps provided a bleak prospect for the hungry gulls wheeling overhead. Tasty leftovers from family picnics were long gone. Rumors of operation 'Sea Lion' the invasion of England, had subsided. The focus of the war would soon take other directions.

Routine duties in the clerical section at Bldg. 2B carried on in much the usual fashion, but by now Karl couldn't wait for Christmas. He'd asked Lilli to marry him and she had accepted. His mother and future in-laws were delighted by the news and were already making preparations for the wedding. Hans was already married to Gretchen, and he had promised to be best man provided he could obtain leave from his naval unit in Cherbourg. Fritz had a back log of time owing, and was looking forward to the event immensely, especially having never been to Vienna. Hans had recently visited the chateau for a weekend and Karl thought he looked fit even though he'd gained a little weight. He introduced him to Fritz and both men got on like a house on fire. All three went into Dreux and ended up roaring drunk. The next day, they visited the local winery, but the aroma of the place all but gave them a second hangover so they didn't stay until the end of the tour.

Relations were beginning to get a little more frigid between the occupiers and the local population, however in Dreux things remained generally relaxed. Orders had been issued that soldiers could no longer go out on their own but must be in groups of not less than three if their destination was greater than 5Km from the chateau. Additionally side arms were to be carried at all times. Minor incidents had already occurred, but so far these had only been verbal in nature. Since delivery of the wine cache, Fritz had received two payments from his brother in Karlsruhe which he split with his partner. Transfer of the wine to the farmhouse had all gone smoothly and apparently there wasn't any lack of customers.

During his last leave in Vienna, Karl opened a bank account in order to save a share of the proceeds. When he deposited the second installment, less than a quarter of the bottles had been sold. At this rate his dreams of owning a Volkswagen would become a reality, if only the stupid war would come to a finish. His sights were set higher now with his forthcoming marriage looming on the horizon. Money towards buying a house was next on the agenda, and hopefully proceeds realized from the treasure would take care of it. Meanwhile, he was more than satisfied having something other than his miserable army pay to look forward to every month.

* * * * * * * *

The wedding took place in the St. Maria kirche. Lilli's parents had gone all out for the celebration. Earlier the prospective bridegroom had a close call which would have put a crimp in the festivities. Through one of his Luftwaffe contacts, Horst Wederman had arranged for Karl and Fritz to hitch a ride on a transport plane bound for Wiener Neustadt, only 30 miles from the capital. The Junkers 52, a three motored aircraft had lumbered along quite happily until just south of Braunau when it developed hydraulic problems necessitating a landing at a nearby fighter base. After a couple of hours, the mechanics informed the pilot it might take two days before the necessary shut- off valves could be obtained. On hearing this, Karl began to feel panicky wishing they'd taken the train. Fortunately, after searching in one of the hangers somebody found overlooked replacement parts, and after a 5 hour delay the Junkers was again airborne with Karl relaxed in his seat.

Coming down the aisle Karl was given a wink by Fritz, standing next to his mother who was wiping away a tear. The reception after the church ceremony had been lots of fun. It seemed ridiculous that they were toasting one another with champagne which Lilli's parents had paid a great deal for. He should have kept a few of the vintage bottles from the chateau Lancour. Oh well, one couldn't think of everything. As it turned out, Fritz had remembered, and was busy pouring a glass for his mother as the happy couple approached their table. Frau Bayer was looking a trifle flushed and Karl couldn't remember ever seeing his mother giggle like this before. Maybe weddings agreed with her!

* * * * * * * *

The honeymoon was spent at a little resort in the Kitzbühler Alpen where the couple rented skis. It was cold and most of the slopes were covered with deep powder snow. Karl wasn't much of a skier, but Lilli was proficient. Her father had taught her when she was small. In his earlier days he had worked part time as an instructor at the resorts in Garmisch while attending school in Innsbruck. Lilli showed Karl how to wax the wooden skis and adjust his bindings properly. Speeding past him down the slopes she would turn at the bottom to laughingly watch as her new husband sometimes tumbled following in her tracks. On the first day, Karl had not gripped the tow rope correctly. It had cut through his glove, giving him a skin burn. After one of his falls Lilli told him "Be more careful, I don't want a hospital case in my bed tonight!" He lay in the snow smiling up at her feeling completely happy.

The resort had none of the amenities of the more expensive places, but the log huts were comfortable, and every night they piled wood into a potbellied stove until hardly able to stand the heat. A Christmas tree stood in front of the main chalet, which had been decorated by the owner's wife. The cabins were less than half filled, but the pair had met three other couples who joined them on the second evening. They drank schnapps and sang the traditional Christmas songs while watching snow falling outside.... it was bliss but so quickly over, and for the first time Karl pondered his future. During the return trip to Vienna the heating system on the train was inoperative. This was hardly noticed by the love birds curled up in each others arms, with Fritz's army great coat spread on top of them. Both were fast asleep when the train pulled in at the Hauptzollamt terminus and were met by Hans and Gretchen. Fritz apparently had taken Karl's mother out to dinner having arrived at her apartment carrying a huge bouquet of red carnations which thrilled Frau Bayer. Fritz was on his best behavior.

18

BARBAROSSA

'OPERATION BARBAROSSA' THE INVASION OF RUSSIA, began in the early hours of 22 June, 1941. The World held its breath. On hearing the news Karl remembered seeing the train load of tanks when returning from leave and wondered if they formed part of the spearheads. Possibly they'd gone to North Africa where German troops had landed in February, or they might have taken part in the Balkan campaign. The Wehrmacht was beginning to stretch like a piece of rubber in some places and feldgrau uniforms were already seen in Crete and Sicily, and now it was Joe Stalin's turn. Everybody at the chateau wondered if the latest events would affect them personally, except for those who never thought about anything at all.

Reserve Lt. Otto Hauser was the duty officer on the last day of August '41. He stood facing a window thinking of the flourishing law office he'd abandoned after recall to his regiment. Otto's father, also a lawyer was getting on in years, but had come out of retirement in order to take over during his absence. Wars had a nasty habit of overturning people's lives, but so far Otto had been lucky in comparison with some of his friends. To date the casualty lists had been sparse but with this Russian affair he suspected they'd become depressingly larger.

Sipping his coffee, the infernal teletype machine started its chatter. Placing the cup down, he walked towards the console and read incoming message formats. For the moment, nothing too startling was being ejected. He eyeballed the latest personnel movement orders. They contained names of only four officers, none of whom were familiar. He gave a grunt of relief noting his own name wasn't listed, thank God. Dreux was too comfortable, besides being a safe haven. If one had to spend time in the army, the area was ideal for Otto! He placed the message forms down on the desk, not bothering to scan a final batch which were applicable to the N.C.O.'s and other ranks. Had he done so the names Freiburg, Wederman and Wittich would have meant nothing. Otto Hauser only arrived at the chateau Lancour five weeks previously and there were lots of people in the building.

The next day Karl read the latest bulletins pinned on the orderly room notice-board… He counted thirty-four names of men about to have their lives radically altered. In fact within two years eleven would be dead and nine badly wounded. His first glance focused on surnames under the B heading. Only four were recorded and his eyes quickly moved down the list until reaching the name Sgt. Frtiz Freiburg… fuck it, why did this have to happen when things were going so well? He visualized faceless types in an army records section putting names into a hat. The whole bloody system was so impersonal. Karl turned away with his hands shoved inside his pockets… piss on everything was all he could think of.

Later, after meeting up with Fritz, he found his friend fatalistic about things. The draft would be moving out early on Friday. Freiburg had already been to a meeting attended by all the Sergeants due to be transferred. Hauptman Kessler had told them their destination was Sicily, and pointed to the island on a small map stuck up on the wall. "Hopefully you will infuse backbone into our gallant Italian allies, please give my regards to Mussolini." A few of the men were granted 48 hr. passes. All that remained was the issuance of pay and travel documents. Questions were encouraged, but mostly the group remained silent contemplating the latest turn of events. The whole thing had lasted less than forty-five minutes.

* * * * * * * *

Francine Cacheux had grown accustomed to seeing the two soldiers come into her father's tavern. She was applying some lipstick using the old cracked mirror behind the bar just as Fritz and Karl entered. Quickly smoothing her skirt, she reached for glasses and a tray, then walked over to the table where the pair sat down. The older one as usual reached out to pat her backside. This didn't displease her so long as her father wasn't behind the bar, but she'd have preferred the younger soldier to do the patting. During their last visit papa Cacheux noticed Fritz being overly familiar, and when Francine returned to the bar he'd slapped a wet cloth on the counter hissing "nom de nom, don't let me catch that oaf touching you ever again." Francine stepped back in surprise, and her elbow knocked a bottle of brandy onto the ground. Her father stared in disbelief at the broken glass and pooling liquid, then rolled his eyes to the ceiling before stomping through to the kitchen.

Francine was learning German at school which had become a compulsory subject since the occupation. She pulled up a spare chair in order to practice her latest vocabulary on the two friends. Instead of the usual beer Fritz ordered champagne which surprised her. He raised his glass and said "Au revoir mademoiselle. I'll be leaving la belle France in the early morning." Francine was disappointed hearing this but moments later was relieved to find out Karl would stay. She smiled at him and said "I don't want to find a new beau who has to listen to my fractured sentences." Karl winked at her and she began to blush slightly as he asked her for a pencil and a sheet of paper. She went off to fetch the requested items before returning to the bar.

Fritz wrote down his brother's address and telephone number, and passed it to Karl saying "This should always reach me and I have your mother's address. Who knows where we'll both end up. Leon will send money drafts to Vienna regarding future sales of the wine, but I've told him not to try and rush things, and that he needs to be careful. Is this all right by you?" Karl nodded. "Incidentally, speaking of being careful, if ever we should need to mention the treasure let's use a code word... how does 'Uncle Lancour' sound?" Fritz laughed, "Sounds pretty good to me. That should do it, if one of those censors at a field post office get nosy. At least there is something good about this upheaval, apparently Pvt. Wittich will accompany me on the Sicily jaunt, which will let me keep tabs on him... kind of ironic don't you think?"

Fritz gripped Karl's hand across the table, "Comrade, this stupid war can't go on for ever. I trust you completely and I hope you feel the same about me. May 'Uncle Lancour' rest in perfect peace until we're ready to wake him up and sell him. When we next meet we'll have a real celebration at the farmhouse. We'll buy ourselves pinstriped suits and have the world by the balls." Both men laughed uproariously and when Francine glanced across from the bar she smiled at them. Fritz called for her to bring another bottle of champagne and poured out three glasses, handing one to Francine. "To Uncle Lancour." She didn't have any idea what this meant, but no matter as both men looked happy, and the drink tasted delicious.

Karl was still asleep the next morning when the Sicily draft rolled through the chateau gates. On awaking he glanced across at Wittich's bed. It was bare except for a rolled up mattress left on top. He hadn't even bothered to shut his locker door that stood behind it. A single piece of paper lay on the top shelf... he'd scrawled, fuck you Karl Bayer your time will come, Karl laughed as he banged the door shut.

* * * * * * * *

Almost three months had elapsed since the departure of Freiburg and Wittich, as Karl sat on his bed writing to his mother. Occasionally, Lilli would stay a few days with her to provide company. Frau Bayer was teaching her how to cook, and Karl was pleased they got on so well. Looking at his watch, he put his pen and writing pad away knowing it was time to report for his shift in Bldg. 2B. He was now doing most of the work Fritz formerly handled and he'd been told his name was down for promotion which would compensate for the additional responsibility.

Somebody had left a newspaper on his desk and he noted that the onslaught against Russia appeared to be slowing after the initial pulverizing attacks. These had gained huge chunks of territory and millions of Soviet P.O.W.'s. The article pointed out that the Russian army was badly led due to lack of military expertise. Stalin had purged his ablest generals before the outbreak of hostilities, and the Russian bear was now suffering the consequences. Karl worried about the R.A.F. bomber attacks which were becoming a regular occurrence over Europe. So far these raids were nothing in comparison to the massed attacks that came in the future, but the fact of bombs having fallen on Berlin made nonsense of Göering's earlier boast of invincible defenses. The possibility of raids on Vienna was more than Karl cared to think about. He hoped the people manning the defending flak batteries were more capable than himself in handling the 88's if bombers should hit the city

* * * * * * * *

Some members of the band unit now used the gazebos for practice sessions. This worried Karl, but he concluded musical activity hardly posed a threat to 'Uncle Lancour' so long as nobody left any lighted cigarette butts on the floor. Occasionally he'd walk over to the gazebo to keep an eye on things. He still went down to the tavern from time to time accompanied by new friends from the clerical section. Francine was making rapid progress with her German and Karl thought about trying to learn French but so far hadn't done much about it. A lieutenant Hauser attached to the signals unit was to teach French classes in two weeks, which might be a good time to start.

Karl went down to the 'Chez Martine' and Francine came over and kissed him on the cheek, much to the amusement of his two friends. He didn't mind their teasing remarks, but was concerned about his newfound feelings toward her… maybe it was just being randy, but he suspected something more than that. Damn, he didn't want to feel guilty about Lilli and needed to keep his nose clean. The girl was too young, but when his companions got up to join a group standing around the piano, he felt relieved being alone with her. She giggled over pronouncing a sentence about 'the postman delivering the mail' as he put his hand on her thigh under the table. She didn't appear to notice, until coming to the end of the sentence she leaned slightly forward and her left hand enclosed his own, he guessed they were on the same wavelength.

Just when Karl suggested she might like to visit the local cinema, Papa Cacheux brought the idyll to an abrupt close by shouting "Francine, I need your help in the kitchen, one of those pipes over the sink has burst." Francine got up quickly and followed her father. Karl felt frustrated as his hand had just moved higher on Francine's leg.

* * * * * * * *

The next morning he felt far more frustrated reading the daily order sheet. This one was signed by General Strecker. Henceforth, none of the personnel at the chateau were to leave the ground unless authorization was signed by the adjutant. Two airmen from the neighboring Luftwaffe base had been found shot. The bodies had been discovered in a ditch and an intensive search of the area turned up an old French army rifle and pistol. The caliber matched with the bullets extracted from the corpses. The initial conclusion was rumored activities of a fledgling French resistance movement had become reality. Posters had been distributed in Dreux and its surroundings by the Feldgendarmerie stating that hostages in the ratio of three to one would be executed if further such incidents occurred. A curfew was imposed, and military police were busily employed making searches of all civilian installations thought to be harboring 'gangster terrorists'. The notice had been countersigned by the mayor of Dreux and its Chief of Police.

* * * * * * * *

A gentle rain had been falling for nearly two hours. Karl looked out of a window in the billet just as it stopped. The sun had broken through the cloud base and droplets of water on blades of grass reflected its rays. He decided to take a walk before making a call from the pay phone in the orderly room. After cutting through the rose gardens, he stopped at the edge of the lake and skimmed a few pebbles on its surface. The last time he'd done this was when his mother had taken him on a stroll in the Franz Joseph gardens. Occasionally his father had accompanied them and shown him how to skim.

He found a cigar in his tunic pocket Fritz had given him the day they'd discovered the wine cache. Searching other pockets for matches he wondered what his friend was doing at that moment. Probably drinking Chianti and ogling the young signorinas he reckoned, and the thought made him smile as he continued walking until reaching the orderly room. Someone was already using the phone, and another soldier was waiting. By the time Karl's turn came he'd almost decided not to bother.

Francine answered on the third ring, which was lucky as it could have been Papa Cacheux, thereby posing a language problem. Karl spoke slowly telling her why he couldn't visit and she seemed constrained. "Perhaps it's just as well, the Feldgendarmarie paid a visit last night. My papa is furious... the pigs broke some furniture searching for heaven knows what. When he protested they hit him twice. I'm afraid Germans are no longer welcome as patrons. I'm sorry Karl, perhaps it will all pass... I must go now." He knew she was crying and felt helpless. Karl replaced the receiver and swore. The orderly room clerk glanced up momentarily catching his eye. "Trouble comrade?" "Shut your damned mouth" Karl responded, retracing his steps and slamming the door. Three days after his phone call, two letters arrived which changed his filthy mood. Lilli thought she was pregnant and Fritz inquired if 'Uncle Lancour' was happy in the rest home.

The changed mood didn't last long. On the way over to Bldg. 2B he saw Oberfeldwebel Ahrens approaching. The mere sight of the man churned his stomach in disgust. Ahrens halted in the middle of the path. "Guten Tag, gefreiter Bayer. I trust you like cold weather?" What the hell was the shithead talking about? "I see from the latest personnel sheets you are going to get your chance to show 'Ivan' everything I taught you about the 88 m/m gun. That is after your transfer to the gunnery school at Beckerdorf." Ahrens had a vindictive grin on his face and Karl's jaw dropped as he stared at him. "What do you mean?" "Exactly what I've just told you. Go and take a look at the bulletin board... in fact I put in the recommendation." Karl angrily clenched his fists while Ahrens continued. "Winter on the steppes of Mother Russia is highly invigorating so I am told, especially as you'll be promoted to sergeant. Who knows, maybe you'll get my job one day." His tormentor laughed. "It's really too bad, as I'm being posted to a training school at Klangenfurt which means you could have taken my 'graduate' course!"

Bayer instantly decided the Eastern front would be preferable, longing to smash his fist into the bastard's face Ahrens picked off a thread from his immaculate uniform. "Well, I must hand in my report to the adjutant… Auf wiedersehen. Kommen sie bald Wieder nach Dreux!" Karl watched Ahrens retreating back, and he was filled with loathing for the army and Dreux. The place was becoming a prison with patrols walking its perimeter with Rottweiler guard dogs. Well, Freiburg and Wittich were gone and now it was his turn to leave. Only one of the three would ever see the place again.

EPILOGUE

PART I

In June 1940, on a road clogged with refugees, a young nun rescued the two Lancour boys from a wrecked car in which their parents had been killed outright. In the turmoil of war the brothers were cared for by two different families. For a long time Martin the oldest boy had nightmares of the terrifying event, but Pierre's age precluded lasting memories.

Following the liberation of France, ownership of the Chateau Lancour passed to the State. A perfunctory search had been made by those responsible which failed to trace the former owners. Claims for war reparations were duly filed by the French government for damages sustained by the estate while under Wehrmacht occupation.

Endless wrangling with Chancellor Adenauer's bureaucracy had yielded nothing. Other greater claims were still outstanding, and the courts moved at a snails pace. Eventually, in late 1946 the Lancour estate was refurbished at taxpayers expense as a center for international trade and adult educational classes. The Lancour name faded in the minds of the locals... just a few elderly villagers recalled it in the subsequent years wondering what became of the family... c'est la guerre.

LETHAL SPOILS

Part 2

IN 1917 A LARGE SECTION OF the French army driven to the point of exhaustion decided they'd had enough of false promises of victory. This led to the largest mutiny in modern history.

Near the site where this took place is a sign that reads. " Now it's your turn all you big shots to climb the ridge, because if it's war you want, pay for it with your own skin."

19

STALINGRAD

WINTER 1942

"THE GERMANS ARE PERHAPS TOO EFFICIENT. Its soldiers have the correct size boots, whereas the Russian soldier knows it's better to wear oversized ones. These can be stuffed with straw, which counters the effect of frostbite." General Georgi Zhukov, Red Army.

* * * * * * * *

By late afternoon, Karl Bayer's battery received their latest movement orders. The guns and support equipment had undergone a badly needed overhaul at Kupyansk in July. Climate and terrain were taking a terrible toll on mechanized equipment of the Panzers, and Col. General Kunder wanted everything to be in first class order for the next blood bath. It was about this time Bayer first heard of the name Stalingrad.

Later on, his worst nightmares couldn't have conceived the absolute hell it came to represent. Mars, the Roman God of War, undoubtedly gloated over the final tally of Russian and German soldiers obliterated by the epic struggle for mastery of a sprawling city along the banks of the river

Volga. Hitler ordered the German sixth army commanded by General Paulus to take the city by August 25th, and Karl's unit had been earmarked to play its part in making Der Führer's order reality. General Manfred Kunder's message was read out to the assembled gun crews. Stirring words about the Fatherland and what their commander expected from each man during the next onslaught on the Bolshevik enemy etc. Karl noted an absence of words regarding what each listener might expect… maybe an iron cross or probably one of the wooden variety was more than likely.

After completing the gunnery course at Beckerdorf Karl was promoted to sergeant as had been forecast by his nemesis Oberfeidwebel Ahrens back at Dreux. He'd received five days leave which was happily spent in Vienna with his wife and mother. Lilli had been mistaken in thinking she was pregnant when Karl was still in France, this time however there was no mistake. Nearly all the new graduates at the gunnery school were posted to Russia shortly after the start of 'Barbarossa', or the great patriotic war as the Russians termed it. In mid-October '41 the Germans were only sixty miles from Moscow and at the beginning of December they'd reached Istra, a suburb fifteen miles west of the capital. By then the population was in panic. The 'Blitzkrieg' was of a far greater scale than the one which brought France to it's knees in 1940.

By Christmas of 1941 the vast Nazi juggernaut was becoming stalled by growing resistance and the terrible effects of winter. The German troops suffered horribly still dressed in summer uniforms worn at the start of the war and they envied the proper clothing issued to the Red army. The Nazi's wouldn't resume their offensive until the spring. Mid-summer saw the great cities of Rostov and Sevastopol fall to the invaders during gargantuan thrusts which sent the Russian bear reeling. Masses of Soviet prisoners were still being taken and huge quantities of equipment fell into the hands of the Wehrmacht. The prospect of survival for Mother Russia was looking pretty bleak. Leningrad was under devastating siege and in July Hitler ordered his generals to prepare 'Operation Northern Light' with the objective of capturing the city by September. Before the siege was lifted close to a million of its inhabitants were to die due to bombing, starvation and cold. Adolf Hitler's main goal however was seizure of the rich oilfields that lay to the south around Baku. This had been spelt out to the O.K.W (Wehrmacht High Command) in no uncertain terms. Germany desperately needed new oil supplies to keep its war machine running. With the intensified fighting on several fronts during the summer of '42 a steady advance had been forged by the Panzers along the great curve of the river Don.

Spearheads of the German 6th army under command of General Friederich Paulus reached the outskirts of Stalingrad in late August. Joseph Stalin knew if he couldn't hold the city that bore his name, little else would prevent the enemy from reaching its objective. The Russian leader had already decreed the Red Army must halt the German formations at Stalingrad and ordered the city to prepare for attack. Any deserters were to be shot on sight. If the city capitulated, oil and food from the resource rich south would be choked off, imperilling the Soviet war effort. The Führer's deadline for capturing the city had already passed and the opposing forces were locked in murderous street fighting amongst piles of rubble. Each and every building was fought over with tenacious fury. Stalin granted General Chuikov's request for transfer of elite forces from other fronts to bolster defense of the city. The deadly combat went on day and night sometimes with opposing forces shooting from alternate floors of abandoned department stores and factory buildings. The slaughter continued for weeks with neither side taking prisoners, it was simply kill or be killed and any semblance of military tactics in the normal sense were ignored, and it had degenerated into a case of mutual genocide. On November 18th reinforced Red Army units simultaneously struck German positions around the city from the North and South. Heavy snow began blanketing the scars of war. Bodies lay where they had fallen as little energy was available for digging graves in the frozen ground. By early December the surrounded German forces were in dire straits with food practically nonexistent and transport horses already killed and eaten. After weeks of horrendous combat twenty-two German divisions found themselves in a steel trap and over 300, 000 men were squeezed into a pocket between the rivers Don and Volga. Karl Bayer was one of these unfortunates experiencing the hopelessness of impending defeat. In later years historians would come to regard it as one of the most cataclysmal battles ever fought and the turning point of W.W.II.

* * * * * * * *

Karl Bayer was almost on the point of crying as the temperature hovered around -28 Celsius. He looked a pretty pathetic figure with a stubbly beard and eyebrows encrusted in granules of ice. Only the eyes were visible between folds of a shawl wrapped around his head and forage cap. He had removed the shawl from the corpse of a Russian peasant woman who'd died beside her hovel near villages where the gun tractors refueled en route to Stalingrad. By then Karl had learned not to pass up any opportunity since the rigors of his first winter in Russia. After leaving Kupyansk, it had taken over four days to reach their new gun emplacements on the banks of the Volga and on arrival the crews viewed the outskirts of the ruined city through high powered field glasses, while potential target co-ordinates were evaluated. Two days later, Karl's crew along with three others, moved up closer to the areas of combat in northern sectors of Stalingrad, where they'd been ordered to act as close artillery support.

To compound his present miseries, a flesh wound in his right leg was beginning to fester from pieces of shrapnel. Low flying 'Stormoviks' destroyed one of the 88 m/m guns and most of its precious ammunition stock. The spectacular explosion had rammed Bayer and another gunner against an abandoned T-34 tank knocking them out. By early December, the crews were exhausted, and on the point of starvation. Apart from a few scraps, they hadn't eaten for days and everyone's nerves were stretched to the limit. The entire Stalingrad pocket had become denuded of supplies. Food and medicine were the worst deprivation, and deaths due to malnutrition and hypothermia were decimating the trapped Wehrmacht forces. Reich Marshall Göering's promised airlift had turned out to be just another cruel propaganda fantasy. Sgt. Bayer's battery was used in the role of firing point blank at buildings selected by Waffen SS shock troops. After several rounds softened things up, these veteran assault groups consisting of nine men or less would leave their cover and attack the target using grenades and flame throwers.

By now Karl had lost all count how many times his crew had repeated these actions and his brain had become numbed. His every movement seemed to be on automatic, no longer in need of commands. During the latest assault the noise factor was deafening, then suddenly everything went eerily quiet allowing him to take stock of the surrounding scene. He slumped against some pitted brickwork pondering over his total lack of feelings seeing the vista of utter desolation. It was almost as if Picasso had tried to paint the Götterdämmerung and given up.

A nasal voice penetrated his consciousness, "Sergeant, we are down to eleven shells." Karl became aware of his screaming "what the fuck do you want from me! Do you expect I can shit some more you cretin?" This sudden outburst on his part startled Karl as he was in charge and supposed to make decisions for his crew. Something triggered within his brain and a semblance of normality returned. He stared at the man in front of him for a few moments. He was a dull-witted Saxon gun layer with eyes like those of a sheep. How could this fool think he did not know the number of shells remaining? It was ironic, but perhaps types like Franz Schultze would end up being the Wehrmacht's salvation. Only simple cannon fodder was the requirement at Stalingrad. The expressionless face of the soldier hid the near vacuum between the ears. This simple ex-farm boy would take all the suffering and hardship handed out and still follow whatever inane orders were given to him. Apparently the man had worked in a slaughter house before joining the army... well he must be feeling right at home in this place.

The day after Karl yelled at the gun layer a heavy snow started falling again. A fierce wind whipped the icy flakes into a temporary whiteout. Apart from the isolated rumblings of Russian howitzers in another sector, an odd feeling of stillness pervaded the gun position. God why couldn't they have sent him to Sicily where his comrade Fritz and that man Wittich had ended up... maybe Fritz was bellyaching about the heat at this very moment, such were the vagaries of war. Karl would have given anything to hear from his wife and mother, but he knew it wouldn't happen as mail had stopped coming into the Stalingrad pocket days ago, ever since the Russian noose tightened around the thousands of encircled Germans cornered like rats. A fraction of the badly wounded had been flown from the pocket in old Ju. 52 ambulance planes, but it was doubtful if the nearby airfields at Pitomnik and Gumrak would be operational much longer, if indeed they hadn't already been captured by 'Ivan.' Karl knew it could only be a question of another day before his unit was non-effective, unless some ammunition and food reached them. He hoped the 'Angel of Death' would be quick when the time came. Karl called Schultze over "Go and see Cpl. Bauer and ask him if he's had any luck getting that field telephone working."

The man was back within minutes. "No Sergeant, he says it's useless." Karl sighed and tried to blow some hot breath onto his frozen finger tips. The answer was what he'd expected. Since the pull back to the river by the other gun crews, only one incoming message had been received on this worthless piece of junk before it finally quit. It seemed like a million years since hearing the faint voice of Capt. Bergman the company commander telling them to stay put until he could send help.

After darkness had fallen the preceding calm was shattered by a salvo of 'Katyusha' rockets landing close by. Bayer was only too familiar with these babies and knew they were launched from self-propelled carriers which the Wehrmacht had nicknamed 'Stalin Organs.' After a third salvo exploded on previously demolished buildings the silence returned for a bit until a wind started moaning in the black surroundings. Karl reckoned the rocket launchers must be located fairly close by. He worried the cushioning effects of snow coupled with wind noise would allow their position to be over-run without warning, unable to hear 'Ivan' creep up in the dark. Karl Bayer began to feel a rising panic taking hold. With the one and only 'Panzerfaust', an anti-tank projectile fired from a hand held launcher, plus the few stick grenades which had already been distributed, the situation would be hopeless should the Russkies strike within the next few hours.

Following the Waffen S.S. attack in the late afternoon none of the shock troopers returned for the usual hurried exchanges with the gun crew regarding the next targets. The 88 m/m had lobbed at least three shells into the lower floors of the three-story building at the start as Karl watched the troops go in using flame throwers. Maybe during the confusion created by smoke and brick dust he'd missed seeing them leave the place, or they could have exited on the far side of the building after flushing out snipers. Supposing it was 'Ivan' that had done the finishing off? One didn't hear noise from bayonets being thrust into survivors. Maybe the Russkies had been on the upper floors and were now waiting for dawn to eliminate the gun crews, unaware of the pitifully small opposition.

Bayer pulled himself together... this kind of conjecturing only stretched his nerves to the limit. It was getting dark and Karl went in search of Cpl. Bauer who was dozing in the lee of an abandoned personnel carrier. "Listen, take Pvt. Kaminsky with you and get down to the river and try locating Capt. Bergman. Explain the situation here and ask permission for the battery to withdraw on my behalf. Make sure he understands we are at the end of our tether... if you are lucky you should be back before dawn."

* * * * * * * *

General Paulus, Commander of the Sixth Army, was holding a staff meeting in his command bunker. It was like a gathering of dead men, which in fact was close to the truth. Under discussion were the consequences of Hitler having rejected 'Operation Thunderbolt' a plan involving a mass breakout of the Sixth Army with assistance from Hoth's 4th panzer forces. It was far too late as Hoth had been halted on the Myshkova. The Führer had ordered a defensive 'hedgehog' configuration be maintained at the Stalingrad pocket until help arrived. Specifics as to how this was to be accomplished were notably missing. General Paulus listened to verbal reports given by each of his divisional commanders before turning back to the map table. His own estimation had been that his army required at least 700 tons of supplies per day in order to continue fighting. Actually this was quite inadequate. The O.K.W. in its wisdom urged the Luftwaffe to fly in 300, but in reality all they ever managed was under 100 at the most. It all added up to pissing against the wind, while in the meantime nearly 300, 000 men were starving.

Bauer and Kaminsky returned about 2.a.m. and reported they'd found no trace of Capt. Bergman the battery commander. Nobody seemed the slightest bit interested wrapped up in too many of their own problems. Karl stared at them for a moment and gave a shrug, then put an arm around the shoulder of each man… "Thanks, I know you did your best." Inwardly he'd expected something like this.

As the first glimmers of daylight appeared, Karl shook each man awake and ordered them to gather by the gun tractor where he ordered Schultze to spike the 88 m/m making it inoperable. When this had been accomplished the men made a quick dash across the snow towards the shattered entrance way of what had been their last target. The bodies of three Waffen S.S. men lay sprawled just inside a long passage. Karl had Dieter Rausche pick up the Schmeisser submachine guns belonging to the assault troops and detailed Schultze to cover the entranceway. The rest of the crew continued walking slowly until they came across several offices containing smashed furniture and broken fixtures. Lots of paperwork was strewn about in each room which occasionally wafted about, caught by the wind blowing through gaping holes in the walls. Shards of glass from broken windows crunched underfoot. Reaching a stairway to the upper floor, Karl motioned the others to hold back. Gripping his Luger he felt his heart pounding. If 'Ivan' was waiting these could be his last moments. He touched the St. Christopher medallion hanging around his neck, given him by Lilli on his last leave. Almost at the top of the stairs he could see a half-opened door. Tucking the Lüger into his belt he removed a stick grenade from the other side, pulled the pin and hurled it through the doorway. The explosion blew the door off its hinges. As it hit the floor, Karl raced up the last couple of steps. With his back brushing the landing wall, he inched along with his pistol drawn, then peered through smoke from the grenade into the room beyond. The only waiting Russkies were three dead ones.

20

THE ABYSS

Perhaps tortured souls still congregate to mourn the horror of Stalingrad.

EVERYONE FELT TOTALLY DEJECTED, THERE WERE no food scraps to fill empty bellies. Karl ordered the men out of the building and back to the gun emplacement. To stay put might increase the odds of being discovered by 'Ivan'. Later, thinking of Bauer and Kaminski's failure to contact the battery commander, Karl wondered if he had done the right thing.

Karl Bayer was looking for Cpl. Bauer and found him with a comrade fitfully trying to sleep in the cab of a gun tractor. Karl cupped his right hand to the corporal's ear "Grab your ground sheet and lead me to that big shell crater nearby." After stumbling along a few yards they slithered into the large hole created by a Russian howitzer shell. Karl pulled his ground sheet over both their heads before lighting a cigarette which he gave to his comrade. Bauer was grateful for the gesture having smoked his remaining one hours ago and didn't visualize another unless he got lucky searching pockets of a corpse. Bauer suddenly asked "What date is it?" Karl was nonplused by this seemingly irrelevant question, besides being unsure of the answer. "December the 28th I think but that's only a guess." Bauer drew on his cigarette "Well the 28th happens to be my twenty-first birthday, I was curious that's all… it will be a miracle if I see the twenty-second." Karl nodded agreement.

Both men gave a hollow laugh as Karl felt inside his tunic and handed Bauer two of his remaining cigarettes "happy birthday friend." Three loud thumps occurred which sounded too close for comfort. Cpl. Bauer observed "the Russkies must be having some sort of celebration music in his honor." Karl was biting his lip due to a sudden pain in his leg but managed to reply "If you are lucky they'll send over some of those Red army girls to dance on our coffins. Pity it was a wasted trip to find the battery commander, but I don't need to tell you we've had it as a combat unit. I once saw a notice saying something about… 'blessed are the decision makers' well, this is what I've come up with. We might as well return to the building and get out of the infernal cold, 'Ivan' won't take long sniffing us out either way. I want you to spread the word among the men to relocate first thing in the morning." Bauer nodded then clambered to the rim of the hole, dislodging some poor sod's dismembered leg which fell on Karl, who mumbled "Thanks, we may need it for the pot tomorrow."

* * * * * * * *

As the first streaks of dawn made an appearance Karl trained his field glasses on the building but no signs of 'Ivan' were evident. He stamped his boots to improve the circulation in his feet but to little avail. The temperature had dropped, and his teeth were chattering convincing him the move was the right choice. Earlier he'd toyed with the idea of lighting a small fire at the bottom of a shell crater using some of the discarded ammo boxes but knew this would be tantamount to suicide with snipers waiting for opportune targets to present themselves.

On reaching the building Karl entered using a side door. A short flight of stairs led to the boiler room which had escaped damage during the SS assault. The room contained three bodies and Karl almost tripped over the first... a Russian officer sprawled face down with a bayonet protruding from his back. His fur cap was clutched in one hand and a Tokatev pistol in the other. Karl pried the weapon loose from the frozen fingers then rifled the pockets of his great coat. Apart from two stale bits of bread and a half eaten sausage: there was nothing. Still beggars can't be choosers he surmised. Two other corpses were on the far side of an old-fashioned furnace... a man in civilian workmen's garb was propped up against the wall with a single hole drilled through the center of his forehead. Karl judged him to be roughly sixty years old, most likely the janitor. A quick search of the clothing revealed nothing except a tattered wallet containing a few rubles and a crumpled cigarette package causing Bayer to swear. The third body lay stretched out on several layers of sacking as if asleep but a glance at the man's Mongolian features left no doubt it was his last. No visible wound was discernible so Karl wasn't sure how the Russian trooper died but he noticed his bayonet scabbard was empty and judged the weapon was the one lodged in the officers back.

Karl stood up and walked over to the officer's body. Removing his forage cap he replaced it with the Russian fur headgear after tearing off the red star emblem. A slight noise caused him to glance back at the doorway where Dieter Rausche stood with a startled look on his face, maybe the fur hat on his sergeant confused him. "What's up, did you think it was 'Ivan'?" The two men walked slowly around the boiler room but Rausche hardly glanced at the bodies. A pile of dirt caked potato sacks were stacked in one corner next to some old newspapers and kindling wood. Several glass bottles stood on rough shelving attached to a wall, one or two still contained liquid. Rausche reached up, uncorked one, then sniffed the content. "Smells like vodka, Sarge." He handed the bottle over to Karl, who, after taking a couple of hefty swigs agreed. "By the saints that feels good, at least this rat hole has something to offer before we die like dogs."

Karl told his companion to bring the others downstairs along with anything worthwhile from the shattered upper floors. "We'll be out of the wind and snow in this place so get Schultze and Harald to lug these lousy 'Ivans' upstairs while you're at it, then share out the potato sacks… they can act as blankets cum shrouds." Bayer gave a sardonic laugh at his own remark as Schultze looked at him blankly. Karl wondered if the man had ever cried. If he hadn't, now was the time as their countdown to oblivion was imminent. A rat scuttled alongside the far wall and disappeared under the pile of sacking before Bayer was able to level his weapon.

Shortly after the gun crew moved into their new location, the Soviet High Command sent a surrender ultimatum to the headquarters of the trapped Sixth Army, which was rejected. The insane killing continued a while longer, until the 'grim reaper' was satisfied. For the survivors there was no hope anyone might escape the hell hole of Stalingrad. Finally on the last day of January '43 Paulus capitulated inside the southern pocket… he'd been promoted to Field Marshall a few days earlier, an act of supreme irony on the part of the Nazi Führer. Surrender of the northern pocket quickly followed bringing to a close an event that reverberated around the world. A bitter looking Field Marshall and his chief of staff General Arthur Schmidt, along with a senior staff officer Col. Wilhelm Adam, emerged from their command post to present themselves as POW's to the Russian 64th army.

* * * * * * * *

Despite having air superiority backing up its ground forces every effort by the Germans to capture the entire city had been stymied. Josef Goebbels the Nazi propaganda minister tried blurring the magnitude of defeat from the home front, failing miserably. When the news was finally announced over the radio it was accompanied by the constant playing of somber music. Thousands of mothers wept for sons who had given their lives for the Fatherland. During a single day at the start of the battle 600 Luftwaffe bombers killed more than 40, 000 of Stalingrad's population providing a foretaste of further horrors for those who remained within the city. Even this kind of hammering proved inadequate for breaking the morale of a people who'd emerged daily from the rubble of their homes and were familiar with hardship and suffering. When victory finally arrived they were left with the name of their city but precious little else.

* * * * * * * *

The finale so far as the gun crew were concerned, happened when 'Ivan' ferreted out the boiler room twenty two hours before the official surrender. Only five of the original crew were left when Russian soldiers burst into the basement during mopping up operations. Pvts. Dieter Rausche and Hans Linderman on the point of desperation had stumbled outside earlier to forage for food and never returned. The remaining men ended up huddled inside the boiler itself in an attempt to stave off the awful cold. Earlier in an attempt to light the boiler furnace a blockage in the flue had caused a blow back and billowing smoke drove them upstairs until it dissipated.

Emerging into the daylight prodded by automatic weapons the men evoked a picture of hell, covered in ashes and filth along with their wild looking beards. Each man was in a semi stupor debilitated by a combination of frostbite, sleeplessness and hunger, and most were barely able to walk. Ninety thousand others were subsequently rounded up like cattle while the leaders of the third Reich climbed into warm beds on a full stomach. Within weeks of this enormous disaster fewer than 10, 000 German POWs remained alive. Starvation and wounds coupled with disease would claim approximately 80, 000 members of the Wehrmacht who'd undergone incredible hardship in an effort to capture a single city for the Führer. The Russian fighters were hardly in better shape despite the stunning victory of the Red Army. History wouldn't be able to record the cost in human life and misery it had taken to achieve. Over two million Russians and Germans were killed in the apocalypse. In later years Stalin erected an enormous monument outside the city to commemorate the struggle, while the Germans for their part would only be left with bitter memories. After Stalin's death even the name of the city was erased… it was to be known as Volvograd.

* * * * * * * *

Harald Schultze and Karl were the only survivors of B battery, and were taken to an abandoned factory outside the town of Primorsk some 60 km from the place of their capture. On arrival each POW was issued an old blanket or greatcoat then looked for space on the oil splotched concrete floor in order to lie down. Hardly anyone spoke while they contemplated their individual fate. Twice daily, minute portions of kasha, a form of porridge were doled out, and a few battered tin mugs were provided for brackish drinking water stored in old oil drums. After four miserable days elapsed, the prisoners were herded into a metal building where long tables had been set up. Originally the place had been used as a machine shop and contained work benches and several antiquated lathes and presses.

Directed to the first of the tables, everyone's arm was jerked up for inspection by a grim faced sergeant looking for tattoos which designated a member of the SS. Whenever the incriminating mark was spotted, the man was roughly dragged from the line and taken through a side door... it didn't take much imagination to guess their fate. Karl noticed a stern looking woman in officer's uniform at one of the tables. Harald, who was behind him, quickly whispered "she's probably one of the political commissars we've heard about." At another table sat a row of Red army medics with a German speaking officer. Badly wounded cases were separated from the others, and taken into another area. Karl's leg was still painful but he decided not to draw attention to it and become separated from Harald and Schultze. At the last table, everyone's pockets were again searched, and paperwork was handed over along with small bags of hardtack.

After another group had been processed, two hundred men including Karl and his comrades were marched eleven kilometers to a small train station. Following a wait of over two hours, a dilapidated locomotive hauling a long string of box cars pulled in, and they were herded aboard by their guards. No one knew the destination was Moscow. After arrival they were marched with thousands of compatriots through the main streets of the city. Harald spoke with bitterness, "I feel like some animal in a circus parade." Karl didn't reply as he no longer gave a shit.

Muscovites, out of curiosity stood watching these specimens of the master race file by, but showed very little emotion. The humiliation of the former 6th Army was complete... newsreel cameras recorded the spectacle for posterity. Stalin never tired of watching the reruns. Shortly after this it was as if a veil had been drawn over the life of Sgt. Karl Bayer. The three men were split up and one ghastly prison camp followed another.

* * * * * * * *

The end of the war in Europe hardly registered with Karl. The winter of 1946 was one of the worst on record. The USSR was stricken with drought and starvation, causing the remaining number of prisoners to quickly dwindle. Following a period spent at a political indoctrination center, Bayer ended up in one of the sealed zones along the Amur River, close to the Russian/Chinese border known as the Khabarovsk territory.

For years he toiled in several saw mills under the supervision of guards who were mostly harsh but occasionally he found humane ones, their lot in life differing little from that of their captives. When final permission was granted allowing Karl to return to his homeland, he knew the age of miracles had not yet passed. How was it he'd survived when so many others had perished? The Karl Bayer who'd first put on Feldgrau uniform would never have recognized the drawn features reflected in the piece of cracked mirror, as he attempted trimming a wild looking beard.

21

SPRING 1945

THE WAR FOR SGT. FREIBURG AND Heinz Wittich terminated in sunny Italy when they went into 'the bag' at Modena Lager #7 towards the end of April '45. After a total collapse of the German front, thousands of men were rounded up and put in temporary POW cages near the city. Although the two men were unaware of their close proximity to one another, each had a thing in common... namely profound relief at having survived in one piece.

Adolf Hitler's greater Reich was crumbling throughout the whole of Europe. Fritz Freiburg sat on a discarded gasoline drum letting his thoughts dwell on Frau Bayer, the mother of his best friend. Using a rusted pocket knife found half buried in the mud near the garbage dump, he'd amused himself whittling scraps of wood. He remembered her words after his marriage proposal... yes, I will marry you once this awful war is over and you come home for good, so make sure you look after yourself.

Hans Wittich also daydreamed while peeling a mountain of potatoes in the camp kitchen. His mother had died of cancer in late 1944 and his father frail and ill, had struggled to keep the gallery in business. Actually his efforts were more to keep him occupied than anything else. Months previously he'd hidden nearly all the valuable items.

By a miracle the building escaped major damage during the bombings of Berlin, but clients had become practically nonexistent. At least someone on the premises was a deterrent to looters amongst an influx of refugees. Most days the gallery owner sat reading at an old desk piled up with bric-a-brac and his 1917 Luger within easy reach. He thought of the remark an acquaintance had made... enjoy the war, the peace will be far worse.

The Russian armies were close to the city and noise of gunfire was getting louder. On the day Heinz Wittich his oldest son was captured, Soviet shells were falling in the Wilhelmstrasse and onto the Reich chancellery... it was all but over now. The only thing preventing him from putting a bullet through his head was the slim possibility of seeing Heinz once more... it was the proverbial straw to clutch at however unlikely it seemed, as the boy might already be dead.

Shortly after joining the Völkssturm Putzi the youngest boy had stepped on a landmine which killed him outright. Nothing his father had said was enough to dissuade Putzi from enlisting in the pathetic rabble of school boys and the elderly, hurriedly formed for defense of the city. Wittich Sr. had turned away after looking into Putzi's eyes and witnessing the stamp of fanaticism.... "I am doing this for mother and Der Führer, Papa, please don't hinder me." Herr Wittich felt desolate watching the poison of National Socialism infect Putzi with its deadly virus, but somehow the indoctrination didn't take hold in Heinz. The father was glad his wife died before the demise of the youngest boy knowing he was her favorite child.

* * * * * * * *

Heinz Wittich realized he hadn't heard from his father in several months, although he hadn't written either. With a small pang of guilt he hefted another bucket of potatoes up onto the bench knowing it was the gallery that was uppermost in his mind rather than his father's welfare. A new life awaited Heinz once he shed his uniform, but this all depended on how long he'd remain a POW. Pushing aside another unending pile of peelings his thoughts focused on his time in the Mediterranean region.

After leaving France the first few months had passed quietly enough spent on a radar complex in eastern Sicily before withdrawal to the mainland, and a steady retreat northwards up the spine of Italy, ahead of the advancing enemy.

From time to time there were prolonged stalemates until the next assault took place. Sometimes things became boring, then suddenly he was terrified by artillery barrages and low flying attacks by fighter planes. In the beginning he'd managed to go on leave in Florence and Rome, spending hours in the museums and art galleries which had been the high lights of his life. Mostly he preferred being on his own, as his comrades were more enthused by the fleshpots these cities offered.

Just as Wittich reached for his peeling knife, the kitchen door burst open revealing the impressive girth of Sgt. Harry Kowlinsky, late of Brooklyn, New York. "O.K. Kraut, when the hell are those goddamned taters gonna be ready?" Wittich's few words of English didn't cover the situation and he sat slack jawed until Kowlinsky's gestures at the remaining sacks of potatoes made the situation quite clear. The sergeant glanced at his watch and glowered before storming out. Heinz Wittich concluded he wasn't going to make the role of a model prisoner. Meanwhile Fritz Freiburg finished another wood carving, eyeing the results of his labor. Disgusted, he threw the crude object towards the perimeter wire. Standing up, something made him think about Heinz Wittich. He remembered how they'd both been posted to the same radar base in Sicily after leaving Dreux.

Using the code name 'Operation Husky' the allies invaded the island in July '43 and fierce fighting ensued. Relentlessly the German forces were pushed back onto the Italian mainland. Following the evacuation of Sicily the two men parted ways. Fritz was assigned to a large supply depot in Hungary on the outskirts of Budapest… this was altogether too close to the Eastern front in his estimation. However it proved to be quite a bonanza for money making in the flourishing black markets. After the Hungarian stay he'd transferred to a communications center in Prague on temporary duty and finally completed a circle when reassigned to army group "C" in Italy. Ironically, Fritz arrived nine weeks before its surrender at Caserta, on April 29th '45. By then he'd all but forgotten the existence of Heinz Wittich. This was not the case regarding his friend Karl Bayer whom he'd not heard from since the Stalingrad débâcle making him fear the worst. At the time Karl's wife and mother were completely distraught not knowing what had become of him. Fritz wondered if this would affect his marriage plans? Time would tell. Worrying about a future out of his control was useless.

Ten days after Fritz entered Lager #7 the rudimentary P.A. system began crackling then blared across the wire enclosures of the various compounds. A tinny accented German voice informed the POWs that contingents would depart for the main processing center in Milan at 13.00 hours the following day. All troops will assemble carrying their bed rolls, eating utensils and any other personal effects, adjacent to cages L and M. Following roll call, selected personnel will be directed to trucks by guard M.P.'s. The P.A. system dissolved into a series of popping noises for a few seconds after which the same message was repeated. Heinz Wittich and Fritz Freiburg and most of the other prisoners speculated on their chances of relocation.

P.F.C. Burt Hall pulled the Studebaker semi-trailer to a halt outside the Lager main gate whistling one of the latest Glen Miller tunes indifferent to knowing he was over ten minutes late. Having burped, Cpl. Dick Kelly his companion in the cab leaned over towards it's driver... "For Christ sake Burt watch it, if the snowdrops smell your breath they'll stick us both in the stockade sure as hell. I don't want to pass up a night on the town and Sgt. Tower said they have terrific clubs and broads in Milan". "O.K., O.K., stop pissing your pants old buddy." Glancing at his partner's service issue.45 Burt grinned. "Maybe some of the master race might want to jump truck... think we'll get some target practice?"

The white helmet of one of the M.P.'s appeared at the driver's window. "Ready to move out pal?" Burt nodded his head then folded the proffered paperwork and stuffed it in a pocket of his field jacket. After a quick glance through the rear window checking his load of humanity he engaged gears and started moving muttering "Enjoy the ride you lousy bums" to no one in particular. Most of the prisoners in the stake sided trailer lurched forward in unison standing like upended cordwood. Dick Kelly checked the remaining bottles left over from the previous night's drinking to see if they were safe under the seat. Both Kelly and Hall were still half cocked but convinced themselves of a need to top up for the run to Milan. Cpl. Kelly was never sure about his companion who had a terrible thirst once he got up steam.

A lead jeep carrying a couple of officers and a sergeant was somewhere up ahead with seven trucks strung out behind them. Once past Reggio everyone set their own pace. Kelly glanced sideways at his mate, the raw Chianti was starting to have it's affect and Burt's driving was becoming increasingly erratic as he kept swigging the wine. Having bypassed the outskirts of Palma, Dick Kelly was beginning to feel pretty nervous despite his own consumption of the liquid.

Suddenly, without warning a mule drawn cart emerged from an opening onto the road, it's ancient driver staring straight ahead. Deaf and blind was Burt's last thought. He'd just lowered the Chianti bottle from his lips and in sudden terror he'd let it fall between his thighs… his dulled reflexes left any evasion far too late. Violent braking and sharp wrenching of the steering wheel on a rain slicked road, precipitated jack knifing of the rig. The truck skidded to the opposite side of the road hitting a low concrete edging of a rain culvert before overturning. Following the noise of the accident an eerie silence fell.

P.F.C. Hall died instantly and Dick Kelly wore a back brace for many months after being shipped to a stateside V.A. hospital in Iowa. Seven POWs were killed when thrown from the trailer and nine more seriously injured. The rest of them were lucky to escape with various cuts and contusions. On the other side of the divided highway a convoy was headed south to Taranto. It consisted of several small vehicles and five ambulances. It halted after seeing the overturned truck with people milling around, and the two convoy commanders quickly conferred. All the seriously wounded were loaded into the ambulances which reversed direction for the military hospital in Milan The medics meanwhile attended to minor injuries before their departure, and the dead were left to be placed in body bags for transport later on. The prime task was to clear the wreckage and open the road again.

Four of the fatalities had been laid out end to end at the edge of the road where Wittich's vehicle happened to stop. Gazing down at the carnage devoid of feelings, he lit a cigarette as he leaned against the top rail of the trailer. "Gott in Himmel, it can't be."

Heinz Wittich needed to be absolutely positive that his initial gut feeling was right. Glancing quickly up and down the road checking to see if any Americans were nearby, he only saw a small group clustered around the officer's jeep further up the road. Earlier its three occupants had stopped for a smoke and to adjust the vehicles canvas top while waiting for the rest of the convoy to catch up. Capt. Allen Baker the officer commanding became impatient after fifteen minutes had gone by, prompting him to turn the jeep around and head back down the road. It didn't take long ascertaining the cause of the delay… the Colonel back at base sure wasn't going to like this one, and Capt. Baker groaned at the thought of all the paper work he would have to deal with.

Heinz Wittich climbed over the edge of the trailer and clambered down until his feet contacted one of the twin tires before dropping the rest of the way to the road. Taking a quick pee he looked to the left and right noting some other POWs were following his example. The rain was falling again and oil from the damaged truck created an iridescent sheen on areas of the road. Buttoning up his fly he quickly strode over to the nearest body which first attracted his attention. He bent forward and stared into the unseeing eyes noting blood which had oozed from gashes in the left cheek. Heinz put a hand inside the man's tunic groping for the dog tags. Reading the familiar name he quickly dropped the tag back on the corpse… Heinz Wittich reckoned Sgt. Fritz Freiburg had probably died of a broken neck just as a voice from the trailer broke into his consciousness. "What's the matter comrade, never seen a dead man before?" Wittich stepped back and turned towards the trailer when someone shouted from further up the road. It was the driver of Wittich's truck returning from the officer's jeep. "Get back in the trailer pronto you Nazi creeps, if you know what's good for your health." One of the prisoners leant over offering a hand to the man on the ground. Wittich's forage cap fell off as he climbed back up and it landed adjacent to Freiburg's right boot. Giving a backward glance Heinz Wittich smiled sardonically, "auf wedersehn you shit head, wear it as a souvenir." He remembered the time Freiburg humiliated him in the storeroom at Dreux, and feelings of anger surfaced within him, soon replaced by the triumph of knowing only one other now stood between himself and the treasure. Who knows maybe he too was also dead.

Heinz lurched forward as the truck moved, banging him into the back of a burly Wehrmacht gunner. The man's elbow jabbed him in the gut but no minor irritation could spoil Wittich's sudden vision of eventually becoming a very wealthy citizen.

22

KIEV

SPRING 1961

LAURA ICHENKO WAS CONSIDERED A BEAUTY of classic proportions by her admirers. They would have been startled to know the tumult she'd experienced in her twenty-eight years. An excellent brain complimented by striking physical features caused envy amongst some of her peers in the G.R.U. (Soviet military intelligence) which she'd joined after graduating from Moscow University.

None of Laura's attributes had been marred by conceit. Well aware fate had dealt her a lucky hand, she had learned how to manipulate these advantages over the course of time: but like an imperfect diamond, there was always a fatal flaw. The girl was completely amoral. This character defect was also part of her father's make-up, so it was likely to have been inherited. Born in the eastern part of Poland, she'd grown up in an old rambling house seven kilometers from the town of Krasnystaw. The homestead had been inherited by her mother and Laura was a late addition to the family. An only brother, Victor, was eleven years old at the time of her birth and attended boarding school in Warsaw. Capt. Tomasz, the father, was a regular army officer infrequently at home due to his regiment being stationed near Poznan.

Left mainly to her own devices, the young girl became self-sufficient and most of her knowledge of the outside world was gained from the three servants her parents employed, plus a tutor who came to give lessons four times a week. Madame Ichenko wasn't particularly close to her daughter, although on occasions they would bond walking by the banks of the river Wieprz which ran past the Ichenko property. Years later, Laura still remembered an incident during one of these strolls. They had sat down on a fallen log and contemplated the river. A convoy of ducks went by and disappeared from view. Laura was daydreaming when her mother's voice startled her with its bitter tone. "You know I was a professional dancer before I met your father, it was all I ever thought about in those days." Laura watched a tear run down her cheek which was quickly brushed away. "Things somehow change between men and women." The girl was too young to understand what this implied, so remained silent, and reached out for her mother's hand sensing the sadness behind the words. Later that evening, Madame Ichenko sat at the piano and played the same piece over and over. Ash from a cigarette in its ebony holder spilt down her elegant dress and onto the keyboard.

Shortly after her daughter's eighth birthday, Madame Ichenko, a long-time alcoholic, committed suicide in her bedroom. A long disjointed letter had been left on her writing desk addressed to the children. Amongst other things, it accused Tomasz of having sold off family assets on the sly to finance a business venture run by his current mistress. Victor never believed this, but Laura felt it might be true. The subject, even in later years, was never raised with their father. Victor crumpled the letter and tossed it in the fire before the police arrived to investigate the death… Few mourners were present at the funeral and Laura and her brother stood next to their father with downcast eyes. The words of unsound mind she'd heard an uncle utter during the inquest puzzled the young girl. It seemed there were many things regarding the adult world she somehow couldn't grasp.

* * * * * * * *

Many years later Laura spent a few days at her father's apartment in Kiev. Stretching back on the settee, she yawned and looked across at the armchair where Tomasz Ichenko dozed. The newspaper had fallen to the floor and his glasses were in danger of dropping off. He looked frail and worn out. Col.Ichenko Ret. late of the Red Army intelligence branch began gently snoring. The daughter stood up and walked across to where he kept the drinks. Pouring a shot of vodka into a crystal glass, she returned to the settee and tucked her shapely legs beneath her and stared at the ceiling letting her thoughts drift into the past. She recalled a somewhat blurred vision of standing in the streets of Krasnystaw clutching the warm hand of Anna, her parents' housekeeper. A long line of soldiers marched down the main street led by men on horseback. She'd seen soldiers before when her mother took her to see ceremonial parades her father participated in but this time something was different... it was the color of their uniforms. It must have been around the middle of September 1939 when the Russian bear had crossed the Polish frontier to claim its portion of the country, the result of an agreement between those chums Hitler and Stalin. She remembered Anna crying watching the stony faced troops pass by. Not long after this there had been the chaos of packing up the house, and the dreadful indecision about what to take of her most prized possessions on the long winter journey to the East. On the train she sat between two large men wearing uniforms of the same color as the troops who'd marched through Krasnystaw. One of the men smoked foul smelling cigarettes throughout the journey which made her cough. Her father was dressed in civilian clothes and rarely spoke.

* * * * * * * *

Later in life she'd heard an allegation that Victor, when still a cadet had probably been murdered by the Russians in the forests of Katyn, together with thousands of Polish officers and intellectuals in order to wipe out any opposition to the new Russian masters of the Eastern part of Poland. When she'd brought this up with Tomasz, he had deftly evaded her questions dismissing the whole thing as rumor, and stated that if a mass killing had indeed taken place it must have been done by the Germans. On her sixteenth birthday, Tomasz became drunk at a party held in her honor. After the guests departed, he'd told her the reasons for their relocation to Kiev from Poland. The Russian N.K.V.D. commandant had summoned him to his H.Q. in Krasnystaw. After being told to sit down in front of four high-ranking Russian officers, one had flipped his thumb towards a thick pile of dossiers on a nearby table. "Well comrade, you can see we have compiled a comprehensive history of your life, and also for most of your erstwhile brother officers." The man fell silent for a moment, then unbuttoned his tunic. "Your career is of interest to us, especially after having read your reports analyzing German military logistics. I offer my congratulations, the conclusions tally with work done by our own people, in fact your data was even more detailed. The other men in the room were taking down notes as he spoke. "You'll be interested in knowing that department S.B. of the army is going to employ you in the USSR." Hearing this, Tomasz was stunned. How could an ex-member of the Polish army be offered this kind of work by its mortal enemy? Tomasz paused a moment before speaking. "With due respect, I am presently employed as a factory administrator since my demobilization. I want to stay here in Krasnytow."

The Russian Officer angrily arose knocking his chair backwards, and thrust his face within a few inches of

Tomasz. "Idiot! Don't you think we know all that? Think again Tomasz Ichenko, unless you want to end up like your son, or at the least, a long term in one of our Gulag's… you'll sign here. Be ready to leave for Kiev at the end of the week, and take your pretty daughter with you. My adjutant will call you tomorrow with details of your relocation. You are dismissed Comrade." Tomasz Ichenko walked out of the building with his brain reeling, knowing his worst fears about Victor appeared to be true. He knew he hadn't any options other than to follow his wife's example, but Tomasz at heart was a survivor.

Listening to her father, Laura now understood the reason for her childhood upheaval which brought them to live in the U.S.S.R. She'd always thought it was somehow to do with the death of her mother. She didn't attach blame to the actions of her father, in fact she enjoyed the privileged position which had accrued, being quite aware how the vast majority of people existed in this 'workers paradise' which also included her former homeland. Tomasz had remained embittered by events which had overtaken Poland in the last twenty-five years. Pondering the past was useless, when it came to the crunch it was everyone for himself. This pragmatic outlook had pushed him up the ladder into a comfortable retirement. Explaining his thoughts to Laura he used the Russian word 'Verkhushka' indicating the top layer of people, as a target to be aimed for. That way you remained safe, led a pleasant life, and if the ship did go down you had the best chance of reaching the shore. Convinced, Laura added her own "Amen" to all this. If it meant going through the motions of allegiance to all the political dogma and the rest of the clap trap, so be it. She supposed it was pretty much the same state of affairs in the capitalistic world.

When Laura went off to Moscow University it was the first time she'd felt really independent. She loved every minute of the six years spent there. Her father's position opened many doors which would have otherwise remained shut on the lifestyle she enjoyed and was determined to keep. A star attraction for male students she also found that several of the faculty made passes at her. Occasionally she had slept with someone who momentarily caught her eye, but each affair was treated with indifference by Laura. Her goals were still far on the horizon and no detours were contemplated. Despite an active social life, she worked hard, graduating with high honors. During the final weeks a summons to the G.R.U. for an interview would prove instrumental in shaping her future

* * * * * * * *

Laura sighed then got up to refill her glass and remove her father's spectacles. The old boy had certainly done well for himself by Soviet standards. The apartment was big and luxurious and she thought about the little places some of her friends were forced to live in. Within a few minutes she'd drifted off into a contented sleep, while a heavy snow enveloped the city outside. About forty-five minutes after Tomasz had gone to bed she was awoken by the ringing phone. Reaching for the receiver Laura knocked over the glass of vodka causing her to swear in Polish. "Good evening, is this Comrade Laura Ichenko? Please be good enough to present yourself at Department 7, Room 3 tomorrow at 9 a.m." Without waiting for her reply, the phone went dead. Laura thought sod them, annoyed by the arrogance of her new bosses, but wondering what would be in it for her. G.R.U. assignments could provide lots of perks when handled satisfactorily.

She stared at her reflection in the mirror and wondered if her new job would be dangerous. Well, she would find out soon enough. Deciding to take a bath she opened up a new package of French soap. Holding it to her nose she smelt its perfume. Her father always bought the best vodka and toiletries at one of the special military co-operatives known as Voentorg. As the warm water of the bath enveloped her Laura smiled. It wasn't a bad life if you made sure to play the game properly… maybe one day she'd end up with a place in Moscow and a dacha in the countryside. Perhaps her father would donate one of the jeweled samovars from his collection as a 'piece de resistance'.

23

A LONG WALK

On a freezing cold morning in late 1945, Heinz Wittich was released from the POW camp at Bernberg. The Americans had transferred him to this former SS barracks shortly after the initial confinement in Italy. Visiting interrogation teams didn't waste much time with Wittich, being intent trawling for much bigger fish. In the compound, most of the talk dealt in rumor and fact about conditions now prevailing in the erstwhile third Reich, but Heinz wasn't sure how much to believe, although one thing was certain however... if he'd been captured by the Russkies his chances of being released would have been about zero.

Myriad thoughts ran through his mind as he exited the main gate without glancing back although some of the others did, being apprehensive about what lay ahead. For Heinz Wittich it was 'fini' to an insane episode of soldiering now left behind with each step. He felt a curious sense of elation obliterating slight misgivings about the future. Apart from two chocolate bars, three packs of Lucky Strikes and a spare pair of socks he'd pilfered from the guards quarters, his sole possessions added up to the soiled uniform he wore, and three stapled sheets of paper with his photo attached.

Several rubber stamped markings with scrawled initials covered each page, and to Heinz Wittich they equated with the holy grail. They proclaimed his status as a civilian. From now on nobody would give a shit what H. Wittich did with his life, whatever success or screw-up he made of it. Heinz was going to be damned careful about guarding his independence in the future.

Following the second day on the road, he was very hungry and cold. Spending the night in a wayside ditch, Heinz found it nearly impossible to sleep. By sunrise a hoar frost covered the fields as he commenced walking. Passing through several villages, he'd asked for food only to be rebuffed by sullen stares. The continual tide of flotsam which swept through these places had hardened the local inhabitants. Earlier he'd helped up a young woman who'd skidded and fallen from her bicycle after hitting an icy patch on the road. Deciding to ask her if she had any food in the carrier bag strapped on the back, he was shocked by the response, "Food? No I don't have any to share with cowards... when you all ran from 'Ivan' did you have any idea what the bastards had in mind for German womenfolk?" Heinz was about to say he'd never seen a Russian in his life, but the girl was already pedaling off towards the next cluster of houses further down the hill.

Wittich sat down by a fence and smoked one of his Lucky Strikes while mulling over initial contacts with the civilian world and felt surprised by the venom the girl expressed. Finishing his cigarette he glanced up the road and saw a lanky uniformed figure approaching at a leisurely pace. The man halted in front of Wittich staring at him momentarily before focusing on the discarded cigarette butt. Bending over he picked it up and managed one last puff before turning to face Heinz. What appeared to be a knife handle protruded from under the left pocket flap of the man's tunic. Heinz Wittich quickly decided to offer him one of the precious Lucky's. Taking it, the man said "Horst

Bruckner… ex Lembach." The latter name meant nothing to Heinz, but surmised it to be another POW camp. After Wittich offered his name, Horst gave a nod and lit up. "Ah, Americano brand, much better than the horse shit ones they hand out in the place where I've come from… Sieg heil, comrade."

Having talked awhile Heinz ascertained his new companion had been on the road eight days and was also headed for Berlin. He had been captured in Normandy by the British just after the D Day invasion in June '44. Heinz related his experiences to date regarding the local population as Horst Bruckner gave him a lopsided grin, withdrawing a kitchen knife from his pocket. "These pighead farmers have plenty of food stashed away in their cellars my friend… they just need a little persuasion in feeding their recent protectors. "Hearing this Heinz Wittich felt relieved thinking he probably wouldn't starve on the journey. Horst ran a stubby thumb along the edge of the knife blade…." By the fifth day after leaving Lembach, only one old graybeard had given me anything to eat… two pieces of rock hard bread and a rotten apple. After night fell I noticed some dim lights emanating from a farmhouse and decided to investigate. I was chilled to the marrow and my guts were rumbling like a freight train as I peered through a small gap in the kitchen shutters. I began drooling seeing a man and teenage girl tucking into quite a spread." At this point Horst Bruckner gave a tremendous fart as if for emphasis before continuing "I was licking my lips I can tell you, so I waited until sure nobody was around then hammered on the front door with the knife handle. I yelled 'POLEZEI' loudly a couple of times then the door opened a few centimeters and gripping the knob I swung it the rest of the way. I grabbed the man by his hair as he stumbled forward." Heinz registered a pretty good picture of the scene causing him to smile.

"What was your next move comrade?" Horst paused for a few seconds "When the old boy realized I wasn't a cop he tried reaching into a back pocket where he probably had a gun, so I kicked him in the groin. After he'd recovered somewhat I demanded food and the lying swine had the audacity to say he hadn't had any himself for the last two days… I even laughed while holding the knife to his throat" Horst paused savoring the memory. "The sorry son of a bitch even offered me his niece if I left him alone… can you believe that?" Heinz wasn't sure if he did or not. "Anyhow, by then I was so mad I tied him up with his own belt, grabbed some food and took the girl upstairs." On reflection Heinz felt he'd skip further questions certain that whatever future problems arose in the days ahead they'd be adequately taken care of by Horst Bruckner.

* * * * * * * *

On the fourth day since the men's initial encounter a keen wind from the north compounded their misery. Sometimes they talked, but generally trudged along in silence. A worn sole on one of Wittich's jack boots started to part company with its upper, now making walking a torture. Horst mentioned he'd worked as a bricklayer before being conscripted and figured the trade was going to be in great demand. All Heinz could think was why hadn't he been a cobbler. The men decided to take a break and flopped down beside an upended cart on the side of the road before crawling inside. Finding some furniture pads they stretched out for a short cat nap.

Resuming their walk all Heinz could think of was his foot… Horst suddenly stopped in his tracks pointing. "Look at that" Heinz had been inspecting his disintegrating boot and followed the direction of Horst's outstretched arm. An American B-17 "Flying Fortress" had crashed in a field not far from where they stood. Climbing over a low embankment the men stumbled through a sugar beet field toward the wrecked aircraft. Its back was broken and a faint smell of gasoline mixed with oil still pervaded the area. As the men circled the stricken bomber it was the first time either soldier had seen one of these machines on the ground and they were amazed by its size.

The plane had plowed long furrows across the field now filled with water and thin ice. The forward section of the plane lay semi buried in piled up dirt with the towering empenage riddled with cannon fire. Heinz noticed the large white circle painted on the tail enclosed the letter 'A'. He wondered about the fate of the crew and how long it had been since the crash. Judging by the weeds and grass growing in the dislodged earth surrounding the nose, it must have been several weeks. Horst crawled through one of the open hatches into the fuselage calling for Heinz to follow. It was a relief to be out of the wind, although occasional blasts penetrated rents in the fuselage. After looking over the unfamiliar interior, they proceeded to clamber into the seats of the pilot and co-pilot. The view through the windshield and side windows was almost obliterated by caked oil and dirt. Settling into the seats was pure luxury after many hours spent on the road. Finishing a shared cigarette, they dozed off and it was late afternoon when Heinz awoke with a start to find his companion was still snoring with his head to one side. After examining the many unfamiliar controls and instruments, Heinz noticed a piece of dark green canvas mashed down beside the seat structure. It was almost obscured by crumpled flight charts and an empty instrument container. There was only room to use one hand and with difficulty Heinz managed to finally yank loose what proved to be a rolled up bag. It was quite heavy for its size and stenciled on one surface was the inscription Capt. Andrew Stephen U.S.A.A.F. followed by a serial number. Holding the bag in his lap, he pulled the zip fastener open to reveal its contents. Two paperback books and more folded maps lay on top, but underneath was a more solid bundle. A khaki sweater was wrapped around a pair of flying boots and Heinz let out a yelp. It was akin to the feeling he'd experienced on seeing the St. Lucien treasure... his exclamation awoke Horst who rubbed his eyes, then stretched. "What's all the noise about comrade, don't you know an ex- soldier needs his sleep?" Heinz clutching the objects didn't bother replying as Horst leaned over for a better look... "Gott im Himmel, what a find."

Heinz levered himself from the seat and walked back to the hatch where they'd gained entrance. Once outside he kicked off his boots eager to try the new ones. They were slightly bigger than his proper fit, but this mattered little. His spare pair of socks could make up the difference. Heinz flung the sweater to Horst who deftly caught it, then put it on. The pair looked at one another and smiled "Things are looking up, eh?" Horst exclaimed. The men decided to hunker down in the bomber before making an early start the next day. The remaining chocolate bar provided the sole item for dinner and later the pair experienced the best sleep since leaving the P.O.W. camps. Heinz drifted off propped up against a bulkhead thinking about his luck... surely others had searched the plane? Well they hadn't unearthed his prize, and he remembered something about not looking a gift horse in the mouth. Soon his snores intermingled with the wind whistling around the fuselage.

24

BERLIN

THE WEATHER HAD IMPROVED DURING THE early morning hours, and after opening a fuselage hatch Heinz squinted at a watery sun breaking through low cloud, noting the wind had abated. The pair stretched and shared a cigarette before making a start. It didn't take long to find it was hard going due to the hilly terrain. Rounding a bend Horst Bruckner was first to see a stone marker on a bridge entry. It indicated seventeen Km. to the next town. Stepping up their stride they eventually came to the main square of Plaustadt a small market town. Heinz spotted a large Volvo truck coupled to a long trailer. The rig bore Swedish license plates. White pennants with red crosses flapped vigorously from two jack shafts on the bumper. Lettering on the cab identified it as property of a voluntary relief organization headquartered in Stockholm. A motley crowd of civilians and ex-Wermacht members had formed a ragged line behind the trailer which had been outfitted as a soup kitchen.

Horst Bruckner halted and sniffed as they approached, "Mein Gott, that aroma is enough to drive any man crazy." They joined the end of a line behind three stout women who momentarily turned and scowled at the newcomers. After one or two minutes one muttered to the effect that "good soup should be reserved only for the burghers of Plaustadt, and not wasted on riffraff." The other two women nodded in unison. Hearing this Horst decided he'd had enough, pulled the knife from his tunic and lightly pricked the loud mouth in her backside. The woman spun around, her face contorted in rage until focusing on the knife in Bruckners right hand. His left hand thumb was cocked in a backwards direction.

Fear supplanted anger in the women as Horst growled, "I'm sure you beautiful ladies won't object to waiting a bit longer for your soup as we are in rather a hurry to leave this sewer!" To emphasize his statement, the vocal one received another prod which tore her coat. The woman's face portrayed livid disbelief, her mouth began forming the start of a yell but Horst clapped a hand over it before anything emerged. "My friend has a pistol which he loves using: just pass along a message to those old crows up ahead to disperse. My companion will be by your side making sure you do so without fuss." Heinz grabbed the woman's arm and walked her along slowly to the head of the line. Horst watched with amusement the hurried exchanges and rearward looks, occasionally holding up his knife for view which pretty soon caused an appreciable shortening of the queue. One of the ex-Wehrmacht men walked back from his spot near the front and spoke to Horst "Comrade my group insists both of you join us. These inhabitants need teaching good manners and you seem to have a knack."

An elderly man and two blond women were working hard operating the soup kitchen. Each of them wore smart blue coveralls sporting miniature flags on their lapels. Occupied in handing out the steaming liquid from two gas fired cauldrons, none of the relief workers had time to notice a sudden reduction of waiting recipients. To them it was the same never ending forest of outstretched arms, day after day. With each portion of potato soup came a slice of delicious tasting rye bread along with an apple. After being served, the comrades carried their dented mess cans across the cobbled street to join a group sitting on the edge of a fountain in the town square. Its water had been turned off long ago, and the filthy basin was filled with trash. Finishing the meal both men tossed apple cores into the fountain and idly watched the passers by. Frowning, Horst noted the three women had returned to the throng around the trailer obviously having overcome their recent scare. If the men wanted any seconds they would have to repeat the performance.

Horst got busy taking a crap in the base of the fountain and giving a grin announced "So much for Plaustadt." Heinz smiled. Just a short while ago such an act would have been totally unthinkable in the Nazi state, and now in broad daylight a bearded unkempt member of the 'Master race' expressed contempt for a town which until recently was probably a bastion of law and order under Adolf Hitler. Evidently it didn't take long for civilization to erode in the aftermath of war. Heinz rubbed his chin realizing it wasn't just his companion sporting a ragged looking beard. He'd walked over to a shop across the square and catching his reflection in the window hardly believed what he saw... no wonder the women in the soup line responded so quickly, no doubt convinced the bulge in his pocket concealed a weapon instead of a flashlight found in the bomber.

About an hour after departing Plaustadt, Heinz heard a rhythmic noise of hooves hitting the road surface and turned to see a decrepit horse pulling a cart loaded with hay. Several ribs on the horse were clearly visible. The driver who looked to be in his eighties was hardly in better shape, however he gave the men a toothless grin in response to a request for a ride. As they clambered up into the hay, Heinz realized this was the first act of kindness he'd encountered by a civilian since departing the camp at Bernberg. The men were asleep within minutes helped by the gentle swaying of the cart. When it halted Heinz awoke to see the old man looking up at him from the roadway.

"Another six hours trek, my friends, and you should be in what remains of Berlin; this is as far as I go. Having served in the Kaiser's army, I know what it's like when it's time to go home." They thanked him, and started off towards the capital. On approaching the outskirts of the city the first signs of devastation became apparent and worsened as they continued. Both men viewed the signs of destruction without comment. It was apparent to Heinz that some of the rumors heard at Bernberg were only too true. In places the roads were completely blocked and others had just narrow passages cleared between vast mounds of rubble. A few old men and hordes of women were busy carting and stacking salvageable bricks. The latter had become known as 'trummerfrauen'… literally 'ruinswomen.' A study released in later years estimated that after the cessation of hostilities, 75 million cubic meters of rubble had been created in Berlin, and thousands of the city's buildings were totally destroyed.

In the few streets that were reasonably clear one or two ancient trucks and horse drawn carts passed by. At some street corners small groups of people stood facing open fires which were fueled by timber retrieved from battered buildings. Heinz felt the population walked about like automatons and noticed there was hardly any conversation or eye contact. No doubt food and the cold dominated everyone's thoughts, as it did for the two colleagues. At least the POW camps had provided regular meals and a roof over one's head. What good was the new freedom if you were either going to starve or die of the cold? Scrawled messages left by people looking for family members were tacked up on any walls still standing.

Horst pointed out some rats scrambling around in a pile of charred wood and brickwork. "Look at those beauties, must be former Gauleiters on the loose!" Heinz didn't appreciate the implied humor, as he'd always had a fear of rodents since a child. By now they'd entered the French sector of Berlin without being aware of the fact, and a few minutes after seeing the rodents two jeeps pulled up alongside. A pair of French soldiers with side arms leapt out of the lead vehicle while four more in the other jeep sat impassive, cradling sten guns on their laps. The taller of the two, whom Heinz assumed to be an officer, spoke curtly in German, "Identity papers". Heinz felt his heartbeat quicken when he first put his hand in the wrong pocket and found nothing, at the same moment he saw how quickly the officer withdrew his weapon. Handing the papers over they were quickly scanned then the officer motioned for Horst's documentation.

By now one of the officers approached carrying a clipboard and a thick book. He laid it on the hood of the jeep and stood there scrutinizing several pages. After checking what looked like a long list of names on the clipboard, the officer once again riffled through further pages. Heinz was able to see black and white photos with notations. The officer glanced up at both comrades for several moments studying their features.

A metal whistle hung from a lanyard around the officer's collar. With a sudden movement he put it to his lips and gave a sharp blast. The soldiers with sten guns reacted immediately to form a circle. Transfixed by the weapons, Heinz felt sick to his stomach… was this going to be a revenge execution? His mind reeled as one of the troopers stepped behind Horst, grabbed him by the neck and hustled him into the officer's jeep. The motors of both vehicles had been left running. Horst raised a hand, palm outwards toward Wittich which was instantly slapped down and he was handcuffed. With a squeal of tires both vehicles took off down the street, leaving Heinz dumbfounded. The whole encounter couldn't have lasted more than eight minutes. Heinz felt completely shaken and wandered off dispirited.

That night he slept in a damaged circus trailer abandoned in a cul de sac. It was sitting at a crazy angle with two of its wheels missing, but at least it provided shelter. He hoped there were no rats in the vicinity, but at this low point did he really care? By morning, still miserable and stiff as a board, he peered out of the only window. No activity was visible on the street outside. It looked like some weird moonscape and he imagined himself as being the last man on earth. Looking down at his hands, Heinz was shocked to realize both were shaking. Turning away from the window he made an effort to dismiss his black thoughts. Today he would reach his objective, the gallery on the Gustav strasse. Heinz Wittich slowly pulled himself together. Jumping down to the ground he didn't bother shutting the trailer door. He was unaware of the fact that until recently its former inhabitants had been a pair of expensive leopards. Having been shot and eaten two weeks ago, it wouldn't have mattered anyway.

* * * * * * * *

Heinz stood on the opposite side of the street, in front of his parent's gallery. Its windows were roughly boarded up and myriad gouges in the stone work incised by bullet or mortar rounds, had left strange patterns in the once familiar facade. Wittich leaned against the wall behind him and tried to marshal his thoughts. Mental pictures originally conjured up about his return, now changed to anxiety. Heinz bit his lower lip having not the slightest idea what to do next. Lighting a cigarette he noticed a slight movement at one of the windows several meters down from the gallery entrance and tried to recall who lived there. The street door slowly opened and a woman supporting herself with a cane hobbled across the street toward him. As she drew closer he found some kind of recollection begin to register. "Little Heinz, back from the wars is it not? I've been watching you for the last ten minutes. You can't be too careful in these times." It then dawned on Heinz it was Frau Rossman. She'd been curvaceous and bubbly the last time he saw her, no wonder he had failed to recognize her initially. In the past Heinz had sometimes thought she might be his father's mistress

Observing the careworn face saddened him, and as Heinz glanced at the cane she remarked, "A little souvenir from one of the raids... well, don't just stand there you scarecrow come inside and share some ersartz coffee." In a few minutes she carried in a tray from the kitchen on which was a piece of bread and two small glasses containing a clear liquid. "This is all I can offer soldier boy, not your typical Berlin breakfast I grant, but the schnapps will keep you going for a bit" Heinz smiled at her.... "Our values have changed in recent years, nicht wahr?" They both laughed at the understatement of his observation. Heinz paused for a while then quickly asked "were you and Papa lovers?" Anna Rossman looked hard at her guest and simply said, "Yes, and it was fantastic" She reminded Heinz her husband Paul had died during an air raid in 1942

Heinz had already been told by Anna that shortly before the fall of Berlin his father was overheard making treasonous remarks by a Nazi official. This had led to a trial at the dread 'Völksgerichtshof' (People's Court). It was the last time any one saw the owner of the gallery. Anna was quite sure only one kind of verdict was handed out meaning Heinz's father was dead, but still couldn't bring herself to say this to the son. There was no need, Heinz guessed what had happened to his father... reversals of fortune sometimes happened in these crazy times, but not very often.

Outside it had started raining again. Anna reached under the cushion of the chair she was sitting on, and withdrew a large envelope. Heinz noted the red sealing wax securing the flap. "Your father slept with me the night before they took him away... previously he'd asked me to give you this in the event you showed up, and anything happened to him." Anna laid the envelope on the table, then wiped away a few tears. "I went down to the 'Prinz-Albrecht Strasse' to see if I could find out anything about your Papa." Heinz knew this was the Gestapo central prison, and to go there required a great deal of courage. "Thank you Anna, you must have loved him very much, I only wish I could have felt the same." Picking up the envelope he felt the outline of a key and some paperwork inside. He walked over, kissed Frau Rossman and headed to the door. Turning before exiting he said, "well, we have two common bonds… my father, and we're neighbors. I will be back later."

* * * * * * * *

He broke the seal of the envelope and withdrew the key. The front door had stuck fast and despite his efforts would not yield. He then remembered the same key was used for the rear door of the gallery. The narrow alley at the back of the building provided a scene of utter desolation. A Russian army truck lay tipped on its side, half demolished by an artillery shell. Piles of broken brick and wood made it difficult to even reach the rear exit. Two scraggy cats slunk away as he inserted the key. This time the door opened without trouble and he nearly tripped over three tires inside the doorway. It was dark inside but flicking on a light switch was useless… electric supply to the Gustav strasse had long ago ceased. It would have been smart to have borrowed one of Anna's candles. After a while his eyes grew accustomed to what little light there was. Reaching the front door he saw what had been the initial trouble. The safety bolt was still in place. Picking up a hammer left on a roll of old carpet, he removed some of the temporary plywood from one of the windows, thinking his papa had probably used the same tool in putting the boards up. Grunting from his exertions, at least he could now see what he was doing.

Pulling up a chair to his father's desk, he sat down

and looked at the contents of the envelope. The first batch of papers were the deeds to the gallery with a signed and witnessed form transferring the place to him. A long letter talked about the death of his mother and younger brother, Putzi, and touched on the desperation his father felt at the time of writing. Attached to the letter was another smaller envelope. Heinz's eyes widened as he read the content. It detailed how to find a steel box bricked up in a wall of the gallery. It noted the Spanish gold coins contained were worth a considerable sum (a 1941 evaluation date was given). Also in the small envelope was a rather dog-eared notebook full of his father's spidery handwriting. It listed all the valuables that Wittich Senior could never bring himself to part with to any of his clients. Instructions as to their various hiding places were given. This was about it. In other personal touches there was a request that Frau Rossman, a 'very good friend' who lived close by at number 37, should be helped by any means possible.

No mention regarding disposition of his parent's apartment was made. Perhaps it didn't exist anyway, along with the thousands of others in this Godforsaken city of rubble. Heinz Wittich's spirits rose, if those gold coins were worth what he'd read, there was hope for the future. Gold always shone its brightest in times of disaster when people sardonically lit pipes and cigarettes using worthless paper currency, while those possessing gold could feed from the trough of plenty. Heinz knew he was a survivor… not like his stupid brother Putzi, with his insane Nazi convictions, look what happened to him. People like Heinz Wittich were going to make it in the new world that was beginning to take place, he could feel it in his veins. The question was how long would it take to achieve his goals?

25

THE SCHOOL

A BLACK ZIS LIMOUSINE STOOD WAITING in the forecourt of the 'finishing school', as it was known by past and present students. The place had served as a hunting lodge in Czarist times and stood in a large expanse of forest land. An electrified fence ran the entire perimeter of the grounds and was patrolled by armed guards night and day.

The crumbling facade of the lodge belied its current purpose for training special agents of the Soviet state, and few people even knew of its existence except in the highest echelons of the government and G.R.U. Security arrangements were designated 1A the highest rating, and annual budget appropriations for running the establishment were a closely guarded secret. Food deliveries and other essentials were brought in by unmarked vehicles belonging to the complex. After their arrival new students were completely shut off from outside contacts until they had completed their training.

Despite its prison like exterior the few visitors to the school were usually astounded by their surroundings after passing through the portals. No expense had been spared on the interior, in fact the lodge was reminiscent of opulent hotels in a bygone era.

* * * * * * * *

For Laura, the day for leaving had finally arrived. A young G.R.U. captain accompanied her and the two Tarasov sisters down the marble steps toward the waiting car. All three women had passed their course with high marks and would embark on a future dictated by the G.R.U. bosses. The whole experience had been very intense for the trio, but now each of the women felt a sense of excitement. During their exit interview an elegant silver-haired man introduced himself as the Director of the establishment but none of the three ever recalled seeing him before. After offering congratulations regarding their various accomplishments, he reminded them of the debt they owed to the State for the time and money invested in each graduate. The Director paused to let his words sink in, before adding, "each one of you has become a member of an elite, and can expect many privileges." After he pushed a button on an ornately carved table, a uniformed man and a maid appeared carrying trays of expensive vodka and hors d'oeuvres known as 'zakuski'. After the glasses had been filled the Director proposed a toast to the women and shook their hands in turn, before exiting through a heavy oak door.

Nadia, the elder of the two sisters, refilled the glasses and said, "Well, my friends, we are certainly changed people from the moment we first entered this place… I wonder if we'll ever revert to our former selves." Laura laughed "Personally I doubt it. It strikes me that 'whores of the state' would be a more apt title for us now." The two sisters exchanged nervous glances wondering if the room was bugged. Nadia Tarasov started to say something as a door opened and a member of the school's security staff came into the room and announced, "Comrades, in ten minutes it is time for your departure. Please leave your Security passes on my desk as you leave the room and pick up your new ones. May I wish you good luck in your future endeavors."

Once in the car, none of the occupants spoke as they sped along a road leading to the main highway which eventually would bring them to Moscow. Laura stretched back in the comfort of her seat as her mind backtracked over the events of the past months. Physically she felt in top form, no doubt a result of the daily exercise training she'd been subjected to. Glancing at the Tarasov sisters she realized how little any of the students knew about each other. Each trainee had been allocated an individual living room and bedroom during their stay, and they'd been told not to discuss their former lives with one another. In any case the intensity of the course had left very little time or inclination for socializing. Maids took care of normal housekeeping chores and meal times included staff instructors at each table who didn't encourage fraternization.

* * * * * * * *

Laura's command of English, German and French had been improved to near perfection and immersion in various cultures of the West proved fascinating and so different from the rigid Communist life she'd known. Western films and reading the latest American and European magazines had whetted her appetite for a change of scene. She had been intrigued by the 'museum' consisting of three rooms containing a potpourri of spy equipment such as devices used for 'bugging', mini cameras disguised as cigarette lighters, plus various ingenious types of concealed weapons. Most items had come into being during the last war. Each student was given an opportunity to examine them in order to become proficient in handling the equipment. The class which had most impact on Laura was designated Sexual Entrapment based on a handbook issued to each student of the school. On their first day of this class Madame Ryashentsev had introduced herself. She looked to be in her early seventies, but her poise and deportment would have been the envy of any Parisian model employed at a great fashion house. Traces of her former beauty were still very much in evidence. She was dressed in a severely cut black suit and white silk blouse with a pin denoting the 'Order of Stalin' attached to her lapel. Everything concerning methods to be employed for compromising a 'target' were instilled in each student. Quite often films dealing with seduction were part of the training, and occasionally various situations were enacted by members of the staff. Looking at Madame Ryashentsev, Laura wondered what role she had played in her younger days. Had she been a courtesan in Czarist times? She could only surmise at the number of men who had succumbed to those marvelous blue eyes of hers.

* * * * * * * *

Laura awoke with a start. They were now into the environs of Moscow. She couldn't wait to see her father after so long a time, as no contact had been allowed during her time away. She wondered what he'd think of her new wardrobe, mannerisms and make-up to be used in the 'seduction assignments'. It was all somehow a little unreal as if she'd been rehearsing a movie part. Basically she felt the same but wondered if an alien quality had become part of her psyche... time would tell soon enough. The word puppet came to mind as the Zis pulled up in front of her father's apartment. Well, if she'd become a puppet to be manipulated in furtherance of the aims of the USSR so be it, as long as her role provided quick advancement in the new career. Standing beside the car while her luggage was unloaded she gave a quick wave to the Tarasov girls, who smiled as Laura turned to ring the doorbell of Colonel Ichenko. Her father would understand the 'new' Laura, after all she was a chip off the old block.

* * * * * * * *

Laura spent the next three weeks seeing old friends from her days at the University. She went out on dates with two men she'd known, but found it difficult to be relaxed, it was hard to suppress putting into effect expertise so recently taught. Her father took her to dinner at two of his favorite restaurants which she'd enjoyed, but felt herself becoming bored. Arriving back in the apartment from a shopping trip to a nearby 'Voentorg' she had just dumped her purchases on the kitchen table as the phone rang. After a ten minute conversation, Laura replaced the receiver and walked over to the window and looked out. So this was it... her first assignment and she would be leaving for Berlin on the following Tuesday. All of a sudden there seemed to be a million things she needed to do, but it could all wait until she had a hot bath to mull things over, then perhaps a quick nap before going to a performance of the Bolshoi later in the evening.

26

AUTUMN 1962

Laura was unaware the code name 'Echo' had been given to her forthcoming mission. She'd taken up residence in a large suburban villa in order to prepare for the assignment. The place had served as an ideal 'safe house' for several years, having been bought for the Soviet Intelligence Service through a Norwegian businessman on the payroll. It was located in a pleasant outlying district of the city. Most of the homes belonged to business professionals who worked long hours and didn't have much time for socializing with neighbors. The dowdy furnishings of the villa were not exactly in keeping with Laura's taste, however this was of no importance to it's owners. Six weeks after arriving at the 'Villa Bekker' Laura was about to find out what her handlers expected of her. Three men and a woman arrived for dinner and after finishing their meal retired to the drawing room where Laura was to be briefed. The two younger men withdrew to a small anteroom and Laura surmised they were bodyguards for the elderly man and woman. Laura proffered the pair drinks, then sat down.

The woman spoke first. "Comrade, delicate arms negotiations are presently being held at a high level between the governments of Germany and Turkey. We understand some aspects are highly detrimental to specific plans we've undertaken. Our main source of information is through a Peter Hahn, a high ranking member in the West German government, but we don't altogether trust him. He is sympathetic to the communist cause we are sure of that, but we need an even stronger lock on the man... just in case he has second thoughts about supplying further information needed for policy decisions. The elderly man got up and lit a cigar while studying Laura. The hooded eyes combined with a long scar on his left cheek created a chilling effect and Laura doubted a name given on introduction was real, and wondered what level of authority he held.

Her thoughts were interrupted when he spoke "You will attend a social evening at the Hotel Brendenhof next Wednesday, Peter Hahn will be present. Ingratiate yourself... I am fully aware of your training, therefore you will decide for yourself the best plan of action to employ. As soon as possible we require film footage of you copulating... this man must be compromised without fail. All information regarding his knowledge of the negotiations is to be given promptly to comrade Valentia for evaluation." Valentia looked across at Laura. "Moscow is vitally concerned about this operation, so do you have any questions?" Comrade Laura Ichenko shook her head and bit her lip knowing failure would be disaster for a newly minted graduate of the 'finishing school'.

Laura knew the whole house was bugged and her performance would be evaluated along with that of the intended 'target'. The bedroom ceiling had a two-way mirror concealed in a light fixture through which top quality Zeiss cine cameras focused on the room below. A technician had given her a detailed tour of the house after she first moved in. A wall safe contained a substantial amount of money along with a small automatic pistol. Hidden wall buttons would activate an alarm system for summoning help should it become necessary. The technician was obviously proud of his various installations, and Laura was impressed by the planning which would help facilitate her task... she only hoped the alarm system wouldn't require activation.

* * * * * * * *

Four days had passed since the dinner when she'd learned of her task and during this time she'd attended several sessions with specialists who explained details of a technical nature, and she also read a lengthy dossier regarding Peter Hahn. At the school Laura had studied photographic techniques to be employed for compromising a 'target' and various methods for counterfeiting documents and correspondence. Having browsed through several old case files she was somewhat surprised to find the low success rate with entrapment operations. Laura had a retentive memory which would be essential during her association with Peter Hahn. All pertinent information would have to be memorized and later recorded on tape. Despite the training she'd been through, Laura's mind was reeling with the amount of information needing to be absorbed. There was to be a final briefing then it would be up to her and whatever fate held in store. A strong vodka eliminated a small whisper in one ear about the awfulness if things went wrong as she stood looking out at the garden, but she knew it was time to prove her mettle.

Having tried on several outfits before deciding which ensemble seemed the best, Laura was finally satisfied with her reflection in the mirror. Absently running a finger around the gilded frame she turned away then perched on the piano stool and lit a cigarette. In a few minutes Olaf would be arriving to collect her. She'd already met her escort and found him to be pleasant and adequately trained for his task. Thinking how handsome he looked she wondered if he'd been a professional gigolo at one time? Possibly he was queer as they often made the best escorts… especially in situations demanding there be no emotional involvement. In different circumstances she could be attracted to him as he made a very amusing companion. This chain of thought was abruptly broken by the ringing of the door bell. The maid went to answer it and Olaf was ushered into the hallway as Laura stubbed out her cigarette…. 'Operation Echo' was about to be set in motion. Olaf had brought red roses for her which seemed a good omen.

* * * * * * * * *

Seven years after returning to the Gustav Strasse, gallery owner Heinz Wittich had become moderately wealthy. A quick brain and nose for money coupled with the economic miracle taking place in West Germany, helped provide the means. When people satisfy their immediate needs and start feeling secure they often spend on earlier fantasies. Heinz Wittich began cultivating the types who were likely to spend lavishly on art for both pleasure and investment, and he was more than willing to help fulfill these needs. Most people thought him an expert in such matters, while Wittich in turn regarded his clients purely as sheep to be sheared… the quicker the better. Heinz found himself becoming a fixture at many house parties and he attended a lot of functions in the artistic community. The bleak early days following his return had been tough. The legacy of gold coins had been carefully used to blunt the worst edges of a harsh life endured by most Berliners.

He'd employed Anna Rossman who turned out to be a jewel. Trustworthy and able to handle the day to day office business freed Heinz of many headaches, allowing him more time to search out lucrative clients. Eleven months after reopening the business, Heinz had taken one of his customers for drinks at Otto's, one of the more popular clubs in the arts district. He'd chosen the place because of its reputation for having some of the best whores in Berlin and a few of them sat around the bar scouting for contacts with money. It didn't take long for the two men to find what they were looking for. Heinz ordered three bottles of the inferior champagne the club offered at exorbitant rates. He didn't want to get too sloshed as the girl opposite looked somewhat of a challenge. At times he'd dozed off after drinking too much making it a waste of money… you paid whether you partook or not, it was immaterial to the girls.

In order to fit his new image as a gallery director, Heinz now wore expensive Italian suits, and had grown a stylish Vandyke beard. He also sported dark glasses, mainly to avoid looking a customer directly in the eye after quoting an outrageous price for a piece of 'Art' junk. One of the girls dropped her cigarette case on the floor which ended up near Wittich's left foot. He bent down to retrieve it, and on looking up realized someone was staring at him. The man sat alone at a nearby table. After a few minutes Heinz excused himself and headed for the washroom in order to get a better look at the stranger. Suddenly it clicked… good God, it was Horst Bruckner his ex POW traveling companion.

Horst still wasn't sure if it was Heinz or not. The suit and beard confused him until Wittich laid a business card next to his glass. "Ring me tomorrow Horst, tonight I'm somewhat occupied." Returning to his table, Heinz turned slightly in the direction of Horst who half raised his glass in acknowledgment. One of the girls asked if it was a friend to which he replied, "No, just an admirer of yours." The girl giggled… the champagne was having its effect. It was time to go, things were moving into top gear.

* * * * * * * *

Wittich awoke with a splitting headache… the girl had taken her money and already gone. A nauseating smell of stale perfume lingered in the air and reaching for his watch he saw it was about to register noon. The phone rang as he returned from the bathroom. "Good afternoon comrade, I didn't think you deserved being awoken any earlier, and incidentally you're the only man I've ever seen smoking a cigar with a drink in one hand the other on a girl's thigh." Horst gave one of his peculiar laughs and Heinz Wittich hesitated before speaking. "Listen Horst, it was great meeting up with you again… let's give it an hour then come round here and we'll catch up on our news."

Horst entered through the new double doors of the gallery, and spoke to Anna as Heinz was on the phone in the back office. When Heinz came back a few minutes later, Horst clapped a big bear paw on his shoulder and let out a whistle. "Mein Gott, they were right about the meek shall inherit the earth." Heinz grinned "Come on back you old fart, in case you scare away any of my high class customers. I've got an expensive bottle that needs opening for a special occasion such as this, although I've only just got rid of my hangover from last night." Horst eyed his companion noting he'd gained a little weight which suited him along with the beard and understood why he'd been hard put to recognize him at first. Heinz hadn't had too much trouble recognizing Horst… the man had barely changed and judging by the way he was dressed it looked as if he'd only just been scraping by. "So, my friend, draw me the picture since those froggie soldiers so rudely parted us as we made the grand entrance into our glorious city.

The men were about talked out when Wittich suddenly offered his old comrade a job. It would be a dual role kind of position in the same fashion as Anna's except Horst's would entail longer hours and an element of danger. The pay Heinz offered was more than Horst could have hoped for so he accepted straight away. The gallery had now acquired a security manager who'd double as bodyguard for the boss when needed. Heinz had already been mugged, and there had been an attempted robbery the previous month. The local crime rate was on the rise due to the infiltration of teenage gangs from poorer districts. Heinz thought it was time to protect his interests, and who better than Horst? Three weeks after the interview Heinz Wittich suddenly had a brainwave... the St. Lucien treasure was never far from his thoughts and a way to get his hands on it presented itself. He lit a cigar and gave a self satisfied smirk before propping his feet on the table...

* * * * * * * *

Within three days of his decision to go after the treasure, an advertisement appeared in two local newspapers. It stipulated a requirement for a fluent French speaker willing to temporarily relocate to a place called Dreux in Northern France. The candidate would negotiate various small business transactions. Due to the short term nature of this assignment, payment and expenses would be generous. The gallery phone number was provided.

* * * * * * * *

Anna had screened several applicants before settling on the one deemed most suitable, even though she wasn't fully aware of the true nature of the project. Heinz interviewed Herr Webber, a middle aged ex-teacher who was looking for some quick money prior to emigrating to Canada. Wittich talked briefly to the candidate outlining plans for expanding the gallery. Because of the acute shortage of building materials in Germany he'd decided to look elsewhere. He'd targeted the area around Dreux in France, as being suitable for his needs. When Webber asked if there was any particular reason for choosing this area, he noted a cold expression came over Heinz's face "No, just business reasons and repayment of a debt." Webber decided not to pry any further, and his curiosity ended right there. A money advance and the amount of his final payment on completion of the job was all that mattered. Heinz stood up handing Webber a typewritten sheet outlining tasks he'd have to perform:

1. Contact of a building supplies business and order certain quantities of roofing tile, beams, bricks and sundry items.
2. Contact a woodworking shop for the fabrication of six Doric fluted columns. Each to be 3 meters in length, and hollowed out from one end for a third of their length. Two oil drums of saw dust and a wooden skid to transport the columns on a truck bed.
3. Rent a barn on short term lease, wherein a truck could be parked and the foregoing items stored, until ready for loading.
4. All paperwork for the import/export of these items to be arranged, and any necessary permits to be obtained as soon as possible.

Webber quickly scanned the list and pocketed the sheet. Heinz proposed they meet again in three days "I'm pretty tied up at the moment but I'll finalize some sketches giving measurements and quantities etc. You can phone me regarding cost estimates and quality when you are there. Here is a map of France and the area where you'll be going is circled." Heinz held out a hand "I'm sure you'll have more questions which I'll try to answer next time." Webber walked out of the gallery feeling pleased the way things had gone. The job didn't seem as if it would be too arduous and it would be the last before leaving the Fatherland.

27

THE WUNDERKIND

THE CALL FROM FRANCE HAD GONE through two days ago. Horst Bruckner settled back behind the wheel feeling rather irritable. The officious little customs man at the border crossing had riled him by wasting time, it was obvious the truck was empty and the paperwork correct as Heinz Wittich had been meticulous, even so it had taken 25 minutes before being waved on through. Nearing the end of the trip he'd missed a couple of turns before finally pulling up alongside the large barn, indicated on the map Heinz had prepared. The last vestiges of light were disappearing when Horst slumped down in the drivers seat and closed his eyes.

Within a few seconds of nodding off, a sharp rap on the cab window made him shoot bolt upright and graze a knee on the dashboard. He unlocked the door with one hand while grasping a steel bar in the other. By means of the meager light from the overhead lamp he was able to discern Wittich's features. "Americano cigarette, Comrade? These French ones taste of shit." Heinz asked if it had been a good trip as Horst climbed down from his seat and stretched "Ja, not too bad." Wittich looked at the truck and asked if there had been any problems en route. Horst said "nothing I couldn't handle." Wittich looked at him sharply "listen Horst… it had better be the same on the return journey because I've too much money invested in this little venture"

* * * * * * * *

Six months prior to Horst's Bruckner trip, Heinz Wittich had returned to the area of France where he'd been stationed in 1940. No nostalgia was involved, it was strictly to check out the chateau Lancour and make up his mind how best he could retrieve the treasure… that's if it was still there. Much could have happened in the intervening years but Heinz refused to let his mind dwell on such an ugly possibility. Traveling by train to Paris he'd stayed overnight before renting a car and driving to Dreux.

It seemed strange being back after so much time had elapsed. A road marker indicating the direction of the Chateau Lancour invoked half forgotten memories. Heinz parked near the entranceway before walking back to take a look at the place through the elaborate ironwork of its gates. As far as he remembered it looked much the same and a feeling of anticipation began to take hold. Smoking a cigarette he glanced at the engraved copper plate screwed on one of the gate pillars. It read 'Center for International Trade and Adult Education'. Heinz went back to the car to fetch extra matches, then remembered seeing a glass fronted notice board on the opposite pillar. Using a handkerchief he wiped away condensation from the glass and read the typewritten page pinned inside. The information contained was in three languages giving details of upcoming adult courses to be held at the chateau. Two of them interested Heinz, one on art history and another on Franco-German cultural affairs. Standing there, a simple way of retrieving the treasure occurred to him, a bona fide way of gaining entry to the grounds. Heinz laughed, he would become a student once again. He drove off elated by a new twist of affairs related to his quest.

Returning to Germany, Heinz filled out the paperwork for enrolling as a student at the chateau, and inquired about reservations at one of the smaller commercial hotels in Venton, a small city about forty minutes drive from Dreux. This would lessen chances of being recognized although his changed appearance made that highly improbable. He'd signed up for two courses in art history and one on new European economics, the latter taught by a visiting professor from a Spanish university. Heinz became convinced the man would have starved in the real world outside of academia, but the art courses turned out to be even worse. The lecturer, a dowdy woman wearing thick lensed glasses constantly pronounced that this or that artist was trying to show… or, it is obvious to the viewer that… how the hell did she know those things Heinz mused unless she was a clairvoyant. He felt little empathy with students who appeared to be in his age bracket and took care in not being overly friendly with anyone, it was vital his mind stayed focused on his sole purpose of being there and he couldn't afford distractions.

* * * * * * * *

At the end of his third week at the chateau Heinz fixed a date for retrieval of the St Lucien treasure. Periods between classes coupled with long lunch breaks allowed plenty of time for reconnoitering the grounds. Other than an elderly caretaker and his wife who had an apartment in the chateau, there was no other form of security. Heinz notified the hotel he'd be away on a business trip for a few days and paid in advance to reserve the room for another ten days. Following the last class of the day Heinz Wittich observed nearly all the students smartly vacated the building, headed to the car park and were gone. Probably the majority stopped off at a nearby bistro. Occasionally small cliques remained behind to discuss issues with their lecturers, then departed anywhere from half an hour to forty-five minutes later.

Heinz dawdled inside the men's restroom then sat on a toilet reading a magazine. Having allowed what he deemed sufficient time he walked out... this was the moment, if he'd done his homework properly. The car park was deserted except for two cars belonging to the faculty who might show up at any time, but Heinz decided to risk it. Starting the Renault while keeping an eye on the chateau, he backed out of the lot and turned right instead of taking the usual direction to the big iron gates. These would be locked by the caretaker after all the vehicles departed.

Heinz made sure nobody was in sight and his movements remained undetected. Rounding the corner past an old cluster of deteriorating billets he'd once slept in, he drove slowly along a track leading to a building selected earlier. In the old days the place had been used for storage and repair of Wehrmacht electrical equipment, prior to that it had been a stable for estate work horses. Now the interior was gutted, most likely by local inhabitants who would have taken anything worth having once the Germans pulled out during the war. He parked the Renault between a wall of the building and hulks of two rusted tractors almost covered in weeds. It was perfect, affording a view of the way he'd approached. Patting his pocket concealing a small Grimaldi automatic, the treasure hunter hunkered down and waited. Getting comfortable he opened his thermos bottle filled with coffee and a dash of brandy. Time dragged at first but soon it almost went too quickly. After darkness fell he soon began to yawn and quickly nodded off.

He was awoken at midnight by the soft ringing of a miniature alarm clock placed on the dashboard. Getting out of the car Heinz stretched several times before reaching inside the car trunk for his leather bag containing an assortment of tools. He walked towards the gazebo where Karl Bayer and Sgt. Freiburg hid their loot. His adrenaline was pumping.

* * * * * * * *

In the morning feeling tired and stiff he downed the last of his coffee. He could hardly believe he'd been so successful after years of waiting for this day, and on top of everything was the sweet feeling of vindication. He made his way carefully through the surrounding trees until coming close to the parking lot he found a suitable vantage point to observe arriving vehicles. Checking his watch he allowed another twenty minutes to be sure everybody due to arrive was now inside the chateau. The lazy caretaker wouldn't show his face for at least another hour. Heinz jogged back to collect his car with a big grin on his face.

* * * * * * * *

Pulling into the car park he saw an end spot next to a green Peugeot. Locking the doors he was startled by the sound of a late comer. Heinz cursed under his breath until he saw it was Paula one of the more attractive students in the place. She smiled and walked over "Bon jour, I didn't see your car on the road ahead of me". Heinz countered saying "I guess both of our alarms didn't go off this morning". Paula laughed, "you look a bit rough, it must have been a hell of a party… next time invite me." Together they hurried up the chateau steps, but the girl had no inkling it would be the last time for her fellow student. Heinz considered leaving immediately after the first class finished, then decided he'd wait until the lunch break. This would allow for a shave and taking a shower before slinging his hook. Something buried in his psyche made him want to look sharp leaving the Chateau Lancour with his treasure. So far everything had gone like clockwork, but Heinz knew there remained a lot of details still to be taken care of and he hoped his luck wouldn't run out.

Several months after the curious disappearance of a

German student, an electrical contractor installing new cables was digging a trench close to the gazebo. When he next saw the caretaker he mentioned seeing several floor boards ripped out and tossed aside. The caretaker walked over with him to take a look. After kicking the boards with a boot he shrugged "vandals from the village... just wanton destruction, some require horse whipping." He'd get around to replacing them at the end of his long list of outstanding chores. Nobody connected the incident with a German student who'd suddenly upped and left........ why should they?

* * * * * * * *

For three days prior to Horst's arrival with the truck, Wittich had been busy working in the barn. All of the items on his shopping list stood neatly stacked against a wall. He had picked up Herr Webber from the hotel in Dreux and brought him out to the barn for the last time. Heinz asked Webber to help him lift the wooden columns onto the saw horses then move some other items, before dropping him off at the local train station. Webber had done a good job and Heinz handed him an added bonus, wishing him the best of luck in Canada.

Wittich set to work unscrewing the square bases at the hollow end of each column, carefully placing the screws in an old tobacco tin. With all the bases removed he allowed the opposite ends of each column to tilt until resting against the floor. Handfuls of sawdust were taken from one of the oil drums and put in the hollowed out sections. Heinz had carefully wrapped each item of the St. Lucien which had remained locked in his car since its removal, and these were inserted into the columns and gently tamped in place with additional quantities of sawdust. It had taken five columns to stash the entire horde and a few items were then placed in the sixth column. Pausing for a cigarette he glanced at the time, Webber must be well on his way by now. Checking to see if all of the screws were tight he ran a bead of wood putty around each joint between base and mating column then carefully wiped off any excess.

Taking a sip of coffee he leaned against a bench admiring his handiwork. The two overhead lights in the windowless barn were barely adequate, and it was getting late so the task of painting could wait until morning. Fetching a sleeping bag from the car, he unrolled it and was asleep within minutes. Waking early, the painting was completed shortly after Horst arrived, and the rest of the day was spent checking everything including the paperwork for the return journey. That night both men slept in the back of the truck and started loading in the morning. Finally everything was stowed and strapped down by lunch time and Heinz took his last look around to make sure nothing that mattered was left behind. The newly painted columns reminded him of gun barrels laying in their special cradles, and they were well protected should the rest of the cargo shift in transit.

Horst drove the truck outside as Heinz switched off the lights and closed the barn doors. Horst followed Heinz Wittich back to the hotel where Webber had stayed. He had already booked rooms for the pair, having chosen the place because it provided locked garage space for its guests. There wasn't much room for the big Henshel, but Horst managed to park it without too much trouble. Heinz dropped an envelope containing the keys for the barn at the hotel desk for mailing back to the owner. After enjoying hot baths the men sat down to a hearty dinner of venison complimented with a bottle of good French wine. Finishing up their meal with brandy and coffee they fell silent for awhile as they sat smoking.

Horst Bruckner knew Wittich was smuggling something back but hadn't a clue what it was, and didn't really care… probably some crazy art he was so hung up on. He thought about the bonus he'd been promised. Despite not wishing to sound alarmist he leaned towards Heinz "They had dogs at the border… I wouldn't be carrying anything they like sniffing at, would I comrade?" Heinz's face remained impassive. "No Horst, dogs are O.K. for drugs but anything I'd take back would only be detected if the beast had x-ray eyes." Horst relaxed "OK. no more questions, I didn't want you to be embarrassed by not knowing a potential hazard." Heinz gave a derisive snort telling his bodyguard he'd do the worrying for both of them, then relented "thanks for looking after my interests all the same".

* * * * * * * *

About nine months after the trip to Dreux Wittich visited Dieter Vogel, an art dealer in Dortmund. They'd first met when attending an exhibition in Berlin and found they enjoyed each others company. In one of their conversations about the art world and some of it's characters Vogel casually mentioned having purchased an impressionist painting by Andre Le Vanne. Unfortunately, since then something he'd read made him think it was stolen property and wanted to unload it as quickly as possible. This news had prompted Wittich's visit who had a rich client crazy for works by this particular artist, and had the kind of money to purchase whatever he wanted. Heinz was already marking up a new price in his mind writing a check payable to Dieter, who for his part was more than pleased ending up with a profit and without the worry of sheltering a 'hot' property… such considerations hardly bothered Heinz Wittich! Yawning, Wittich put on his top coat rather wishing he'd declined a final brandy. Waiting for his taxi to arrive he decided to cancel a reservation on the night train and told the driver to drop him at the Metropole. The painting had been wrapped by Dieter Vogel and was placed in the hotel safe by it's new owner. Waking early after a good night's sleep he ordered coffee sent up, then showered and dressed and made arrangements at the lobby for a ticket on the evening express. Trying to remember when he was last in Dortmund, Wittich decided to refresh old memories by setting off on a walk.

Close to the central part of the city Heinz came across a former gallery for sale. A particularly handsome wrought iron arch formed the main entranceway complimenting Dutch tiles on the adjacent walls. The place looked as if it had been standing empty quite a while, and badly needed a paint job. Jotting down information regarding the rental agency from a faded card in one of the windows, Wittich crossed the road and entered a cafe. He polished off a light breakfast and went over to a phone booth and called Dieter. "Good heavens that place belonged to my old friend Wolf Siedler. He died about eighteen months ago. If anyone was thinking of buying they could probably get it cheap... I don't think the heirs have had any serious lookers so far." After hanging up, Heinz contacted the rental agent and they agreed to meet at the Metropole for lunch. His mind was almost made up, he wanted the place if the price was right. Over lunch he studied photos of the interior then informed the agent he might return for serious discussions the following week-end if they could close the gap between the asking price and what he was prepared to offer. As the Berlin express pulled out from the terminus Heinz Wittich dimmed the overhead reading lights in the compartment and poured a jigger of brandy from a silver hip flask before leaning back against the comfortable cushions. Heinz Wittich always traveled first class nowadays and he was becoming tired of Berlin. The four power occupation, and a possibility the 'Russkies' might suddenly turn the cold war into a hot one made him think about relocating to a less hostile environment leaving a manager to look after the Berlin gallery.

* * * * * * * *

Wittich had been back two days when he received a telegram. The agent had spoken with Wolf Siedler's widow and she was anxious to meet him. Heinz knew it was a pure impulse purchase on his part... somehow the challenge of starting from scratch, as opposed to his having inherited the Berlin gallery motivated him. The second gallery could exhibit modern art forms which had interested him for some time. Financially it could be risky but also worth the challenge.

Five days later Wittich treated Vogel to dinner at the 'Golden Bear', one of the best restaurants in Dortmund. After placing their order Dieter raised his glass "My congratulations to the new owner of the Horizon gallery, may it be a happy and profitable venture". Heinz paused for only a second before replying... "I hope we will always remain friends even if we are destined to become competitors... and incidentally, I sold the Le Vanne for nearly three times its purchase price. I hope your feelings won't be too hurt." Dieter grinned and replied "only my wallet is pained, my friend." Six months after the dinner the owner of the Horizon gallery also bought a villa on the outskirts of the city, and set to work refurbishing the place. A newly employed housekeeper and cook soon became accustomed to the frequent live in girl friends with Berlin accents that came and went at the 'Villa Wittich'. Their boss provided generous paychecks as a strong inducement in keeping their mouths shut when tempted to gossip with any of the locals, he'd been emphatic on this point. The smell of pot was often detected by the servants when guests stayed at the villa. At other times the staff were left to their own devices and had the use of the pool and a car belonging to their boss. All in all it was a pretty cushy number besides being lucrative. They were often amused witnessing some of the antics of bizarre characters who showed up if Heinz happened to be in residence.

* * * * * * * *

At a later date there was very little of substance the staff recalled when questioned by a chief inspector Steiner regarding their erstwhile employer and his guests. It had been rather like the movies for the housekeeper and cook and having left the theater everything had become dimmed somewhat in their recollections. Steiner cursed under his breath but he'd seen the same thing happen in previous cases. Probably the pulp magazines would have a field day emblazoning their pages with lurid exaggerated goings on at the 'Villa Wittich'. No doubt some of the featured players would receive fat checks for their embellished stories... it was remarkable how money helped rejuvenate lapsed memories.

28

CANNES

THE WORKING RHYTHMS OF THE GRAND hotel 'El Fenix' were inaudible to the occupants of room number 109. Laura lay back in an old fashioned bathtub letting soap bubbles encase her body while idly surveying the ornate antique fittings. After years of use they were starting to lose the original gold plating and she smiled wondering how many beautiful women had stretched out in this very spot she occupied. Maybe there had been one or two plain ones, but somehow she was doubtful. Earlier in the lobby, she had overheard a woman describing the hotel to a friend "It has the reputation of bankrupting a girl's lover if they stay too long!" It seemed that half the aristocracy of Europe were residents judging from the names and titles she heard being paged at the desk... the whole place smelled of 'old' money.

* * * * * * * *

Peter was still asleep when she ran the bath. He had turned over on his back while Laura waited in the doorway admiring his tanned body. She was amused to see his

232

member was still rigid before padding over to the bed in order to pull the top sheet over her lover. It reminded her of setting up a tent when she was a small girl. God the man was a tiger, he could be rough in his lovemaking one minute, then quickly switch to being thoughtful and gentle. This was the fourth night they had slept together. The first time Laura faked an orgasm but the other three hadn't required anything phony… it was only too real on her part which began worrying her. She leisurely soaked herself and lay back again bemused that her nipples were still sore from the exquisite attention they'd received recently.

Carefully she went over all the things Peter had talked about to date as these pieces were fragmented and her brain needed to correlate all the details. At first Laura insisted he should not be telling her these things. This bluff had worked… Peter seemed almost eager to unload his mind. Of course the amount of Veuve Clicquot they'd imbibed had been a great lubricant with regard to his tongue. Laura had surreptitiously tossed most of her drink over the balcony rail whenever an opportunity arose. She needed a clear head to assimilate all of the information she was tapping into. Twice she'd become apprehensive thinking Peter might nod off while telling her about proposed stratagems regarding the talks with Turkey. She couldn't believe he was so indiscreet, but it certainly made the mission easier and highly enjoyable at the same time.

Laura laughed at the absurd aspect of the whole thing just as her lover put his head around the door. "Want your back massaged?" She nodded, as he walked across the tiled floor towards her naked and still erect. She leaned over the edge of the bath and kissed his most prominent feature eliciting a huge grin. "Well what's the plan for today my sweet?" Laura thought quickly as she needed to meet her go-between for a transfer of information gained from the previous night. "How about the casino in Monte Carlo?" Peter thought for a moment, "sounds good to me. I feel in a winning mood today." After breakfast on the terrace Laura was able to make a quick phone call to her contact, arranging a casino rendezvous. It had been Laura's idea in coming to the south of France and Peter had agreed without hesitation, taking care of all the arrangements. Laura had agreed with her superiors that she would require a contact who would be available at all times.

* * * * * * * *

The building had a faded look of bygone opulence and Laura thought some of the elderly dowagers clustered at the tables had a similar appearance. In a way the place reminded her of the finishing school except a majority of the players looked to be in their dotage with sallow skins derived from too many years spent indoors. Some of the women were laden in jewels although their evening dresses seemed to date from the Czarist era, and a few of them spoke in an old fashioned idiom. Laura supposed they must be 'White' Russians who had made their home in France after the Bolshevik revolution. Standing observing these people placing their bets, she suddenly realized a curious fact... no emotions were displayed whether they lost or won. Laura reckoned they would make good recruitment material for her own bosses. Suddenly she spotted her contact standing close to a roulette table. The woman was wearing the distinctive brooch mentioned earlier in the phone conversation as a means of identification. Slowly she made eye contact and Laura returned the required hand signal before walking across the room, and at the same time glancing towards the black jack table.

She noticed Peter was suitably engrossed before making her way to the ladies room. There was hardly time to admire its sumptuous decor before Laura's contact entered and walked quickly to the far end of the room unnoticed by an elderly attendant dozing on her bench. Only one of the stalls was occupied but after a few moments a woman came out, washed her hands then inspected her make-up in the mirror. It was a hopeless case and she sighed before leaving to rejoin her party. Standing at adjacent wash basins the contact slid a small tape recorder towards Laura's purse on the counter. "My chauffeur Rossi will be in a light blue Bugatti parked close to the entrance. He is one of us by the way, and will drive you around while you carry out your dictation and then he'll bring you back to the casino. Leave the recorder on the back seat as you get out of the car."

Once in the Bugatti Laura entered her code name and number taking about seven minutes to complete the message. The recorder was of Russian make familiar to Laura, but for safety she played back a portion making sure everything was O.K. Satisfied, she rapped on the glass panel separating her from Rossi who nodded and reversed direction. Back at the casino he opened the door and saluted while eyeing her shapely legs. The man had a smirk on his face… cheeky bugger Laura thought making her way up the steps, but by now she was used to men evaluating her body. Within a few minutes she bumped into Peter who was busy making some entries in a small black book. "Hello princess… I was beginning to wonder where the hell you'd got to. By my calculations we are now several thousand francs better off." Laura laughed at him, "O.K. you can buy me some premier champagne and caviar out of your winnings, then perhaps I'll nuzzle your ear." Peter smiled putting an arm around her bare shoulders while they headed to the bar.

* * * * * * * *

A large bouquet of roses with an attached note arrived at Laura's Berlin address. Her bosses were demonstrating their delight with the progress of project Echo, and hoped even more information would be gleaned in the future. Laura crumpled the note having read it a second time, then arranged the flowers in a crystal vase. Russian intelligence analysts were frantically digesting a windfall of high grade information provided by Anton Kirov, the Berlin station chief of the K.G.B. There was a smile on his face for the first time in several weeks... perhaps an additional bonus could be had by blackmailing this German V.I.P. when Echo was wrapped up. Everyone connected with the project agreed that things had been handled in a text book fashion and probably there was a lot more gold to be mined in the future.

Unfortunately for Anton Kirov a fly had recently landed in the ointment. Despite all her training the star agent of Echo had begun feeling something more than attraction towards her quarry. In-built warning signals had started buzzing but were being ignored, an indication of extreme danger. Laura felt depressed, she needed a few days off to be by herself allowing some of the pressures to settle down. The case officer granted her request for a few days of freedom, then mentioned a recommendation for promotion had already been forwarded to Moscow. Nearly all case officers are extremely careful to shield promising agents from unnecessary stress, and Laura was no exception. From past experience he was well aware that pushing too hard would lead to burnout and careless mistakes.

29

OCTOBER 1962

IN THE SPRING OF '61 PETER Hahn discovered the Gustav gallery. He'd been searching for a recommended framing shop but had mislaid the piece of paper giving its location. A sudden downpour prompted stepping inside to browse and avoid getting soaked. It was the year Heinz Wittich gained a reputation within the Berlin art dealers association. He spent inordinately long hours at the establishment, but on the day Peter dropped by he happened to be at the dentist, and it was almost two months before the men met for the first time.

Peter frequented the gallery on a regular basis occasionally buying gifts for visiting foreign dignitaries, and sometimes purchasing a painting or sculpture for himself. The collection was beginning to grow quite rapidly, despite his dislike of having to negotiate prices. This was mostly due to a lack of expertise concerning monetary values, but Peter was a quick learner. His more savvy friends were usually reassuring admiring any new acquisitions and the bargain struck... Peter hoped they were not merely being polite.

Laura's phone rang. "Hello tigress, do you feel sinful enough for a present?" Laura laughed, "Good or bad, I am always ready for a present, do I get it in bed?" It was Peter's turn to laugh. "No, but you need to be ready in 35 minutes, I'll pick you up on our way to the Gustav strasse." She was about to ask what happened there, but her lover had already hung up. It was one of those exhilarating autumn days with the sun shining. Although the air felt slightly crisp, the couple agreed it would be fun to lower the top of Peter's convertible. Threading their way through city traffic few words were spoken. Peter was lucky finding a parking space almost in front of Wittich's gallery, and waited while Laura inspected her face in the car mirror. The owner stood looking through the gallery's window enjoying the sun's reflected warmth. Peter Hahn introduced Laura and with a big grin on his face announced it was her birthday. My God, she had forgotten herself what day it was, but remembered Peter having asked when they'd first met. Heinz Wittich stretched his arms out in welcome "Perhaps the birthday girl would like to explore and see if there is something she'd like for a gift, I suspect Peter is very indulgent."

Laura wandered around the gallery, while Heinz motioned Peter towards the back office where a bottle of deluxe cognac and glasses sat on an ornate table. "I'm sure you'll give me your opinion on it's pedigree" Peter laughed nodding assent, and while the two chatted Laura took her time before poking her head around the door. "Aha, you men are already boozing I see, " Wittich poured out another glass for Laura and reached for her hand which he lightly kissed. "Every time I'm confronted by exceptional glamour I become nervous, which requires alcohol to counter it." Laura wondered if he had always been such a smooth talker as Peter walked over and put his arm around her waist "Listen, we've been invited by this reprobate for a long weekend at his villa near Dortmund, the place sounds luxurious and has an indoor pool, which isn't surprising with the disgusting profits he makes."

Heinz laughed, and they worked on a date which suited everybody. Heinz Wittich turned to the girl "Well did you pick something out?" Laura paused then mentioned a painting hanging in the upper level. "Ah yes, that's an excellent choice, it's done by a young Polish artist. He'll be big in years to come, let's go upstairs and take a look at the inscription on the back. The watercolor measured a little under a square meter and Heinz took it from the wall and held it out to Laura. "Happy birthday" Peter reached for his checkbook but Heinz waved a hand at him "No my friend, I like beauty to associate with beauty and as you know I'm rich enough to indulge most of my whims." Laura reached up and kissed his friend exuberantly. Peter wondered if accepting the invitation had been such a good idea. It was time to leave and Heinz handed them printed instructions for finding their way to the Villa Wittich.

Driving back to her place Laura leaned over in the car seat and bit Peter's ear. "You are not jealous of my birthday gift are you?" Peter stuck his tongue out at her before replying "Of course I am you delicious tart!" Actually he thought Heinz was somewhat over the top, in fact there was a character on the Turkish negotiating team very similar in manner. However, he had to admit Wittich was extremely good company having the 'Berliner mentality' fast, funny and worldly which women seemed to adore.

* * * * * * * *

Heinz Wittich had reserved a seat on the 11:05 am train to Berlin. Before leaving he summoned the cook and housekeeper to his study, and presented them with a bonus for their hard work and discretion. They were told their boss didn't plan on returning before Christmas as unfortunately several problems had arisen in connection with the Berlin gallery demanding his attention. Wittich wished them both an enjoyable time in his absence.

Four days later he received a phone call necessitating a change in plans. It was the housekeeper "Herr Wittich, a severe storm hit the Dortmund area last night. Perhaps you've already read about it? The villa is O.K. but the police rang saying several sections of the Horizon gallery roof had blown off in the high wind. I have taken the liberty of arranging for a company to pump out water inside the building and install tarpaulins to prevent further damage. Happily the art objects seem to be OK, I hope this meets your approval?" Heinz commended her actions saying he would be back in Dortmund sometime the following day after meeting a client, and would take care of anything else that needed attention. Putting the phone down he swore and leaned back in his expensive leather chair. Swiveling slowly to face the bay window he lit a cigar and watched blue smoke curl towards the ceiling while allowing his irritability to dissipate. After a few moments he phoned his insurance agent in Dortmund, and arranged a meeting. Considering the outrageous premium fees he paid, Heinz didn't foresee any particular problems concerning repair costs on the gallery.

Happier thoughts entered his mind knowing that both galleries were financially sound according to his accountant. The Horizon was showing better than expected profits, which should take care of any increased premiums resulting from the storm. The weekend invitation to Peter and Laura was still on, and the timing dovetailed with the Dortmund trip except for his leaving Berlin earlier than planned. The staff hadn't been informed about weekend guests since their services weren't needed and Heinz had given them a few days off.

He tapped ash from his cigar and reached for a notepad to compile a list of places his guests might like to visit. He wrote down a reminder to call that blockhead Bauer who'd originally installed the villa's security system. It had been malfunctioning and Heinz wondered if it was on the point of quitting altogether. If the man didn't respond quickly he needed to look elsewhere. Apart from having the brakes on the BMW checked, and replacement of two pool filters, that seemed to cover the items needing attention.

Picking up mail lying on the desk Heinz listlessly scanned the contents, mostly bills and catalogs, but a large envelope on the bottom of the pile drew his attention. Inside was an enlarged photograph clipped to a thank you letter from the secretary of the ex-comrades reunion committee. The picture had been taken by a professional photographer at the last Munster get-together. It showed Heinz Wittich making a speech... he liked it so maybe he'd have it framed for posterity. Heinz returned to Dortmund on Wednesday the 22nd and the insurance agent invited him to lunch at the station hotel before taking him on to the villa to go over the forms regarding his claim settlement.

Wittich apportioned Thursday to prepare for his guests who were expected sometime in the afternoon on Friday according to Laura's phone call. She'd told him they'd opted to drive instead of taking the train. Peter wanted to stop for lunch at a place called 'Der Adler' about 50 Km outside of Dortmund. Two diplomat friends of his had highly recommended the place so they looked forward to something special to eat.

Reaching into a kitchen cabinet for more of the crystal wine glasses, Heinz experienced a peculiar premonition of impending disaster which he brushed off after a moment. Feeling suddenly tired mulling over various problems, he lay down on a sofa and began to snooze and didn't wake up until hearing the crunch of tires on the gravel. Sporting a large grin he ambled over to the door just as Peter bounded up the steps followed by Laura. "Welcome to the humble abode of a struggling antiques dealer" Wittich added a low bow along with his bullshit and was rewarded by a mock cuff to the head by Peter who laughingly said "Shut up you lying hypocrite, and provide your thirsty guests with something pronto." Laughing, the three walked into the lounge and sat down. After a cursory tour of the villa, and several cocktails, everyone decided a quick dip in the indoor pool prior to the evening meal sounded a great idea.

The dinner turned out to be fabulous, and also very expensive. The place Heinz had chosen was a refurbished 18th century mill on the banks of the Meisse river. Four large bay windows afforded an excellent background of reflected lights on the water. Carefully selected wines complimented a fine menu. After enjoying hors d'oeuvres the men settled for boar's head cooked in a red wine, while Laura chose imported Scottish river salmon. Throughout the meal both men outdid one another telling jokes which were both risqué and witty and Laura realized she hadn't laughed so hard in years. Heinz finished a chocolate mousse before ordering a round of cognac and Turkish coffee, then proffered Peter a cigar. Laura extracted a Balkan Sobranie cigarette from a gold case, a gift from her father. Placing the cigarette in a holder, she was amused by both escorts offering lighters in unison. There was no doubt the threesome had reached the mellow stage... Laura glanced at her watch and saw it was getting late.

Coming back from visiting the washroom she saw her companions had an arm around one another, laughing raucously at something probably outrageous. The maitre d' cast a slightly quizzical look in their direction. Seated at the next table were two couples whom Laura summed up as being typical Junker types. The men, both silver haired and choleric looking, stared arrogantly at Peter and Heinz. Their dumpy overdressed wives, slathered in jewelry were half swiveled in their chairs to better follow their husbands focus. Laura decided the pair looked like ex-Nazi war profiteers akin to the cartoon characters she'd seen depicted in the Moscow newspapers. She began to laugh and sashayed in an exaggerated manner towards their table. Stopping directly in front of the men, she pulled up her dress sufficiently to expose a shapely thigh while pretending to adjust a black garter. Dropping her hem she gave a dazzling smile exclaiming "Good evening gentlemen, don't make it so long before visiting again." One of the burghers almost dropped his monocle in the soup tureen, as the other one went slack-jawed. Both women stared goggle eyed and one emitted a strangulated gasp... Laura blew both of them a kiss, and by now Peter and Heinz were on their feet applauding.

Laura decided it was time they left and Wittich clumsily stuffed several bank notes into a hand of the hovering maitre d' muttering it would help restore tone to the place, then promptly negated his words by stumbling over a potted plant. Laura suggested she should drive back on the narrow twisty roads. Heinz slightly slurring his word remarked it sounded a brilliant idea. The men were still chortling about her impromptu performance, and Laura thought it satisfactory enough for any fascist pigs putting on airs. Peter soon closed his eyes as his head lolled on Laura's shoulder while Wittich sitting in the back launched into several ribald soldiers' songs sung off key. Laura was thankful she had taken it easy on the drinks otherwise they might have ended up sleeping in a ditch.

Arriving back at the villa she made coffee then told her companions she was off to bed. She felt the start of a headache and apparently her stomach wasn't feeling too happy. The men folk wished her 'Gute nacht' in distinctly thick tones, as they picked up their drinks and moved to the luxurious study. Wittich topped up their schnapps as Peter drooped in a chair, his tie loosened and looking disheveled. The host remained silent for a bit before saying. "Tonight my friend, I have a very special treat... something I am certain will astound you."

Heinz Wittich had adopted a rather theatrical tone and knew he was pissed causing his tongue to loosen even more. Peter Hahn was in worse shape although still capable of absorbing Wittich's words. By now the host's ego superseded his natural caution. He was anxious for someone of the right caliber to laud his expertise, paying homage to the talents of a first class collector.

Walking unsteadily to the far side of the study, he fished a key from his pocket and unlocked a door. Leaning against the door jamb he beckoned to Peter who'd already started sliding from his chair looking glassy eyed. It was obvious he couldn't hold his liquor, in fact it didn't look as if he would be able to get on his feet. Testily Wittich maneuvered him from the chair, and with a supporting arm steered his guest past furniture before dumping him onto a sofa in the adjoining room. Heinz then pressed a concealed wall button and a section of paneling opened exposing a steel safe. Peter watched the proceedings struggling to stay awake, but it was very much touch and go.

Heinz dialed the combination then swung the heavy door open, and transferred the contents to the sturdy oak table in the center of the room. Peter's effort to pull himself together allowed him to register interest in his surroundings. Despite his dulled senses his eyes riveted on a magnificent jewel encrusted cross inside a wooden case. After what seemed an eternity, he managed to avert his eyes and take in the rest of the pieces. He shook his head in disbelief... it must be some form of drunken dream. Heinz switched off the main lighting then activated spotlights in the corners of the room creating a stunning effect. Peter Hahn sensed what Howard Carter must have experienced on entering King Tutankhamen's tomb. With arms folded Heinz spoke softly "This my friend, is the treasure of St. Lucien. Take your time and savor the beauty and craftsmanship... I doubt you'll ever see anything like it again."

Peter had seen many exquisite artifacts in museums and homes of the super rich, but nothing had engendered the excitement he now felt confronted by such marvelous objects. He tried regaining his composure but it was hopeless. Heinz smiled, delighted by the reaction of his guest who was slowly examining everything on the table. Peter kept muttering "Mein Gott, truly fabulous" or similar expressions as Heinz stood to one side savoring every nuance bolstering his vanity.

Standing at the table Heinz fleetingly thought about his bleak days at Dreux and the curious twists and turns his life had taken since then. He wondered what his father might have thought had he been standing in the room, seeing the very things now mesmerizing Peter Hahn. The host was aware his life had reached a certain apex, but was still undecided about future plans. Peter knocked over his drink spilling schnapps on the Persian carpet, ending Wittich's reverie.

Part 3

30

THE REUNION

Karl Bayer sat enjoying a late lunch in a restaurant on the outskirts of Bremen. Over a second Belgian beer he checked his appointments calendar, and saw that two remaining clients had to be contacted before the company shut down over the Christmas break. A reminder scrawled on the back of his calendar showed he'd accumulated six personal days since starting his employment. Not wanting to be alone over the holidays he'd booked a mini tour of southern Spain arranged by a travel agency. Picking up the tickets would be his last port of call for the day.

After the years in Russia it had taken a long time adjusting to a civilian environment. On his release and return to Vienna he'd been devastated to learn Lilli and her mother along with hundreds of others had been rounded up by Russian soldiers during the final weeks of the war. Karl heard rumors to the effect that periodic sweeps were conducted to supply slave labor in the undamaged factories beyond the Urals. The orders had been signed by Stalin himself and it was dangerous to even approach the Soviet occupiers asking questions, and the few people who did inevitably came away empty handed.

As the months passed Karl sometimes forgot he'd ever been married. Feeling depressed with only finding dead-end jobs, he'd decided once again to head for Germany with the hope prospects might improve. Standing in line waiting to buy a train ticket he realized history was repeating itself. He thought of the time he'd first left home to find work, it now seemed like a half forgotten dream. As the line moved, Karl ground a cigarette butt under his heel.

Karl Bayer decided to start off in Bremen, and a lucky break enabled him to land a job with the 'VASA' pharmaceutical company. After a few weeks he enrolled in various company training programs and eventually became a sales representative selling medical items to hospitals and nursing homes. The company had originated in Sweden before moving to Germany in 1870 where it had become celebrated for the excellence of it's products. 'VASA' had made huge profits during the war years, in fact Karl found he rarely needed to use any hard sell tactics at all. He was allocated a company Volvo every eighteen months and provided a clothes allowance on top of his monthly salary. All in all it added up to being a pretty good number. Karl didn't mind the travel necessitated by the job, but was sympathetic towards the married men who found it hard on their families. Being technically single he'd adopted the old adage about having a girl in every port. Maybe later he'd find that somebody special and form a steady relationship, but until then he was happy the way things were. Perhaps a miracle would occur and Lilli might come back into his life, but the idea was becoming harder to hang on to with the passage of time.

His final places of business were in Munster and Dortmund, the latter being the most southerly city of his territory. It was also third in importance so far as sales potential and Karl always tried to allow extra time there with his clients, and hopefully a day would suffice for Munster. After lunch he'd driven into the city center which had been greatly revitalized since the end of the war. He collected his tickets from the travel agency before visiting his bank in order to make a deposit. After a coffee he made a phone call to Rosa, one of his girlfriends, to see if she was free that evening. A surly man's voice answered the phone and Karl hung up. Fishing out a tattered card from his wallet he dialed the number for Paula... she was a great party type and terrific in bed... he couldn't think why he didn't call her first!

* * * * * * * *

Not long before Heinz Wittich's unexpected return from Berlin to the villa, Karl Bayer stood looking out of a lobby window at the Storch hotel which was situated in the central area of Munster. He felt peeved having to make another trip to the hospital he'd called on that morning. The Herr Director seemed to be extra fussy this time, demanding Karl recheck everything and asking far more questions than usual, which had left him with a headache. The purchasing department was still working on additional requisitions that would probably need Karl's input in certain cases. However, he wasn't too unhappy about the situation, with this size of order the commission would go a long way in paying for his vacation. Karl picked up the local newspaper and checked to see if there was anything worthwhile at the movies, and decided there wasn't.

Lighting a cigarette he flipped to the back page and was confronted by obituary columns and further down were notices of farm auctions and various upcoming meetings. As he was about to toss the paper back on the table something caught his eye... it was the single word 'DREUX'. It was like seeing a ghost from the past, which in a way it was. Bayer hurriedly focused on the notice in the right hand corner of the page.

DREUX

To all ex-members of the Werhrmacht stationed at the Chateau Lancour during 1940. You are cordially invited to a reunion to be held at the club KESSLER 12 Borg strasse, A2 Düsseldorf Friday November 17th. Festivities starting at 8:30 p.m.

COME AND MEET OLD PALS. (Bring photographs!)

Listed were three names with phone numbers to contact for information regarding purchase of tickets. One of the names was a certain Heinz H. Wittich! It was like being kicked in the stomach, and he sat for a long time staring at the page feeling tingling sensations at the nape of his neck, the odds of coincidence seemed incredible and yet the notice was real enough. Karl paced up and down the room… so it looked like the creep had survived the war and unfortunately he also knew about the treasure. Anxious thoughts erupted. Had he and Freiburg overlooked anything back at Dreux? It was unthinkable but also possible. Pouring himself a stiff drink Karl sat brooding, but the longer he sat the worse it became. Conjecture and indecision were getting him nowhere. His curiosity won out, and on impulse he went downstairs to the lobby phone and ordered a ticket for the reunion using a fictitious name. There was a slim chance of learning something useful at the get together but if not it didn't really matter.

* * * * * * * *

Not long after returning from Russia Karl visited the central War Casualties office to inquire if a Sgt. Fritz L.A. Freiburg was listed in their files. Both men had exchanged service numbers and addresses during their time at Dreux. Finding a page in his battered diary containing this information, Karl showed it to a records clerk which helped facilitate the search. Returning after forty minutes the clerk laid a mimeographed copy of Sgt. Freiburg's military record on the counter. Karl edged the copy closer to him. Across the top of the page he read Fritz's full name, age, rank and service number but it was the next notation that crushed him... it gave the date and place of death. He gripped the counter edge to steady himself, feeling desolate. The past few years in general had inured him to death, but this was different. The clerk noted the look of pain showing on the face of the man in front of him.

After a few moments Karl jotted down the remaining information on the sheet, including the fact that Fritz was buried in a German military cemetery outside Florence in Italy. Poor Fritz hadn't survived the years of madness, however it was better to know than just wonder about his fate. Karl was also curious to see if a Heinz H.Wittich was listed in the records, but lacking a service number the clerk drew a blank and said if Karl left a contact address he'd keep on trying. Karl had a gut feeling he was still alive and kicking. On finding out about Fritz's death Karl vowed that when his finances improved he'd retrieve the St.Lucien, but sadly he realized it would be a solo effort.

Notice of the reunion had his juices running. Maybe the time had arrived for planning a visit to Dreux, and he knew Fritz Freiburg would be there watching over his shoulder helping him to succeed.

* * * * * * * *

The club Kessler looked as if it had seen better days, at least from the outside. An old man in the kiosk just inside the entranceway said "Welcome Kamerad." Karl grinned... he certainly did not remember him. For his part Karl was sure nobody would recognize him from the old days. Since coming home he had grown a beard and wore his hair fairly long, it had turned prematurely white in Russia. He told the old man at the kiosk his ticket was reserved. "What name friend?" Karl hesitated a fraction... "Hans, Hans Linse."

The old boy fumbled around in an ancient cigar box before extracting a ticket marked 'LINSE' from a stack secured with rubber bands. "Ah yes, here it is, that will be 25 D.M. Three percent goes to charity. The first drink is on the house, after that you start paying, hold on to your stub". The club was situated in a cellar, and the music wafting up the stairs was deafening. Reaching the bottom, he pushed aside a heavy curtain to find more bodies milling about than he'd somehow expected. Lighting was provided by five or six overhead spots shedding multi-colored beams onto the crowd. A five piece band dressed in lederhosen provided most of the noise.

Quite a few of the ex-comrades were already half smashed, no doubt having loaded up before their arrival. By now the relating of war stories proceeded at a fast clip fueled by large quantities of exaggeration. The safer a person had managed to remain during the conflict metamorphosed into their becoming war heroes with the passage of time. Karl almost puked on overhearing some of the conversations at the bar. Looking around at the crowd he felt relieved not seeing anyone he knew. One or two faces were vaguely familiar, but none showed any recognition on their part.

About an hour later the band gave a drum roll and additional lights were switched on at the far end of the room. A large table draped with the old war flag stood in a corner with several chairs lined up alongside. Suddenly a side door opened and a rather stupid looking type goose stepped towards the table and remained stiffly at attention. It was all Karl could do to refrain from laughing. Another man then entered and after some heavy breathing into a microphone, launched into a spiel about the welcoming committee who'd organized and put up money to make the reunion possible. This got a big hand, with everyone clapping and whistling and a few stomping the floor like young bulls. Karl suspected the local hookers later on would do a roaring trade with all this available spare energy. Two morons in the crowd did a self-conscious 'Sieg Heil' causing nervous giggles from some of their friends.

A clarion bugle call was sounded, and one of three names listed as a contact in the newspaper, stepped smartly forward and launched into a few corny platitudes. Karl yawned as another comrade got up who thankfully didn't have too much to say. It was the last speaker that riveted Karl's attention. This time a drum roll with trumpets accompanied the speaker when he climbed onto the table with the aid of a chair. The audience fell silent as the previous speaker glowingly introduced him as "our great benefactor and committee chairman... Heinz Wittich." Loud cheering erupted as Karl stared at him through a smoky haze, convinced it was the man he knew. The beard and smartly tailored suit had confused him. Karl closed his eyes listening intently. He recognized the tone and accent of the Heinz Wittich he remembered.

Somebody brushed past Karl clutching steins of beer in each hand heading towards comrades clustered in front of the speaker. On impulse Karl followed in the wake of the beer carrier and with judicious elbowing ended up almost within reach of the chairman's highly polished shoes. Ostensibly Karl reached for some leaflets piled at the edge of the table as Wittich raised an arm to emphasize a point. Karl's gaze was drawn to the hand as the arm lowered, leaving him sick in the stomach. It had taken but a few seconds to confirm a terrible truth, he was looking at the very ring examined in the gazebo. Its distinctive design and beautiful workmanship were etched in his mind for ever, providing a clincher regarding the wearer's identity.

During thunderous applause Wittich was helped down from the table by two beefy cohorts, as Karl made his way back to the bar enraged. It seemed hard to accept but it was evident Wittich had somehow recovered the St. Lucien. As Karl downed his beer he ruefully recalled contemplating wearing the ring until dissuaded by Fritz Freiburg. Karl stayed at the club just long enough to elicit some information from one of the ex-comrades to whom he had offered a drink. The man said he understood Herr Wittich was an art dealer in Dortmund and thought he also had a place in Berlin.

This gave Karl enough to go on for the moment, so giving an excuse of needing the washroom he got up and made for the exit, but before reaching it his left foot snagged the leg of a display stand supporting a blown-up photo of the Chateau Lancour. It wobbled slightly before Karl managed to steady it swearing under his breath, certainly not wanting to draw any attention to himself at this point. Five minutes later he was in a taxi on the way back to his hotel.

31

RECONNAISSANCE

Arriving in Dortmund Karl headed towards the hotel Luxembourg where he'd made a reservation. Having stayed there often he'd grown to like its ambiance. The exterior was somewhat dilapidated and in general the building was past its prime, but the interior was kept spic and span and the beds were comfortable. Sitting on his bed in room twenty-seven, Karl tried relaxing listening to a music program on the radio. He felt keyed up and soon reached for a telephone directory sitting on the dresser. Turning to residential listings under the 'W' heading he ran an index finger down until stopping at 'Wittich' which produced a small grunt of satisfaction. There were seven entries but only one was followed by 'Heinz H.' making his pulse quicken.

It couldn't have been simpler, just the act of consulting a phone book provided the address. Karl leaned against the headboard cradling the back of his head with both hands, letting his mind work out various stratagems. With Fritz out of the picture, Karl had assumed he was the only one knowing the treasure's location, but having seen that extraordinary ring his world had turned upside down. How in hell did the bastard get his hands on it? The thought was paralyzing, Karl felt as if he'd been cheated out of an inheritance. One thing was certain, if Wittich had his paws on the treasure, a reckoning was long overdue. Stretching out on the bed his mind in turmoil, he eventually fell asleep dreaming about Dreux and his pal Fritz.

Early next morning after finishing a hearty breakfast, Karl walked to a nearby newspaper kiosk. He bought a large scale map of the city and its environs before returning to his room. Spreading out the map he studied it for a while and made one or two notes. It wasn't difficult correlating Wittich's address with a grid reference which Karl circled. Feeling upbeat he grabbed his coat and went downstairs. After calling his department head at VASA on the lobby phone, Karl requested a few personal days off which was O.K.'d as it was a slack time of year.

Karl collected his car placing the folded map with the relevant portion uppermost on the passenger seat, and headed south out of the city sprawl. The number of houses began dwindling and he was soon into rural surroundings. Pulling over to the side of the road he glanced at the map and it became obvious he'd overshot the last turn. Reversing into a muddy lane and back tracking almost three kilometers, Karl turned right as the map indicated. The gravel road inclined gently and glancing in the mirror he noticed the edges of the city were still enveloped in morning fog. Cruising approximately five minutes he slowed to inspect what appeared to be several vacation cottages standing back from the road. The area was heavily wooded making it hard to ascertain if more places were further back. Driving slowly, it was only a few minutes before Karl saw an expensive wrought iron sign bearing a familiar name. He could hardly have missed it, the name WITTICH was emblazoned on a background of five stars. The driveway ran straight for a short distance before disappearing around a bend.

Karl drove a little further along the road then stopped.

Releasing the hood catch he got out and stood in front of the vehicle pretending to look at the engine, while studying the immediate vicinity. He figured this deception would allay suspicions of any passers by. Walking a short distance in both directions he found nothing of any particular interest. Karl Bayer decided to take a chance and jogged up the villa's driveway. If he met the owner he'd bluff, mentioning car trouble and needing a phone. Rounding the first curve he saw yet another in the distance, but within a few minutes had his first glimpse of an opulent residence. Karl was shocked to see such obvious wealth and was filled with unease. Had the St Lucien treasure provided the wherewithal?

From where he stood it was hard to discern any activity inside the villa. Despite being a cold day no smoke issued from the chimneys, leading him to hope it was vacant. The villa stood on a raised mound culminating in a steep hillock on the far side, the top of which looked almost level with the villa's roof. Most of the slope was covered by mature pines reaching up from dense undergrowth. Karl instinctively knew this provided the ideal location for an observation site. He made a quick sketch of the general topography before stuffing the notebook back in his pocket and walking away. The Eastern front had ingrained finely honed awareness to danger, making him reasonably sure his scouting foray had gone unnoticed.

Reaching the car he slammed the hood down and sat for a few minutes allowing the heater to warm up. Moving off he felt pleased with the way things had gone. In the first three kilometers he saw only an old man walking a dog, a couple of motorcyclists and an ancient Opel delivery van. Back at the hotel he checked the front desk for messages before going to his room where he indulged in a hot bath. Stretched out on a sofa with his feet propped up, he began orchestrating how to proceed with his surveillance mission. He jotted down reminders about canned food and the necessity for a good vacuum flask, winter stake outs could be cold and boring requiring a great deal of patience. A second scan of the list assured him he'd pretty well covered anything needed to put him in business. He'd start making purchases first thing in the morning.

* * * * * * * *

The owner of Schmitter's "Jaeger Haus" helped Karl load the car and wished him a good hunting trip. Bayer smiled wondering what the proprietor would have thought if he'd realized his customer was after a two legged quarry as opposed to the wild boar mentioned earlier. Karl drove a short distance then pulled into a park and checked his purchases which included warm underwear, boots and an expensive sleeping bag. The costliest item had been second hand Zeiss night glasses still bearing a label imprinted with Wehrmacht serial numbers.

Karl wasn't too concerned with the cost of items, but he wanted to make sure he hadn't overlooked anything. He placed a stubby hunter's knife in the dash compartment, a wicked looking weapon with finely ground edges sheathed in a tooled leather holster. Inside a small bag on the passenger seat was a flashlight, rubber gloves and an old Austrian automatic recently bought from a shifty character in a bar. The man had thrown in two boxes of ammo as part of the deal. While halted in traffic, Karl looked out of his window at an advertising kiosk plastered with movie posters, one in particular caught his attention. It promoted Oskar Lemmel and Heidi Frommer in 'Late Revenge'. It summed up the present situation quite well he thought, maybe he could get to see it. A car behind him honked as traffic began moving again, prompting Karl to give a crude gesture.

* * * * * * * *

After settling up his hotel bill Karl drove towards the villa and continued past the spot where he'd previously parked. Nearly a kilometer further on he spotted what appeared to be an abandoned stone quarry. Six open boxcars stood rusting on a spur line where tall weeds and grass partially obliterated the rail tracks, Karl decided they would provide excellent cover from the road. Returning to the car he drove it along the bumpy ground and parked on the far side of the rolling stock. It was risky and everything might come unglued if he were careless, but for the moment he couldn't think of a better idea and wanted to start surveillance as soon as possible.

Karl carried the heavier items of equipment from the car and stowed them temporarily behind a stack of logs on the hillside, then returned for the smaller items. It took him a while but finally everything was transferred safely to the observation point earmarked earlier. He tried making himself as comfortable as possible knowing a long waiting period might ensue.

The following day brought a sharp drop in temperature and he blew on his hands trying to warm them... a waiting period wasn't a problem, years of deprivation in Mother Russia had already conditioned him. Information was the thing of prime importance to formulate the next move. Waiting until mid afternoon he made his way circuitously to the west side of the villa. Only a trained person could have detected his movements. Since the start of his vigil only one or two small animals and a few curious birds had been sighted, but there was no sign of any human inhabitants in the area.

All he needed was for Heinz Wittich to show up but there was no assurance it would happen, maybe it would require a lot more than just being patient. In a worst case scenario he would have to bury the equipment somewhere using the trenching tool, and return at a later date. Reaching the hidden side of Wittich's place he lay in the long grass checking out the villa's features. What looked to be an insubstantial wooden door faced him, probably the entrance to an utility room. Then he spotted something he stupidly hadn't thought of... wiring for an alarm system. The slipshod installers had simply run exposed wires along the underside of the eaves. Pulling on rubber gloves then checking to see if the coast was clear he made a dash for the door.

On second thoughts cutting the alarm wires could prove highly dangerous, so the door looked more promising. It had a hinged glass window in the upper half and was locked from the inside. A wire mesh insect screen was in front of the glass. Using the blade of the hunting knife Karl pried up four molding strips on it's periphery, poking and twisting the knife blade to expose a gap between wood and metal. Gently he eased out the whole assembly and leaned it against the wall. Risks taken so far were paying off... no alarm bell sounded when Karl reached through the aperture and turned the key still in the door knob.

Hardly believing his luck he replaced the door window carefully, tapping the molding nails back in place with the butt of his automatic. Pocketing the key he entered the villa and moved out of what appeared to be a storage room and found his way to the main living area. A few beads of sweat ran down his face which were quickly wiped away but he was elated. Had the alarm activated it would have been a different story. Maybe there was a secondary system that could trip at any time, and Wittich, or a complete stranger could surprise him so he didn't want to get cocky. The important thing was entry had been gained without creating obvious signs, it was like Russian roulette some of his comrades had once played and could prove just as deadly. Karl had no doubt Heinz Wittich would eliminate him without a second thought if he found out who he was, but Karl wasn't about to give him that opportunity.

The inside of the villa was sumptuous but Karl barely noticed, needing to concentrate on finding the best place for concealment when he returned for an impending confrontation with Wittich. He would pick a moment, then strike like a cobra... he could hardly wait to find answers to questions that tormented him. He knew the right methods to make his opponent talk, as the Russian camps had taught him well. To avoid errors in an unfamiliar and possibly darkened villa interior, Karl noted carefully the placement of furniture. Giving a final look around Karl left the way he'd entered. Leaving the utility room door unlocked he reluctantly left such comfortable surroundings in exchange for a spartan hideout... hell, the place even had a pool, but caution demanded leaving while ahead of the game...

32

UNEXPECTED CORPSE

HAVING VIEWED THE ST LUCIEN TREASURE, guest and host returned to the lounge where Heinz unlocked a desk drawer and withdrew a small plastic bag filled with white powder bought from one of his Afghan contacts in Berlin. He'd spooned out a small quantity into two saucers placed on the table, and carefully pushed one across the shiny surface. As the effect of the drug took hold, Peter couldn't contain the demons swamping his mind and felt extremely agitated. Stumbling over words, he'd rambled on awhile before demanding Heinz sell four artifacts he coveted. Peter was prepared to pay almost anything... my God, surely the man knew how he felt? Going beyond the bounds of reason he even offered to throw in Laura, if a deal could be struck.

Spilling drink down his jacket Heinz just laughed in his face saying "My friend, pull yourself together... these things can never be sold to anyone, they are mine... mine forever." Despite the thin lipped smile Wittich's eyes narrowed to slits. Possibly it was at this point that Peter developed an overwhelming dislike for the man before him. Too many drinks coupled with drugs caused a throbbing inside his head as Wittich carried on talking. "You can't begin to understand the euphoria of possessing such an exquisite collection." Later, through gaps in a murky fog, Peter Hahn recalled these final words spoken by his host.

* * * * * * * *

Although blotted out in Peter's mind, he'd issued wild threats of using his power as a minister of state which only gained scornful looks from Heinz, who'd shrugged them off in a derisive manner. In the extremely hostile atmosphere both men had argued vehemently. Sounds of raised voices had awoken Laura, who'd padded over to the open railed balcony and yelled "What the hell is going on down there? For God's sake why don't you come up to bed." Not feeling up to investigating further she'd gone straight back to their room and slammed the door. Peter Hahn crawled on his hands and knees up the stairs before blacking out.

Around mid-morning Laura opened her eyes and couldn't think where she was. Her head pounded and it took a little time before realizing her lover lay sprawled out on the floor snoring fitfully. He looked disgusting with traces of vomit still clinging to his shirt. Laura rolled over, closed her eyes and drifted off again. Approximately an hour passed before she awoke the second time, got out of bed and headed for the bathroom. She showered and donned a robe before glancing at Hahn noting his inert form still in the same position breathing heavily. Laura badly needed coffee, and gingerly made her way downstairs. Filling and plugging in the percolator she half pulled back the kitchen curtains waiting for the beverage to brew. She walked across to the lounge looking for a magazine she'd leafed through the previous evening before they'd gone out to dinner.

Suddenly Laura tensed then froze... Heinz Wittich's body lay crumpled in one corner, and even a quick glance indicated a corpse. Walking over for a closer look confirmed the impression, the eyes stared blankly up at the ceiling from a white rigid face which had a small trickle of congealed blood in one corner of the mouth. A knife handle protruded from his chest just below the heart and a pool of blood had soaked into the thick carpet forming a surreal pattern. Laura walked back to the kitchen where the coffee was ready and poured out a cup. Today she needed it strong and black. "Oh shit, this is exactly what I need right now" she muttered to herself, the pounding in her head had returned with a vengeance.

Laura Ichenko picked up the phone and dialed a number putting her through to a covert K.G.B. sub-station in Berlin. She heard four clicks signifying auto recording before beginning to speak. "The patient is terminally sick… I require the services of Herr Keppelman. Urgent." The number she'd dialed identified her agent code name and the message signified her 'patient' needed immediate relocation. This team were adept in disposal of unwanted cadavers that might cause embarrassment. They were sometimes referred to as 'garbage men' within the organization.

After replacing the phone Laura smoked another cigarette then went back upstairs. She started dressing as Peter stirred slightly and opened one eye. Kneeling beside him her robe fell open revealing her sexy underwear. Despite a terrible hangover Peter was still able to appreciate the superb body. After managing to raise his eyes to the level of her face he immediately knew this wasn't going to evolve into a bedroom romp of any kind, he felt far too sick and Laura's face was hard as stone. "What's the matter, Liebchen?" Laura continued staring with an expression that registered both distaste and anger.

"You stupid bastard, do you realize you've killed him?" The words took a few seconds gaining his attention one hundred percent. Peter struggled to concentrate, breathing deeply. "What on earth are you talking about, I couldn't kill anyone even if I tried." Laura eyed him coolly. "There is always the first time, anybody can, under certain circumstances, and your turn apparently came sometime last night. We need to go downstairs and survey your handiwork, then you can tell me again how you couldn't kill someone, but before you do I need to tell you I've already checked the place out and there are no signs of a break in, but if you want to look for yourself go ahead. At first I didn't want to believe you'd done it, but what else am I to conclude?"

* * * * * * * *

Peter felt sure Laura had it right as he stared at the corpse, God was he really responsible for this? As he got out of a chair and began walking unsteadily up the stairs behind Laura, he felt like throwing up again and had a hard time moving. He shuddered at the realization he'd become a murderer. Slumping against the banister rail Peter supported his chin with both hands until Laura broke the silence. "I'm going to make a couple of phone calls and meanwhile I suggest you pour yourself black coffee and add a stiff dose of cognac." Normally Peter Hahn was regarded as a fairly impassive character, and if he'd only been able to recall more of the evening's events his behavior when seeing the treasure would have astounded him... His outburst was totally alien to his nature. Peter Hahn hadn't the foggiest idea how long he'd stayed downstairs with his host. Unfortunately, however hard he tried to remember, the worse the horrific turn of events all became. Sporadically, fragments from the previous evening came into his mind then instantly evaporated... nothing seemed to connect properly in the crazy mosaic. He recalled at one point leaning against a wall staring at the magnificent treasure overwhelmed with emotion.

* * * * * * * *

After making her phone calls Laura looked at her lover and shook her head before remarking. "I guess you totally lose it when you are drunk... unbelievable!" Peter didn't reply, absorbed by the catastrophe he'd caused. Unless some sort of miracle occurred he'd be swinging from the end of a rope in a federal prison. This prospect terrified him as he conjured up the stunned reactions of his political colleagues... the newspaper headlines weren't hard to visualize. Sadly he thought of the shock to his ex-wife and their two children when the news broke, and wondered how they'd cope with the disgrace. Ironically, he wondered if anyone else knew about the treasure, but a fat lot of good that did him in the present circumstances. He'd thrown away his career, and certainly lost Laura in one fell swoop. Soon his very life would be added to the list, and black thoughts made him contemplate suicide.

Shortly after Peter's twenty second birthday he'd been invited to a wild stag party and when it broke up everyone stopped off at a grungy wayside bar. While sitting at the end of the bar an evil looking gypsy woman sidled up with an offer to foretell Peter's future if he crossed her palm with silver. Other than himself, only one of his friends took up on the gypsy's entreaty. The crone predicted a dire event of some sort for Peter Hahn... He'd laughed it off, though a small twinge of nervousness made his mirth a little forced. He never asked what she'd predicted for Paul, as he seemed somewhat withdrawn after the session. Seven weeks later, at a level crossing about a kilometer from the bar, Paul's car was hit and demolished by a freight train. He was pulled from the wreck by a farm worker, but died in hospital the following day. Peter was at his bedside, as Paul's last words whispered to a doctor were "the gypsy was right."

* * * * * * * *

Peter winced remembering the prophesy as Laura sat down next to him interrupting his chain of thought. "O.K. Peter, make sure you listen to what I'm about to tell you very,

very carefully." She began divulging the true state of their relationship and his jaw sagged as he listened. "You work for the Soviets? I just don't believe it." Laura lit another cigarette before taking his hand, "Well you better believe because it happens to be true, I really was starting to fall in love with you, what a waste but there's no way of turning back the clock." She remained silent a moment in order to help Peter regain his composure. He seemed incapable of absorbing further assaults to the mind. "This is what is going to happen, you will drive to Freiburg near the Swiss border. Book in at the St. Anton hotel and ask for the owner who is one of our operatives and will be expecting you. Stay in your room, your meals and anything else you need will be brought to you. Park your car in the courtyard and leave the key under the driver's seat. The vehicle will be disposed of by K.G.B. agents, known within the organization as the 'vultures'."

Laura's face allowed the merest hint of a smile while saying this, as she stubbed out a cigarette. "Be very careful not to show your face any more than necessary en route. Keep a sharp look out when you stop for gas or enter a toilet. Wait until you arrive at the St. Anton before eating, and wear one of Wittich's hats, there are some hanging up in the entranceway. I will join you at the hotel as soon as I can." Laura stood up and smoothed her skirt then went to the kitchen for more coffee. After setting down two cups, Peter immediately asked "What happens in Freiburg?" Laura noted his acute anxiety, eyes blinking rapidly while a nerve in the left cheek twitched spasmodically. She remembered an instructor at the finishing school talking about such symptoms in people experiencing extreme stress.

"It all seems totally incomprehensible to me…" Laura cut him off "You bloody fool, just do as I tell you if we are to survive this fucking mess, my friends will take care of Wittich, and as for yourself, get used to the idea of assuming a new identity, I take it you prefer to go on living?" Peter wasn't sure he'd heard correctly but nodded assent, earlier contemplation of suicide had receded. "Our people will do such a good job that by the time they are finished, you won't even recognize your own features. Weeks ago a contingency plan was devised for the kind of situation we are into, although nobody believed it would need to be activated. The murder was unforeseen, but the possibility of getting you out of the country was factored in from the beginning. We didn't want the Federal Protection Agency putting the squeeze on you if things turned sour, thereby finding out what information the K.G.B. possessed regarding the treaty talks. It is a lot better politically for both sides if you just disappear into thin air.

You will be disguised to look like an elderly academic. Forged papers and anything else required will be provided by the owner of the St. Anton prior to crossing the border. You will be in a wheel chair accompanied by a female attendant." Laura flicked ash from her cigarette, then continued. "I think you will be injected with a drug called 'Axelone' which simulates the symptoms of a person suffering from Alzheimer's disease. It doesn't cause any long term effects as far as I know. The K.G.B. laboratories are quite proud of their new toy developed last year. It has already been used quite successfully."

Peter thought the whole thing sounded like science fiction and Laura noted the incredulous expression. "Do you doubt what I am telling you? Just remember this plan was orchestrated before we ever met. The K.G.B. is very efficient Peter." Hahn bit his lower lip and nodded then spread out the palms of his hands. "It's just so bizarre somehow, but with my neck in the balance I suppose I don't have any options?" "No frankly you don't." Laura snapped, by now even her nerves were starting to fray a little around the edges. "I suggest we both eat something before your departure as our agents will probably arrive shortly after it gets dark." Peter lay down on the couch with his head on a cushion as Laura went into the kitchen to prepare sandwiches. He again tried recalling events that happened just a few hours previously, but it was hopeless… if only he could relax a little.

Standing up he slowly walked over to Wittich's body and stared once more at the murder victim. His eyes were again drawn to the knife buried in the man's chest, the one he must have gripped when killing his host. Where had he got it from? Was it from the kitchen drawer? He felt certain he had never seen it before. Peter hated seeing anything killed let alone perpetrate such an act. It seemed implausible, but during a drunken state combined with mind altering drugs he supposed anything was possible. Suddenly, standing there, further disjointed snatches of the previous night's argument penetrated his head… Leibe Gott, he must have entered a realm some termed hell on earth. The St Lucien treasure and its late owner had combined in creating a terrible nightmare. Despite everything, Peter felt a compelling desire for a last look at the treasure, which was thwarted by Laura calling him to come and eat.

They ate their snack in total silence. Finishing, Peter pushed back his chair and brushed away a few stray crumbs from his lap. "Well I had better get going I suppose." Laura nodded, without looking up. As Peter put on his raincoat she handed him his small travel bag and reminded him about the hat. He took one off the rack, thinking it looked like something a game keeper might wear. Somehow it didn't reflect the image of its ex-owner.

Glancing at his features in a hallway mirror he was startled by the pale reflection. His face had the same pallor as the corpse, and combined with the hat he supposed it offered some sort of disguise. With a slight grimace he walked through the door and got into the car as Laura followed him out. She stood by the driver's door as he rolled down the window. "Just don't get stopped for a stupid traffic violation, O.K.?" She turned on her heel, as Peter lit a cigarette and watched her retreating figure. Christ, she hadn't even said good-bye. He let in the clutch. Pity he couldn't engage his mind in like manner, then perhaps he could begin hating her despite the fact she was saving his neck. Everything was too exhausting to contemplate... maybe, just maybe it would all come together later on. Meanwhile he needed to stay alert for the long drive ahead. Laura half turned, with tears in her eyes, in time to watch the car disappear past the first bend.

33

CAT AND MOUSE

PROPPED UP ON ONE ELBOW, KARL lay hidden in the undergrowth for what seemed a long time. Every so often he would scan the villa with his field glasses... it was getting boring, there were no signs of life except for the occasional rabbit and one or two squirrels chasing one another. He mulled over when to insert himself in the villa as an uninvited guest.

Although restless, Karl wasn't about to discard his natural caution. Nearly a day had passed since the initial break-in. Feeling hungry he'd made a snack of wurst and stale cheese and was wiping the rim of the vacuum flask when he spotted a car coming up the driveway... Heinz Wittich was returning from his business trip to Berlin.

Grabbing his field glasses just in time, Karl watched his nemesis emerge from the passenger side. The driver was a tall man holding a bulging briefcase. Karl memorized the license plate in case he needed to check out the car's owner. By now Karl's pulse rate had quickened realizing how fortuitous the snack had been in delaying his second entry of the villa. About an hour later the man with the briefcase shook hands with Wittich on the doorstep and drove off.

For the remainder of the day nothing else transpired and as night fell the windows of the villa remained darkened. Karl assumed the owner was in a room on the far side. Around 10.40 p.m. the main entranceway light was extinguished probably signifying the owner was off to bed. Karl continued to watch the villa for a while before falling asleep.

* * * * * * * *

Shortly after breakfast next morning Wittich hurriedly got into his car and headed for the central part of Dortmund. He was running late for a meeting with his accountant, and also needed to see two other people regarding damage incurred at the gallery. It was almost dusk before he wrapped things up and returned to the villa. From his vantage point Karl saw the bluish light from a TV reflected in the lounge windows and knew this was the time to confront Wittich, but a sudden bout of indigestion knotted his stomach. Knowing he needed to feel fully fit meant he'd have to postpone things until later the following day. When the stomach pain eased somewhat Karl pulled out his mini flashlight and diary from an inner pocket and crawled into his sleeping bag in order to shield the light. In the blank page for Friday the 24th he wrote 'Adios HW.' then closed his eyes. In the morning Karl found all traces of indigestion had gone, only to be replaced with an attack of the runs. He swore vigorously at whatever 'gremlin' was responsible for making his task so difficult, however by mid-afternoon he felt back to normal and decided to move at dusk, and by the time his mission was completed darkness would prove to be a helpful ally. Karl was revved up… this was the chance he'd waited for. Minutes after making his decision, yet another car came into view… it was a blue Porsche roadster with it's top down and a man and woman inside. Karl felt disconcerted… who were these people, and what was their connection with Wittich? Extra people on the scene could only complicate matters.

Finally Wittich and his guests left much to the relief of Karl Bayer.

* * * * * * * *

Using the utility room key Karl entered the villa and headed for the spot picked out initially. A big built in cupboard had seemed the best choice, as it was located in a narrow room close to the lounge and ran the length of one wall. Three louvered doors on tracks provided access and convenient listening to any nearby conversations. Karl rechecked the interior. Two cedar boxes of the type used for shipping loose tea sat on the floor containing old electrical appliances and rolls of miscellaneous wiring. One of the boxes would provide a seat while he was in hiding. He had no way of knowing how long he'd be stuck in there, so with that in mind he'd refrained from drinking anything once inside the villa. Miscellaneous golf clubs and gardening tools were propped up at one end, and piled up on one of the tea chests were boxes of children's games. Idly he looked at a couple of them. The first was a jigsaw of a medieval castle being attacked by knights in armor and the one below had a photo on the lid showing a little girl sitting at a school desk. She was diligently decorating a small Christmas tree. On lifting the box something rattled inside and curiosity made him take a look. Three sections of contoured Styrofoam obviously fitted atop one another to form a tree. The rattling noise had been caused by tiny colored beads intended for decoration. Two tubes of adhesive were provided for affixing them to the Styrofoam. Karl replaced the lid, then quickly glanced inside a third box containing a wooden kit for assembling a sailing ship. He vaguely wondered why Wittich kept such items in the villa. Briefly his thoughts skipped to boyhood remembering his best friend Hans, and the way they had shared their toys… where was he now he wondered?

Apart from two paintings with broken frames, and a stack of flower pots, this about completed the inventory, so leaving a door of the cupboard open Karl stepped into the room. The mini flashlight helped locate a downstairs toilet… a welcome luxury considering his recent privations. Choosing an armchair not far from the cupboard he settled back to wait hoping it wouldn't take forever before the threesome returned. He tried shutting out thoughts of drink and food sitting in the darkness… the vital thing was listening for the sound of tires scrunching on gravel. Headlights ought to be visible through the far window of the room which was more or less in line with the drive and the position of his armchair. Karl was confident he'd have enough time to hop back into his hiding place where risk of discovery was unlikely, but anyone brash enough opening a door would be looking at the business end of his automatic

* * * * * * * *

The capital city of Bavaria was experiencing another cold snap during the winter of 1962. Chief Inspector Leopold Steiner felt tired and slightly depressed. Glancing at his watch he noted it was already 7:30 p.m. He re-entered his office after having stepped out for a plate of wurst washed down with a 'Franzisker spaten'. A file sat in the middle of the desk with its routing list stapled to the outside. His name and title headed a list of three other people, and in one corner of the cover the nomenclature 'URGENT AND CONFIDENTIAL' was stamped as if to taunt him. Having seen these words too often he knew what lay in store, they always spelt trouble. While he'd been eating his snack a few minutes previously he'd hoped the damn file might disappear by some form of osmosis, but a long police career taught him not to expect such miracles. With his feet propped on the desk, Steiner wondered why any person in his right mind would spend a lifetime poking about in the fetid dregs of humanity… it certainly wasn't for the money, his latest bank statements were ample testament on that score.

The early days on the beat following graduation from the "Ritterhelm" police academy had been exciting and any boring periods were mostly forgotten. Promotions had been slow, but with the passage of time he'd worked up the ladder without getting overly involved in departmental politics, apart from the disgusting era when official duties forced co-operation with Gestapo thugs. He supposed his contributions in fighting the 'War on Crime' accomplished something useful over the years for the citizens who helped pay his salary, at least he hoped this was the case, but with the new breed of criminals nowadays it was getting harder to tell. A culture of violence and drugs was beginning to blur any picture of real achievement.

The soft purr of the phone interrupted this chain of thought. "Leo?… I thought you might have left by now. Please drop by my office before you do." Leo groaned, replacing the receiver knowing his boss Kurt Stroebel, the Police Commissioner, wouldn't be ringing this late unless it was trouble on the horizon. It was hard enough to get hold of the man if Leo had matters to discuss, but when it was the other way around Stroebel wouldn't hesitate getting him out of bed. Putting on his jacket, Steiner yawned regretting he'd not gone straight home after eating.

* * * * * * * *

Leo Steiner was part of 'UNIT H' responsible for so called 'Special cases'. The Chancellor's office decided when a crime fell into this category. They were comparatively rare and usually very complicated it seemed to Leo. 'Special cases' always took precedence over 'normal crimes' handled by the unit most of the time. They had been relocated to an upper area of a multilevel building until renovations now under way at the main police H.Q. were completed. The commissioner's office was on a floor below Steiner's, and taking the stairs rather than the elevator, Leo walked down a carpeted corridor and tapped on the end door.

"Come in, my friend." Kurt Stroebel rose from behind his desk indicating two easy chairs. "Drink... whiskey, brandy?" Leo indicated the latter. As his chief poured out drinks into glasses on a rosewood credenza Leo's eyes wandered over the expensive furnishings and potted plants, before focusing on his boss. He speculated they must both be in the same age group. A tall handsome man, Kurt was wearing tortoise shell rimmed glasses pushed back on top of well tonsured hair. 'A smooth political animal,' as someone had once described him at a police party. Steiner wondered if having the same traits might have put himself in the commissioner's spot by now? Perhaps, perhaps not. Inwardly he knew he had a better track record than his superior, so far as solid police work went, and a gut feeling told him this was the reason for his latest summons to the almighty. "Well Leo what do you think?" The chief inspector sat hunched slightly forward cradling a brandy goblet between his hands. "So far I've only been able to skim the content of the file, but it seems to be one of the more bizarre cases I've come across."

Stroebel stood up and was pacing in front of his desk. "Well, its going to be another one like the Olaf Lundgren case all over again. You recall that particular horror I'm sure." Leo remembered all right, how could he forget? The murder of a Swedish trade delegate had taken place three years ago. Eventually he'd solved the case, and although the regular police investigation was bad enough, pressure from Bonn and the media nearly sent him to the 'funny farm' before its conclusion. An ironic part was having done all the donkey work and Stroebel hardly lifting a finger, it was his boss who'd reaped all the glory. Yes, he remembered that particular case, together with others which catapulted the commissioner to the top of the heap. "My phone has been ringing off the hook all day." Kurt had a hurt expression on his face, the man would have drawn rave notices if he'd chosen a stage career. "I'm getting the usual stuff from the politico's, and now the media boys are onto it." Stroebel sighed. "Anyway, I've been able to tell my superior I've got the best man in the department heading things up. There's going to be pressure Leo… lots of it. I'll do my best to keep the mosquitoes off your back, but I can only do so much, which I'm sure you'll appreciate."

Leo swallowed his drink and sucked on his pipe. Looking at his chief he mused… shit, go play your violin somewhere else. Stroebel's words "I know you'll give it your best shot" irritated him as he walked back to his office. The whole meeting had taken less than an hour, and already a panic clock was ticking away. Leo took the elevator to the underground parking area and walked quickly to where his B.M.W. was parked. He had bought the car three months ago. It was luxurious, but somehow it didn't give him particular feelings of well-being, although a few years ago he'd have given his right arm to own one. In fact nowadays material things didn't rate high in Leo Steiner's life, even if to a casual bystander seeing him pull into traffic might have pegged its driver as a symbol of the new German 'Wirtschaftwunder' arisen from ruins of the third Reich.

His only son Otto a fighter pilot, had been shot down and killed in 1940 during air attacks against England, and three years later his wife died during a night bombing raid on his home town of Halle. This had occurred while he'd been away from the city on police business and on his return Leo fought back tears gazing at a pile of rubble which had once been the house they'd scrimped and saved for. The tragedy triggered a nervous breakdown and Leo spent three months in a psychiatric ward exhibiting very bizarre behavior until treatment allowed a reversion to his former self. The doctors were slightly nonplused by his quick recovery tending to attribute it to an experimental drug 'Zeton A' used on their patient, but unfortunately they weren't able to produce the same results on others having similar symptoms. Before the war one of the doctors would have written a paper about Steiner's case... but at the time such a luxury was out of the question in a rapidly collapsing third Reich. Leo's police salary continued during his absence from work and his new superior had offered a few days of convalescent leave before resumption of full time duties. Leo had expressed his thanks but declined the offer. With nobody for companionship he didn't see much point staying idle.

In the beginning he'd managed remarkably well shutting out black thoughts from his mind. As time went by however, memories flooded back. To overcome anger and loneliness, he turned into a workaholic and recluse. Although this eased the pain for a man without an inner core, it left only a battered husk to old friends and co-workers. Then out of the blue he met Hannah... sweet wonderful Hannah, the woman who began pulling him back from the brink of a black hole where his mind had teetered too long. Afterwards he couldn't pinpoint when the metamorphosis took place but knew fate had stepped in at the last moment to restore his sanity.

34

A POLICEMAN'S LOT

NORMALLY THE JOURNEY FROM STEINER'S OFFICE to his apartment on the outskirts of the city took about forty minutes. A forecast storm had already started it's full assault and Leo knew it would take much longer. A bitter wind from out of the north was causing the first snow drifts to accumulate in it's path. By now, most of the city's inhabitants had already reached their homes in the suburbs, and having finished their evening meal were watching TV, as Leo's car approached the Krensler building on the Lindwurmstrassse. Suddenly, the car slid sideways on the glazed road surface, and just missed hitting a stalled truck. Swearing, he decided to concentrate more on his driving and forget the day's events as the wet snow plopped on the windshield with hypnotic effect. A few brave souls on the sidewalk threaded their way carefully, heads bowed against icy blasts, while occasional vehicles spewed showers of frozen slush across the curb compounding their difficulties.

Steiner noticed a conspicuous absence of taxis on the streets; typical he thought, never there when needed. A few traffic policemen, and one or two road crews looked as if they were fighting a losing battle. Criminal activity throughout the city would be minimal as the 'break and entry' boys had sense enough to stay home on nights like this, and no doubt there would be a sharp increase of 'fender bender' incidents entered into the log books of the traffic department. Finally pulling into his apartment parking space, Leo gave a sigh of relief. Loathe to leave the comforting warmth of the car, he kept the engine running with the heater on high. Slouched in his seat he ruminated on the reason why he hadn't opted for full retirement after reaching his sixty-fifth birthday three years ago... what an idiot! Now, he felt burnt out with endless case assignments demanding grueling hours, not to mention getting home late from the office especially if it was shitty weather. One last hurrah, then he'd turn in his resignation... Leo laughed out loud thinking about his nickname 'Dinosaur' which some of the detectives used behind his back... so be it. These young bucks in their Italian tailored suits could take the ball now and see how far they got from square one. He would monitor progress of the new high tech crowd simply by watching the popular TV show 'National Crime Watch' from the confines of an armchair... Leo would no longer be found in the trenches, thank heavens.

Pocketing the ignition key, he slammed the car door and made his way along the snow encrusted pathway towards the lobby. Returning at the end of a hard day always gave him a lift especially whenever his spirits sagged. Max, the Siamese cat jumped down from the sofa, stretched and came over to rub against his legs. After walking through to the kitchen, Leo loaded the coffee maker and switched it on before moving to the bedroom. Sitting on the edge of the bed for a moment he gazed at two photos mounted in embossed silver frames. One showed his son Otto wearing Luftwaffe uniform standing beside an Me 109 fighter... it had been taken shortly before the fatal flight over England in August 1940. The other one was a picture of his wife on their second anniversary and Leo felt tears welling up and blew his nose before removing his suit and tie. Next on the agenda would be a hot bath, read the newspaper, and perhaps fill out the tax form that had been sitting around for days. Hopefully Hannah would call him sometime before he climbed into bed.

Stretching out in the bath water was pure heaven, and Leo felt the last vestiges of irritability slide away allowing his mind to become blissfully blank. He'd almost finished toweling himself when the phone rang... if that was the commissioner... no, it must be Hannah. "Hello, Steiner here." Hannah's laugh made him smile. "You pompous old goat. Did you think it was the police calling?" "Er no, not exactly but it could have been... and I'm not pompous, I'm naked." Hannah laughed again. "In that case I should be around in the blink of an eye, but it's late and the weather is filthy, so let's make it tomorrow." They chatted a while longer before ringing off. In fact Leo was quite pleased to be on his own. With their relationship it wasn't necessary to be in one another's arms every five minutes, just knowing they had each other when needed was sufficient. He felt drained as he slowly poured a little cognac into the coffee.

* * * * * * * *

Thank God the paper didn't have more screaming headlines about this latest murder which was going to employ all of his savvy before resolution, and it would get resolved because this was his last effort. Snuggling down in the bed Leo switched on the electric blanket a younger brother in Canada had sent the previous Christmas. The gift had necessitated buying a transformer but the cost was worthwhile, and he let his body enjoy the comforting warmth. Normally he'd fall instantly asleep, but tonight he lay awake in the dark listening to the wind buffeting the bedroom windows as if it was trying to enter the room.

Thoughts generated by the file pictures of the corpse

were interspersed with ones of Stroebel and Hannah... but he tried very hard to concentrate on Hannah, by far the nicest subject. They had met eighteen months ago at a birthday party where a mutual friend introduced them, and they'd instantly hit it off. Hannah, a widow was younger than himself and also a good-looker. At the time he'd wondered why she hadn't remarried after her husband had been killed during the latter part of the war. She'd come to live with her only daughter in the western sector of Berlin after renting out her house on the outskirts of Leipzig. Rental payments had long since ceased, after some official in the East German 'nomenclature' commandeered the place for his family. After leaving the DRG Hannah secured a job with a large department store in Berlin, and worked herself up to become its chief buyer which necessitated a move to Munich.

Since their initial meeting Leo and Hannah felt their respective lives had taken on new meaning. They would eventually marry, but for now the relationship was perfect the way it was. Both felt a need to exorcise specters from the past before taking the final step. Leo rolled over and drifted off as Max jumped onto the bed to share in the warmth.

* * * * * * * *

The business of transporting Peter Hahn across the border between Germany and Switzerland had taken place without problems. Before the transfer Laura had taken the night train to Berlin for a meeting with her case officer. He'd received fresh orders from Moscow. Afterwards she visited her bank and did some shopping prior to catching a plane to Basle, where she rented a car for the short journey north to Freiburg. Laura needed to double-check the new arrangements for Peter Hahn's defection. Moscow central had been explicit, making known it wouldn't countenance further foul–ups regarding the Hahn case, and Laura took note of the veiled warning.

After talking with the owner of the St. Anton she went upstairs to Peter's room and knocked on the door. After identifying herself, Peter got up from his bed where he'd been reading magazines and newspapers. When he opened the door Laura hardly recognized her recent lover. Peter seemed listless and indifferent to her presence, which in the circumstances made the final parting somewhat easier. Finishing a cup of coffee she handed him two cartons of cigarettes and a box of Swiss chocolates, then asked if there was anything else he needed. Peter slowly shook his head. Leaving the room Laura promised they'd be in touch. Each of them knew this was highly unlikely, given the changed status of their relationship. Laura was aware the Keppelman boys had disposed of the BMW and Peter's car. It was easier to be rid of material things than people. With Peter it would be hard but also necessary. She gave a small sigh and turned the ignition key of the rental car.

35

THE KILLING

AFTER THE HEATED ARGUMENT OVER THE treasure and departure of Peter Hahn for the night, Wittich returned to his study. He sat down and leaned both elbows on the table staring at the artifacts. Dimming the lights to see what effect was produced, he became mesmerized the way various jewels were pinpointed in the semi-darkened room. The events of the evening had left him feeling hot and sweaty. He needed a shower and bed, but somehow couldn't summon up the necessary energy to move. After a big effort, he stood up and removed his shirt and tie which fell to the floor. Feeling distinctly unsteady he collapsed in the nearest chair, and within seconds of flopping down his chin drooped on his chest as sleep overtook him.

From his hiding place Karl Bayer had heard a good deal of the exchanges between Peter Hahn and his host. At the sound of the visitor making his way upstairs he knew his moment had come. Pulling on a black ski mask and removing shoes and socks Karl crept from his hiding place. Barefooted, he silently stalked his prey and had almost reached the dimly lit room before hearing Wittiich's rhythmic snoring. Karl hesitated in awe on seeing the glittering St. Lucien spread out on the table. Revenge along with repossession of the treasure was within grasp and Karl felt a vindication for everything that had transpired since Dreux. A few strides placed him directly behind Wittich's back. He tightened his grip on the knife handle and his fingernails dug into his palm.

Heinz Wittich felt a viselike hold on his shoulder... surely that fool Peter Hahn hadn't come back? Halfway up from his seat he turned sufficiently to see the upper torso of a masked intruder. In horror Wittich's eyes registered a knife blade aimed at his chest... a robbery ? If so he might save his skin by not resisting. Any hope was dashed hearing the chilling words "This my friend is a memento from Sgts. Fritz Freiburg and Karl Bayer". Cold terror took over and the hand gripping his shoulder turned him a few degrees until he fully faced his assailant. Karl's earlier thoughts of questioning the man dissolved in a blind rage at being outsmarted by Heinz Wittich, and he knew he must finish things now. Like a rabbit mesmerized by a snake Heinz saw the glint of a blade describing an arc before penetrating his body. Attempted screams of desperation were stillborn and giving a sickening gurgle he crumpled, falling from the chair. As last vestiges of his life ebbed, his final thoughts revolved around the names uttered by his assailant... but it was too late, the execution had been carried out by an expert.

Karl pulled the mask from his head and although feeling inwardly cold he was sweating as Heinz had seconds before. The physical act of killing meant little having participated in so much slaughter on the Eastern front. The mechanics were merely routine making him immune to acts of violent death. What had occurred hadn't necessarily been on the agenda, but Karl felt a sense of closure. The big question was how to deal expeditiously with the treasure and cover his tracks.

Karl previously had noted various items of camping equipment in the utility room. He fetched four of the sleeping bags and several towels before re-entering the study. Dividing the artifacts between bags he padded the valuables with the towels as well as he could. Almost finished, he froze… somewhere upstairs a phone was ringing. Jerked from a stupefied state, Laura reached over for the receiver, dropped it, and flopped back on the pillow. Peter Hahn was in total oblivion and therefore heard nothing, it was doubtful an explosion would have awakened him.

Karl paused, awaiting resumption of the ringing tone but there was only silence. Breathing easier he would have liked a shot of brandy from a bottle in the next room, but knew it was high time to leave. He paused a moment making sure nothing was left. The prospect of apprehension on a murder charge gave impetus to get moving, therefore his next actions defied logic.

Had it been someone other than his nemesis, Karl would have departed immediately, but now he decided the victim required a farewell token. During the dreadful years of captivity he'd sometimes thought how he would salvage his life if the day of release ever came, but this was only conjecture. At least it helped pass the time and gave strength for daily survival. Maybe resentment regarding the contrast between the art dealer's style of living, and his time in Russia caused the present aberration.

Karl hurriedly retrieved the cross from the sleeping bag he'd just finished packing, then fetched the Xmas tree kit examined earlier. Putting the items on a chair seat he began rolling the body over until it was facing the floor. The knife handle caused a humping of the back suiting Karl's purpose. Using a sharp corner of the cross he rapidly incised a vertical and horizontal ragged cut in the back of the cadaver, roughly duplicating the artifact's profile. Using a towel he blotted blood from the cuts and reaching for the tube of adhesive, squeezed its content into each incision before tamping down a handful of glass beads with his thumb. He rolled the body back to its original position then replaced his socks and shoes. He glanced at the body and muttered "O.K. Herr Wittich, I hope you'll enjoy this souvenir of your precious keepsake in the next life… it would be too wasteful leaving the original with you."

The man had paid the ultimate debt and the saga was ended. Karl hastened outside the villa dragging the sleeping bags across the grass towards a wooden garden shed. Leaving them temporarily propped against its far wall he jogged to his vehicle alongside the boxcars. Driving without lights and in low gear, he returned for the sleeping bags, placing two in the trunk and the remaining ones on the back seat. Having removed his rubber gloves he lit a cigarette as there were no apparent signs of movement within the villa. No doubt Heinz Wittich's guests were soundly sleeping off the effects of good food and drink, while the owner lay sprawled in the deepest sleep of all.

Karl carefully drove along the bumpy ground with the St. Lucien cross lying reassuringly across his thighs and stopped as close to the observation site as he could manage. Shielding the beam of his flashlight he climbed up through the undergrowth feeling exhausted. Gathering his belongings he carried them back to the car having given a final check and deciding everything had been accounted for. Karl drove away in low gear until parking beside the boxcars. He'd try and grab a quick nap before moving off at first light. Awakening from a bad dream just as daylight was chasing away the last vestiges of night. His mouth was parched and he brushed away ants crawling over his forehead. Karl started the car and made his way to the main Dortmund road. He'd stay for a night there before moving on.

* * * * * * * *

Had Karl remained longer at the observation site he'd have been mystified keeping tabs on the villa. The appearance of a white van marked J.Heiderberger, plumbing company, would have struck him as odd considering both house guests were unlikely to be concerned about plumbing problems with a corpse lying in the lounge. He would have been baffled seeing three men emerge from the van wearing mechanics overalls, one carrying a collapsible stretcher. They re-emerged twenty-five minutes later with what could only be a blanket draped body. This would have erased any ideas of a police investigation... only undercover agents used purported commercial vehicles.

Separate departures of Peter Hahn and his glamorous companion would have also been noted, especially as the woman used Wittich's car. It was risky, but probably her only means of transportation available. But of course, during all this time Karl Bayer had been busy elsewhere.

* * * * * * * *

Once the van departed Laura poured herself a stiff vodka. She hadn't bothered watching as the 'garbage men' carried out their tasks, probably it was all routine for the Keppelman boys. She gathered her belongings together and walked into the lounge to pick up her lighter and cigarettes. After lighting one she noticed the irregular patterned blood stain which had soaked into the expensive carpet. By the time the police examined the villa the guests would be far away, and the owner wouldn't be talking to anyone.

Laura had watched Heinz hang up his car keys after returning from their dinner at the restaurant, and she took them from the peg on the kitchen wall. Buttoning her coat she picked up her bag and walked out of the front door. Having backed Wittich's B.M.W. from the garage she drove off at a fast clip.

* * * * * * * *

Finding a parking spot in Dortmund, Karl rang the Luxembourg and made a reservation. To while away the time until the room was made ready he visited a nearby Turkish bath. Finishing with a cold shower and massage he felt completely relaxed and more like his old self which justified an expensive lunch. After the meal he entered a small cinema specializing in vintage Hollywood movies. When his eyes became accustomed to the semi darkness it was obvious there were less than twenty other patrons. Karl reclined in the seat hoping his mind would be distracted by the film, but much to his annoyance it didn't work. Finally he gave up and let his thoughts wander.

Perhaps the villa's house guests would panic on finding the corpse, realizing they might be the main target of suspicion. Maybe they would bolt to avoid being involved in some sort of scandal, but this was all pure guesswork. Whatever the case Karl felt reasonably sure he'd taken the necessary precautions in covering his tracks. Watching the screen but unable to concentrate he got up to leave. Once outside he walked the short distance to his parked car. The press would have a field day when the news broke regarding murder of a prominent local art dealer. Stories about the man's social life would be blazoned across their pages based on interviews with people coming out of the woodwork. It would all make good copy Karl supposed, providing titillation for the good burghers of the city. Maybe he'd buy newspapers later on and read all about it.

36

CRATED CADAVER

In accordance with the promise given her boss to keep an eye on the property, Wittich's cook bicycled over to the villa. Letting herself in she went upstairs and noticed unmade beds, open drawers and empty cupboards as if someone had left in a hurry. Downstairs she trod on small beads scattered on the floor, but it wasn't until spotting an ominous looking stain in the lounge that puzzlement changed to fear... it definitely looked like dried blood to her. Trying to stop a rising panic the cook took a deep breath, thinking about her blood pressure, then hurried to the phone. She tried her boss's Berlin number three times but the calls remained unanswered, so finally mounting her bicycle she pedaled off back to her cottage. Her husband Max could sort it all out for her after returning from work, or so she hoped. The cook took one of her pills and lay down on the bed trying to fathom what it all meant, but couldn't shake a feeling something terribly wrong had occurred at the villa Wittich.

* * * * * * * * *

Leo Steiner opened his eyes and stared at the ceiling... schiess, he'd forgotten to set the alarm clock for the second time in a week. Swinging his feet out of bed he padded over to a window and peered at a desolate and messy scene below. It had almost stopped snowing, and Leo gave a chuckle seeing the cars had large white boxes of the stuff on their roofs. Tire tracks and footprints criss-crossed in geometric patterns in the dirty slush, but this time Steiner winced thinking about road conditions before he climbed back into bed. To hell with it... he'd call and tell his secretary he wouldn't be coming in. Renata also might not make it as she lived outside the city. He felt sympathy for people in the department working the graveyard shift. It must have been hell going in and the same heading home. He supposed the basement cafeteria had done a roaring business dispensing coffee and schnapps... at least it was a warmer place than most of the offices in the building.

* * * * * * * *

Leo idly watched melting snow trickle down the window waiting for his bath to fill. At nine forty-five the phone rang, it was Stroebel at the other end sounding particularly unctuous. After initial small talk was dispensed with, Leo was told the commissioner was sending his chauffeured Mercedes to pick him up. "If the case wasn't so urgent I wouldn't dream of bringing you in on such a rotten day, but in the present circumstances it's the least I can do. Please drop by at your convenience after you arrive." Leo made an uncouth gesture at the phone before replacing the receiver trying to recall the gist of his thoughts which had been interrupted by Stroebel... but it was no good, they had dissolved like spilt butter on a hot stove. Damn the man and his pushy manner, he never changed.

Shortly after his second cup of coffee, the big Mercedes drew up outside the foyer entrance and Leo climbed into the rear seat, sinking into the luxurious upholstery. He immediately closed his eyes until sensing arrival at the underground parking area of the police HQ building, causing him to give a small sigh before getting out. Renata and her boss walked into the office simultaneously. She was clutching a small bunch of roses which she handed to Leo once they were inside the office door. "Mein Herr, this is a token of the five years we've worked together." Leo was startled and slightly embarrassed having no idea it had been that long and gave Renata a quick peck on the cheek and thanked her. "How very thoughtful of you... I can't begin to think how many bumps you've flattened out for me during that time." She was like that, always reminding him of dates he'd otherwise forget. He couldn't wish for a better secretary. Renata was one of the old school, and he was indeed very lucky, so many times she'd relieved him of tiresome tasks. After a few minutes Leo called over his shoulder. "Renata, I'm not to be disturbed for the next hour, then I have to see Mr. Big. No calls, O.K.?" "Of course, Chief Inspector, exactly as you say." Renata knew the routine as well as she knew her boss, today was no exception.

For a case to be allocated to the federal police H.Q meant it was of special significance. As yet Leo was unaware of its classification, his boss was keeping it under his hat for reasons of his own. The file lay undisturbed where he'd left it and Leo felt a twinge of malevolence seeing another one lying on top. Either Stroebel or one of the detectives must have placed it there before his arrival, most likely it contained preliminary forensic and ballistic information. Leo pushed it aside and picked up the original one, it wouldn't be just a skim-through but a proper evaluation for which his mind had been trained.

Starting with the typewritten pages prepared by Hans Zahn one of the senior detectives, Leo mulled over details regarding the corpse shown in attached photos. A call had been logged at 10.00 a.m. December the 2nd., at police station #14 located in the Bauer district. The caller was noted as being Arno Walther, general manager of the Zeller Transport and Storage Co. whose telephone number and address was listed. Apparently a large wooden crate consigned for pick-up hadn't been called for on the given date. Shortly afterwards an employee in the shipping office smelt something bad emanating from the box and reported it to the supervisor who in turn had spoken to Zeller's general manager. Authorization was given for removing the lid which was nailed shut. It only took a few seconds for the manager and supervisor to ascertain the content didn't match a waybill listing secondhand books.

Arno became sick on the spot with the combined effects of stench and what he'd glimpsed once the lid was lifted a few centimeters. Overcome, he'd staggered back to his office and reached for a bottle of spirits kept for calming frayed nerves whenever business pressures became too much. This was far worse than anything he'd experienced while working at Zeller Transportation. Both his hands trembled putting through a call to the police after the supervisor looked up the number. Fortunately for the supervisor Arno's back had obscured the view. The dreadful smell was more than enough for him. Hans Zahn accompanied by a policeman arrived at Zeller's within a half hour after receiving a call and verified the manager's gruesome discovery. He arranged for removal of the crate to the police labs and put all the paperwork concerning the shipment into his briefcase. Before leaving he told Herr Walther his presence would be required at the police station later that day in order to make a full statement and answer further questions.

* * * * * * * * *

Payment for transportation of the crate had been made in cash at a Zeller branch office. The consignor's name and address in addition to that of the bookstore which was supposed to pick it up proved fictitious. Leo grunted, working through the initial procedures, and doubted anything garnered at this stage would prove significant, but you could never be sure... it was all part of a jigsaw needing a lot of work. Steiner opened the second file and as he'd surmised found it contained preliminary ballistics and forensic reports. Reaching across the desk he pulled a writing pad towards him and jotted down the following:

1. Male aged 35-45. Caucasian. Blonde hair.
2. Scar 8 cm. long on outside of left leg.
3. Cause of death : knife thrust though the heart. Weapon: Hunting knife removed from body, and bagged under ident.23/a.
4. Body in initial stages of decomposition.
5. Upper torso bare. Suit jacket, shirt and tie found inside crate. Corpse wearing suit pants, boxer shorts, socks and shoes. Superficially it looked as if all these items had carried expensive price tags. The maker's labels had been removed from the suit jacket and pants.
6. Examination of the cadaver revealed a ragged cross shape incised in the upper back by a chisel or similar tool. The cuts were approximately 2 mm. deep in places. The vertical incision was slightly to the left of the spine having a length of 26 cm., and an 18cm. horizontal cut ran between the shoulder blades. Probably household glue had been used to secure colored beads in the incisions. They appeared to be of the type used in cheap costume jewelry. Congealed blood had melded with the adhesive, but several beads had loosened and were found in the crate.

Leo glanced at the photographs which had nauseated him the previous night. He couldn't begin to fathom the killers state of mind, although this was nearly always the case in mutilation murders he'd handled. Leo reread his notes before recording personal effects found with the body.

Signet ring. Rolex wrist watch (on corpse).
Notebook, key ring with keys.
Gold cigarette case and lighter.
Roll of 35mm film (exposed). Handkerchief,
small piece of string.
Jeweled case containing tooth picks.

Leo back tracked and was slightly puzzled at not finding a wallet listed although he didn't think robbery was the motive for the killing. Lighting his pipe he realized more than fifty minutes had elapsed since starting his task.

He buzzed Renata, but she was one step ahead of him announcing that coffee was already brewed. She asked if he'd like something stronger to go with it before his next port of call? Leo responded with a faint smile and nodded. Renata knew his work habits and doubted this case would be handled differently from the others, but with Leo there was always an element of surprise. It was time to go and see Stroebel, probably the man would hint at lack of progress, which was his usual opener.

* * * * * * * *

A watery sun struggled with angry looking gray clouds, while keen winds whipped up the remnants of the recent snowfall. Work crews were hard at it clearing secondary streets. Many spots remained treacherous after melted snow had refrozen overnight creating polished surfaces for the unwary. Chief inspector Steiner yawned as he watched people bundled up against the cold hurry warily along the sidewalks. His mind had become sluggish deliberating about what to do next until a hunch made him opt for a return visit to the morgue. He placed a call to Detective Hans Zahn asking him to come to his office. Hans had been the first one of the team to view the body. There was a faint chance a second look might yield something missed during the initial examination. Apart from anything else, Leo felt a compelling urge to escape the office before the Commissioner came nosing around.

Detective Zahn held open the heavy main door of the mortuary, while Leo stamped off slush covering his boots. The two men were approached by an elderly custodian who looked slightly annoyed by the intrusion. Steiner always hated the antiseptic smell of the place and was not too thrilled by the attitude of its staff. The custodian learning the purpose of the visit sniffed and wiped his bulbous nose on a sleeve before ushering them into a large white tiled room. The appearance of the far wall reminded Leo of a giant's filing cabinet. There must have been over fifty drawer pulls, each with a number stamped on it. The custodian glanced at his clipboard, then pulled open #57 for inspection.

The corpse lay face down covered by a heavy plastic sheet which Zahn tugged back, and then checked the identification tag tied to a toe, merely from habit. There was no doubt about it being the same cadaver they'd viewed previously. Glancing at Leo, Hans said "Not a pretty sight, I reckon." Leo nodded agreement while reflecting on the sicker side of human nature. After checking the original report and verifying the information, he congratulated Hans on his thoroughness. "O.K. I don't think this beauty has anything more to tell us, however I still want to look at the crate he arrived in while we are here." Hans summoned the custodian who took them to a store room at the end of a dimly lit corridor.

Effects found with the body were spread out on a trestle table, all of which had been noted in Leo's dossier. Everything was neatly bagged and labeled, and Leo turned towards the heavy crate placed in a corner. Peering into the interior as he pulled on a latex glove, Leo reached over and extracted a blood-soaked newspaper partially stuck to the base. The paper's masthead proclaimed it to be the 'Dortmund Examiner' dated seven days prior to the gruesome discovery by Zellers general manager. Finishing a cigarette Zahn shrugged and said, "I don't feel any bolt of lightening strike, chief." Leo nodded in agreement, but still felt somehow he'd overlooked some important detail. Back in the office he reopened the manila file and riffled through its content, an oblong blue card dropped onto the desk. It was the consignment ticket for the crate, listing a place called Blaustein as point of shipment. Leo gave a smile of satisfaction and closed the file.

* * * * * * * *

According to a dog-eared police directory Blaustein came under the jurisdiction of the Dortmund division regarding major criminal investigations. Leo flipped to a stapled telex near the front of the file which detailed an interview with the shipping clerk. Leo slapped his forehead, that's what he'd tried to recall while at the morgue . When looking at the newspaper inside the crate the word Dortmund somehow hadn't registered. A Blaustein location stamped on the telex made Leo suspect a possible link between the two places. At first he'd focused on the text, and the consignment location didn't seem of special significance, now it could provide a clue in establishing an area of domicile for the corpse.

The telex noted the shipping clerk had only furnished fuzzy descriptions of the two men who'd brought the crate in for shipment. He'd been extra busy that particular day due to his assistant failing to show up for work, and hadn't recalled anything untoward concerning their appearance. He did remember they'd paid using small denomination bank notes, as it helped the cashier who was running low on small change. The customer's signature was indecipherable which was of no great surprise. The consignment ticket had been examined by the fingerprint and handwriting department who'd promised a report for the following day, but Steiner decided not to hold his breath knowing how overly optimistic these people often were. At this stage of the investigation he knew it would be premature to reject or prejudge anything. Checking the location of Blaustein he estimated the place to be roughly thirty-seven Km. north east of Dortmund.

Glancing at his watch he remembered to get moving having promised to take Hannah for dinner. If he left straight away he could manage to squeeze in a nap before changing into the new suit she'd cajoled him into buying. The policeman's mind began shifting into neutral, and putting on his hat he struggled into his heavy topcoat. His mood had changed for the better, police work was often a hard slog coupled with monotonous drudgery but occasionally it paid off unexpectedly, an inspired moment or even a lucky guess helped solve otherwise intractable cases.

Usually it took many years on the force before policemen developed the ability to harness these gifts, and with many it never happened. Certainly it had helped Leo's career even though he'd never given it too much thought. Classes on police methods, and manuals dealing with detection theory never touched on these aspects… they couldn't, it was indefinable. When Leo first enrolled at the police academy one of the professors talked about 'Fingerspitzengfuhl'… the feeling in the fingertips regarding a situation was worth a whole bag of theory. As he stepped outside the main door of the building an icy blast almost slammed it back in his face, but this minor annoyance didn't detract from Leo's anticipation of meeting Hannah later that evening.

37

VANISHING MINISTER

THE WEST GERMAN FEDERAL PROTECTION AGENCY is headed by an appointee solely responsible to the Chancellor. Few citizens are aware of it's existence. Budgets are seldom revealed, and its operations rarely publicized. Political clout wielded by the agency along with it's infinite resources make it unrivaled in government. Their operating method arouses jealousy and the perception of arrogance. For some citizens they portray more sinister aspects reminiscent of the Gestapo era. Occasionally at dinner and cocktail parties ministers railed about this autonomous branch of government, but only within earshot of trusted friends.

Weeks prior to the start of the arms talks between Germany and Turkey, discreet tails were placed on members of each team. Several photographs of Peter Hahn, the chief German negotiator had been taken, and one showed him with Laura Ichenko and Heinz Wittich standing in front of an art gallery on the Gustav strasse. A notation on the back of the print identified Peter Hahn in conversation with Heinz Wittich the gallery owner. The girl hadn't been identified.

An agent obtained the photo while sitting in an unmarked

Opel van parked across the street. All surveillance pictures are automatically enlarged, date stamped, then indexed prior to deposit in central archives. Only people with the requisite security clearance and a 'need to know' basis can access them. Unknown to most members of the police a restricted directive N/47 requires morgue photographs and biographical data, on a certain category of victim, to be forwarded to the W.G.F.P. agency. When a chief inspector (or higher rank) has been assigned as investigating officer, copies of all data are automatically sent to their boss who is responsible for the case. Stroebel had been hand picked by the chancellor for the latest job, and was aware serious political ramifications were involved.

The N/47 directive had come about as part of a modus operandi for dealing with the large number of cases involving Russian and Warsaw Pact operatives. Often disguised in the role of military attaches or scientific delegates, too many had turned up dead for normal accountability and such events led to embarrassing scandals for the German government, especially when it became obvious blatant errors had been incurred by counter intelligence. Sometimes innocent business men and eminent academics ended up on a morgue slab, and after these stories broke the media went ballistic with sensationalism in efforts to increase their circulation figures.

The extraordinary powers of the agency allowed for subversion of justice and sometimes they'd closed an investigation prematurely when a case was considered too hot to handle. Certain departments dealt exclusively in the arts of manipulation and blackmail, and occasionally their tentacles were even directed against fellow upholders of law and order. Throughout the early sixties few people tried subverting orders that had been O.K'd by the chancellor. The Federal State was on the road to democracy, but still had a lot more tarmac to traverse before representing the interests of its citizens.

* * * * * * * *

Helga Nordlund, a senior W.G.F.P. photographic evaluator, finished studying shots of the corpse transmitted by the Munich police commissioner. Helga found herself intrigued by the curious disfigurement of the body, but it was the face that riveted her attention... she'd seen it before. Halfway through a cup of coffee she was hardly able to contain her excitement. She'd already seen the picture of Wittich, Ichenko and Hahn together earlier in the week. By now it was probably labeled and awaiting transfer to the archive department.

Helga swallowed the rest of her coffee then dashed down the corridor to retrieve it from the mailing room. The photo was fifth from the top of a pile lying on the table, and after signing it out at the wicket Helga returned to her office. Taking another hard look she mouthed the word 'Eureka' knowing this discovery could burnish her personnel file. She was elated and there was little doubt in her mind. The corpse had acquired a name besides a photo index number. Heinz Wittich had been seen talking with Peter Hahn the missing minister just days previously, according to the date stamp on the back of the picture.

Helga attended the deputy director's meeting when the announcement was made that Peter Hahn had vanished. The attendees were told not to discuss any details outside their departments. Later on bulletins would be released to the media on a managed basis regarding this latest shock, but chances seemed slim that the arms talks would resume any time soon. They had already been placed on hold, although the chancellor let it be known he wanted them restarted as quickly as possible. Apparently he was furious with the turn of events, and he'd been overheard shouting at an aide "just what I need with fucking elections around the corner; I can't believe it."

* * * * * * * *

Helga put a call through to the police commissioner. After listening to her for a while he took a deep breath. "Congratulations agent Nordlund you've done excellent work, just keep this information strictly to yourself for the moment. I will be writing a personal letter commending your efforts to the director of the agency." Replacing the phone, Stroebel jotted down the text of her message from his recorder before erasing the tape. Taking the file of the corpse from his locked drawer he placed the text of Helga's message inside. He stuck a gummed label on the cover and wrote on it CORPSE # 57. Only the few people already involved on the case would know this identified a mutilated cadaver in the morgue.

Two days after talking to Helga Nordlund, Stroebel received a call from his wife. He'd just retrieved the file from his drawer and placed it on his desk. His wife sounded hysterical as 'Putzi' their prize Schnauzer had somehow got out and been hit by a truck. Stroebel told her to calm down saying he would come home immediately. Replacing the phone he grabbed his jacket and hurriedly left the office. His secretary decided his departure gave her an opportunity for an extended lunch with a friend…

A few minutes later, Leo walked in carrying a sheath of departmental paperwork and vouchers requiring Stroebel's signature. However, his main purpose was to corner his boss and talk about the latest developments in the case. To his mind it was exhibiting some rather odd aspects. Finding nobody around Leo decided he'd wait inside Stroebel's luxurious sanctum. While marshaling his thoughts, he helped himself to a Cohiba from the ornate cigar box sitting on the desk, and in doing so his attention was drawn to an open file next to it. Despite feeling furtive Leo glanced at the content outlining Helga's phone call.

His features tightened and any guilt feelings evaporated – so the man wanted a miracle and at the same time withheld information, what was the point? Well perhaps Leo might provide the miracle by solving the case with or without cooperation, but after that it would be 'Adios commissioner'. A photo of the cadaver had a note clipped to it listing details about the man which Stroebel had omitted to mention. Apparently the victim owned a gallery in Berlin and Dortmund. Another photo featured two men and a woman outside a building identified as being on the Gustav strasse. On the reverse side it had been signed and dated by an agent. So the identity was known... how about that Leo thought feeling embittered.

A terse memo inside the file carried the embossed heading of the chancellor's office. The head of state had written to the director of the agency expressing utmost concern regarding Peter Hahn's disappearance, one of his most trusted aides. It also indicated that many heads would roll if things weren't quickly resolved. Leo ran off duplicates of the file's contents on the secretary's copying machine. It was risky as she or Stroebel might come back at any time, but Leo's luck held. He shoved everything into his briefcase and opened the window sufficiently to dissipate the cigar smoke. Leo then turned on his heel and shut the door.

Back in his office the chief inspector relished the remainder of his Cohiba before turning back to his paperwork. Leo stuck his neck out by dialing Helga Nordlund's number. She might refuse to give out further information, but on realizing he'd seen the photos this would indicate his actions were cleared by the commissioner. In fact it didn't even enter Helga's head... she was happy to co-operate with any higher echelon types within the police. One never knew when helping out might prove useful, especially if a small favor was required. Leo turned on the charm. "I hear you have done some excellent investigative work." Leo was beginning to choke upon his syrupy tone. "Oh one more thing, could you run that shot showing Hahn, Wittich and the woman past your counter intelligence people… it's only a hunch of mine, but she could be KGB."

* * * * * * * *

Helga called back soon after lunch. "I have another name chief inspector, the girl is named Laura Ichenko. She is suspected of being an agent, but to date nothing incriminating has been tied to her. The fact of having been recently escorted by Hahn has lots of red lights flashing now." Leo oozed his appreciation. "Can you order me photos and background data on this Ichenko girl?" Helga said she could and Leo gave his confidential routing address with a code number for forwarding the package directly to his office. Leo ended up by saying. "Perhaps we could meet for drinks sometime after this whole business is resolved."

He didn't want to be egotistical, but sensed his words caused a slight stir of interest at the other end of the line. "I shall look forward to that." Helga was conscious she'd stammered and blushed slightly when replying. Between phone calls Helga had looked up a picture and biography showing Leo in a current year book, she thought he was extremely handsome. Leo knew the shit would hit the fan when his boss found out he'd been talking to Helga Nordlund, but what was he going to do? Stroebel's head could be on the chopping block and he would need Leo to save his bacon. Leo chuckled… that might teach him to be more up front next time!

38

LEO TAKES A TRIP

WHENEVER FEASIBLE LEO STEINER KEPT HIS office door shut for the first hour of the working day, to allow study of accumulated data on each case. If he didn't, his time was consumed by meetings and routine police matters. On this particular day he required quiet time for a different reason, Leo's head felt as if the hammers of hell were all striking in unison. He fumbled for the aspirin bottle in one of the cabinets then asked Renata to bring him some mineral water. It was the quantity, not the quality of wine imbibed at Hannah's birthday party the previous evening... the inspector was suffering from a first class hangover.

Before the drinks started exacting their toll, some fragmented ideas had surfaced regarding his present case. He was somewhat amazed he could remember anything at all. Now the trick would be recalling their substance with a mind still battling an alcoholic rearguard. Pouring another glass of water he gulped it down and closed his eyes trying to concentrate. Suddenly something clicked, it wasn't to do with viewing the cadaver that had fidgeted his mind, but something Stroebel mentioned during the initial discussion of the case.

Why had the man been getting 'the usual stuff' from the political types? At the time Leo wondered what caused them to show interest in this particular homicide, apart from its lurid details. He decided he'd probably committed an error not being more forceful with his superior. Was there more he hadn't been told, and if so for what reason? Tapping his teeth with a pencil Leo concluded Peter Hahn must be the key factor in the equation, but how did the girl and the owner of the gallery fit in? If Stroebel was withholding information it could only make things tougher. He rubbed his nose annoyed for not picking up on earlier vibes, probably lack of attention which was unusual for him. Now he'd have to operate via the back door, but there was something else needed to be taken into account... was his boss becoming slightly paranoid, or just being more devious than usual?

Renata brought in a pot of coffee with the morning paper on a tray. After checking her outgoing box for anything requiring attention she withdrew. Reaching blindly for the coffee pot Leo knocked off the lid spilling hot liquid on his hand making him swear. Grabbing a napkin he dabbed at it before swabbing the widening pool on top of his desk. His mother had been right, he was clumsy as she'd often told him as a child. He unfolded the newspaper and spread it out. The headlines screamed back... MYSTERIOUS DISAPPEARANCE OF GOVERNMENT MINISTER. A press release emanating from the chancellor's office described the importance of Hahn's work but little else of value was to be gleaned from the story. An adjoining column carried a file picture of Hahn attending some society function surrounded by elegant women wearing ridiculous hats. He stood next to the chancellor holding what appeared to be a glass of champagne looking as bored as his boss.

The chief inspector bit his lower lip turning to a page in his diary under the M tab. Müeller, yes Hans Müeller was the man he needed to talk with. Their friendship went back to police academy days when both were cadets. It had been a long time since they'd spoken to each other. He thought it must have been around the time Hans was promoted to the number two spot in the Dortmund division. Picking up the phone he dialed a coded number... "Müeller here" the voice barked. Hans was delighted to find out it was Leo at the other end, and after a quick exchange of pleasantries Leo mentioned he was on the verge of retiring and said this final assignment was bothering him more than usual.

Leo outlined recent events until Hans broke in "Listen, you know I'll do anything to help. It's an odd thing but I think I can do so, right away in fact. I received a report from one of my men and have just finished plowing through it... have you read today's newspaper? Well, we've all been slaving hot and heavy on the Hahn disappearance this end. I hear on the grapevine all those politicos are shitting their pants as usual, especially now that the tail assigned to Peter Hahn lost him along with his female companion. It happened somewhere in traffic during Hahn's trip from Berlin to West Germany. I'll have a copy of this report sent by courier, but meanwhile this is the gist."

Leo tucked the receiver under his chin reaching for a notepad. "At the Adler hotel in Feltersberg, on the evening of the 24th a statement was made by a waiter to one of my detectives. The hotel incidentally is about 70Km. east of Dortmund. The man served lunch to the minister and his companion. After the couple had left the waiter raced from the dining room with Hahn's cigarette case which had been obscured by a napkin... the waiter noticed the name P.L.HAHN prominently engraved on the lid. Cutting across the lawn he caught the couple just as the convertible was about to turn on to the highway. The grateful minister rewarded him with a fat tip for his alertness. The waiter thought the vehicle was either black or dark blue but was unfamiliar with it's make, terming it a sports car. Starting back to the dining room he'd momentarily glanced back and saw the car turn left in the direction of Dortmund. In the waiter's opinion the female companion was an outstanding looker he'd recognize again.

A pre-wedding party had also attended luncheon at the Adler. Sonia, a freelance photographer was busy taking pictures of the guests. My detective Paul asked to see them after they were developed, and in three of the shots Hahn and the girl happened to be in the background. Each of these prints were of good definition." Hearing all this Leo gave a smile of satisfaction. "Several guests were discreetly questioned as to what they might have noticed regarding the couple but this produced nothing of significance, and as you know that's not unusual as public amnesia quickly sets in when the police start asking questions." Leo knew the feeling and chuckled. "This is great stuff Hans, pictures of Hahn with the girl and your report will be a tremendous help." "It's all yours old friend" Hans replied. "I hope it gives you something to get your teeth into, and don't leave it so long before calling again." Leo promised to keep in touch before ringing off.

Later, comparing the Berlin and Adler photos there was little doubt it was the same girl in each shot, now things were beginning to percolate. When Renata walked into the office the following day she saw a cryptic note propped in front of her day calendar 'Gone to Berlin, back soon. L.S.' A little dinosaur figure was drawn in one corner, and she laughed knowing how he was referred to by some of the younger detectives. It was typical of her boss when he was hot to trot. About an hour later Stroebel stopped by looking for his subordinate, so Renata passed him the note. The commissioner read it and scowled "bloody unprofessional". The secretary smirked at the retreating back as he strode out of the office slamming the door...

* * * * * * * *

Before leaving Munich, Leo contacted Harald Henze, a police photographer, who'd taken the shots of the Ichenko girl standing next to two men in front of the Berlin gallery. Henze had been told to accompany the W.G.P.A. tail assigned to track Peter Hahn's movements and contacts. Henze and the agent witnessed the couple emerge after visiting the gallery followed by Wittich. The threesome chatted awhile before Hahn and the girl drove off and this interlude provided Henze an opportunity for more photos. The photographer told Steiner it was somebody else who'd added the note identifying Heinz Wittich on one of the prints. At the time Henze only guessed the man might be the gallery owner. A street number on the building shown in the background provided an answer Steiner was looking for. Pleased by his discovery, Leo took a train to Berlin and on arrival tried phoning the gallery without success. Finishing a meal in the station buffet he left and hailed a taxi to take him to the Gustav strasse. He was impatient to confront the gallery owner for questioning.

Leo drew a blank seeing a notice pinned on the door reading 'Temporarily Closed'. He had a premonition the man might be the recent occupant of a shipping crate. Normally he would have obtained a search warrant at this juncture, but considering Stroebel's devious behavior, Leo opted for a different tack. The inspector booked a ticket to Dortmund on the night express after calling Hans Müeller to let him know he was on the way.

* * * * * * * *

He had prints made from the film found in Wittich's jacket, but was disappointed that only five frames were marginally readable. The remaining negatives turned out to be blank making Leo wonder if the camera had been inadvertently opened. Before arriving in Berlin, Leo had the police photographic lab. do a rush job making enlargements from the usable frames. Two out of focus views showed an exterior face of a building taken from different angles, while the remaining ones were interior shots. Leo had twenty copies of each in his briefcase for distribution by the Dortmund police.

He checked his watch reckoning it would be ten minutes before the train reached its destination. He looked at a city index to find the location of the 'King of Prussia' hotel where he was to meet Hans Müeller for lunch. The following day the two men spent a long time over their meal. Waiting for coffee Leo opened his briefcase and showed Hans the photographs. "There's an outside chance these were taken in Dortmund, my friend… as you can see definition is lousy but a cop on his beat might recognize the place having walked past it many times. Could you have them displayed on your station bulletin boards?" Leo got up from the table "maybe I'm just grasping at straws, but I need to try everything." Hans looked his friend in the eye "of course, you've always had the best gut feel of any cop I've known, it will be taken care of straight away."

Hans had provided Leo office space, so for the rest of the afternoon he was able to catch up with back paperwork, and declined an invitation to the theater preferring to have an early night… a headache was probably due to the several Dortmund beers consumed at lunch time. He scanned the headlines of a couple of newspapers left in the office before phoning Renata to let her know when he expected to return. They both had a good laugh when she related Stroebel's annoyance when finding him gone. Leo asked her to tell Hannah he'd call later that evening. Gathering his stuff together he dialed for a taxi and in less than five minutes reached his hotel. Sitting on the edge of the bath waiting for it to fill he mulled over events trying to connect the dots in his precise manner.

* * * * * * * *

Leo got lucky once again after police officer Zengler signed in for the graveyard shift and glanced at the station bulletin board. Part of his beat took him past the building shared by the Horizon gallery. Zengler reckoned he'd walked down the street for a seeming life time, knowing it like the back of his hand. Being a conscientious type he always shone his flashlight over doorways and windows when passing, looking for any signs of a break-in. During recent years there'd only been two or three robberies, and for months everything was 'in ordnung', which suited Zengler. Maybe the local crooks knew he was not a sloppy type and his attention to detail helped pass the hours until returning to the station house. Before signing off he usually took a quick nip of schnapps from a bottle stashed in his locker then promptly left, but this time he stopped for another look at the bulletin board. The pictures didn't ring any bells but as he continued to peer at the inferior quality prints he recognized the familiar pattern of bricks flanking an entranceway. Suddenly it was obvious, it was part of the art gallery facade.

Replacing the phone following Zengler's call, Leo felt relieved. Driving a short distance he picked up the officer who then directed him. Zengler had remembered the gallery's name just before the phone call, and having reached the Horizon it took only a few moments to establish that the pictures matched the building in front of them. In fact it was easy to pinpoint the spot where they'd been taken from... Zengler hammered on the door but elicited nothing in response and the officer looked at Leo who shrugged, then congratulated Zengler on his astuteness. Dropping off Zengler at his home, Leo returned to the station house and cornered Hans who knew his friend was ready to pounce before he'd opened his mouth. He'd seen the look before.

Hans walked over to the desk sergeant who'd already tracked down the residential address for the Horizon's owner. Steiner felt exhausted, so both inspectors decided to check out the villa the following evening. Hans needed to attend the funeral of a senior officer in the morning, and was scheduled to meet with the mayor of Dortmund for lunch. Both events would be difficult to avoid and Leo knew about these 'duty' appearances; politics played a significant role in the life of an inspector. Müeller suggested it might be prudent having a radio squad car monitor the villa's driveway for any traffic. He would be able to call his boss if he witnessed anything. Steiner nodded in agreement ruefully adding "we'll need Zengler along as neither of us can handle potential scuffles the way we did in the old days".

* * * * * * * *

Karl Bayer drove in the direction of the hotel Luxembourg munching some fruit he'd purchased. Signing in at the reception desk he felt distinctly hot and suspected he might be running a temperature. Looking at him the clerk politely inquired if he felt O.K "Is there anything I can get for you?" Bayer thanked the man and asked that black coffee and a package of aspirin be sent up to his room. After closing the door he rang housekeeping and told them he didn't want to be disturbed before 10:00 a.m. The most important thing at the moment was the luxury of a proper bed. The St. Lucien would be safe and sound locked in his car. Having slept like a log he awoke to discreet tapping on the door by one of the hotel maids. Padding into the bathroom he caught sight of himself in a mirror. The view wasn't flattering, and despite feeling a lot better realized his appearance still looked like hell. He rang and ordered a late breakfast in the dining room, and went down to the lobby where he bought newspapers and selected three cigars from the rack.

Only one couple was in the room and Karl chose a table in the corner. By the time his coffee arrived he'd scanned the papers for anything that might cause alarm, but the pages seemed to be filled with boring stuff not worth reading. However this was good news in itself. Karl's spirits perked up and he decided a brisk walk in the nearby park would stretch his legs before the long drive north. Maybe it would be smart to rent a vacation cottage in one of the less traveled areas close to the Baltic coast. This would afford privacy, and at this time of year they would be cheap.

He would lie low for a bit and see what repercussions arose over the Villa Wittich affair. By listening to radio reports and checking newspapers he'd know when the time was ripe to move on. For the moment he had enough money, but this wouldn't last indefinitely and also there was a possibility of having to flee the country. If his name showed up on a missing persons roster it might require an identity change which presented difficulties. The biggest problem at the moment was the St. Lucien treasure, not knowing how to safely go about turning it into cash. If only Fritz was still around the man would have a solution. Karl needed someone with the right expertise in a hurry, and these kinds of people would be hard to find, but once the problem was solved his future would be considerably brighter, assuming he had one that is. Returning from the walk Karl took the elevator to his room and kicked his shoes off before sitting down. Gazing at a picture on the opposite wall he rubbed his chin reflectively realizing he'd forgotten to shave, a sloppy omission on his part. The stubble stirred memories of POW days when circumstances dictated wearing an unkempt beard... perhaps now was the time to grow another but kept in trim.

Suddenly Karl felt slight uneasiness, then it hit him like a thunderbolt... those bloody night glasses! In all probability they were still hanging up at the surveillance site. He remembered looping them over a tree branch before taking a piss. After buttoning his fly he'd sat down and removed one of his boots intent on finding a sharp nail which inflamed his big toe. Now, try as he might he couldn't remember retrieving the damn things, Gott in Himmel, how the fuck had he been so careless. His fingerprints must be everywhere, and though a long shot, conceivably the police could trace them to the place of their purchase. Should the sales clerk give a detailed enough description, wanted posters would soon be plastered all over the place. He'd messed up big time, and for a moment felt tears of frustration after scrabbling through his few belongings which yielded nothing.

Feeling a panic button had been pressed Karl dashed downstairs to the lobby and waited impatiently for the desk man to locate the garage keys. Handed one with #16 on the tag Karl hurried across the hotel courtyard. Opening the car doors he rummaged about in the front and back swearing under his breath. The St. Lucien lay undisturbed beneath the cover on the rear seat, and in the trunk, but that was it… nothing. Back in his room Karl sat chain smoking trying to think up ways to rectify the disaster. By now he was in a foul mood, but had no one to blame but himself. Nothing brilliant came to mind and Karl knew they had to be found before someone else came tramping around the site. He decided daylight was too risky so he'd wait until darkness for the attempt. He called the reservations office and booked an extra night at the hotel.

Stubbing out a cigarette Bayer pondered his future course of action once he'd accomplished the next task, but his brain seemed to be on hold, and finally he lay down on the bed and dozed off. After awakening from a dream he sat perched on the edge of the bed regaining his bearings. He walked over and closed the bedroom curtains. It was almost dark and he reckoned it was time to get going. At one point while dozing he'd visualized the night glasses swinging to and fro from a branch like a felon on the gallows and he thought there'd been enough bad vibes for one day without his imagination running riot. He knew he'd over-reacted and began to feel confident again that he was going to be successful. Once he'd recovered the glasses and Dortmund disappeared in the rear view mirror, the happier he'd be. He jotted down a reminder to extend the car rental date which was almost due.

Having made a few more notes, his mind centered on the St Lucien treasure. Whoever he contacted for its disposal would more than likely be crooked, so how was he going to shield himself from blackmail? Putting on his jacket and topcoat he locked the door and went down to the car. Once inside the vehicle he felt relaxed, and there was no need to refer to the map. Unfortunately, he wasn't to know Inspectors Steiner and Müeller had also decided to pay a visit to the villa using a van borrowed from the undercover branch. Before leaving, Leo and Hans checked out sidearms from the armory not knowing what might develop.

39

DEADLY ACCIDENT

KARL BAYER DROVE PAST HEINZ WITTICH's driveway and again parked alongside the rail boxcars. As he made his way to the observation site he felt irritated by his stupidity at having to return. Reaching the search area, and using his shielded flashlight, it didn't take long to find what he was looking for. Grabbing the carrying strap he slung the night glasses over his shoulder and headed back to the car.

The cutting wind was bringing more snow making him thankful for not having to spend another night outdoors. Whether it was finding the glasses, or the prospect of getting back into a warm bed which influenced his next decision would never be known. Whatever it was Karl made a cardinal error. The weather was definitely worsening, so rather than return the way he'd come over the rough ground he opted to head towards the villa and pick up the driveway providing an easier and quicker route to the hotel. Had he paused, probably caution would have kicked in, but tonight he was in a hurry to wrap things up.

* * * * * * * *

He drove off whistling a popular tune and turned right on reaching the driveway. After shifting into top gear he suddenly gripped the wheel much harder as headlights pierced the darkness over on his left. The beams were at an angle as neither vehicle had reached the intervening bend. Du liebe Gott, who on earth could it be at this time of night? Within moments he was abreast of the other vehicle. It appeared to be a van of some sort, but in the time it took to pass he couldn't be sure. Karl's initial reaction on seeing the lights was the thought 'POLEZI'. It was far too late for commercial deliveries by his reckoning…

When Karl reached the main road he jumped out and stood on the rear bumper looking back in the direction of the villa. He couldn't make out if the other vehicle had continued on it's path, but within seconds a beacon emitted red and blue flashes. Karl realized the vehicle was heading his way but was still closer to the villa than the road. He felt a small twinge of fear knowing he was now the target of a hunt. Scrambling back into the driver's seat he took off at a fast clip. The bulge in his jacket concealing his automatic gave reassurance. Of course there was a chance the vehicle might be an ambulance, but Karl knew this was wishful thinking. If pursued he would give them a good run for their money on a road becoming increasingly slick and dangerous.

* * * * * * * *

During the initial approach of the vehicle Karl switched his headlights onto high beam, causing Hans to flinch on the unfamiliar driveway. The dazzle caught him off guard and temporarily blinded the inspector. Suddenly he veered right in the wet snow and both curbside wheels sank into semi frozen slush almost up to their axles.

Hans wanted to yell in frustration wishing he'd cut off the oncoming car as he wrestled the steering to avoid bogging down. Leo Steiner and Zengler jumped out and began pushing while Hans rhythmically changed from reverse to low gear and back, rocking the van until gaining traction on the driveway. The two men hurriedly jumped back in and the van continued for a few meters until reaching a stand of trees. Steiner pointed to an adjacent patch of ground used for stacking logs. "Go slowly my friend, that looks a good place to turn." Leo partially opened his door and swept a flashlight over the area. "O.K. let's return to the main road pronto." Hans remembered comments regarding the van's lousy turning circle wondering if there were drainage gullies obscured by snow. He made the turn wishing he'd left the driving to Zengler. Leo keyed in the police channel. "RJ4, RJ4, we are following a suspect… probably connected with the villa Wittich, meanwhile send two of your men to check the place out… over and out."

* * * * * * * *

By the time they'd regained the road it was almost too late, Karl's tail lights were just disappearing over a hill a kilometer down the road. Both inspectors had been glancing in the opposite direction when Zengler leaned forward glimpsing the last vestiges of red. Hans Müeller cautiously increased speed as Leo got on the radio calling in map references and the probable route of their quarry. It was difficult map reading due to vibrations of the vehicle, and Steiner hoped he'd got it right. With any luck a police cruiser might be in the general area and hear the transmission.

The information wasn't much to go on, but at least it provided the probable make of car… a Taunus 17. Hannah owned one, so Leo was familiar with the type. Hopefully the local police would be quick off the mark establishing road blocks. Leo said to his companion "the radio car reported nothing regarding any traffic to and from the villa, and the officer didn't leave until we showed up, so it has to be our boy up ahead... pretend you're at Le Mans and see if we can nail him." Hans gave a raspy laugh as Zengler remarked "You are asking a lot from this old tortoise, but it's still pretty gutsy." The vehicle had been used mainly for stakeout operations, and high speed chases unfortunately weren't part of the design specifications.

* * * * * * * *

Karl widened the gap between himself and the van, although he'd no way of telling by how much. It was urgent he maintained his lead but because of the slippery road and unfamiliar territory caution was paramount realizing a spinout would be disastrous. The idea of turning onto a side road occurred to him, but was immediately discarded as the twisty rural lanes would only slow him down. He reckoned his best bet lay in outrunning his pursuers by staying on the highway. Scudding clouds partially obscured the moon, but the falling snow had eased up somewhat.

The landscape looked increasingly bleak, and he was finding the worst hazards to be bridge surfaces akin to skating rinks. Rounding a sharp curve Karl made out a large body of water, and came to a halt at the junction of the road paralleling the river Meisse. Looking back he was relieved by the absence of lights, but was hesitant over which direction he should take... crossing his fingers he opted for the left.

Karl scrabbled in the glove compartment for cigarettes and his lighter, then checked the gas gauge which registered a reassuring three quarter mark, making him feel slightly more upbeat. He remembered the times on the eastern front awaiting the signal to attack... once things were underway he always felt better whatever dangers lay ahead. The road ran close to the river's edge, and passing a couple of octagonal signs he stopped and peered at the third one, which warned of possible flooding for the next thirty-five kilometers. Karl cursed, it was imperative to maintain his lead to give time finding another vehicle. He doubted a description of his car had already circulated but wasn't banking on it. Sooner or later he'd encounter road blocks remembering tactics of the military police in Russia following partisan attacks behind the German lines. If the police employed similar methods, Karl's euphoria over possession of the St. Lucien would be quickly dampened by a cold dose of reality.

* * * * * * * *

Dieter Rausch, having visited his latest girlfriend Rosa Hildebrandt, was headed home. Both of their parents owned and operated prosperous farms about nine kilometers apart, but despite this proximity they'd only met occasionally outside of school. It had been nearly a year since Helga, Rosa's sister moved out of the house and enrolled in a nurses training college near Hanover. Rosa missed her company, but secretly felt envious of her sister's new-found freedom. It was lonely without a sibling to share interests, however inheriting Rosa's bedroom had been a consolation. Neither girl had much enthusiasm for life on the farm, but there weren't many jobs locally if you happened to be a teenager.

Rosa had run into Dieter at one of the farm stores just prior to her seventeenth birthday. A celebration had been organized by several friends, and they'd invited Dieter to help as he was the only one with a car which proved invaluable for running errands. The party room was already booked at the hotel Schwann in Obermeisse, the nearest town of any size. Parents and friends pitched in with food and there was enough money in the kitty to hire a small band for dancing after the meal. When the music began the birthday girl felt exhilarated every time Dieter held her in his arms and it seemed none of the other males got a look in. During the past year she'd been out with several boys from the village but none of them attracted her in the same manner as Dieter. When the party came to an end it was quite late and Dieter offered to drive her home in his DKW and was then introduced to slightly dour parents still waiting up who succeeded in making him nervous. Since the celebration the pair dated whenever able to get away from their respective chores on the farm, which wasn't often.

Rosa's parents were hard working people, who invariably went to bed early. If Rosa happened to be meeting her boyfriend for a late tryst she'd pause outside her parent's bedroom door listening for sounds of stentorian breathing before creeping downstairs. Rufus the family dog wasn't much younger than Rosa… now partially deaf he sprawled in front of the dying fire where embers provided a last vestige of warmth. As Rosa hurried to the door and lifted the latch, he merely opened one eye before falling back to sleep dreaming of chasing rabbits…

A gentle slope ran from the farmhouse past a large wooden machinery barn, and Rosa's heart was beating somewhat faster than usual. The last time Dieter held her she'd been on cloud nine and although still a virgin, she felt this condition was about to change and didn't know whether to feel concerned or pleased. Dieter was a few months older than Rosa, and was both handsome and gentle, seemingly a perfect match for her. He sat in the barn on a tractor wheel in the total darkness. On hearing the barn door creak open, he shone his flashlight downwards to stub out a cigarette and also signal Rosa his whereabouts. Dieter had been waiting almost twenty-five minutes since he'd parked his car alongside the barn with the nose facing down hill. When the time came to go he'd coast down the slope in neutral to the road before switching on the engine and lights in order to minimize chances of awakening Rosa's parents. Dieter had already heard rumors about Herr Hildebrandt being quick reaching for his double barreled shotgun when aroused from sleep, and he'd been meaning to ask the daughter if this were true.

Rosa carefully picked her way over to Dieter by now leaning against a hay box, and they immediately began kissing passionately. Quickly she felt a hand working under her sweater, while the other one massaged her thighs. Rosa gave a small sigh before pulling Dieter's head close to her lips. "Wait, I've a great idea, there are some horse blankets in the tack room… why not make ourselves comfortable… shine your light in the far corner and follow me." Dieter laughed at her orders… it didn't require a fortune teller to know what would happen next as they sat down on the blankets. Rosa felt she was aboard an express train being vainly signaled to halt on the track, and felt Dieter's heart beating as he nuzzled her neck. She lay back as Dieter's hormones went into overdrive… he lowered himself gently onto his companion. After what seemed an eternity both lovers felt spent by their mutual efforts and remained still for a long time… One or two pangs of remorse flitted through Rosa's head but were quickly banished as the pair clasped one another in an afterglow of affection and quickly fell asleep.

* * * * * * * *

Waking with a sudden start Dieter realized if they didn't get moving there'd be all hell to pay. God only knew what time it was, as he fished around for the flashlight to check his watch. After shaking Rosa by the shoulder they shared a cigarette before he pulled her onto her feet. He walked over and pushed the barn door ajar before slipping into the cool night air. Rosa followed quickly, then she paused and called softly. "Until Saturday, lover boy" and hurried towards the house. Dieter raised a hand in acknowledgment and grinned to himself walking towards his car.

Reaching inside he released the hand brake, pushed hard on the dashboard and jumped in behind the steering wheel as the vehicle began moving. Regaining the river road he pulled the choke and starter buttons and sat waiting for the engine to warm up. Feeling a sudden urge to pee he hopped out and crossed to the opposite side of the road. Standing almost at the edge of the river there was enough moonlight to notice the surface had risen alarmingly. It looked to be just shy of flood level. Buttoning his fly he thought of Rosa and what had taken place in the barn. It had been one hell of an evening.

* * * * * * * *

At the inquest Dieter couldn't remember when he first saw Bayer's car on that horrible night... possibly the crash occurred while he'd fumbled a fly button. Lying in the hospital bed, he surmised it must be akin to spotting the first blip on a radar screen... what kind of time lag was there between the eye and brain? However, he realized it was within a flash that Bayer's vehicle materialized around the bend roughly twenty meters from where he'd relieved himself.

A fractured muffler on the DKW made a loud burbling as the engine idled, and this combined with a gusting wind completely blotted out the noise of the approaching Taunus until the final impact. A terrible cacophony of rending sheet metal and screeching brakes registered seconds before Dieter lost consciousness.

* * * * * * * *

Rosa's boyfriend was extraordinarily lucky to have survived – his bandaged head throbbed and his right arm was in a splint. His injuries were caused by metal blasted from both disintegrating cars. The police questioned him at the Obermeisse hospital, but he'd been unable to add much to their report. Asked if his car lights had been on, Dieter lied hoping to deflect blame from himself. His D.K.W.

was nothing but a charred wreck judging by some photos he'd been shown, making contradiction of his statement unlikely. Dieter told the police he supposed the other car was driven without lights, otherwise he'd have had some warning of its approach.

Karl had in fact turned off the lights after reaching the Meisse, as moonlight provided sufficient visibility. It would also make it more difficult for his pursuers to estimate what kind of gap separated them from their target and whether he was even on the same road. Wrapped up in his thoughts Karl's speed had increased recklessly, until suddenly confronted by a sharp bend, flanked by craggy rocks. Braking on the ice slicked surface, the car skidded wildly around the bend. Stark terror supplanted an oath, within split seconds of Bayer's death.

40

WHAT THE MEISSE CLAIMED

A TRUCK DRIVER COMING FROM THE opposite direction of Bayer's car witnessed a large fireball erupt ahead of him. At the wreck site the impact had ruptured the D.K.W.'s gas tank which exploded causing debris to spew in all directions. A sheared door handle ricocheting off nearby rocks gouged Dieter Rausch's head in it's trajectory. Shortly after reaching the scene, Police officer Zengler found Dieter face down in mud, with the Meisse almost lapping at his feet. Told about it in hospital Dieter shuddered realizing how close to death he'd come.

Following brief initial questioning he'd slept for over nine hours, and awoke to find two new policemen sitting reading in his room... after reflecting for a few minutes, he asked one of the sergeants for a smoke. The man put his paper down and pulled a chair up alongside the bed. Dieter asked "So what happened to the occupants of the other car?" The policeman struck a match and lit a cigarette before replying... "Singular is the word, and very dead, according to one of two inspectors who'd been chasing the car." The other policeman came over and sat on the edge of Dieter's bed... "The victim was being tailed, and they hope to find the remains once the river is searched by a dive team already on its way. Nothing overtook the police van during the chase, so they are sure they will be looking for only one body. There is a side road about 45 Km further back from the site, but according to the inspectors it was virtually impossible for anyone else to have come between them and their target during the pursuit. Even supposing someone had, wreckage of the DKW completely blocked the road and the truck driver was trapped on the far side. Judging from skid marks it appeared the Taunus was deflected towards the river after striking the DKW then catapulted into the water by the force of the explosion.

Dieter visualized this scenario while dragging on his cigarette. "Poor bastard... who was he?" The sergeant shook his head. "Who knows, but he was important enough to have two inspectors after him. Our station received a class 'A' on the radio, and I was called out of bed to set up road barriers not long before the incident occurred. In fact we'd already erected one about 2Km. further up the road." The sergeant asked a few perfunctory questions before getting up and folding his notebook. "Well I need to get moving, take care and good luck." As both sergeants departed Dieter lay back against his pillow feeling exhausted, not relishing a forthcoming visit from his parents... he just wanted to sleep some more and didn't feel up to answering any more questions for the moment.

* * * * * * * *

Karl's scream of horror was only half uttered as his head contacted the dashboard knocking him cold. Split seconds earlier he'd instinctively jammed on his brakes, but it was already too late... the Taunus hit the surface of the Meisse and began submerging. Absence of a rear door wrenched off during the crash provided access for a surge of water which engulfed the car's interior. A powerful undertow propelled the battered Taunus towards midstream where a vortex swept the St. Lucien treasure from the rear seat. Nearly all the items were carried down stream before fetching up against a ridge of sediment while others were randomly strewn elsewhere. One of the sleeping bags Karl had used for carrying the treasure was discovered several days later entangled in floating driftwood and almost ripped apart. It had taken only moments to consign the St. Lucien once again to obscurity... except for one item, the premier piece still in it's container.

During his stay at the Dortmund hotel, Karl replaced the cross in its beautiful satin lined rosewood box measuring 51x71 cm. The hand-crafted container had been made for M'sieu Bauten during the thirties, and fully complemented the magnificent object it housed. When the torrent of water filled the sinking car, a twist of fate allowed ornate handles on the box to snag on the fractured front seat structure, trapping it in place.

* * * * * * * *

Steiner and Müeller turned up their coat collars as they stomped their feet. There were certain aspects of police work Leo abhorred and the waiting game happened to be one of them. Leaning against a rusted stanchion, he stared balefully at the Meisse's turgid water. The river looked cold and uninviting as Hans reached into his pocket and passed a small flask of brandy to his friend. "Here, have some for medicinal purposes, if you want to see your pension." The men had been standing around over an hour on the deck of the Phoenix, an old recovery barge chartered from the Meisse river authority.

A keen wind was making things pretty unpleasant until one of the divers popped his head up alongside raising both hands, indicating his descent had been successful. After a short interval the crane operator started paying out steel cable and a grapple... a mood of expectancy registered on the faces of those aboard the barge. After another lengthy wait one of the dive team gave the O.K. to start lifting operations and the crane's cable began rewinding on it's drum. Slowly the battered weed-encrusted Taunus broke the water's surface, and after it was clear by two or three meters, it was rotated laterally and deposited on the barge deck. It looked a forlorn sight caked with oil-stained mud and small streams of water pouring from its interior. Fortunately the divers had hooked onto the rear axle prior to the lifting phase, otherwise out-rushing water might have dislodged the remaining artifact and sent it back to the bottom.

Both inspectors stepped closer to the wreck waiting for a photographer to finish taking pictures. When he was done two of the divers began extricating the car's sole occupant. Bayer's body had become wedged firmly between a crumpled steering column and the driver's seat, making it extremely difficult to extricate. Once the corpse was finally freed members of the recovery team stood by with a canvas body bag. After glancing inside the vehicle Leo was surprised at finding it empty except for two sodden blankets and torn newspaper pages wadded under the forward seat structure. A fold of blanket obscured one end of a flat wooden box until Leo tugged it aside. The inspector sucked in his breath and gave a wintry smile, stepping back to pull on a pair of rubber gloves, he called out to Hans. "We may have something here."

Leo twisted then gently pulled on the end of the box wedged between the front passenger seat and door. After a final pull he managed to extract it. Giving a grunt of satisfaction he leaned against a cabin wall to catch his breath.

The solving of murder cases often hinges on lucky breaks... such an instance occurred when recovering the St. Lucien cross. As Hans stood watching, Leo placed the box on top of a hatch cover then sat down beside it. He flipped two ornate catches and pushed up the lid… "du liebe Gott in Himmel". Both men simultaneously sucked in their breath and remained silent at first overawed by what they were looking at. Leo muttered "Well let's get back on shore with this baby, as I think it may have something to tell us." Closing the lid he wiped off greenish gobs of muck to reveal a small brass plate screwed into a recessed area. Leo peered at the engraved lettering and read the inscription.

> *Claude F. Bauten*
> *Rue Felix Conte*
> *Paris A.D. 1932*

Reading the notation Hans bit his thumb nail. "Yes this may give us some answers." "Maybe so, maybe so." Leo replied. The lieutenant in charge of the recovery team had already started shutting down operations and placed marker buoys at the spot where the car had been lifted from the river bottom. Hans and Leo agreed with his decision as darkness was rapidly descending and the Phoenix needed to head back to its berth.

* * * * * * * *

The inspectors took their seats at the preliminary inquest held in the Obermeisse town hall. The investigating magistrate seemed rather pompous, more interested in preening before an infrequent audience, than following proper procedures. It became apparent to Steiner the afternoon would likely end up being a waste of time. About half an hour into the inquest, Hans was called upon to explain the sudden appearance of two out-of-town inspectors at the accident scene. Leo was impressed by how much his friend managed to say, while revealing so little. There was a hush after he sat down and his companion was hard put not to laugh out loud.

Following desultory questioning of the two local police sergeants, the session came to an end. Summing up, the magistrate stated a full inquiry would be held at the end of the month, and stipulated that a final police report be submitted to his office within the next five days.

Stepping outside the building for a smoke both inspectors lit up. After a pause Leo remarked "so having listened to that load of weighty nothingness including your brilliant song and dance I might add, what's next on the list?" "Dinner, then after a good nights sleep, return to Dortmund. I want our discovery checked out quickly by the people in central forensics, and I have a hunch we'll get some interesting answers." The following day both men were driven to the Obermeisse bahnhof to catch an early train as Zengler had already departed with the van.

While the train gathered speed Leo glanced through a local newspaper before opening his briefcase. He thumbed through photos of the cadaver retrieved from the Taunus finding them distasteful, then reached for an envelope containing images of the victim's fingerprints. After a few minutes he slipped the envelope and its contents inside a plastic cover protecting the container of the St Lucien cross... Hans looked up as Leo tapped the box... "I can't wait to find out what other prints the lab might find on this work of art, besides those of our friend in the photos. I'm betting some belong to the corpse found in the crate... if that happens you'll get that bottle of Napoleon brandy you are always on about." Hans emitted a chuckle. "You can't afford it, and I wouldn't share such ambrosia with a ruffian like you." Leo farted and closed his eyes murmuring "Greedy pig" before allowing himself to relax. It had been another one of those long and tiresome weeks.

* * * * * * * *

Back in his Munich office Leo Steiner finished digesting reports from Dortmund. Included was a memo from Obermeisse concerning the body fished out of the river. A wallet Hans Müeller found in the man's jacket showed him to be a Karl Bayer. Calls by the Dortmund division traced the Taunus to a rental agency. Detectives had done their plod-work and the license bureau provided Bayer's age, and other information. Digging up stuff for a detailed background profile had proven more than tedious, but pieces were beginning to fall into place. Leo yawned and clasped both hands behind his neck just as Renata popped her head around the door. "Mr. Big needs your presence now, if not sooner Chief Inspector."

Leo ambled into Kurt Stroebel's office within five minutes of his summons noting the enigmatic smile on his boss's face which was mildly disconcerting. It usually signified something he'd be allergic to having been down this same road before. Stroebel got up from behind his desk and came over to his subordinate putting a hand on his shoulder. "So, how did things go in Dortmund? I'm sorry you had to leave so abruptly." Leo ignored the sarcasm then moved a step to one side turning to face Stroebel. "Very good chief, and getting even better." Kurt looked slightly surprised hearing this, but quickly reverted to smile mode. Leo distinctly felt his boss was only listening with half an ear, still something must be in the air judging by his convivial demeanor. The commissioner proffered a cigar and waved him to a seat. "I have good news, look at this…." Kurt held up a folded telex lying on his desk. "It came in last night." Leo was somewhat mystified seeing striped color bars in the corner of the envelope. The bars signified a minimal circulation amongst department heads, making Leo wonder about the content.

Stroebel loosened his tie before speaking… "Go ahead, read it man." Leo fumbled for his glasses and eyeballed the text. "Good grief, I never cease to be amazed in this job."

The telex had been sent to the German chancellor via the foreign service department, and in curt terms announced the defection of minister Peter Hahn. Apparently he'd recently asked for, and been given asylum by the Soviet government and late breaking newspaper and TV reports emanating from Moscow were quoted. A hand written appendage at the bottom of the page noted no attempts at denial were required by West German spokesmen. Leo gave a look of surprise seeing the chancellor's signature scribbled below that of the foreign service chief. Kurt Stroebel contentedly puffed on his cigar as Leo still stared at the telex. "So, you see the man's alive, and thankfully no longer a problem for us and above all, the pressure is off my... er, our backs." After a pause he continued "I wish to thank you for all your efforts and co-operation." So that was it, you never knew with Stroebel, the next thing he'd be inviting him to his club. Leo winced and made a quick excuse for returning to his office.

Sitting down he mulled over the commissioner's words, never mind that your government was being highly embarrassed on the international stage by a renegade minister, it was because the dogs had been called off which was of prime importance to his illustrious boss. Depending on his mood at the time, Leo was either amused or irritated by Stroebel, there was hardly a halfway mark. Occasionally, when Leo pointed to flaws in Kurt's reasoning the reply was usually asinine such as 'mea culpa' accompanied by that insincere smile, the man had been born with a slippery skin. Kurt was intelligent, there was no doubt about it but their philosophies were far apart. And so the world turns Leo surmised, scratching at his neck with a wry look on his face wanting to laugh but feeling too tired to do so.

41

FINIS

Leo stayed at home for a couple of days due to a cold, that felt like the hammers of hell were beating on his head. On returning to the office he dictated case notes to Renata, most of which were culled from a daily journal. The man at the W.G.F.P. fingerprint section called as Renata shut the door. "Good morning chief inspector, this is supervisor Bergmeister. I have good news regarding your artifact, and rest assured maximum security has been afforded it under my care. What a beautiful object, in my estimation it must be worth a fortune." Leo gave a discreet cough hoping to set the caller back on track. "Well my findings are as follows... the lower vertical section of the cross has several discernible thumb and fingerprints. Most are smudged, however two are of sufficient quality enabling them to be matched with corpse #57. The same applies to the photo negatives in your envelope marked 'Obermeisse', in fact we were able to 'lift' three excellent prints that dovetailed. However, regarding your set identified 'P.H.' we couldn't come up with anything. There are other prints on the cross, but possibly you're not interested in those. A report of my research has already been compiled for you. Leo propped his feet on the desk, "indeed this is excellent news and no, I'm only interested in the prints you've matched up and I'll come over to your office about 10.a.m. if that's O.K?"

Renata came into the office bringing coffee. "You look like the cat who has licked the cream.".… "Ate the mouse as well I reckon, " Leo replied smelling the coffee aroma. Sipping his drink he thought how easy it had been obtaining Peter Hahn's prints. Steiner reckoned an old boy's club permeated the caverns of bureaucracy sometimes making investigations much harder than necessary, especially when it involved people in the higher echelons of state. This time Leo had been surprised by Stroebel's helpfulness in obtaining prints from the minister's office, and it now seemed Hahn could be ruled out as a murder suspect. Kurt Stroebel had used his influence, and the minister's prints were passed to Steiner in record time. In the past even minor requests were stymied unless heavy clout was brought to bear.

The following day Steiner drove to the W.G.F.P. agency building to meet the senior supervisor he'd previously talked to. Klaus Bergmeister met him in the reception center and held out a hand as Leo approached "You've come at an opportune moment chief inspector. I've just returned from our forensic laboratory. After our telecon., I took another look at the cross under one of our most powerful microscopes and discovered tiny slivers of flesh tissue embedded in the jewel settings of the horizontal arm."

Klaus coughed then resumed "I tried calling you but the line was busy, so I took the liberty of taking the artifact to our lab people for an analysis and preservation of the specimens." Leo commended Klaus for his initiative and congratulated him on the results. "I would like your forensic people to also take a look at tissue samples from corpse #57 at the same time if you can arrange it." Leo lit Bergmeister's cigarette and his own. "I'm positive the flesh tissue you discovered belongs to my cadaver and coupled with those print matches it will prove a certain Karl Bayer committed murder and disfigurement. As Bayer is now dead, it's more a case of tying up loose ends." The two men continued chatting for a while before the inspector took his leave and drove back to his office.

* * * * * * * *

Leo phoned Hans Müeller "you have a fancy dinner on your agenda next time we meet." Hans chuckled, knowing things must be going right for his friend. Leo paused a moment before speaking "I've got fingerprints taken from the cross... although they wouldn't clinch things at a trial, forensic reports confirm tissue specimens embedded in the cross came from Wittich's back. Incidentally, just to be rock certain I had a pathologist confirm it was the cross used to mutilate Wittich. Incision patterns and other marks conclusively tie it to the bizarre killing."

Hans took a deep breath then almost yelped "Congratulations my friend, things are definitely looking up, eh?" Grinning to himself Leo agreed. "By the way, Peter Hahn's prints didn't show up on either the cross or it's container, which almost certainly rules him out... he is guilty of treason, but murder I think not. However as both he and the girl have flown the coop, it doesn't look as if anyone will end up in court as the whole thing is somewhat academic now." Hans glanced down at his desk jotter "By the way, how did Wittich end up inside a crate?" Leo thought a moment. "Ah, my friend that one puzzled me and I can only guess Bayer had an accomplice who took care of things. Perhaps they hoped to find a shady dealer who'd buy the cross, then they'd split the proceeds, but who knows. The knife that killed Wittich hasn't been found... it wasn't in the Taunus and could have been discarded anywhere, so I really needed the flesh tissues and fingerprints to clinch things." Hans interjected "funny thing, all that searching and Wittich was in your back pocket all along." Leo chuckled "well Stroebel is happy now and so am I. The only bad thing is I'll have to make good on that bottle of special brandy." Hans coughed, "don't send it, come up here and we'll evaluate it during the dinner already promised, how does that sound?"

Apart from reports and minor details requiring attention the investigation was at an end. Like a jig-saw puzzle, pieces representing Karl Bayer, Heinz Wittich and Peter Hahn fitted into their proper places and could be scratched off Leo's list. Perhaps the antique dealer surprised Bayer in the act of stealing the cross and ended up with a knife in his chest. Leo reckoned the minister was shown the artifact being one of few people who could truly appreciate it, however he must have simply viewed it in the case without touching it. Leo hadn't an inkling the cross was only one single piece of a priceless treasure. Something still puzzled him, had the motive been just a case of simple burglary that went badly wrong, or did Karl Bayer happen to know what was inside the villa? The man wasn't entered in any Interpol files and appeared to be a law abiding citizen. Perhaps it tied up with some events in the past, but Leo Steiner wasn't about to dig any deeper... his job was completed. Stroebel was off his back and it was time to wrap things up.

* * * * * * * *

Leo doodled on a piece of paper lost in a jumble of thoughts. He'd nearly always resolved cases satisfactorily and this one followed the pattern. A final step was required that would take but a few moments. He straightened up reaching for the phone to dial Kurt Stroebel's number which was answered by the secretary. "Steiner here... tell your boss I am on the way up to see him." As she cleared her throat, he put the receiver down to cut off the standard nonsense about his not being in, or was attending a conference. Leo was not in a mood to hang about waiting for call backs. Reaching into a small desk drawer he extracted a letter of resignation and added the current date. With a slightly sad look on his face he licked the envelope, transferred it to his jacket pocket and headed for the door.

Seeing her boss's purposeful stride, Renata wondered what was going on. A few minutes later she returned some files to Leo's office and noticed a desk drawer half open. Realizing what this implied tears welled up in her eyes as she pushed it shut. She'd been the one who had typed the letter and placed it there over three months ago. Renata didn't even want to think about working for someone else… but she also needed a job. When Leo returned, he placed an arm around her shoulder. "Grab your hat and coat Renata… we are going out for the best lunch in town." His secretary laughed while reaching for her purse and gloves. "Why thank you kind sir, and to what do I owe this honor?" Leo held the door open for her. "I'll tell you all about it over drinks, but my guess is you know perfectly well."

* * * * * * * *

Not long after Bayer's Taunus plunged into the Meisse, another accident occurred on the same stretch of road. This time it happened during daylight when a large truck swerved violently to avoid a careless motorcyclist. The truck carried a load of toxic waste from a chemical plant in Hamburg, and seventeen metal drums ejected into the river as the truck toppled onto it's side parallel with the bank.

When news of the incident reached the local police sub-post it was relayed to Dortmund. A decision was made to send a dive team to the scene to make sure all of the drums were recovered. It proved a tricky business as some of them were buried in a heavy oily sludge. Over the course of time two large pockets of silt had formed on the river bottom, and most of the drums ended up in these areas, complicating the recovery task. The divers told their supervisor that in order to avoid the possibility of further damage most of the surrounding silt and debris needed to be removed. The Meisse river authority was contacted, and the Phoenix used in salvaging Bayer's car was anchored close to the spill area.

A smaller barge had been tethered to the side of the mother ship whose twin hoses would carry goo into it's hold. After the dive leader gave a signal indicating the suction nozzles below the surface were properly positioned, the Phoenix's owner Rudi Webber switched on the pump motors and almost immediately sediment began spewing forth. Paul Ullrich, a nineteen year old deck hand employed by Rudi was leaning nonchalantly against a bulkhead having a smoke, when suddenly he gripped the railing... something had glinted twice in one of the grayish streams being directed into the hold. The stuff was rising quickly as Paul yelled at Rudi to cut the pumps, and within seconds each flow became a dribble. In the past Paul had often seen various objects brought up which usually turned out to be odd pieces of kitchen appliances or junked car parts etc. but sadly nothing of value.

This time Paul's instinct urged him to investigate further and grabbing a rake clamped to a stanchion he scurried down the starboard ladder and started poking about in the sticky sediment. Within a few minutes the rake caught onto something solid, and Paul carefully brought it to the surface. By this time the goo was almost level with the tops of his rubber boots, but was unnoticed in his mounting excitement. The snagged object resembled the silver chalices he'd seen in church. Rudi, who'd been watching from the top deck gave a low whistle as Paul climbed back up holding his find. "Give me a few more minutes boss, there could be more stuff down there."

Rudi started wiping the chalice on his sleeve "O.K. but make it quick or we'll have those divers wondering why the pumps quit." Paul hurriedly pushed the rake back and forth using semicircular sweeps edging back to the ladder until he felt the rake contact something else. This time it was a small golden urn with ornate handles. Rudi switched the pumps back on as Paul scrambled topside holding the urn and rake with one hand while pulling himself up the rungs with the other. As his head cleared the edge of the deck he saw Rudi holding the chalice as detective sergeant Braun, chief of the dive team, was writing in a notebook... suddenly it didn't look as if Paul was going to keep the objects and split the proceeds with his boss.

Once the drums had been recovered and thoroughly inspected, the search continued for more valuables on the authorization of Inspector Müeller, and two additional divers were brought in. Over a period of nine days a further seventeen artifacts were discovered. News of this find produced a mini hysteria in the press and raised a lot of questions and speculation about the Meisse treasure. After reading the reports Leo contacted his friend Hans Müeller. "It looks as if the motive for killing Wittich had more to it than we supposed."

* * * * * * * *

After the Stalingrad disaster, Lilli waited in vain hoping to hear news about her husband Karl, but as the long months passed she finally gave up hope. She decided to take the child with her to Germany, where she quickly obtained a job at an aircraft factory in Regensburg. Gradually, memories of Karl dimmed, and her despondency disappeared after moving in with a Belgian volunteer worker who was a foreman at the plant. Lilli's life began to change, and when the war terminated the pair moved to Antwerp, where they found jobs to support themselves and a child who was never told anything about his real father. Lilli had long ago stopped mentioning Karl's name in an effort to wipe out the past and help her adjust to a new life. Jan, her companion treated her well and she was reasonably happy with the way things had turned out.

* * * * * * * *

Having kept Peter Hahn on ice for eleven days at the Soviet embassy in Berne, Igor Strolov, a K.G.B. colonel holding diplomatic status finalized arrangements to have Hahn spirited off to Moscow aboard an Aeroflot plane. After arrival, he was held incommunicado at a large dacha on the outskirts of the city until long after ramifications concerning the German/Turkish arms talks had dissipated. A Russian major general known only to Hahn as Oscar visited him every five weeks and interrogated him about German governmental policies, and some of his closest colleagues. Occasionally Peter was dumbfounded by the information Oscar already knew. Soon the two men got on well together, and Peter began looking forward to the visits which provided a source of happenings in the outside world.

There were no radios or newspapers in the dacha and the staff who ran the place refused to engage in conversation other than about domestic matters. Halfway through his third year at the dacha Peter found himself responding to questions for the last time. Two stony faced men dressed in civilian clothes sat down at the table and grilled him while Oscar was busy writing notes in what appeared to be Hahn's dossier. After three hours Peter began fighting off sleepiness when suddenly the interrogators stood up, nodded to Oscar and left. Oscar smiled at him and told him he was about to embark on a new phase of his life, and to pack his things and be ready to leave in the morning.

Peter Hahn was about to spend the next sixteen years in the Russian capital, living in a nondescript block of apartments typical of many throughout the city. Rental of his accommodation was paid by the state and he also received allowances for food and heating furnished by one of the city's agencies. Aware his living conditions were much better than those of most Muscovites, it still didn't prevent Peter Hahn from thinking wistfully about his former life style. Despite a fairly comfortable existence he felt it was akin to living in a cage, especially after a warning from the K.G.B. informed him that any attempt at contact with the Western press corps would result in dire consequences. In the beginning, this had caused lingering resentment, especially as some of the other guests of the Soviet were encouraged to give controlled interviews on T.V. Eventually it ceased to bother him, and he ended up becoming almost a recluse. With the passage of time Peter became fluent in Russian which was self taught, enabling him to obtain a position teaching German and French at a prestigious military cadet school near to the Kremlin. The job got him out of the apartment and eased his financial straits, but a vodka habit was now beginning to dull his brain at an alarming rate. Hahn chafed at a restriction keeping him from traveling further than fifteen kilometers beyond city limits, especially after the snow and ice disappeared at the end of a hard winter. Applications for temporary permits were routinely turned down on vague security grounds, and eventually he gave up trying.

After several years, few people in the West ever recalled the once celebrated Hahn case and its associated scandal. Occasional magazine articles would briefly bring it back to light, but a proposed three hour TV documentary was eventually shelved, due to funding problems. The former minister of state ended up bitter and disillusioned and died of a heart attack six weeks prior to the Berlin wall coming down.

Very few mourners attended his funeral, and only a brief obituary appeared in the Moscow papers. Laura Ichenko occasionally thought about him, but this hadn't happened recently. Reading Hahn's obituary she briefly contemplated their relationship which now seemed so long ago. Since their final parting Laura had moved steadily up within the ranks of the K.G.B. and now secure in her position she'd considered paying her ex-lover a visit for old times sake. She had ditched the idea... to do so might still endanger future promotion given the paranoia of her superiors, and Laura was still ambitious. She had phoned Peter's apartment one time but had replaced the receiver as it started to ring.

* * * * * * * *

Laura decided to attend the funeral... they'd forgive her for that. At the Vaslovsky cemetery a few Muscovites walking along a narrow pathway near the burial site noticed several black Zils parked close by, and an outstanding looking woman. She was wearing a sable coat and hat with expensive looking boots. Laura had placed two dozen red roses on the coffin, and was now shaking the hands of a small group of elderly men in dark topcoats. Onlookers momentarily wondered who had reached the end of the line at the Vaslovsky, before they moved on without further curiosity.